Last Man Home

Last Man Home

CD Wilkinson

Edited by Kelly Powers

Published by Nishihara/Wilkinson Design, Inc.
P.O. Box 624, Turlock CA 95381 USA
1.209.668.7627 | www.nishwilkdesign.com

Book design copyright © 2020 by Nishihara/Wilkinson Design, Inc.
All rights reserved.

Cover design by Ron Wilkinson
Cover photo by the author and Ron Wilkinson
Center spread photos by the author
Back page photo courtesy of Bob Massie

Published in the United States of America

ISBN 978-0-9990229-3-1
Fiction / Historical - Fiction / War and Military
17.05.16

CHAPTER 1

AN INCONCLUSIVE, COSTLY, crummy, little ten-year war, nobody saw this coming. Here they are, US Navy pilots flying out over this green sea of North Vietnam's vast jungle, making BDA[1] flyovers a simple procedure of photographing big holes in the ground so some political bastard back in the "world"[2] knows that our pilots did not waste taxpayers' money dumping their bombs into the deep blue sea.

Don't they know this is not healthy? The North Vietnamese really do not like US planes flying over their country and try their damnedest to put a stop to it. What input does a pilot have? They fly when and where their commander demands, he may disagree, but this disagreement stays within his helmet-encased head. This mission is no different than most—a quick routine low-level flyover just like the rest. Go to an orbiting station miles from the bombers' run-in on the target. Once the bombs are away, the Navy F-4 Phantom drops out of its holding pattern, powers down, rolls in on the target following the same path as the fleeing flight of B-52s. It's all so close the pilot can see secondary explosions, throwing debris mixed with dirt, foliage, and shrapnel high into the air along the targeted strip of jungle. Flashes of fire and flame are sending big black bellowing puffs of smoke,

---

[1]   Bomb Damage Assessment

[2]   "World" used in Vietnam by US military personnel referring to their homeland, the United States of America.

rising above the lush green landscape. Finishing his run over the three-mile long target, the pilot throttles up for a fast climbing exit. Suddenly, coming out of this mass of green, a column of thundering gray and white smoke with a fiery red tail pushing a telephone pole-sized missile right up the jet's exhaust, the plane is dealt a shuddering blow on impact, sending it immediately into an uncontrolled gyrating spin, plummeting toward earth, accompanied by loud explosions and a whole lot of fire and smoke. No time for thought, pulling the ejection ring sends the pilot, still in his seat, right past the canopy, out into the cold silence of nothingness. Not for long, gravity is going rear its ugly scientific head, pulling his ass down to earth. Falling through a pillow of blue, he can see what was once his almost-new, not a dent or scratch, F-4 on fire, leaving a trail of flaming smoke, along with a lot of used parts spread out across a once beautiful sky. The only good thing from all of this is his plane, or what's left of it, is sailing off to the north. The pilot is headed down and to the south at a fairly good rate of speed.

There is really no need to try and find an opening to land; nothing but solid tree tops. The pilot's thoughts during his descent, *This is really going to hurt, could even leave a scar. Put your legs together, try and save the boys, leave helmet on, protect the head so they can identify the body.* Amazingly, three years of intensive naval flight training is suddenly kicking in.

Almost dark in the jungle's embrace, spiderlike webs and lightning bolts of sunlight breaking through the canopy dancing across an almost silent forest floor, two hunters quietly approach a group of small Vietnamese deer. Strong gusty winds and divine fate silently bring the pilot descending directly over the deer and our two unsuspecting hunters.

Crashing through the treetops, breaking his right leg, rendering him unconscious with multiple cuts and abrasions over various parts of his body, this loud thundering crashing sound is interfering with the silent jungle, startling the deer and scaring the living crap out of the two hunters. The young one lets out a bloodcurdling scream as this unidentified object comes within inches of his face, hanging a few feet off the ground. The pilot, with his white helmet, green-tinted visor, along with its oxygen masks, expandable rubber tubing hanging down, gives him the appearance of something from outer space, which by all accounts he is.

After recovering from the initial shock and surmising what has just happened in front of them, the old hunter and his companion approach with crossbows at the ready and a whole lot of caution. The old one removes a bamboo-sharpened arrow from his quiver, moving slowly but deliberately in the pilot's direction. Not moving or responding to probes from the arrow's pointed tip, the old man informs his partner they are going to take this strange creature from the sky back to their encampment.

With the expenditure of much effort and time, they succeed in bringing this green-suited white-helmeted body to the ground. Without wishing to linger, the old one directs his friend in helping him secure the pilot in what are the remains of his parachute. Tying this bundle to a long bamboo pole enables the two men to carry this weight with relative ease, trying as much as possible to clean the area of broken branches, twigs, and any and all signs of them, or the pilot ever being there, realizing there is nothing they can do about the huge hole he has ripped in the overhead canopy.

Using jungle skills learned over years of experience, the two hunters move off in the direction of their camp. Being careful not to leave a trail away from where they found the pilot, continually checking for intruders, cautiously and diligently covering any tracks they are leaving, most importantly, they're doubling over their own back trail, going through every stream or river they come across, knowing that members of the NVA[3] will be search-

---

[3] North Vietnamese Army.

ing for their wayward friend, probably bringing tracking dogs with them.

Because of the different directions of the pilot and the plane, it takes two days for the NVA to locate the site where a huge hole has been torn in the canopy, where a pilot made his entry into North Vietnam. As suspected, they bring along their dogs. After fruitless hours of searching, finding nothing but the landing site, no substantial trail to follow, in frustration, they depart the area.

The hunter's journey, lasting several hours, has awakened the weary pilot. Finding himself in pain, enveloped in near total darkness, apparently encased in some kind of cocoon, not knowing the circumstance of his journey, he tries not to utter a sound except for a moan every now and then. Struggling to keep their 180-pound bundle moving, not dropping him or running him into too many trees, is taking a toll on these people of small stature. Nearing their encampment, the old hunter stops their procession, laying their package down, not all that gently, and starts to untie their newly captured prize. Finding the pilot in a dehydrated and somewhat of a comatose and delirious state, they quickly remove his remaining wrappings, discovering an olive drab green in color military jumpsuit clad figure with boots, a belt, and a .45-caliber Colt model 1911 semi-automatic pistol. Over the left top front pocket of his flight suit is a leather tag with the words, US Navy, under this, LT JG T. Bigelow. Removing these items and his helmet, for the first time before them, lies a once formidable enemy, not so in a T-shirt and boxer shorts. Telling the young hunter to stay with him, the old one takes the pilot's belongings, wrapped in the remains of his parachute, into the bush, placing them in a cache, where only he can find them.

Upon his return, he is surprised to find his companion sitting on the man. Asking in Vietnamese for an explanation, the reply is simple and to the point. "He woke up, tried to stand up, fell face first onto the ground, just holding him down until your return." With the help of the boy, the old one struggles and stumbles, finally getting the pilot in a modified fireman's carry, then they proceed with their homeward trek.

Greatly relieved to have reached their final destination, they are traversing a heavily forested hillside covered with a thick-bladed ten-inch tall grass with small clumps of scrub brush among a scattering of rock formations. The sun is desperately trying to disappear behind a black-silhouetted tree line, exposing the dark gray outline of their humble abode. In this part of the world, home translates to a one room, bamboo and thatch hooch with no indoor or outdoor anything, except for two rolled up sleeping mats in one corner, a shelf on one wall with a few utensils and cloth bundles. On the floor under a straw mat is the hidden wooden-covered entranceway to the all-important family escape tunnel. Once the old man is satisfied that they are alone and no one has paid them a visit while gone, they place the pilot on the floor, and for the first time evaluate, not only the ramifications of the days' actions, also the condition of their captive, who at this very moment, is starting to move his extremities and serenade them with choruses of moans and groans.

The old hunter and the young man have a short hotly contested discussion as to the pilot's circumstance; it has been swiftly and aggressively won by the one with experience, knowledge, and compassion for his fellow man, the older and the wiser of the two.

After a short meal of cold rice and dried fish, they begin their medical chores on the pilot. Seeing the discoloration, swelling, and angle of the right leg, they know it is broken. Luckily, there are no bones protruding through the flesh. Using the bamboo pole they carried him back with for splints, they strap these to the sides of his leg with twine made from stripping plant vines. Now that his leg is splinted, they start on his cuts, scrapes, and scratches, again using their knowledge and plain simple jungle savoir faire, making a healing poultice out of ground tree bark, plant root, and mud, mixed into a damp moss, tied with twine where possible, smeared into or simply placed on other wounds.

As the next few days pass, the pilot's condition is an issue of concern for the old man, with his open sores showing swelling and redness due to infection. His inability to maintain consciousness for any length of time makes it hard to keep him hydrated; they keep trying by pouring as much water into him as they can.

Keeping an open wound clean and dry is paramount. The jungle is a tough place to heal from any type of wound or ailment, with its damp night air, especially on the side of this mountain where the passing clouds have their undersides taken off and deposited among the trees like a coastal fog. Monsoon season keeps this place in a vigorous state of lush green growth, bringing with it a constant state of dampness that invites infection and mildew. With time, the pilot knows there is someone caring for him, but he is not sure who. There are no sounds but for the shuffling of feet and an occasional smattering of voices that are foreign to him. When there is stillness, he dares to open his eyes, trying to recognize and familiarize himself with his surroundings. Doing so at night leaves one feeling blind; no light from moon or stars can break through this veil of green. Daylight is not a whole lot better. In the day's faint light, he can see a ceiling and walls constructed of bamboo poles covered with thatch made out of palm fronds. Catching a glimpse of his caretaker every once in a while as he moves about, feeling his hand supporting his head and shoulders while being fed and watered, is a comfort and puzzle. After weeks of care with the daily changing of his poultice smeared moss dressings and careful rearrangement to the splint on his leg, Lt. Bigelow is finally able to sit up and for the first time, help in his own feeding and the drinking of water. The only communication between the patient and caregiver has up to now been smiles, head nods, and some abbreviated hand gestures. He also knows there is more than one individual taking care of him, one older and one in his teens. From body language and smug glances from the younger one, the pilot knows he is not all that welcomed.

Time is of no importance. Days and nights float together in his clouded reality. After time, his concentrated feelings and thoughts guide him into some realm of understanding: he has lived through a plane crash and parachute descent, injured upon his landing in the trees, taken prisoner by some unknown indigenous persons. Prisoner is a little strong as he can sit up, move his arms, and scoot his butt across the floor. The way his splint is attached makes it impossible to stand at all. It's like having a stilt on one leg; there are no restraints on his hands and arms or his one good leg.

For some time now, the routine is for the two hunters to go about their daily chores after all three having downed a small breakfast and an attempted conversation consisting of the pilot's English, high school French, and frantic facial and hand expressions. His replies come in Vietnamese, beautiful roll off the tongue French, and stares of disbelief to most anything he says or gestures.

In the cool of the evening, the pilot ventures out the doorway; not being able to go far, he sits and listens to the strangely archaic echoes of the jungle choir, soothing most of his thoughts but doing nothing for the big lingering questions: *Where am I? What am I doing here?* On most evenings, the old man retrieves one of the cloth bundles that are kept high and dry on a shelf in their hooch. He carefully unties and unfolds it to reveal old-age, tattered, and well-worn school books along with some scraps of paper and pieces of old yellowed notebooks. He is using them in a teaching attitude with his young friend. All this is somewhat of a surprise to the pilot. Not only has this man spent considerable time and compassionate effort in his healing, and now this, what's next?

The old one and pilot seem to be having a harmonious relationship, but the young one does those little things to provoke some sort of reaction. For a while, he was sneaking up on Bigelow and poking him with a stick. He was good at it. Lt. Bigelow twice saw him approaching and had the agility and speed to grab the stick, pulling the youngster so close he could take his nose between two fingers, twisting it while adding a "Three Stooges" downward slap with his other hand, thus putting a stop to this childish and irritable poking habit.

As time passes, the old man removes the pilot's bamboo splint and makes him a wooden cane with intricate carvings trailing around and down the shaft to aid in his walking and the sport of stick dueling with the younger one, their new way of bonding. Occasionally, there's the sound of jet aircraft, along with the formation of high altitude vapor trails—the only reminders that a war really exists in this part of the world. As the old man's teachings with his friend progresses, Bigelow ponders the thought of offering his assistance to the math-struggling youth. Although he can clearly see the old one knows his stuff. He can also see the frustration and dismay on his face and the concern in his eyes at the young one's dismal progress in this one seemingly difficult subject.

So on a warm late afternoon, Lt. Tom Bigelow launches his first collaboration with the enemy; moving over to the pair sitting under a huge tree as they look questioningly in his direction, he proceeds to scratch out the math problem in the soft earth with his cane. After doing so, he realizes the problem facing him involves algebra. This kid knows some math; he must have had years of teaching to get to this point. Extending his hand to the old hunter, indicating a desire to look at the schoolbook being used, his examination of the inside cover reveals its origin, the University of Moscow, year published 1949. Bigelow spends many warm, shadowy afternoons under this massive cathedral-like tree, helping to teach the young man algebra, after they return from their daily food gathering trips.

As for Lt. Bigelow's military training in E&E,[4] the rules of engagement here are not all that clear; for starters, he really does not know if he is a captive. After he was finally able to hobble

---

[4]   Escape and Evasion.

around, his two companions simply pick up their crossbows and fade into the dark recesses of the wood line every morning. This is but one blow to the theories taught in the Navy's E&E class. Another critical point is that he has no idea of his exact location, which brings us to one of the most important things you must know in any escape and evasion attempt. Where are you, who are you evading, and in what direction are you going to go? With these factors in mind, he finds it prudent to stay right here where there is food, water, companionship, and for the moment, no war.

The schooling of the young man seems to be progressing well. Not only is Bigelow helping with the math issue, they have all started dabbling in the learning of languages, with the pilot using rudimentary English and French, trying hard to understand their Asian responses.

For the past few days, Lt. Bigelow has been watching the old man working on a new crossbow about four feet in length and two and a half to three feet across at the bow head. Made of a dark hard wood rubbed smooth, first with a piece of bone, then a fine sand was applied by hand rubbing, he finished the smoothing process with a piece of leather.

The final adornment was the stringing of the bow, which he accomplished with the use of animal gut played down to a strong elasticized bow string coated with bees wax supplied by local hives.

It's hard to keep track of the days. Bigelow tried maintaining a daily count, but it did not really seem of any importance with one day pretty much like the others.

Over the last thirty or so of these days, the pilot finds he's getting stronger in his walking and has been doing some vigorous calisthenics to help in the process.

From the looks of him, Lt. Bigelow has dropped a good thirty-five to forty pounds, yet he doesn't feel any fatigue or ill effects due to this dramatic weight loss.

To keep Bigelow clothed, the old one has made a pair of shorts out of the pilot's jumpsuit with a crudely made matching shirt vest. He has not seen his boots since his reentry to earth; all three go shoeless. This soft-soiled forest floor is covered with layers of decaying leaves. There's no real need for footwear. Besides, it's hard to track a man going barefoot in the jungle.

On a clear crisp morning, a few days following the completion of the magnificent new crossbow, the old one and his young friend came to Lt. Bigelow with as much pomp and circumstance as they could muster and present it to him as a gift. What total trust and affection they must feel toward him. Now for the first time being able to hold this heavy mechanical wonder in his hands, his close inspection has brought real wonders to his eyes. The stock of the bow is carved into a slightly elevated hand grip toward the front, wooden dowels hold the artfully arched bow in place, and the trigger mechanism is a total wonder. The detail in hinging the trigger to the stock is amazing with the fitting and dowel work, making it functional. No metal parts were used in its construction. No nails, screws, springs, or wire.

Looking at the butt end of the stock, which has been carved down, making a cheek rest similar to that of a rifle, upon closer scrutiny, Bigelow discovers intricately carved inscriptions on either side of the stock. On one side, there is carved a small star with the formula Pi-R Squared, followed by another star. At first, the inscription on the other side of the stock looked like a shooting star or possibly a comet arcing across the sky with its tail crossing a half moon, finding that when the bow is placed butt plate on the ground, with the bow in the vertical position, this comet becomes a parachute with its shroud lines converging on the star, carrying it to earth for a safe landing, a true picture of how Lt. Bigelow entered their world.

The three spend their mornings making arrows for their upcoming hunts, in the afternoons, its trail discipline, tracking, and archery practice with the evenings still devoted to the young hunter's school learning.

After all this time, Bigelow has wondered where his and the others' food stuff is coming from, knowing that there is fish and meat readily available but the rice was a mystery until one day, on a short excursion into the dark side of the tree line with the old man. Walking up to a small rock formation on the downside slope of a small hillock, not more than fifty yards from a tranquil little stream, the old man stopped. With a sweeping hand motion, he begs the pilot to observe. Not really knowing what he is to look for or what he's observing, with a confused look on his face, Bigelow throws his hands up in defeat. The old one reaches down, grabbing a small scrub brush, which is in a pot, lifting it out of the ground, exposing a granite rock slab approximately three foot by three foot. Rolling this rock aside reveals a cave storage facility. Within this cold storage den are two or three twenty-five pound sacks of rice with the shaking hands US Aid logo stenciled on the side of the burlap bags. After retrieving a portion of the rice, the stone is rolled back into place, potted scrub brush returned. A branch with leaves is used to obliterate any tracks leading to and from this food stash. On another occasion, Bigelow was introduced to the family kitchen, another short walk from their hooch. This consisted of a small underground oven. You cook by stoking the oven with small twigs and dried grasses. Smoke is drawn through two chimney pipes, depositing the smoke at ground level over fifty feet from its source, almost odorless and undetectable. This man has impressed and literally amazed the pilot with his supreme knowledge and mastery of his environment.

Becoming somewhat of an accomplished tracker and marksman, Lt. Bigelow is cordially invited on one of the hunter's adventures into the forested jungle. It's more, way more than he ever envisioned, believing he was in good shape; this turns out to be a continual uphill trek. He knew the trees directly behind the hooch, which he believes is in an easterly direction, are taller than the others as they delay the sunrise each day, but he never expected that the land was rising at such a tremendous angle and on a narrow-forested and fern-covered ridgeline.

Hiking for hours, they stop to rest their exhausted friend, the two hunters always on the lookout for game, unwanted intruders and being especially alert to the sounds, or the lack thereof. In the jungle, there is plenty of mystery and intrigue. There are unknown things out there that make big bump in the night sounds. There are snakes and animals that can kill in seconds, not minutes. The best alarm to impending trouble or harm in a jungle is silence. If there is sudden quiet to the normal jungle background sounds, you're in deep shit and should be at that very moment in time in the "stop and drop" mode.

Reaching the crest of this richly vegetated mountain, approaching and climbing a jagged outcropping of rock, Bigelow is stunned beyond belief. Laid out before him is a vast landscape of green valleys and endless tree-covered mountains, turning slowly to take in all this heart-stopping view, suddenly, there it is, a faint blueness on the horizon, just a small glimmer of the South China Sea.

They descend the ridge into the dank darkness of a ravine, continuing their hunt for whatever game they may encounter. On Bigelow's first outing, the old hunter brings down a rather small monkey, their only take this day, leaving Bigelow with visions of the deep blue sea dancing through his head.

Their daily routine is almost predictable, early to rise, fix a little rice with whatever meat, poultry, fish, or vegetable that is handy thrown into the pot. After the meal, the two hunters discuss the day's hunt direction; and by midmorning, they trudge off to see how many of God's little creatures they can annihilate with their sharpened bamboo arrows. Bigelow's marksmanship is being challenged by his fellow hunter's abilities to bring down almost anything, including running small deer, monkeys, rodents, and sitting birds. The pilot spends most of his hunting time retrieving wayward arrows. His first victim was a small, not so furry rodent with a slow problem—he did not move fast enough to avoid almost sudden death, only to be wounded. It takes Lt.

Bigelow three more arrows to bring this monster down, to the pronounced joy of his fellow hunters.

On an early cloud-covered and foggy morning, the routine is broken. After a hurried meal, the old one starts placing some rice, dried fish, and beef jerky type substance, along with their bedrolls into an American rice aid sack. Placing this aside, the three hunters gather all the arrows they have stockpiled and load their quivers. Without much discussion, the three depart on a southeast track, going into the tree line to be swallowed by its vast expanse of dense musky-smelling jungle. The trio is now at an easy downhill gait. They're only a few hundred yards from their debarkation point when they scare up some deer. Trying to make the first clear shot of the day, the pilot takes aim, only to have the old hunter reach up and pull his bow gently down as the deer moves off. Not understanding the old one's actions, they continue on their way. After hours of bone-weary travel, the three stop by a slowly moving river or maybe just a large steam. His two companions, without embarrassment or any hesitation, unceremoniously disrobe and dive in for a swim. Looking on, Bigelow decides to join them, invoking some light laughter because of his lily white butt. After their swim, the three refreshed and clean travelers take a short lunch break. Afterward, the little band continues their journey at a steady, predictable pace, only as fast as the slowest man can manage.

Hours go by, more animals are sighted, but the old hunter does not seem that interested. He just keeps moving in a determined direction, not caring about the change in terrain, down into ravines, over rock formations, through thick stands of bamboo, swampy marshland, and through thick jungle. This is a determined individual with a mission in mind.

As darkness descends over the forested jungle, the sounds change. The bird calls cease, small animals quiet their hurried rustling sounds, and the crickets stop their constant chirping. The approaching night brings with it a definite chill to the thick musty air. Breaking out their supplies, food, and bedrolls, Bigelow prepares for his first real night under the stars, if only he could see them, the thick canopy still not letting any moon or starlight through. At this time, on this very scary, darker than dark night, Lt. Bigelow would like to ask the old man about Asian Tigers but does not know how; and besides, he doesn't want to break the night's silence.

Back at the hooch, the mosquito problem was, to an extent, under control. Here in the open, they not only desire your blood, they're also after body warmth. That's how chilly it's gotten. The night passes but not without those wide-awakening screams and howls that leave you sleepless for what seems like hours, hoping not to hear it again. So you just lie there, waiting.

Again with the rice and fish, but as the two native hunters prepare themselves for the day, there seems to be a lighter mood in their relationship, the spirit and tone of their almost whispered voices, as if they knew something Bigelow did not, as is the case most of the time.

After an hour's walk, the jungle and trees along with leg grabbing "wait a minute" vines[5] are all dramatically thinning. The direction they're going in is leading the three hunters into an open meadow. Before moving into the clearing, the old one goes to one knee. Lt. Bigelow and the young hunter follow suit. Scanning this opening in the jungle, with its grass maybe eighteen inches tall, total area about one and a half acres. There are a number of cleared track, not man-made, these furrows were carved out by the frequent use of a good-sized animal. All the trails are running north to south, not a one coming directly at or away from them in an east to west direction, seemed strange to Lt. Bigelow, but not for these two. They just watch the clearing, every once in a while, giving that ever-present Asian smile to each other.

---

[5] Term used by American GIs to describe vines that snag ankles and legs impeding one's progress.

Sitting in the heat with the sun glaring down on him, Bigelow, with his sweat-covered back pressed to a tree, is seeing nothing in the clearing. The expectation of the other two is unmistakable, intense concentration on the field before them. The old hunter sticks his finger in his mouth, wetting the tip, holding it aloft, checking on wind direction, reassuring himself they are downwind of whatever they're waiting for.

It's past midday. Bigelow has been silently napping; he is now being brought out of slumber by a slight tug to his foot. Opening his eyes to the sun's sudden glare, squinting, rubbing at them to clear his focus, there they are, Asian water buffalo–big black, massive-headed, with huge inward swooping sharp-tipped horns. Simply put, they are really big ass, nasty looking, Southeast Asian water buffalo.

Thinking quickly of past hunts where arrows were on target and bounced off birds, monkeys, small rodents, especially wild pigs, Lt. Bigelow does not know much about the native water buffalo. From his present location, about sixty to eighty feet away, they pretty much look like one and a half ton trucks with real nasty hood ornaments combined with four-wheel drive and a tough outer body. By the sounds and foamy-looking crap coming from their nostrils, they could be powered by steam engines.

Not knowing what the hunter's intentions are, Bigelow tries desperately to keep one eye on the buffalo and the other on the old, hopefully wise, hunter. Not a savage but definitely a native hunter posture is being taken by both hunters. Bows cocked, two arrows tip down in the earth before them, one arrow held between their teeth, crossbow in the left hand, another arrow in their right, not kneeling, their bodies in a coiled squat, calf mus-cles bulging, veins popping out over every part of their bodies in anticipation of what is to happen in the next minute of their lives. Bigelow hurriedly prepares himself for the inevitable, taking a quick glance up just in time to see two arrows fly toward their intended victim: one striking behind the head, glancing off its horns; the other striking the shoulder, breaking in half, bouncing off the tough hide falling to the ground.

Believing it's time for action, the pilot loads his weapon, swinging it into play. He is witness to two more arrows headed for this, now stopping, turning toward them, really agitated, pissed-off buffalo. These two projectiles penetrate: one in the chest, the other into the upper front thigh. Bigelow's first try at this now snorting, ground-pawing, hate-driven beast has passed harmlessly over the animal's back.

The next and last two arrows from the hunters are on the way. Both hit hide and sink into flesh: one in the ribs, another in its back side. Lt. Bigelow prepares his bow for his next attempt. While bringing it into action, he can't help but notice two very important things: his two companions have abandoned their crossbows and are now climbing trees as if they had stairs cut into them, and the other noticeable event is the real close and fast moving, black haired freight train barreling down on him.

Taking great aim at the heart, or where he thinks it should be, Bigelow lets his arrow fly, a miss, not even close to the heart. It seems fate, alignment of the stars, directional pull of the earth's rotation have all played a role. His arrow has struck the right eye of the beast, penetrating three quarters of its shaft's length, surely penetrating the brain. The animal, no more than forty feet to the front right of the pilot, goes completely ass over teakettle landing on the ground with its four feet bent beneath it, looking the pilot right in the eye with its only remaining good one, sounding like a steam engine boiler that's been punctured letting out a bleating, shrilling cry–truly, a devilish sound straight from hell.

Life is not done for this majestic old bull. With concentration, amazing determination, and agility, the wounded brute brings its front legs up to a standing position followed by the rear ones. Bigelow readies his next shot, looking up, taking aim as the beast rises to his feet, once more pawing the earth, blowing and drooling foaming white globules mixed with blood out of its mouth and nose. This sight and sound is shattered by an explosion. Not understanding what has just happened, looking toward the buffalo, he can see that most of the back of its head is gone with rivers of blood, brain, and tissue oozing onto its right shoulder, pooling on the ground beneath it. Looking to his left, the young hunter, still in his tree, has a bewildered facial expression. The old hunter is lying flat on his back with arms and legs splayed out, looking somewhat dazed, the pilot's smoking .45 caliber pistol resting in the dirt at his feet.

Reaching down, picking up the gun, looking at it for the first time in months, finding it in good clean condition, helping the old one to his feet, standing facing each other, for the first time, Bigelow has the upper hand with his captives, yet here comes his second act of collaboration with the enemy, putting the safety in the on position, grasping the gun by the barrel, hands it back to the old man.

Now focusing his attention on the carnage and mayhem that has been inflicted to this once tranquil little meadow, he can not only see the remaining buffalo stampeding their way south, he can finally hear their bleated snorting cries now that his hearing is slowly returning after its deafening interruption. Viewing this scene, he can only wonder what the old one's intentions are with such a large chunk of meat. Knowing they are a two-day trek away from hooch sweet hooch, with the road bumpy and long, this added weight will make this a big, ass-kicking journey.

Turning back to the hunters, the young man is picking up his and his friend's crossbows while the old man places the Colt into the old rice sack and retrieves, to Bigelow's bewilderment, a US military issue Ka-Bar Marine knife that he hasn't seen before. This does not come as a shock or surprise, after almost ten years in this country, Uncle Sam's war machine must be scattered all over the Asian continent.

As all three are standing surveying this scene, suddenly, there is an eruptive spontaneous bellowing of laughter, joined by bird screeches and monkey howls, bringing great relief and joy to the three stressed out and tired hunters.

Moving to the task at hand, first thing the two indigenous do is drink a sampling of the animal's blood. Being offered the same opportunity from a rolled leaf cup, Bigelow for the first time tastes the clotted, acrid-smelling, warm, strangely bitter-sweet nectar of life.

The old hunter moves onto the carcass with the finesse and skill of a professional butcher: carving nice thick steaks from behind the lower shoulder, moving into the interior of the beast itself through an incision running neck to bowel, retrieving unidentifiable white and yellowish blood-covered organs that are being wrapped in banana leaves by the young one. Once done with the bisection and removal of the intestines, with bloodied hands the old hunter marks an area of the hind quarter, handing the knife to the pilot, indicating he should remove the entire rear leg section, including the massive hip.

As they gather their bundles, the large portion of the hind-quarter lashed with vine hangs from a bamboo pole. The remaining parcels are bundled in a banana leaf package to be carried over the shoulder. The old man and his companion intend to burden themselves with the pole-carrying task, being closest to the same height, this will make traveling a little easier, leaving the rest for Bigelow to carry.

Before their final departure, the old hunter, who up until now has been carrying the old rice sack looped through a rope belt holding his shorts up, steps over to Lt. Bigelow and again showing his respect and utter faith, holds out his hand and offers up the sack for the pilot to carry, the sack his Colt pistol is in. Bigelow accepts the offer, flinging this sack along with the load of freshly harvested buffalo parts over his shoulder. He is ready for their adventure home.

Taking the lead, the old one moves a little deeper into the clearing. Turning south at one of the buffalo trails, this is something the pilot's never seen them do, follow a trail. Not just a path, this thing looks like a bulldozed, one lane highway with dark menacing tunnels cut through the thick brush. It has taken many, many years of buffalo migrating to plow this out.

Following this track for some time, the trail drops toward the southeast into a deep looking ravine. At this juncture, they turn in a southwesterly direction, skirting a somewhat imposing mountain. This track seems a little more subdued in its terrain and obstacles. They did not depart until mid afternoon so the sun will not stay in the sky much longer; it's already casting long dark, tinted shadows across the landscape, bringing a close to their day.

Setting up their makeshift campsite, placing their blood-soaked parcels down, the pilot sees another possible opportunity to ask about the Asian tiger and its amazing ability to sniff out a fresh blood source. Their meal this night consists of cold thinly sliced pieces of raw meat, tartar style, combined with rice, making for a very satisfying and hearty late evening meal. Bigelow's worry and fear over tigers, lions, and snakes is overcome by his sheer physical and mental fatigue. He plunges into a deep restful sleep.

A fresh, new morning, the air seems crisper, less heavy. The birds, trying to outdo each other for clarity, pitch, and loudness, simulate war planes with their swooping dog fighting and dive bombing of each other. Lt. Bigelow, after one of his best night's sleep in a long time, is feeling fully refreshed and rested, ready for the day's long journey, trying not to contemplate thoughts of steep mountains and those unpleasant claustrophobic ravines, hefts his assigned load.

The slope of the hill they're on is wooded with light green two-foot tall ferns. Every so often, they scare up a pheasant type fowl when bursting through the underbrush, startling the three travelers. This route back seems easier than the trip to the buffalo field, not as much heavy tangle-footed vines. The trees are not as close growing, but their combined overhead canopy is not allowing the forest floor to receive much light. By midday, the heat with its humidity has drenched the hikers in sweat, coating their clothing with a caked on white film of salt, irritating the flesh when and where it's touched or rubbed.

Not stopping for a lunch break, sucking on a piece of dried fish and a gulp of water during short rest and recoup stops, the old one is on a mission, pressing on as if on some sort of schedule. Again the old man changes direction, moving from the side slope they are on for a more direct assault of the mountain itself, bringing a new challenge to their already bone-weary bodies. Moving in an slumped over posture, trying to maintain forward momentum has changed the order of march, with the old man and his companion slowing caused by them dragging the heavy hindquarter. By natural chance, Bigelow takes the lead. There is no protest from the hunters as he slowly trudges past them. Nearing the end of their endurance, the old man whistles for the pilot's attention; as Bigelow turns, the old one simply points to the left. Again moving on an angled slope, the trees growing farther apart with more ground hugging cover, making each step difficult and tiring, it seems they are racing the sun. Clomping along, trying not to distance himself from the others, Bigelow slows his pace. Suddenly, he has an unnatural deep gut feeling that he knows for the first time in days, his almost exact geographic location. Not more than twenty yards to his right front, hidden among the ground cover and tangles of vine clumps, is the stream that quenches their daily thirsts.

Lt. Bigelow, waiting for his fellow porters, lends his hand in assisting the slightly out of breath old man. Receiving the obligatory smile of approval, they stand at the last moment of another dying day, enjoying this approaching quiet time. A few birds shouting their nightly displeasure to the vanishing sun as it hides beyond the distant tree covered mountains. Once the young hunter has gained his breath and composure, the old one leads off in the direction of their storage cave. Not more than a few yards around a small grass and fern-covered hillock, removing the potted shrub and rolling the stone obstruction aside, he opens the buffalo parts' package Bigelow has been carrying. Looking through these carefully, he examines and separates some of the parcels for storage.

Not looking at nor paying any concern to Bigelow's reaction, the old one removes the Colt form its rice sack storage, replacing it into its issued US military holster, placing the Ka-Bar knife aside, returning the belt, holster, and revolver into the sack, then placing it in the far corner of the cave.

Backing out with the knife and selected intestinal organs, replacing stone and potted shrub, moving off in the direction of the hooch with Bigelow and the young man doing the pole carrying, the old hunter was out front in an intense investigation with his approach using his instincts, glancing from ground to grass, checking scrubs for signs of disturbance, looking for any tracks or foot prints visible in the waning light. Finding none, he signals them to advance.

Initially, the buffalo hindquarter is placed on the ground; it will eventually spend the night tied high in a nearby tree away from blood-sniffing rodents, snakes, tigers, and the ever-present pesky ravenous ants. This herculean task will be performed by the young man, the only one with any strength left after their five-day arduous adventure.

The strange feeling of security, comfort, and belongingness is slowly washing over Bigelow, that same sensation he has dealt with before on shorter but nonetheless strenuous expeditions. This flimsy, no door, fire trap of a structure, allows Lt. Bigelow worry-free, sound sleep. Someday, somehow, he must ask for an answer on the Asian tiger question.

CHAPTER 2

F OR THEIR MORNING meal, the old man cooked up some excellent tasting buffalo bacon-flavored meat mixed with vegetables and the ever-present clump of rice. This early morning feast is leisurely taken under clear skies, the air not yet full of chaotic bird screeching or monkey chatter. There will be no forays into the wilderness this day. While Bigelow is scurrying among the underbrush for suitable pieces of firewood, the young one is in the process of digging a pit in which they will roast the huge chunk of buffalo once the old man finishes the careful removal of hide and the stripping of various blood vessels, fat, and muscle attachments.

Starting an open fire like this has never been done before, at least not with the pilot's knowledge, building a roaring inferno in the three-foot deep pit, letting it burn down to red hot embers, covering these hot coals and cinders with softball-sized rocks then placing more fuel in the hole. Once this has flamed down, the old man finished with the meat preparation including its encasement in banana leaves. With Bigelow's help, they gently lower this bundle into the pit of hot rocks and red glowing embers; the final task in this process is to fill the pit over with dirt, after covering the meat with palm fronds.

Near midday, the ground covering the cooking pit is dribbling out small wispy spirals of the most wonderfully smelling smoke, attracting and filling the air with swarming little black fly-like creatures with a high-pitched buzzing, voicing their approval to this undertaking. Time has not been wasted, moving from storage cave to cook stove, quick trips to various locations in the nearby forest, returning with food stuffs the pilot has never before seen, mixing these and other ingredients. The old man has assembled quite a diverse menu.

Before the start of the impending sunset, with the old man tending the cooking pit, Bigelow and his young friend are not far off in the wood line gathering broad leaves. As sudden as death itself, without any warning, the surrounding trees and jungle, all the earth has fallen silent in a heartbeat. Monkey sounds and bird calls have all vanished.

The old man, stopping interest in the fire pit, moves in the direction of the hooch, searching for his crossbow. Bigelow and the young hunter are farthest from the hooch, also weaponless. Their reaction is go to ground scanning their front and flanks for movement. The sun casting long shadows is sending bolts of light, splashing through the woods, not helping with this detection. Straining to hear any strange sounds indicating unwonted visitation, the two move in a low slow steady advance in the hooch's direction.

In a hurried moment, the old hunter is moving toward the big canopied tree just a few feet north of the hooch with bow in hand, one arrow poised for flight, notched end balanced against a taut strung bow string, low posture, quickly scanning his front, moving to the thick sprawling tree trunk, peering around it looking for any signs of danger. Lt. Bigelow is the first to see him, just a dark-silhouetted lone individual, short and stocky, fireplug-like build, advancing slowly out of the concealing darkness, slowly showing himself purposely, revealing a primitive loinclothed, head-banded, indigenous tribesman. Not so primitive is the Kalashnikov—folding stock, thirty-round magazine—AK-47[1] he's holding waist level pointed directly at Lt. Bigelow's midsection.

---

[1] Russian-made assault rifle.

Glancing up at the old man, not knowing if he has also seen their guest, looking for any recognition that he has, none is forthcoming. Quickly turning to the young man, finding him with a shit-eating grin on his face, showing little or no alarm, facing his formidable foe, lifting his head, slightly viewing his surroundings, Bigelow discovers ghost-like figures wafting through the forested jungle like an early morning fog being pushed into existence on a wave of stealth. From a short assessment, he counts three to five, maybe more, doesn't really matter; first one had them outmanned and gunned. Coming to his knees with his arms still raised over his head, turning in the old man's direction, finding that same smile on his face as his young friend, leaves Bigelow thinking he has not been fully informed as to the evening's complete schedule.

Coming close to the pilot, the only one in the group wearing shorts is revealing himself in the remaining vestiges of twilight. He turns, slinging his weapon over his shoulder. Advancing toward the old man with his arms outstretched, the two men embrace. Bigelow, a little confused while witnessing this encounter, is surprised even further when the young hunter comes brushing past him, stops abruptly, standing before this man with hands clasped held to his chest in the typical Asian prayer posture, then rigidly bows. The remaining newcomers, shouldering their weapons, converge on the smiling, hugging, backslapping trio. All but one, he remains vigilant within the tree line, AK-47 leveled at Lt. Bigelow's churning stomach, eyes never leaving his intended prey, paying no interest or concern to the surrounding welcoming commotion. Separating from the others, the old hunter adjusting his attention toward Bigelow, who by now is more comfortable with the situation and has defiantly, if somewhat sheepishly, lowered his arms but is not yet standing.

Arriving at the warrior's side, the old man leans close to his ear, whispering some form of greeting or command, moves only a few steps back with a smile, bringing his hands to his chest bowing from the waist. Then, and only then, does this sentinel lower his weapon, flicking on the safety, collapsing the stock, slinging it over his shoulder, letting it rest in the small of his back, he walks off joining the others.

After hugs and much backslapping, the old man confronts Bigelow with a big grin on his face, extending his hand to assist bringing him to his feet; once standing, the pilot finds himself the focus of interest and much curiosity. Standing among these natives, even in this dim shadow riddled twilight, they are not your normal run-of-the-mill Asian. These people are short and stocky with dark brown skin, muscled arms and legs—the consequents of many long treks through this challenging and most demanding terrain.

Faces, these people have more of a South Sea Island, Chinese look, flatter nose, fuller in the cheeks, larger lips, taller swept-back foreheads, where as the typical Vietnamese have more delicate facial features. Bigelow's wandering eyes pick out other movement coming from the wood line, figures carrying tribal adorned, masterfully woven baskets. They are loin-clothed, bare-breasted native women with anklets, armlets, and necklaces of what looks to be rolled gold or brass.

Taking this all in, Lt. Bigelow watches as the old man walks hand in hand[2] into the tree line with what appears to be this group's leader, the one in shorts. They're accompanied by two armed escorts. The young hunter, joined by the three females and two others from the newly arrived, begin the task of unearthing the cooked buffalo flank. Once exposed, it floods the air with its delicious aroma. This package of meat is set aside, unwrapped, and distributed on plates made of banana leaves. Out of the deep jungle comes two people carting a large wild pig dangling beneath a bamboo pole already gutted with the hair burnt off. After carefully restocking the fire with wood, replacing the rocks, they untie their offering, placing him carefully into the pit and recovering it. Again surprising Bigelow is the building of an open fire, some-

---

[2]   Not uncommon among Asian males.

thing the old man has never ventured to do, but no one is voicing their disapproval of this blatant disregard for night security.

Lt. Bigelow is sitting with his butt all the way down on the ground. He admires but cannot duplicate the indigenous way of relaxing with their feet flat on the ground, knees high and wide with their butts slung low beneath them, pointed toward the earth but not quite touching, one could say in a relaxed low squat. Sitting in the glowing firelight, more details of these people's characteristics are coming into view; the women's and some of the men's teeth seemed at first black. After closer inspection with the light offered, he realizes they are the darkest of purple, stained over years of chewing betel nut, a seed like berry of the areca or betel palm. When chewed, it gives a narcotic jolt to the system, suppressing hunger, reducing stress, and heightening the senses. The men's head and arm bands along with the waistband of their loincloth, which is a tight, fine, hand-woven material of what appears to be made of thin delicate fibers interlaced with a natural grass or other dark green plant matter to lend a greenish tint to the flowing repetitive diagonal design played out over a muted tan and yellow background. Each of the men are wearing gold bracelets with finely detailed tribal symbols notched into them; the same symbols appear on the woman's adornments.

Appearing out of the tree line, walking through smoke and firelight gives the two returning friends the illusion of floating out of the midnight black night. Moving through the scattering of light, the one in shorts is slowly coming into focus, strolling gently through the small groups of eating and happily chatting tribal warriors, giving and receiving small quick head bows, wide mouth purple-toothed smiles followed by a funny mannish giggle.

Noticing not only their jovial, friendly banter and playful easy physical contact with this man, Bigelow could see the admiration, loyalty, and utmost respect they hold for him. Speaking briefly with the old hunter, he is handed something by the old man; looking at it resting in the palm of his hand, with a nod, he turns in the direction of Bigelow who is seated off to one side of the fire eating with the others, but really by himself, alone in a thousand thoughts, a myriad of scenes right out of *National Geographic* magazine playing out before him.

Not knowing if he should stand, remain seated, or run like the wind, he was quickly answered by the approaching visitor's open hand gesture, signaling him to stay seated. He placed his meal on the ground, hands on his cross-legged thighs, bringing his eyes up, making contact with the darkest of charcoal gray pupils set in midnight eyes he's ever seen, bowing slightly, showing gold front teeth through a polite smile. Coming to rest in the firelight, sitting beside Lt. Bigelow, this man extends his right hand, displaying the tattered leather tag torn from the front of Bigelow's jumpsuit. Not understanding this gesture, the pilot, for the first time since his arrival in North Vietnam, is astonished and unbelievably shocked when he hears, "How you are, hoping you to be well or as you Americans say, okay," spoken in almost-perfect English.

Not wishing to let this opportunity pass, the pilot asks his first, not brightest, but his only and last question of the evening. "You speak English?"

This man's wise and funny response is delivered tactfully. "Yes, to your deduction that I speak English, you must have other more pressing questions you would like answered. Lieutenant Bigrow (Ignoring the *E* and *L* entirely, giving the *G* a grunt like sound and butchering the letter *R* as most Asians do), this is not the time. Tonight is to the feast and the rejoining of old friends. Morning is only a short sleep away. In the early light, we shall walk, talk, and decide your fate. Enjoy your meal." With that said, in one quick flash of movement, he is once again among his own.

Finishing the best meal he has had in ages, Bigelow stands, navigating his way through this maze of low voiced, almost song-like, delicate chattering groups of tribesmen. Being recognized and greeted by the always persistent quick nodding head bows and courteous smiles, accompanied by a faint giggle, as he heads for the comforts and imagined safety of the hooch. Lying within the dark confines of this dwelling, peering out the doorway, framing the most beautiful and tranquil natural jungle night scene he's ever viewed, knowing full well that sleep is something this night will not achieve. With the flame of the fire drawn down, the embers are giving the night a grayish fog-like veil, letting only the senses feel movement not witnessing it. No sounds giving location or direction, just a slight disturbance as breeze-blown swirling smoke climbs its way through the trees.

Before early light, that time when you're alone in the deep confines of thought, the outside world not yet reaching you, the dawn hanging onto the silence of blackness, Lt. Bigelow is not quite sure what this day will bring. He knows the priority of questioning when the fingers of impending light claw and scratch its way through the trees, bringing life to the forest floor. Stirring the dying embers into low-flying red hot sparklers, someone places a fresh log onto the fire. This added light exposes a small mound of cooked pig, apparently unceremoniously exhumed from the earth during the night, obviously not witnessed by the ever-vigilant, never sleeping pilot.

Ready to face the unknowns of this day, splashing cold mountain water over his head, shaking off like a dog removed from a bath, he clears his sinuses with hoots and snorkels of exhaled air through his nostrils to the delighted amusement but somewhat apprehensive natives. Not at first seeing much, Lt. Bigelow, standing outside the hooch doorway, observes four of the men, seemingly fixing a meal of rice and pig, rolling this mix into a broad leaf, tying it with twine, leaving a large loop for hanging over their shoulder. Finished, they pick up their weapons and move off into the gray shadows of the wood line, each in a different direction.

The old man and his companion did not spend the night within the confines of the hooch, preferring the stars, a warm glowing fire and the camaraderie of their fellow natives. With the early light brings a bristling of activities, storing of sleeping mats, folding of American-issued camouflaged poncho liners used as blankets. All this and packaged food is stuffed into the women's baskets. It's at this time that Lt. Bigelow notices four not previously seen individuals approaching from the same directions the other four disappeared to earlier. Moving to the one in shorts, participating in a short conversation, putting down their weapons, they sit down to eat a meal. Lt. Bigelow slowly comprehends what he has seen. Last night, there were guards or listening posts stationed around this little camp. These people are not slack with security. Is it fear of the tiger or their fellow man? Another question to be asked.

Finishing a tasty meal of succulent roasted pig, Bigelow spots the old man, and his young friend emerge from the hooch. The young hunter is now garbed in the traditional Montagnard attire: head and arm bands, loincloth, and gold anklets. The old one is still wearing his faded black VC[3] shorts. Licking his fingers, sucking them clean, drying them on the back side of his pants, Bigelow finds himself more than ready for this day's unknown consequence, his fate in the offing.

Approaching head-on into the early morning light puts a different face to this man: he has a flat nose, not as broad as the others; eyes dark, not set as deeply as his comrades, more of a European influence; skin tanned from exposure to the sun, not a natural dark brown tone. Reaching Bigelow, he waves an inviting gesture to join him for a walk into the wood line in the direction of their ever present water supply, the stream up and around the corner from the hillock near their storage cave.

Finding a pleasant streamside location, they sit in the early morning's defused light with the sound of running water battling to be heard over the waking monkeys and still perched but loudly squawking birds. They are not alone. Fifty feet to their flank, just across the stream from them, are armed sentries. The two are secure for their scheduled morning conference, removing

---

[3]   Viet Cong

his camouflaged boonie hat, revealing a short cropped military style haircut. The orator begins.

"Lieutenant Bigrow, I know there are many desires you have to ask questions. First, I say to you the wishes of my brother Dinh, his hope for you to have fulfilling, prosperous, happy, and long life. May your god be with you."

Dinh, that's the old man's name, never did get into the name thing, never seemed relevant. Bigelow asks, "Young man's name?"

"Nhu is his name, but he's not blood of my brother. I am called Bao. I call Dinh my brother because we grew up together. My parents ran an orphanage here in the north. They were missionaries—my mother French, my father Montagnard. They met at her parent's church school when they in their teens, fall in love, make her parents angry for long time. Dinh's parents were teachers in the south. During one of the many rebellions, like most uprisings and revolts for some reason, they kill the teachers. Dinh, not yet one-year-old, was brought up north by refugees and deposited at my parent's orphanage."

The pilot contemplates his first real question, one more important than that of tigers. "Bao, I knew my location at the moment my plane was brought down, but I do not know where I am at this time. I do have one question, why am I here with Dinh?"

Thinking on this inquiry, Bao, preparing his answer prudently and carefully, gives a golden smile to the pilot. "Bigrow, this could take some time."

"Besides your company, all I have is time," Lt. Bigelow gave a curt response, as quick as a cat. Laughing at this, Bao stands and moves a step or two toward the stream conspiring with his thoughts and feelings, turning, retracing his steps, once again sitting beside Lt. Bigelow. He begins almost from the dawn of time.

"Vietnam was first populated some four thousand years ago. Some believing Chinese from the north migrated south about the same time Polynesians and other island natives were exploring the bountiful coastal areas. The meeting and mingling of these wanderers became the first true race of peoples in this part of Indochina, Montagnards. These people believe they are true decedents of this coupling, *Dega*, a term used by these people. It's meaning in the western world, Adam and Eve, they were the first residents of this land. They are maybe a simple wayward group at times, but with their skills and understanding of their environment, they survived, forming different clans or tribes all over South and North Vietnam. These clans include the Bru, Jarai, Rhade, and Koho among others. They are primarily a nomadic people, practicing slash and burn agriculture, fishing and hunting until the resources are depleted, then they move to a new location.

"Confucianism, a religious sect made up of a Chinese ethnic group, started migrating south out of northern China flowing into what is now Vietnam. This rushing influx of educated, commerce-oriented village and town builders, along with experienced farmers, pushed the Montagnard off any good land, driving them to seek refuge in the high mountainous regions away from their fertile plains, coastal hunting, and fishing grounds. Much like what the white man in America did to the native Indians.

"From its conception, this diverse region of Indochina has been in an almost constant state of turmoil and conflict. Note that this land has had fifteen names, its current name affixed by France in 1945. The French also gave the nomadic hill people their first public and acceptable unifying tribal name *Montagnard*, meaning mountain or hill dwellers. Until that time, they were just an interracial migrating group of unknown and unnamed people."

"France's colonialism starting in the mid 1800s did nothing for the solidarity of this land, with its religious factions, political groups, and the communist all trying to carve out and secure territory for themselves. Things got even worse during the first and second world wars. Some of the biggest losers in all of this were the Montagnard, forced into becoming everyone's coolie laborer, virtual slaves.

"The first glimmer of hope for a united, unified country was following the defeat of Japan at the end of World War II, France holding land but not political influence. A brash patriotic warrior statesman by the name of Ho Chi Minh, already a party leader and world traveler, went to the Geneva meetings attended by all the so-called free world leaders, thinking, praying, and hoping against all odds of achieving independence for his beloved country. Not having this granted, France being allowed to return to its prewar colonialists ways, lead us to war in 1946."

Removing his hat, wiping his brow, Bao continues, "Dinh and I were educated at my parent's orphanage school, all necessary studies allowing me to go to Moscow University getting an engineering degree. Dinh studied hard, gaining knowledge from books and my mother's political ranting. He excelled in the knowledge of forests and jungles. This schooling was provided by my father on many of their scavenging and hunting excursions. Dinh's main goal, his soul purpose in life was the revenge of his parents, parents he never knew but loved deeply. In the early fifties, I traveled to Russia studying for my future. At eighteen, Dinh joined the Vietminh, Ho Chi Minh's army at the time. Not satisfied with the everyday life and mundane duties of regular line troops, Dinh volunteered to become a sapper, a highly trained individual in the art of stealth and mayhem. These are the guerrilla fighters that crawl, almost naked, undetected through an enemy's barbwire defense, removing trip wires, booby traps, and reversing claymore mines to detonate back in the defender's direction. Once through the wire, they use their only weapon, the satchel charge, a carrying bag full of high explosives to destroy and terrorize camp personnel. Most missions were considered suicidal. Dinh enjoyed and excelled at his trade.

"We were both sent south in the early fifties, our destination Dien Bien Phu, the last and deciding battle of the war with the French. I spent my days and nights, along with my new engineering degree building roads, bridges, tunnels, and cave structures off in the distant mountains. These caves housed hospitals, munitions, and were used for food storage. Most important, artillery pieces that were hidden in these caves were rolled out and fired than returned after being used. The French air and land observers could never find them."

"Dinh, on the other hand, was on the valley floor, digging narrow slit trenches under constant mortar, small arms, and machine gunfire so he could get up close and personal with his enemy. This was fifty four. We were back up north in fifty six, the year of the unification vote that never happened, pissing off Uncle Ho and starting one more costly war for everybody involved. I returned to school. Dinh spent the next few years recruiting, training, and equipping a sapper battalion. These later would be segmented into smaller groups, platoon size to you Americans, sent south to disrupt and or destroy your Special Forces camps strung out along the Laos and Cambodian borders.

"These groups were joined up with large ground forces, the sappers always initiating a surprise attack doing as much damage as possible, causing confusion and chaos among the camp's defenders. His actions and deeds of extreme bravery and courage did not go unnoticed. My brother was decorated and given the rank of lieutenant in the North Vietnamese Army. I too was an officer. My promotion achieved through my engineering skills while working on new roads, bridges, and the constant road maintenance and repairs following B-52 strikes on the Truong Son Route[4] running the entire length of Vietnam crossing into Laos, Thailand, and back down into Cambodia. We both spent many years in the south, returning north for short periods of time, visiting my parents and our friends. All are veterans, all suffering the rigors, shortcomings, and tragedies of war.

"In late 1966, early 1967, Dinh took part in the siege at Loc Ninh, a Special Forces camp seventy miles northeast of Saigon, almost on the Cambodian border just off highway 13. During the final assault, Dinh was badly wounded and was taken into the surrounding rubber plantation and given inadequate medical attention. On the brink of death, they took him to a jungle loca-

---

[4]   Ho Chi Minh trail.

tion to let him die. Being of strong will and body, he lay for days in the harsh elements before being discovered by Montagnards of the Jarai tribe who were out hunting, following the hostilities. Bringing my brother into their encampment, working their jungle medicine and magic, they did for Dinh what he did for you: healed his wounds, let him recuperate, and gave him time to settle his inner being, making peace with his soul. He had been witness to much destruction and death.

"Dinh thought he was master of his domain. He was one with the world, the surrounding forest, and jungle was his provider. As you well know, you have survived on only what he has appropriated from this seemingly endless source. He was awed watching the Jarai deal with their environment. Their skill and techniques as hunters is amazing. They use animals, not only for food but also the many applications of its byproducts. Their medical prowess was amazing, using just plants and roots along with various tree barks, assorted leaves, and plants. Most impressive was their awareness and understanding of their surroundings. They used primitive conservation and preservation of the jungle itself.

"It took time, six months he thinks, before he could half ass take care of himself and move around on his own. His time in recovery was spent sharing a hooch with one of the tribe's elders, his wife and two children, a young boy, maybe eight or ten years old. The other, not only charming in her shy approach when tending his wounds and administering food and drink, she was a beautiful thing all of sixteen.

"This Jarai tribe is no different than the others, caring and compassionate. They respect all peoples, practicing their beliefs, never thinking twice about taking a Vietnamese wounded soldier into their care, even with the animosities felt toward them by most Montagnard peoples. He lingered in his recovery for almost a year, moving once to a new location, helping not only in camp construction and local food gathering. Once he was physically able to do so, Dinh joined in the hunts. Time was not wasted on romantic endeavors. Dinh and his Montagnard nurse fell in love.

With her mother and father's blessing, they were married in a traditional hill tribe Montagnard ceremony.

"His ability to speak Montagnard, learned from my father, a Rhade clansman, did more than ease relations. Within his new family structure, he was able to give help and advice in their struggles with this most confusing and constantly changing modern war, where fire and death come suddenly from above without warning from fast-screaming silver-winged birds and giant dragonflies.

"There came a time for Dinh and his wife, not only to move from the hooch, they were sharing with her parents. Dinh convinced all concerned that the three should migrate up north. His wife's parents wanted an education, some semblance of safety and what most parents wish for, a better life for their son, far better than what they could provide him. Two months traveling on the Ho Chi Minh trail was not the most pleasant of journeys. Dinh and his small family spent many uncomfortably anxious moments avoiding NVA troops going south. The 1968 Tet offensive depleted their fighting force in the South. The North was frantically trying to bolster its legions."

Again standing, Bao moves to the stream, kneeling. He scoops up a handful of water, drinking in its refreshing coolness. Taking a short minute to revue his surroundings, Bao continues, "I know this is maybe more information than you need to know. I just feel with the situation we are all in, you should know and try to understand the reasoning of things. Why are you with Dinh? He was simply trying to save your life. At this stage of our little war, your country signing a treaty, washing their hands of this whole mess, the South not being able to defend itself, you were no longer needed as a bargaining chip. No need for any more POWs. If you had been taken by government troops, torture and a slow agonizing death would have been your fate.

"You were in the same predicament he was in at Loc Ninh when the Jarai hunters found him. He saw a way to return a grateful deed, to give back a life. Lieutenant Bigrow, you have your life back. You are blessed to be here. Dinh would like to see you returned to your country so that you could tell your people how the Montagnard saved your life and helped in our rescue. Maybe they will someday help the Montagnard."

Pondering all this, visualizing for a moment what could have been, Bigelow now moves to the stream, splashing water on his face. Cupping his hands, he drinks in the freshness, relieving his cotton mouth, now able to speak. "This is good fascinating information, Bao. I know I owe a great deal more than just my life to your brother. But I must ask why this isolated mountainside, and how did he know you were arriving on the particular day you did?"

"My answer again is not short or simple. Let me continue. As for our arrival date, over eight months ago, I told Dinh we would return on the first quarter moon, following the second rainy season. That was last night. As for this location, my father would bring Dinh and me to these mountains when we were just boys. We spent wonderful days hunting followed by many splendid nights in front of a warm fire listening to my father's Montagnard growing up childhood stories. This place was discovered by my father while on an extended hunting trip because game was scarce in the lower hills and meadows one year. After you Americans entered the war, he saw what he thought was indiscriminate bombing of the North as a prelude to invasion and occupation. With this possibility in mind and it taking five days to reach here from any heavily populated village or town, we started visiting more often, eventually building a hooch, cooking area along with a storage cave. With plenty of game, fish, and drinking water from the nearby stream, this makes an ideal spot for a hunting camp or someplace difficult to find. With the knife edge ridges at steep angles and ravines plunging almost straight down to nothing but black despair discouraging hunters, woodcutters and heavily burdened army troops from venturing up this high, my brother has been up here for nearly two years. He does not wish to be found."

Speaking quickly before Bao can go on, Bigelow asks probably an unneeded, unnecessary question, "Why?"

Stifling a laugh, Bao smiles, the light giving a sparkle to his gold front teeth, moving his neck and arms in a quick stretching motion. "Beginning in the mid-seventies, my brother and I were both at my parent's orphanage for the first time in many years. Conditions were verging on deplorable. Father was hunting when he could, but the influx of orphans from surrounding bombed villages and towns was overwhelming. The communist cadre and medical personnel denied services and aid to them. We did what we could, but the pressure and hardships were too much for my mother. I'm sure she died of a broken heart.

"At this same time, Dinh's wife was preparing for childbirth, this was not to be. Having complications, they traveled to a clean communist run, Vietnamese staffed hospital. When he entered to inquire about help for his wife, they treated him well. Once they saw she was Montagnard, they simply refused to see her. No one would even console his wife, ending their visit by insulting Dinh and his wife, calling her *Moi*,[5] left a deep burning hatred in Dinh, once a respected and valued member in this country's communist army. Two days later with the help of a local midwife, not to her discredit, Dinh's wife died. The child could not survive the rigors of its birth, also died. With much grieving and sorrow, Dinh did what any well trained, experienced, totally pissed off sapper would do. Dinh assassinated the doctor and destroyed their spotlessly clean and sterile operating room, the very one they had refused his wife. This was accomplished with the use of a satchel-charged explosive. Taking Nhu and little else, he retreated into obscurity amidst his beloved highland mountains.

"With all this personal family tragedy, turmoil, and stress, trying to just keep the children fed, clothed, and housed took its toll on my father and me. I was spending most of my time gathering food from any available source. Without funds,

---

[5]   Meaning savage or barbarian in Vietnamese.

charitable donations dwindled as the populous was burdened with more and more government requests of rice and other farm produce including their livestock. Having not many options available, we took the few Vietnamese children in our care to a Catholic-run refugee camp near the coastal plains. The rest of our entrusted hoard consisted entirely of Montagnard boys and girls. My father and I packed them up, moved out, and headed into the Rhade tribal lands among the low-laying foothills of the western mountains. As my father predicted, these people graciously accepted this tragic pathetic result of war. Putting each child with a family, they also arranged lodging and care for my father in his waning years.

"These people could see what was in store. The Northerners were on the move, taking traditional Montagnard lands, kidnapping young men, using them as forced laborers in their farming and construction endeavors. The Rhade people of this tribe were trying to defend themselves with primitive almost stone-age weapons compared to the modern weaponry of their adversary. With my military background and training, I started recruiting young tribal hunters, young men who knew the ways of tracking and traveling quietly through the forest and thickly vegetated jungles. I was building a small guerilla band of warriors.

"After some training in the techniques of ambushing, patrolling, and live action maneuvers, we ventured out to raid, plunder, and pillage distant villages and government facilities. Our first forays into battle netted us some much-needed fire power and munitions, this being our first priority, rice and food stuffs second. This band of Montagnard guerilla fighters is only one of many roaming the countryside. With the communists struggling in the South, having their storage areas and undermanned resupply convoys ambushed in their own backyard, they have brought large military units in to secure supply depots and furnish troops as road security. Once this was done, we simply and diligently moved our operational game of ambush to South Vietnam's supply system. This proved bountiful as well as profitable. We started selling our surplus material and food in a thriving black market down South as well as up here in the North. We not only have a marauding guerilla band of warriors, we maintain a large and well-armed security force. Our group provides three Rhade encampments and their inhabitant's protection from kidnappers, raiding bands of bandit thieves, and murderous and resentful government troops. After translating the story of England's Robin Hood one night, my troops started referring to themselves as the Band of Merry Men. Following this example, they started giving portions of their plunder to the poor impoverished Montagnard villagers."

This was a lot of information to absorb, the day now showing through the forest canopy, giving the stream a sparkling shimmer of life. This breath of light has given rise to the bird's morning song, disturbing the slumber of tree dwelling monkeys. A black spider with yellow-and-white-spotted markings scurries across Bigelow's outer thigh, traveling in a hurried motion down his leg. Reaching down with his finger, he flicks it to the ground where it vanishes into the grass. Lt. Bigelow looks up from his endeavor, catching a quick glimmer of light, reflecting off Bao's gold teeth. Bigelow lines up for another shot at some meaningful personal questions. "Do you know the date? I would like to know how long I've been here."

"From what Dinh has told me, you appeared from the sky shortly after my departure. That would be a little over eight months. I cannot give you a specific date. We calculate our time through moon phases and seasonal changes," Bao replied.

Lt. Bigelow thinks this time lapse is inaccurate; if it is correct, he was incoherent lapsing in and out of consciousness for quite some time. Luckily, Dinh and his jungle medication worked its healing, magical wonders. Knowing the where, having the why explained brings Bigelow to his only logical question. "Bao, what do I do? Where do I go from here? You mentioned fate being discussed this morning. I fully understand your brother's intentions. I am more than just thankful. I'm indebted for life. My concern at this moment is the future."

"Bigrow, I came here not only to see my brother, delivering news of family, and other matters, my main mission this trip is to return with Nhu. It's time for him to enroll with school so he can advance to a university, his father's wish. When Dinh mentioned coming up here to live and ready Nhu for school, I sent with him my old school books and material beneficial to this task. It was much surprise to find you here. We have talked long on your future, what would be best for you and realistic for us. This debate must continue with your input and desires known."

Waiting just a brief moment before answering, Bigelow responds with, "My desire and ultimate goal would be to return home, as any ones would. This task seems somewhat impossible from my standpoint, there being a lot of miles and a lot of water before reaching a safe shore."

"We will have some food, sit, and further our understanding of the situation. Bigrow, our desire is to see you off this continent returned safely to your home shores, alive and well."

This being said, Bao stands, signaling his men; extending a hand to the rising pilot, they depart this tranquil sitting. On their way back, coming from the opposite direction, three beautiful young Montagnard girls carrying five to six each, of what appears to be hide covered gourds with leather straps attached for the carrying of water. They are headed for the stream accompanied by two armed escorts. While passing, one of Bao's sentries, with a low mischievous tone in his voice, says something to the passing group that gets a shy giggle out of the females, a loud knee slapping laugh out of the men.

Coming into the small clearing that was the burning pit area the night before, Bigelow sees that the mound is gone, along with the fire ring, no sign of ashes or burnt logs. They have spread leaves, small twigs, and a few broken branches over the ground, giving the night's bivouac an unused, natural look.

Moving up to the hooch, Lt. Bigelow can see that their guests will not be staying long, gathered round the front of the entrance, in that half squat sitting position only Asians can master, their meager belongings and weapons by their side waiting for marching orders. Followed by the burning stares of these small yet impressive people, Bigelow enters the hooch with Bao on his heels. They find themselves facing a red-eyed Dinh and a teary-eyed puffy-cheeked Nhu in a farewell embrace. Head bowing, hand clasping, smiles all around, the four sit down, all the way butt on the ground down. Nhu, in his Montagnard attire, looks all the part of a jungle native warrior. He says something to Bao. Their conversation carries with it some hand gesturing and moments of silent contemplation. Once they are through talking, Bao turns his attention to the ever-patient Bigelow.

Slowly speaking with one hand on Nhu's shoulder, the other hand on the pilot's, speaking in French, Dinh softly tells Lt. Bigelow, "Bigrow, Nhu knows and believes you were, at one time in our past, his and his father's feared enemy, sending fire and destruction down to their place on this earth. He feels you have learned respect, understanding, and temperament of the jungle's vibrant heart. It lives in you. Pulsating through your blood are medicines from the trees and plants, from the earth itself. He asks that you take your newfound life, your newfound understanding back to your home. Tell your brothers to never foul nor desecrate this or any other forest again. He wishes to thank you greatly for your help in his schooling. Someday he hopes to be smart like his father, myself, and you. He wishes to be your friend forever."

After Bao has finished translating Dinh's message into English for Lt. Bigelow, Nhu stands up and moves to the wooden shelf, removing a small leaf-wrapped package. Handing it to the seated pilot, without further comment, no hand clasping, no head nodding or bowing, he turns and exits the hooch. Not knowing what to think or do, Bigelow just sits, holding his little bundle, turning it over and over in his hands.

Sitting next to him, Bao states a fact, "Bigrow, it's a gift to you for being a friend, teacher, and brother. Open it."

Unfolding Nhu's gift, carefully peeling off one then another leaf, there lying on this green bed of flora, is a delicately woven, cream-colored, with beautifully entwined dark green and blue lightning bolt pattern designed headband with leather ties for securing, along with a pair of matching arm bands. "God, they're beautiful," tumbles from Bigelow's mouth.

Dinh, speaking French, directs his attention toward the pilot stops and sheepishly looks toward Bao. He suddenly turns his palms up, lifting his elbows off his thighs while shrugging his shoulders. He turns to Lt. Bigelow. "Bigrow, you welcome to stay my friend long time." This is one of the longest English sentences spoken by this man in the pilot's entire time here. Not knowing what really he should do or say, he turns to Bao then Dinh.

"I wish also to be your friend forever, Dinh. I will never be able to repay you for your help, your care, and understanding."

This brings wide grins and a short burst of laughter from the two brothers, turning those coal black eyes in Bigelow's direction. With a stern look on his face, Bao proclaims, "Bigrow, my brother's happy you two are friends, happy you are now healed and strong. When he says you're welcome to stay, he means stay to live here with him a while longer. My mission was to stop here and take Nhu back down to civilization for enrollment at school so he may qualify for university. Finding you here has brought new problems to bear. The situation here in the North is neither good nor healthy for Montagnards, refugees from the South, Vietnamese who assisted you Americans in your war effort and of course, lowly US pilots that have fallen from the sky. We cannot take you with us, Bigrow. I must first check with people I know in the dealings of black marketing and overseas shipping in the hopes of obtaining passage for you to the Philippines or some other safe port. So sorry, this could take some time and doing, maybe three four months. I can say best time for our return would be after the next rainy session. It is only a five- to seven-day trip from this place to the coast. During the monsoons, this treacherous, flash-flooded trip can take weeks, and there's no telling how long the negotiations with black market gangsters will take or what they will ask in return for such risky cargo."

Somewhat stunned and startled but not speechless, Bigelow stammers on, "If that is how it must be, then so be it. I can live here easily with your brother. My time here has been a huge learning process in survival skills, tracking and hunting techniques and all of this with the calibration and cooperation of two diverse cultures without a lot of understanding of languages. My time schooling Nhu was a glimpse into the Asian mindset. His ability to understand and grasp mathematical and engineering problems in this environment was phenomenal. I had trouble with the same equations in a good public school system when I was his age, so I'm good with the stay if it's necessary. I do have some questions before you depart."

Knowing Bigelow had some pertinent questions, Bao flashes a slight smile, beckons with a hand wave, and nods to continue. "You really think it would be possible to leave this country by ship without any papers or a passport? With little to no working knowledge of the Asian language, I'm going to be at a big disadvantage and in grave danger among any ship's crew. My small understanding of French learned in high school has helped Dinh and I communicate in our daily conversations, but my inability to learn or even repeat often spoken words in Vietnamese is most discouraging. I'm wondering if going south would be better than trying for the coast. There are no more American personnel down there. Possibly, friendly Southerners would help or heading into Cambodia or Thailand. I have doubts about a sea voyage."

This brings a quick response from Bao. "Going south is out of the question. NVA are all over the south doing their communist thing: purging of peoples and religions opposed to their ideals and political beliefs; placing good, honest citizens and village rice farmers into concentration camps they call indoctrination and learning centers; and refuge holding areas. What's really happening, their land, personal belongings, and their very lives are being completely taken from them by the victorious, vengeful Northerners. There's too much trouble in the South. Moving into Cambodia or Thailand at this time could be worse. They have just begun their communistic war for survival. Guerilla and bandit gangs, along with private guerilla armies, are roving all over the rice rich lowlands. Throughout the hills, valleys, even the high mountain plains and strategic passes are being held for ransom. Travelers have heavy fines and taxes extracted from what little they have. The abuse of the Montagnard is rampant. Land and life is lost, slavery and hardships for the young. Even with our skills, fire power, and tenacity, we do not venture across their borders. In our part of the world, we travel in familiar forests where we know the lay of the land, the people, and our enemies. We know what to expect, how to react to different situations and obstacles that arise. No, we have never tried to procure passage on a ship before. The black marketers we do know on the coast have dealings with unscrupulous ships, captains selling their cargos illegally, preferring profit over honesty. It's the only choice we have at this time. My country will suffer through this terrible transitional stage of war and revolution, striving for a peace it has yet to find after hundreds of years of turmoil and unrest."

Coming to his feet, Bao offers a hand to his seated companions. "This is the only option right now, Bigrow. I wish to be open to your desires and ideas, but I must look to my understanding of today's situation within my country and its neighbors. Things sometimes change quickly, sometimes not so quickly. I have not received any new reports in the last three or four weeks and will not reach any populated areas large enough to have updated war news for another week or two, so, my friend, you may stay here and await my return. Try and learn as much of our language as you can. Refresh your French." This being said, the two indigenous exit the hooch, leaving Lt. Bigelow standing alone in the darkness of his thoughts, taking in all this profound new knowledge of his future, trying to envision two, maybe three months more of this isolated haven. So far, he has found pleasure and gratification through his ability in adapting to such primitive conditions, foraging for their very existence, challenging life itself each and every day.

Knowing that on his own, there's not much chance of making it to the coast or anywhere else from which he could make his escape. Bigelow's only alternative, the only sane alternative, is to stay and wait for Bao's return. Taking a few moments to adorn himself with his newly acquired native treasures, standing tall and most proud, the pilot joins the others, readying for their departure.

All movement outside the hooch comes to a slow halt, the men slinging their weapons, women harnessing their woven backpacks. In silent respect, they all clasp hands in a prayer gesture, bowing at the waist, giving the all-important smile to a fellow native warrior.

Walking up to the pilot, Bao speaks, "Bigrow, you look as if you belong with the Rhades. You have lived our life. You now know our feelings, desires, and our hopes for you. May the gods watch over you and Dinh while we are gone. It is my wish to remove any doubts you might have about our mission. As one of your famous generals once said, 'I shall return.' Bigrow, time moves past morning. We must start our journey. Are there any small questions you need to ask? There is no time for large ones."

"Well, there is one, really more than one, but this one I've thought about many times. Are there tigers in this part of the world?"

Bao says something to his troops that brings wide-eyed stares of laughter in response. "Yes, we have the tiger in our midst, a very cunning and most secretive animal. You may find paw prints near water, animal carcass hanging from a tree, but seeing one is remote. If you did and it saw you first, that would be the last thing you would ever see. Do not worry, all the times Dinh and myself have hunted in this area, we have seen tracks but have had no sightings. They seem to stay near the grasslands below the forested tree line, waiting the passing of water buffalo, their favorite meal. Hoping this satisfies your concerns in this matter."

"Thank you for that kind, unsettling bit of information. One other thing, when will the rainy session start?"

Bao's reply was analytical. "The monsoons are moving across the oceans as we speak, scooping up thousands, maybe millions or even billions of gallons of water, filling the darkened belly of the thunderous giant beast. North winds will blow it onto Vietnam's shores, sending it racing across the lowlands, crashing headlong into our mountain with walls of water. Skies will be black with rain night and day. Rivers will overflow the valleys, pushing flash floods down onto the lowlands, carving new canyons across a large flat expanse of grassland. The rain will be here soon, my friend. That is why we must leave."

Picking up the rest of their belongings, Bao's troops quietly chat among themselves as Dinh and Nhu say their farewells. Bao approaches Bigelow while pulling the bolt back on his AK-47, slamming a full metal-jacketed, 7.62mm round into the chamber; he fires one loud, echoing blast through the overhead canopy into the midmorning sky. "This is to bring in our security, sorry, easiest and fastest way. Bigrow, you stay well and healthy while I'm gone. Talk with Dinh. Learn more of his ways. He will miss Nhu. Good-bye, my friend." He holds out his hand, smiling his golden smile, bowing his head, and bringing those coal black eyes into direct contact with Bigelow's soft blue stare.

Reaching out and shaking his hand, Bigelow utters his farewell. "May your god be with you and help guide and protect you bringing you to a safe and quick return."

The group has broken up into small organized platoons for marching order. The four members returned from security duty, grab their equipment, and are handed freshly filled containers of water as they migrate into the file of lingering troops.

Turning away from Lt. Bigelow and Dinh, in a controlled officiated voice, Bao gives a command sending two man teams to the left and right, as flanking scouts and one highly skilled trooper leading the way as their point man, Bigelow's little fire-plug buddy.

No more relaxed posture with these people, bolts being drawn and released, sending live rounds into rifle chambers. Moving off at spaced intervals, no sound, save the slight screechy crackle of dried leaves being scuffed by so many bare feet. Moving past the massive learning tree, across and down the small rocky grass clearing, they pass into the shadows of the far tree line. Vanishing into this green mass like smoke filtering through the tree branches climbing for the night sky, in one breath, they are there, the next they're gone.

Not as quick as its death, sound is slowly returning to the trees and surrounding jungle. First the birds, always the birds—they are the jungle criers, their songs announcing to the heavens that once again it is safe to fill the air with the sounds of life, screeches and chirps the howls, grunts and groans, the everyday banter and chaotic clatter that dominates this part of the world.

Standing next to each other, together but really alone with their thoughts. Neither wishes to break the silence of the moment. Lt. Bigelow finally turns to Dinh. "Just you and me, my friend." There is no verbal answer from Dinh, just a red teary-eyed grin and quick nod.

CHAPTER 3

THE NEXT FEW days or a week maybe, the two need not hunt. They have plenty of cooked meat from their previous culinary adventure. The old man has been doing things Bigelow is somewhat curious about. One morning, Dinh started a horseshoe-shaped trench, two, in some places three feet deep and maybe two feet wide on the uphillside of the hooch and continuing along both sides. Bigelow, suspecting the old one's reluctance to communicate is due to Nhu's absence, makes himself busy and scarce as possible while doing menial chores around their encampment. Finally, one evening, Dinh engages the pilot in a short conversation, in understandable English. "Bigrow, we go two days looking for monsoon. Bring back food."

The next morning the two prepare for their monsoon adventure. Bigelow is a little uncertain as to why they must go and look for this storm if Dinh knows it's on the way, but they do need to replenish their dwindling food supplies, and Lt. Bigelow could use the trek to chase down a cure for the cabin fever he has been feeling lately.

Packing for this trip is light: sleeping mat, water, dried and some cooked meat, cleaned and oiled crossbows with plenty of sharpened arrows. They are ready; moving out of camp in an early morning mist brings a chill to the pilot. Can this be the change of weather that has prompted this foray or the need for food?

They start off in a northeasterly direction moving over a small hill at a brisk pace, not quite a jog or run. The old man is headed into a thick bamboo stand, running parallel to a slow dropping jungle-choked ravine, like a pinball weaving his way through the thicket. Dinh pushes off bamboo stalks with such force it sends him into a quick change of direction, grabbing another sturdy bamboo stalk, spinning himself in a different direction, his feet barely touching the ground, like a monkey swinging effortlessly through the treetops.

Bigelow keeps pace using the all-American football technique—shoulder, forearm, hip check, straight arm, legs churning, head down, eyes up move to the left move to the right, fight, fight, fight, no cheers, no boos, just the sound of breaking bamboo shoots, brittle old lifeless stems and the crunching of dried leaves. Emerging from this maze of yellowish green bamboo, they stand on the edge of darkness. Before them lies a devilish steep and deep ravine covered in tangles of vine and moss-encrusted trees, leaving Bigelow to wonder about the old one's true intentions with these kinds of physical challenges.

Dropping off the ridgeline, moving down into the blackness, Dinh travels only twenty or thirty yards and stops, turning to the pilot, pointing out a small animal trail moving across this angled hillside. With a wave of his hand, they follow it bent at the waist using this tunneled out opening like a high speed trail, except for the sudden jerky stops from ankle- and arm-grabbing snags and vines, the going's not that bad. Reaching a fork in the trail, Dinh moves to the right, up and away from the abyss. This portion of the trail brings them back to the steep ridgeline they have been following most of the day; this exit point brings them close to a small clearing with a defused lighted view of five fawn and white spotted deer grazing in the last vestiges of a cool sunny day.

Both men on one knee, the old hunter turns, making eye to eye contact with Bigelow. Pointing to their victims, indicating to Bigelow that he should dispatch the one on the far right, with this unvoiced understanding, Dinh positions an arrow in his bow, second arrow held at the ready between clenched teeth, with deliberate hesitation, ensuring their arrows will fly at the same time they do.

Striking tender hide and soft flesh, both projectiles bore into two very startled and dead young deer. Within seconds, a third is down, leaving two escaping wide-eyed panicked sons of Bambi crashing headlong into the jungle. This bloodlust seems to have relieved a lot of tension for the old man. Standing, smiling, light on his feet as well as his mood, he slaps Bigelow on the back with a little giggle and a congratulatory comment of, "Good kill." This is taken by Bigelow with glee and the humbling fact that Dinh brought down two of the deceased deer.

The task now is to bleed out, gut, butcher, and skin these small Vietnamese high mountain forest deers. With fading light, only the one knife for carving flesh and sawing through bone, the two must prepare this little clearing for the night. After butchering their kill, they dig a shallow hole to bury heads, hooves, and other unusable parts. The salvageable meat and usable parts are wrapped in broad leaves and hung suspended high off the ground with vines cut and thrown over a large overhanging tree branch. Moving to the opposite side of the clearing, arranging himself in such a way to have a clear view of their dangling booty and the downhill approaches to this hastily built camp, in this dark shrouded landscape, Dinh unrolls his sleeping mat. With a slight wink and a nod in Bigelow's general direction, he retires for the night.

Feeling the strain and stresses of the day, sleep comes quickly for the restless pilot, falling into slumber with the lingering tiger issue scrolling through his subconscious mind. During this cold and wind-chilled night, both men find their sleep interrupted by the body's vibrating spasms reacting to the colds numbing discomfort. Lt. Bigelow, finding it hard to distinguish between unconsciousness and sporadic spastic sleep, is suddenly jolted into midnight black existence, bringing his knees into his chest, wrapping his arms around them, squeezing for the warmth that will never come.

Waking with a startled suddenness, it's still dark with a heavy low fog, chilled to the bone. Bigelow lies in the quiet predawn. Challenging his mind for a recall of last night's miserable experiences that only bad dreams are made of, bad weird dreams, like that of a large cat, possibly a tiger on its two hind legs spinning like a top.

As early morning rays of sunlight brighten the surrounding treetops, the birds beginning the day's chants, Lt. Bigelow, focusing through this haze, does not see Dinh. His bedroll is in place, his carrying sack still lying there but no quiver, arrows, or crossbow. Not thinking much more about the old one's departure, Bigelow stands and starts stomping his feet, flapping his arms, crossing them over his chest, thinking this maneuver will somehow, someway, warm him; it won't, but the movement alone helps awaken the body and his senses. With more of a steady light breaking through the trees the pilot's world is slowly coming into view. His immediate area, sleeping mat, quiver with arrows, crossbow, and carry sack, still arranged as they were the night before. Looking up in the direction of the hanging meat bundle, he can see strips of shredded hide, dripping blooded meat shards pulled from the leaf packaging. The ground beneath the overhanging limb looks like it has been plowed. The grass, small shrubs, the earth itself is ripped open and thrown about with furrows two and three inches deep. Confused and skeptical but sure something is not right, Lt. Bigelow moves quickly to his crossbow and quiver, not stopping until he's in the dark shadows of the wood line.

Looking for any movement, listening for any sound, his sudden dash has quieted the few early morning bird calls. His own heart echoing like a drum beat throughout his body, any rational thinking seems frivolous. A cat, upright spinning like a top, a large cat, maybe a tiger, maybe a dream, maybe not. An animal's crying screech trumpets from the bowels of the distant jungle, heightening Bigelow's anxiety and tension. He turns slowly, checking all approaches to his present location, kneeling with his back to a tree. This is his only defendable position.

Not a sound or a reflection of light, a shadow moved, a light ray broken, something's there. Pulling back the bow string readying his arrow for flight, Bigelow tries desperately to locate a target—nothing, just a world of silence. Time is at end, and the earth's rotation has stopped. Movement, ever so slight, flowing through the grasses like a soft morning breeze, there's just shadows and the splashing of the sun's gilded fan bringing color to this black and gray landscape. Lt. Bigelow sees it now, just a dark shape, not very big or tall. It's not moving. Without a word, just holding his bow up like a cross, Dinh slowly stands, revealing himself to the primed and ready pilot.

Releasing a sigh of relief, relaxing tension on the bow string, Bigelow moves back into the clearing pleased to find his companion but startled to see a pale, drawn, tired, and obviously distraught old man.

Reaching the disturbed soil beneath the hanging remains of their now shredded deer meat, Dinh, forcing a half smile, half grimace, bends down, places his fingers into the furrows, tracing their path through the dirt, patting the ground. He stands almost on his toes, like a pirouetting ballerina, arms reaching out clawing, scratching for the blood-dripping meat hanging overhead, dancing and spinning like a top, sounding out like a tiger. Motionless, shoulders in a defeatist slump, looking up, Dinh says the only thing he can. "Tiger, Bigrow."

What a revelation, the old man using broken English, French, mixed with dramatic body and hand gestures. Dinh starts telling his story of the tiger.

Waking in the dark, cold and fog misted middle of the night, Dinh thought he saw shadowy movement across the clearing. Not returning to sleep, he gathered his crossbow and arrows and moved silently around and to his left deeper into the wood line. Once positioned in this new vantage point, he waited. His patience was rewarded a short thirty minutes after settling in. Finally, there it was, a large black shadow, eyes of yellow fire, hunched back, legs pawing through the grass in a low crawling, slow moving, cautious approach into the tiny clearing. When the tiger reached the ground beneath the suspended deer meat, the cat pawed the earth, spinning round and then leaping on its hind legs, clawed and spun grabbing, trying for the prize. On his third leap, the old hunter fired a single sharp-tipped bamboo arrow into the big cat's angel white, thick-furred underbelly, digging into its soft unprotected stomach. Reacting violently with super-sonic speed, it bolted across the small clearing, leaping over the sleeping pilot before scrambling wounded into the night.

Moving around the little campsite, Dinh points to the evidence of his encounter. There's the ground disturbance under the hanging deer meat. Dinh points out a blood trail along with paw prints leading through the clearing over the mat Lt. Bigelow was sleeping on then disappearing into the forested jungle. On closer inspection, Bigelow can clearly see for himself spilt blood and tiger prints leading directly to and over his sleeping mat. On the one side of his mat, there is a clear, fully splayed left front paw print; just ahead of that is the right, shorter knuckle tight push-off point. Five feet on the other side of his mat, there are four closely spaced paw prints indicating the cats landing. Other prints and a blood trail are leading off into the dark unknown.

As for the old hunter's reaction to all this, he followed the wounded animal trying to kill it. Not an easy task, it's dark, and Dinh is making too much noise crashing his way through the tangles and branches. The snapping of twigs, the grinding of dried leaves, these sounds are being echoed through the foggy dark night, letting the cat know something is following. Fearing that the tiger will wait in ambush or clover leaf over his own back trail trying to outwit his adversary, knowing he is being preyed upon, Dinh wisely abandons his hunt and returned to their night's encampment.

Lt. Bigelow is in a state of not shock but rather disbelief. *How could this happen?* In the confusion of cold restless sleep and a ground-hugging fog, the dream of a dancing tiger has past him over, literally. Both men sit cross-legged on the edge of Bigelow's mat, not saying a thing, just sitting staring off into the darkness that is the jungle, each in his own way, thinking of what ifs!

Rewrapping the remaining deer meat, tucking this and their sleeping mats into their carrying sacks, not wishing to remain, not even taking the time for breakfast, they start the day's adventure. They proceed with a lot more noise discipline and greater caution. Dinh leads off in an easterly direction straight into a thick stand of trees so tightly spaced sunlight never reaches the forest floor, resulting in little or no ground cover. Making for a quick advance or a hasty retreat, either one, they are covering a large stretch of territory very fast. Slowing the pace, they begin a gradual climb through thicker ground covering. Moving halfway up this incline, Dinh changes the direction of their march. Bigelow thinks they are now traveling due south, bringing them to the base of a ridge that looks to be a much steeper climb. Resting for a quick snack, deer jerky, and water, Dinh once again starts his assault. Moving bent to the angle of the slope, almost on all fours, grabbing vines, young tree saplings, tree roots, anything to help in their advance. Cresting the top of this ridgeline, Bigelow finds himself on a narrow and treeless strip of land pointing east. Moving up this finger of earth, no wider than three feet, the treetops slowly receding on either side the higher they climb. Coming to a dog leg right turn forcing them back to the south, suddenly, Bigelow sees a familiar sight—the jagged outcropping of rock from which he viewed the South China Sea on his first outing many long months ago.

Again, Dinh has arrived at a known location without traveling the same route. He must know this forested jungle like the back of his hand; he seems to always be in navigational control. Reaching the base of the rock out cropping, Lt. Bigelow can see a definite and ominous change on the horizon. Climbing to the utmost edge of this jagged pinnacle, gaining an unobstructed view of the vast forests and jungles laced with snaking rivers and streams that make up this little corner of Southeast Asia.

Lt. Tom Bigelow, with all his accumulated flying time, in all types of conditions, has never seen a storm front this impressive.

Not only is it dark and menacing, this wall of black clouds covers the earth from horizon to horizon from the earth itself to the highest reaches of the heavens. There are bolts of lightning popping out in all directions, filling the afternoon airwaves with thundering bursts of impending gloom and doom. Turning to face the east, he finds clear and bright skies with the wind moving across the treetops like a rolling white-capped wave making its approach to a waiting shore. Reversing his thoughts and direction, Bigelow heads down the rocky outcrop, stopping in front of Dinh. He asks, "When?"

The old man's response is simple and brief. "Soon Bigrow, soon."

Moving off the ridgeline, they start a leisurely downhill trek, weaving their way through the forested jungle most of the afternoon. On their last leg of this journey, without much to show for two days hunting, a small wild pig, being suicidal, crossed Dinh's path. After simply gutting his find, they continue their homeward trek. Again, before entering his camp, the old hunter checks for signs of any unwanted visitors; Feeling they are safe and secure, they enter their tiny compound. Their first goal is to cut the remaining deer meat into thin strips for drying, the first step in the process of making jerky. The young piglet is being readied for a barbecue pit full of hot rocks.

The mornings are slower to arrive. It's taking the sun longer and longer to reach their secluded little encampment. Its arrival being delayed by the season, it's been windy and overcast, but so far, no rain. While eating a small but delightful breakfast one morning, the two strain to hear and understand the commotion and sound coming through the trees out of the south. Suddenly, Dinh jumps to his feet, shouting, "Monkeys," as he snatches up his crossbow and arrows. Bigelow, somewhat confused and off guard, realizing the noise of screeching monkeys is getting closer and closer, reaches for his bow in time to witness a strange phenomenon—monkeys, hundreds of the scampering little bastards are literally flying through the trees. This spectacle is brought on by the monkey's hasty retreat from the rainstorm chasing after them. Between the two men, seven little monkeys will not be getting wet this rainy season.

For two days now, Bigelow was certain it would start to rain, sky's so dark and ominous, winds steady out of the south, the sounds of exploding thunder causing startled birds to take flight.

Their encampment is being improved upon daily. Besides the horseshoe ditch on the back side of the hooch, yesterday, Dinh gave Bigelow hands-on instructions on how to interweave freshly cut palm fronds into the old hooch roof, preventing major water leaks. The outside walls are having the same broad leaves woven into any cracks or openings. Included in all this hooch remodeling is the construction of a leather-hinged, bamboo-framed, and broad leaf-covered door.

Preserving food is basic—thinly sliced strips of meat dried and smoked into jerky. Some vegetables and what fruit they come across are also dried. Cooked rice is balled up and wrapped in leaves, tied with twine, later to be thrown into a fire's hot embers, reheated easily for a quick addition to any meal.

Then one morning, the skies did not just open up with rain, the skies burst forth with a tsunami-like wall of water. No sprinkles, no light drizzles or intermittent rains. The only prelude to this wall of water was the lightning strikes kissing the black earth with loud crackling booms, akin to canon fire, sending a thunderous roar, echoing through the forest like a freight train rolling through a quiet sleepy town. The pummeled earth answering back with groans of ambivalence.

Heating food in the hooch on a small stick fed fire helps keep the room warm against the rain's chilling cold but makes for a smoky unpleasant experience for the two occupants. Except for personal "natures" calling, they do not venture out of their confines for days on end due to the relentless down pouring of water. The thunder pelting the earth with a drumming rhythmic tattoo of blistering X-ray light is filling the darkened forest with blinding brightness.

Water is running everywhere, soaking everything, giving off a mildewed funky dank odor. Their daily chore is to plug up rivulets of water running through the hooch. All this water has brought other more menacing problems. Ants, these little red devils, normally stay high up in the surrounding trees. All this rain has inundated their living quarters and turned the tree bark into small rapids. These carry the struggling, drowning little buggers round and round down to the ground where they try and find comfort and dry places among the walls' ceiling and floor of this ever more crowded hooch. Their sharp little pincer type bites produce painful bright red welts.

Leeches, these nasty black blood-sucking, blood-gorging finger-sized slimy bastards attach themselves wherever skin is exposed. Removing these blood-filled creatures entails the use of a fire-reddened hot-tipped stick, burning and squeezing your blood puffy skin, forcing them out, making sure their purplish pink head has been fully extracted. Once out, they leave an ugly open bleeding sore, causing one to itch and scratch where they were attached.

Two and a half weeks of confinement in their water-soaked home has left them a little agitated and irritable with each other. Bigelow's French has improved, but his understanding of spoken Vietnamese is still lacking, although, conversing in English seems easier for Dinh now. Certain points don't get across. The majority of questionable meanings usually get worked out with gestures in mime, finger air drawing, sometimes including frenzied pointing and grotesque facial expressions.

Their immediate food source is running low, to the point that they are presently on a vegetarian diet, something neither man enjoys. The current situation is not allowing them to venture out as far as their storage cave; the down pouring of water along with the flash flood like runoff is keeping them isolated for the time being.

Finally, there is a small hint that this massive storm is starting a slow withering death, the early morning wake-up call delivered by the forested jungles voice of revival, birds. Just a few to start with, many more of the winged inhabitants are returning to the treetops as the rains slacken. Lightning strikes are fading to the north. The all elusive sun is starting to show faint whispers of breaking through the tall trees. Opening the door, they are greeted by the refraction of light rays playing off the mirrored surface of the many water puddles that have formed in pockets across their small clearing. A little alarming, but not unexpected, is the amount of debris and downed trees in the area.

This morning, their first in many weeks without a substantial rain fall, will be one of adventure, amazement, and disappointment. Upon leaving the hooch, evidence of the storms furry lies before them. Branches and limbs, large and small, litter the ground. Leaves, brush, and other debris is wound in, over and through a mound of clogged waste, like fish caught in a net. Looking up into the massive tree just a few feet north of their hooch, Bigelow can see large openings where branches, stems, and leaves have been completely ripped out, letting the skies show through. Moving to the right, facing the north side of their hooch, things look fine; mud and debris have gouged out the trench dug by the Dinh, obviously diverting large amounts of water from traveling a more destructive course. Stepping around to the back side reveals some of the same evidence. Dinh's ingenuity, combined with his knowledge of the jungle and years of experience dealing with the monsoons, has saved their little home from certain and utter destruction.

The south facing side of the hooch has a fair amount of mud and tree debris stacked two to three feet up its exterior wall. Continuing to the south, headed in the direction of the storage cave, they find themselves in a new and strange environment.

The storm has not only altered the landscape. Gone is the tranquil babbling brook sound their little stream used to make, replaced by the roar of rushing water. This muddy mix of broken branches and limbs, chunks of dislodged trees and other debris, is being pushed downstream by the swollen, swiftly flowing waters.

Looking for but at first not finding the storage cave entrance, Dinh finally discovers the top portion of the entrance rock, protruding a mere three to four inches above ground level.

Using broken pieces of limbs, the two start digging mud from around the entrance stone. This arduous task takes them into midday. Finally clearing away mud, rock, and unruly tree debris from the cave's approach, they maneuver the cover stone aside. To their astonishment, the cave interior is intact, somewhat damp and musky, but intact. They remove most of the contents, bringing them out to dry in the day's warm sun.

Taking a few bites of limp, soggy deer jerky and some cold precooked rice balls, they stop work for a quick late day meal. Once finished with this little feast and respite, they proceed to their cooking area. En route, they come across an unusual sight; on the edge of a small ridge that drops off into a mud swollen gorge, they see, lying much like fallen dominoes, a row of trees, the first tree uprooted toppling into the others, resulting in the downing of at least half a dozen big old trees. The giant spiderlike root balls of these big trees are huge, measuring twelve or more feet across and some eight feet thick that have created big holes that are filling with water from the heavy rains and runoff.

Getting close to where the cooking cave and oven should be, they again find a changed environment. The hill or where it once was located is gone. In its place is a sunken mud pit surrounded by tree and clay pipe debris, this pipe residue coming from the two chimney flues. The clay oven has been blown right out of its hillside enclosure, replaced by mud and water. Large pieces of the broken and destroyed oven were carried off by the rain's destructive force.

They make a return trip to the storage cave, replacing items that have been out drying in the sun. They will follow this procedure for the next few days, drying out the remaining deer jerky, along with the two surviving bags of rice.

For the next few days, Dinh and Bigelow spend their time removing tree and wind-swept debris from around the hooch.

Their hastily built door that gave them great service during the high winds and heavy rains is now tied in the open position, with the aid of a leather strap.

The earthen oven is being rebuilt using handmade bricks. This brick-making process must be thousands of years old. Dinh starts with river mud, working it into a medium wet slab while mixing in some chopped up grass stalks, building simple forms out of split bamboo lashed at the corners with twine. Fill these forms with the clay mix, smooth off the top, and let them cure five to seven days, or until they are fully dried, carefully remove from forms. Now you have a somewhat rough and simple usable brick. The flue pipe is simply made by loosely packing this same clay mixture around a smooth straight stalk of bamboo. During the drying process, the bamboo shrinks just enough, making it possible to slide the pole out, leaving a hollow cylinder. You now have yourself a clay pipe three feet long. Building the oven into a hillside helps it retain heat and keeps the fire box above ground level, making it more efficient and easier to use. Digging the front portion of the hill out, leaving a base to start building from, Dinh first puts down a layer of flat, smooth river rock, then starts carefully stacking bricks in an overlaying pattern. Each layer cantilevered a few inches over the previous one. Using his mud mixture as mortar to hold everything together, he continues this process until he has a dome-shaped structure. Taking some of the wet clay, using just his hands, Dinh smears a smooth coat of mud on the inside of the oven walls, leaving two small openings in the top rear ceiling of the oven. Dinh places the flue pipe in an angled ditch running twenty or thirty feet up the hill, wrapping the butted joints with broad leaves and covering this coupling with his mud mixture. Once everything is dry, they cover the flue pipe and completed oven with mud and dirt, leaving the fire box and oven entrance exposed. Again, they have the capability of cooking in an oven.

It's been awhile since the last big rains, leaving the pilot to pounder if this destructive weather system is through. Mother

Nature must think so; the grasses and small shrubs uprooted and washed away are replenishing themselves, popping up everywhere. The large mounds of plant matter and tree debris is turning into compost in record time due to its moisture content being sucked out by the humidity and relentless heat of the sun. This decomposing brings with it clouds of musky-smelling steam, leaving the far tree line in a day's long fog bank. New growth is witnessed among the trees and surrounding jungle, bringing a virtual rainbow of new and varied shades of green.

Food is starting to be bothersome; their supply is dwindling at an alarming rate. The only fresh meat added to their meals of late has been two small turkey-like fowl brought down by Dinh. The pilot has been able to kill a three-foot long tree lizard.

The conditions for hunting will improve once the grasses and plants eaten by deer start to flourish and thrive. The monkeys seem to be taking their sweet time in returning to this part of the forest. Their food source, consisting of fruits, nuts, and seeds has been ravaged by the wind and rain. The birds are enjoying the treetops all to themselves for the time being, sounding their approval with day-long serenades.

They are unable to postpone their hunting trip any longer. They move off early in the morning, headed into the higher tree line to the east, no game or signs of any all morning. It is well into the heat of the afternoon before Dinh sights movement in a tangle of vines. Being silent and methodic in his approach, he is almost run over by two very large and aggressive wild boars that come within inches of goring Lt. Bigelow. These two boars are followed by three sows and about six or seven piglets. As they scamper by, Dinh and Bigelow end the life of one sow and a piglet, both sounding a squealing protest to their addition to the hunter's upcoming meal. These two morsels are easy to carry back to their encampment. Neither one weighs much—the sow not more than ten pounds, the piglet maybe five. Not much for an all-day hunt but welcome and real tasty.

Within the past two weeks, Mother Nature has kicked butt in the recovery department. Grasses, along with deer-loving ground cover, scrub brush, and vines of all types, are seen flourishing throughout the jungle and across the forest floor. The distinct high-pitched screeching and rapid chattering of monkeys is starting to return to the canopied treetops, encroaching upon the bird's sanctuary. On a short morning outing while gathering edible plant stalks and bulbous roots for use in cooking, they spot a small wandering herd of deer across the receding river, signaling the opening of hunting season.

Comfortably familiar with his surroundings, a little too relaxed in his approach, Lt. Bigelow walks on a hunt while daydreaming, almost costing him his young life. While passing into recently decomposing matter covering the floor of the forest, it's another bright early morning, they're facing a sunlit panorama of green jungle with steam misting from the vegetation disturbed by passing feet. Bigelow pays no heed to the almost invisible, yellowish, light green with dark green dime-sized spots running down its side, as big around as your thumb, snake. This is one of the deadliest snakes in all Southeast Asia—the bamboo viper, whose bite can kill in less than a minute. Dinh is amazed at the pilot's dumb luck, his leg just being missed by this fanged killer. Bigelow did not see the snake until Dinh dispatched it with a head-removing blow from his razor sharp knife. From that moment on, Lt. Bigelow sticks to a full 110 percent awareness of his surroundings, instilled with a new attitude of never ever trusting this very much alive deadly monster of a jungle!

These tranquil sun-blossomed days are why this place is so damned appealing at times. Bigelow feels very much at home in this environment even with all its trials and tribulations. He finds himself enjoying the experience. He has found plenty of those worldly possessions and conveniences that he can live without. This simple life, this "live off the land" existence, has a strange appeal for him. Something seems right and good about his present life style.

This is all subject to change, on a clear sunny midday of light camp chores and general relaxation after repeated one-day hunting trips. Suddenly without warning, sounds of the jungle are hushed. There is an immediate stillness, one indicating alarm and danger. Something has gained the attention of the lofty, ever-present sentinels, the birds. They have ceased their afternoon clatter of songs. Dinh and Lt. Bigelow are reacting to this alarm with speed and purpose. They grab crossbows and arrows then head for defensive positions in the underbrush bordering the hooch. They are too late. They find themselves surrounded by well-armed, highly skilled stealthy little, brown-skinned, loincloth-wearing tribal warriors. The pilot's little fireplug-built adversary is moving on his prey with his AK-47 at the ready and a big purple beetle nut smile. They're back, Bao and his little Band of Merry Men.

After all the smiling, hand clasping, and bowing, Bao, after greeting his brother Dinh, walks up to Lt. Bigelow, bows, quickly flashing his golden smile while extending his right hand in a very western style, warm and inviting handshake. Speaking first, Bao proclaims, "Bigrow, you and my brother have lived and survived one of the worst monsoons in many, many years. It is good to see you, my friend."

With a grin on his face, Bigelow jokingly replies, "It is good to see you also, my friend. I thought at times, we could just float to the coast, saving you the trip up here."

The remaining warriors gather in the small clearing after emerging from the far tree line in groups of twos and threes. To Bigelow's eyes, they look road-weary, used, and abused. The three female followers are not only carrying their woven baskets full of supplies, they are also struggling with four military type rucksacks belonging to the troops left in the jungle as listing posts and early warning security. Not wasting the day's fading light, the women, along with their male counterparts, start preparing for the evening meal. They are fixing a lemur stew with deer and monkey meat thrown in along with some vegetables and root stock. Others are rolling out sleeping mats, some relaxing in little clumps of chattering bliss. Bao is moving through their presences, checking with each one, a smile, a laugh, a curt bow of the head, an arm on a shoulder for confidence, then on to the next, letting them know he cares and believes in them. As a leader of a primitive people, he is their equal. He is family. Bao's name has a meaning these people know well—"protector."

By the time their evening meal is over, so is the light of another day. Sitting by a dying fire, sleepy and full, Bigelow lies in the cool, soft spring grasses, watching these wonderful little people, feeling comfortable among them, yet not quite fitting in. Bao and Dinh are across from the fire, off by themselves, talking through their dinner, continuing long after the meal is done.

Bao, now moving through the firelight, acknowledging the smiles and the head nods of his troops, is on his way to Bigelow's location. He sits next to him in the grass, removing the camouflaged boonie hat he always wears. He speaks in a soft, almost-whispering voice. "I too marvel at these ingenious little people. Everything in this jungle seems to come so easy for them. They are so aligned with Mother Nature and the environment that she lays out for them. Be it good or bad, they somehow take it in stride with a lot of pride and dignity, their courage and tenacity working together for the good of all. Bigrow, my brother, Dinh, has told me that you faced the tiger. You are still with us. You won this time." With a mighty laugh and a slap to the pilot's knee, he adds, "Try not sleeping next time."

Bigelow joins the laughter. "I think it's better to dream of the tiger than really face one. I won nothing but another chance to be a future meal. Dinh probably told you about my encounter with the bamboo viper? Well, I was asleep on that one too."

With a chuckle in his voice, Bao continues, "Yes, he said something of your encounter with a snake, but he did not call it sleeping. He said your head was up a dark place. Listen, Bigrow, things happen here you can never see coming or have control over. You have been lucky. These bad things have made you think, and that's a good thing. They awaken your senses, giving you a new perspective and a better feel for this place.

"Before we talk of things to come, I must first convey a message from Nhu. He would like to thank you for the helping of his math. There are problems with officials and school administrators, but he is doing well in his studies. He wants you to know that he misses Dinh and you, along with his beloved mountains. Wishing me to say hello to you and hoping you are in good health.

"I'm sorry for not wishing to talk further with you tonight. Our trip here has been long and at times very dangerous. The monsoons have left behind mudslides, blocking the passes along our mountain routes, fallen trees, along with broken branches litter the ground. New temporary streams are cutting through the forest floor, causing constant directional changes in our march. These hazards posed concern and much physical danger for my men. Trees are leaning one against the other, needing only a breath of wind to bring them all crashing down, rock and mud trying to slide its way farther down the mountainsides, flowing into the ravines. This has been a long slow filthy mess of a trek. My present plan is to rest two to three days, do some hunting, cleaning of equipment and our dirty, muddy bodies. Bigrow, we will have plenty of time to talk. I for one am looking forward to it, but for now, good night, my friend."

With that said, along with a grunt of physical exhaustion as he gets up, Bao replaces his hat. After doing the Asian hand and head gesture, he slowly glides his way through sleeping bodies, disappearing into the wispy spirals of smoke being lifted to the heavens by a gentle breeze. Bigelow does not bother with the hooch tonight, finding comfort and sleep in the earth's warm embrace.

The morning shines bright and clear; some of the Montagnard's are off cleansing their muddy, grubby little selves. A few, including the four night guards, are gathered near the lifeless fire pit, eating a morning meal. Bao is not among them. Standing, stretching himself awake, Bigelow approaches the hooch, ready to enter when he hears laughter and giggling coming from the direction of the stream, its swollen waters rapidly receding; it is once again being used for bathing. Bao, along with five of his men and the three women, are returning to camp. In passing, Bao gives the pilot a good morning greeting, tosses him a rough woven, clean towel. "Bigrow, the water is fine, almost too cold for leeches. When the rest of my people trek to the stream, join in, my friend. They will set out security. Relax, enjoy your bath." He moves off with the others into the small clearing to begin their morning meal. Refreshed and replenished after a cleansing swim and a quick breakfast, Bigelow is again anxious to resume his conversation with Bao, this time being more assertive with his questions. Bao and Dinh are walking in the pilot's direction; Bao says something to some of his men. Immediately, three men grab their weapons, one takes point, the others move out flanking the three men. Security set, Bao invites Lt. Bigelow to join him and Dinh for a midmorning walk.

"Bigrow, I have been telling my brother of the many changes taking place all over this country. This you may not know, don't be too surprised, but the United States's involvement in this war is over. Your side negotiated their way out. The North rolled over the South. It's over, kind of, sort of. Hostilities are still taking place in Cambodia. Other skirmishes are taking lives up and down the Vietnam border. The people of the North are rebuilding and devouring land as fast as they can, cutting down large stands of trees, clearing the under growth and surrounding jungles with fire.

"Not more than four, five days march south of here, we had to divert our line of march to avoid woodcutters, many men with axes and chain saws. They had with them regular NVA as guards, not just for their protection, we feel these workers were civilian and political prisoners. They were pulling the logs by water buffalo to a collection point a few kilometers south to a newly cut single lane dirt road for loading onto trucks. Once the timber is removed, they will simply light their fires and let this clear the land for them, until it burns out.

"This movement for land and lumber will not come into these high mountains. Timber is too hard to harvest up here, but their hunting parties will venture this high for the deer, monkey, and wild pigs that thrive in these woods. Driven by the need to feed their slave laborers, they will be here! Dinh knows he must move on to another farther isolated area. He and my father visited many ideal locations during their numerous hunting and gathering trips. I believe he will be all right. My only worry is he will not keep a weapon here, says it is too hard to keep rust and gunk out of the working mechanisms. After time, the bullets retain moisture, powder gets wet, and cartridges corrode and swell to the point that they are useless. Besides, the crossbow is silent, drawing no attention to one's self."

Continuing their walk and conversation, bringing each other up-to-date on the hurriedness rainy session that has just passed, Bigelow and Dinh tell Bao of the days and weeks of confinement imposed by the torrential rains, coupled with tree-shredding winds and explosive lightning. Bao's experience on the coastal plains resulted in some of the same treacherous conditions, including large areas that were flooded, entire villages wiped out by mudslides, with many lives lost.

"This trip, I bring good and some bad news. We have talked of Nhu's progress, of Mother Nature's unleashed fury over these past months. Bigrow, I have done my best. I've visited every black marketer that I know, that I have dealt with over the years, some owing me favors. None, not a one would risk his life, his boat, or the chance of ending up in prison by boarding a round eye for departure on one of their ships. Stowing away is not a plausible solution either. A captain could not only lose his ship, he could lose his head. They tell me the northern government is boarding every vessel before leaving port, placing all crew members on the aft deck. And with dogs, they sniff out any contraband or human stowaways. This is a dangerous way to try and get anyone out of this country. Going down the coast won't help. The North has open access to the entire Vietnam coastline now that your navy has withdrawn. They're boarding hundreds of boats a day, not necessarily looking for an American. Their primary interest are officials that during the war demanded and received large amounts of money in bribes, black market profiteers that dealt in food distribution, people pilfering from government supplies than selling the munitions and medical supplies to gangsters and bandit gangs. The government's not real happy with these people, besides the communist purges, rounding up unsuspecting citizens on the slightest provocation. The government needs all the workers they can get for their forced labor parties. There's a lot of rebuilding to do.

"There is a ray of hope, my friend. In Ha Dong, a town southwest of Hanoi, lives an old French priest, longtime friend of my family. The last time I was visiting with him, he mentioned that the Swiss and French delegations were seeking information about the POW, MIA situation. He told them he did not have any information regarding this subject, said if he heard anything of interest, he would contact them through their embassy in Hanoi or the small satellite embassy in Ha Dong. During my brief visit, I did not mention your existence, not before I had a chance to discuss this with you."

"Discuss what? Bao, what choices do I have? From what you're telling me, the government of the North has this entire country under lock and key. Do you believe your priest friend can make successful contact with an embassy, keeping my identity a secret? Some of your black market friends could have already passed this information to the communist officials for money or favors. Do you think now that anyone would have safe transportation available? I know this is a lot to ask. You probably can't answer until you speak to your priest friend. I am anxious to start, no matter where it leads. My time here with Dinh has been not only a great adventure but also the experience of a lifetime. He has taught me more about the true meaning of life, not only through the ability to live off the land, but also the importance of some type of self-preservation within one's environment. He is a true free soul.

He has the ability, spirit, and faith to treat his fellow man with respect, dignity, and kindness. All this considered, I must try and return to my homeland. It's the nature of man."

Bao gives a direct and honest reply. "You are correct. I don't know all the answers to your dilemma, but I make you this promise, with all my heart and soul, I will try and make your return home a success."

The old man and one of Bao's troops are preparing for a short hunt, hoping to procure food for tonight's meal, as well as meat for their return trip to the coastal plains. Dinh and Bigelow's fireplug-shaped Montagnard buddy are headed in the pilot's direction. With the help of Bao, Dinh asks Bigelow if Ung, this being the indigenous fireplug's name, might borrow the pilot's crossbow. They did not bring along their own, and Dinh wishes them not to fire weapons in the vicinity of his living area. With Bigelow's permission, the two depart.

The remaining troops are breaking down their weapons for cleaning; the young women are removing ammunition from the magazines, cleaning the rounds, and reloading them. A few of the troops who were on guard duty during the night are sleeping; others are sitting in small groups, smoking and chewing betel nut while engaged in conversation. Bao and Bigelow, sitting apart, engrossed in their own thoughts of what's to be, how to achieve their common goal.

Returning from their day-long hunt, the two men place before the fire pit five good-sized monkeys, one wild boar, and two turkey-sized birds of some kind. Two of the females stop their rather arduous and tedious reloading chores and begin the process of meal preparation, skinning, de-feathering, disembowelment, butchering, and the cleaning of today's bounty. Bigelow heads into the tree line looking for firewood. While picking up some sticks, he notices the intent interest Ung has in him. He seems to be keeping an eye on Lt. Bigelow no matter where he goes, showing interest in whatever he is doing; this is not troubling but rather annoying at times. Returning to the small clearing with his firewood contribution, the pilot asks Bao about the interest showed to him by Ung. Bao's laughable answer sounds strange. Knowing little of these people's knowledge and understanding of the real world, Bigelow accepts this simple explanation. "Ung has been told that you, the round eye, came down from the heavens. That you were brought down by a fire-belching dragon, a rocket, that you are a flyer. He knows not about pilots and their planes. He believes you can fly, Bigrow. He's just waiting for you to flap your arms and take off, or at least for you to try."

The evening meal is good. The meat, rice, and vegetables are done to perfection. Well, Bigelow thought the meal was adequate. The day's end is taking longer now, early evening spurts of sunlight relinquishing their hold on the depths of the jungle, not quite reaching the earth, only shadows being thrown about, drifting into total darkness.

The small groups of chattering people, once sitting by the dying fire, are now in a quieter, relaxed posture readying for the upcoming trek. Bao and Dinh are standing by the old giant tree in deep conversation. Bigelow removes himself from the cool night and enters the hooch.

Moments later, two silhouettes break the darkness of the hooch's doorway. Sitting down, one of them speaks to the darkness. "Bigrow, myself very much happy to be with you all this time. You have given to me much help with Nhu, not only for his study, but for letting him see and understand the meaning of compassion for his fellow man. You learn fast and good, Bigrow, the ways of this place. Just remember to stay one step ahead of the jungle, always know your next move before you take it. This place does not give up second chances very often. You have had yours, my friend. Please go tomorrow with my hopes to you for a safe homeward journey. I will be your friend till the breath, I can no longer take."

In this tunnel of darkness, the sound of silence is deafening. It is now shattered by a loud intake of cool, late evening air. Bigelow speaks after his exhale. "Dinh, my friend, I owe you, in the simplest of terms, my life, no matter the outcome of all this, my time with you and Nhu, especially my time here in this jungle paradise with the master, the ultimate master of his domain. You move through this maze like a small ship windblown across a still, calm sea. The perfection in your skills, your knowledge, understanding, the love for your environment is unquestionable. You are the heartbeat that echoes through this forest. Your spirit drifts through the jungle like the ghostly early morning fog. You were the light that shone my way through this dark labyrinth. You will always be in my heart. Thank you, my brother, and may you live in peace, all your long days." With that said, the silence is returned to the night.

Sleep was hard to come by this last night on Dinh's mountain. As Lt. Bigelow exits the hooch, he is bursting into the early morning with a new awareness, new purpose, and an overwhelming guilty feeling about leaving a home that he has known and enjoyed for so long, a lifestyle and friend he will miss. He will cherish the memories of this place and the time he spent here. These thoughts were the ones that kept sleep at bay.

"Bigrow," Bao calls out to the pilot as he approaches the group gathered in the small clearing. "Bigrow, I have something for you." Coming closer, Lt. Bigelow can see Bao holding his holstered .45 Colt pistol attached to its belt. "Dinh thought you might need this more than he did. It's been cleaned and found to be in good working order. You only have six rounds left. We don't use .45 ammo. We can probably find some somewhere along the way. Until then, aim carefully before firing."

Turning his attention back to his troops, Bao was giving quiet but precise orders, switching the safety of his AK into the off position, aiming for the heavens, and then fires a single resounding shot skyward. Bao is standing next to Lt. Bigelow as their procession starts off, point man out, flankers headed out into the tree line. The retuning night guards gather up their equipment and put their rucksacks on. Bao turns to the pilot. "Bigrow, you are my unknown, untried warrior. I shall ask, with no disrespect, that you walk in line between the second and last of our women. Keep your head up, eyes off thighs and butts. This is serious shit. No sleepwalking on my patrol."

Before departing, Bigelow asks Bao, "I have not seen Dinh as of yet this morning. I would like to say good-bye."

"My brother accepted your good-bye and gave you his last night. He awoke early, went into his forest to hunt this day's meal. He did not wish to show his displeasure and sorrow with your leaving. He is watching, that I am sure of."

Leading off at a military manner, conversation and noises has died off completely, no grab ass, smoking, no steps taken without purpose. Lt. Bigelow can see these people glide through the jungle in the marveling way that Dinh uses—no effort, no sound, just a steady flow. There is no other way to describe it—flow, smooth, uninterrupted movement.

Throughout the morning and early afternoon, the pace never slackens. Rest is not an option. The terrain is allowing for a fast advance toward the coast. Bao, letting Bigelow demonstrate his skill in the use of the crossbow, stops for the night. Sending him out with Ung, within thirty minutes, they return with two good-sized tree monkeys, supplying a small, tasty addition to their evening meal, eaten by nineteen indigenous troops and one round eye.

Within two days, they are running out of dense jungle. Deer and monkeys are scarce. The jungle's demise is due to the natural thinning of trees. The farther down the hills you go the tree lines are now opening into meadows, grassy plains with swamps nestled among mangrove and palm stands. The disappearance of the deer and monkey population is due solely to the encroachment of man.

In the early evening of the fifth day, stopping in the shadows of the only cover, bamboo, Lt. Tom Bigelow, for the first time in more months than he can remember, hears the distant sound of civilization, woodcutter axes, shot like echoing sounds of metal striking solid wood. Waiting for the day's fading light to burn out,

Bao not only sends out his normal nights four- to five-man camp security, he also dispatches Ung and three others on a reconnaissance patrol in the direction of the now silent woodcutters.

Settling in for an uncomfortable night in this bramble and bamboo thicket, Bao has the remaining troops, including the women, lay out in a wagon-wheel pattern, everyone's feet touching their neighbor's, toes pointed inward, everyone facing out, every other person awake, trading off, sleeping every two hours. Lt. Bigelow is oblivious as to how they managed this, never seeing a watch, clock, or other timekeeping device. The stars and moon are spectacularly bright when not blocked from view by the branches and leaves of the overhanging tree canopy. In this darkness, with the natural light provided, Lt. Bigelow, for the first time, can see the young girl's face close up, not bad looking at all, moonlight reflecting off her jet-black eyes, the warm touch of her thigh, a not-so-unpleasant earthy smell generated by her closeness. Then she smiles at him, there it is, the only thing preventing his advancement in her direction—purple teeth.

In the early dawn, commotion to Bigelow's right causes a hurried exchange between two or three people still out of sight. The quiet murmur around him is insurance that all is well. Coming into view are Ung and his three companions, giving waves of recognition as they move into the defensive perimeter.

In the center of their little camp, Bao and Ung are having a rather animated but quiet conversation. Ung moves his hands in a rapid, jerky, jumble of pointing in various directions, counting off numbers by taking the index finger of his right hand, striking the index finger of his left. The high-pitched whisper of Ung's voice and the look on his face show signs of a startled and panic driven individual, characteristically not an emotion seen in these fearless little warrior tribesman. This confrontation not only has Bigelow perplexed, the entire group now seems to be in a worrisome questionable state of mind. Short head-to-head conversations, hand cupped to mouth, whispering directly into each other's ears, something has these people in a tizzy. Once their talk is finished, Bao orders four of his men to retrieve the night security personal, not wishing to us the typical shot in the air method giving his position away to any nearby enemy.

Quiet orders are given to quickly devour any cold food available. There were no fires last night; there will be none this morning. Movement is brisk and silent in the sterilization of their overnight camp. Once these people leave, it would be hard to find any indication that twenty humans spent the entire night bivouacked among the bamboo.

Lt. Bigelow is not all that sure what's happening as he gathers his meager possessions. He fingers his Colt for self-assurance, placing his bow and quiver within arm's reach. Looking for any sign of true panic, none is seen. Not one person seems out of sorts with the task at hand. As Bao and Ung move in the pilot's direction, Bao is delivering orders and smiles of confidence to his followers. Reaching Bigelow, Bao stands close and leans in using a soft, undertoned voice.

"Bigrow, we seem to be in the middle of some sort of military exercise or training maneuver. Ung reports many cooking fires all through the plains and forests to our front. These fires are being tended by uniformed soldiers. We are traveling in a southeasterly direction at the moment. The woodcutters, with a heavy contingency of solders, are occupying the cleared portion of wood line to the northeast, unwittingly but effectively blocking our path. I would like my friend and best soldier Ung to walk with you. You stay real close to him. Where he goes, you go. What he does, you try and mimic. Ung will not let you out of his sight. Bigrow, consider him your personal bodyguard for now. We have no more time to waste. Our new trek will be due north, back into the mountains. At times, it will be a little unpleasant. In three or four days, we should reach a high mountain Rhade tribal village. Once there, we can rest and plan our final approach to Ha Dong. Stay especially alert these next few days. The troops sitting around those fires last night are going to be hungry later today. Some of their fellow comrades will be in our vicinity with hunting parties. Be careful, Bigrow. I'm starting to like you." With that and a few quick words with Ung, Bao moves down the column of troops.

Starting out first are flankers. Bao moves to the front of the column and surprises Bigelow by taking point; they all move on. More spacing between troops, slower, quieter pace, heads turning side-to-side a little more frequently, weapons not shoulder slung, carried at the ready, rounds in cambers, safeties off. Bigelow remembers Bao's departing words at the start of this jungle voyage, "This is serious shit. No sleepwalking."

They start off in a northerly uphill direction, not leaving the tree line, skirting any grassy open areas. This sometimes forces them to trek through leech- and mosquito-infested mangrove and palm swamps. The hills are getting steeper, trees growing closer together, sunlight defused by the overhead canopy, the forest floor starting to be covered in low-growing foot-grabbing vines. Indeed unpleasant, not only the hardships of dealing with the terrain, the approaching midday sun is baking the forest and driving the heat and humidity to amazing heights.

On the edge of a ravine, preparing to drop into its dark recesses, the clatter and screeching of monkeys is heard coming from the south. Suddenly, breaking through the natural volume of the jungle, sounding like a tattered tattoo of trumpets, the rapid, rhythmic, rapping of automatic gunfire, six to eight rounds, close enough to alarm and alert, far enough not to be overly worried about. Moving into the dark and dank ravine, Lt. Bigelow realizes they're now following a very narrow animal trail, can't be but eighteen inches wide. The indigenousness are having no problem moving through, the wide-hipped and shouldered pilot is having a harder time of it.

Wading across a small stream at the bottom of the ravine, most of their party on the other side, the sound of rifle fire is again heard. This time closer and directly to their front, not the desperate auto fire as before. These are single purposeful soundings, true hunters, someone with a target in their sites, not a random spraying of bullets hoping to hit something.

Reaching the other side of the stream, Bigelow follows Ung into some concealing brush beside the trail. Quietly waiting, Lt. Bigelow, not sure for what, sits poised for any trouble that might come along. Through the still heat-drenched jungle comes the sound of tiny hoofed deer feet. Tapping and clapping their way past Lt. Bigelow's position, a mere ten feet away, passing quickly, they are followed closely by three men. The first to go by is an older individual clad in the typical Vietnamese working clothes, black pajamas wearing a straw conical hat, carrying an older bolt action rifle. The other two are wearing green NVA military uniforms, carrying automatic AK-47s. They pass, not noticing twenty hidden killers, just a few feet away.

Staying in the confines of their concealment until the sound of footsteps fade, waiting for the little birdies to start their tweeting, now is the time to move. Not down this well-traveled trail, Bao has them about face and advance up the wall of jungle onto the higher ridgeline. It's a difficult task being performed by the indigenous with dedication, determination, and the skills of a mountain goat. Lt. Bigelow grabs roots, shoots, and clumps of shrubs. Sweaty, muscle sore, he crests this rock-cluttered pinnacle. No view from here, the trees are too tall. Listening to the silence, finding it a comfort, Bao, after resting awhile, points his nose to the north and follows it.

All this day and the next is a repeated encounter with steep, jungle-clogged seemingly bottomless ravines. Constant motion, little rest, Bigelow wonders how these people can do this all day long. The answer may lie in their purple teeth. Betel nut!

Chapter 4

ON THE FOURTH afternoon, Bigelow is coming out of a very deep, steep-walled ravine, thick overhead cover refusing the sun's advancement. Looking to his right, surveying the southern expanse of green forested jungle, he is stunned. Before him lies Vietnam's Shangri-La. On the face of the adjoining hillside is a terraced patchwork of rice paddies and vegetable gardens being tended by black pajama, conical hat-wearing natives. Some are using water buffalo as farm implements, working among the varied colored fields looking much like bees on a bouquet of flowers. Nestled among the neighboring tree line are hooches. They have reached the high mountain Rhade village.

Skirting the open fields, not alerting the workers of their presence, climbing the hillside in silence while working their way closer to the main village, their advance is halted by two—one, they could have dealt with, but two naked dirty runny-nosed three-year-olds giving the alarm, you're caught.

Approaching from the uphillside of the village, first thing noted are the varied blinding of smells, pig pens, cooking fires, chickens, ducks, and the pungent order of animal and human waste collected and used as rice paddy fertilizer. In the day's heat and no breeze, this can, at times, be stifling.

Dogs are just now starting to give the alarm, mange and flea ridden, curly-tailed scruffy cute little future meals, not many kept as pets, monkeys hold that distinction with these people. The villagers are now coming out of their hooches, stopping whatever chores they are engaged in, turning their attention to the armed troops being lead into their compound by two young crying and stumble-running captors. The two brave boys fold into the loving outstretched arms of their mothers.

Bigelow is seeing far more hooches than he'd seen from that exposed ridgeline they used to first view this place; there must be quarters for fifty or more families. There is an open common area with logs arranged for sitting, focusing on a rock ringed fire pit still smoldering from the night before. Off to the south of this is a large elevated bamboo post and beam, open-sided, palm-roofed communal longhouse, a tribal gathering place for this village.

This communal hut is where Bao, Bigelow, and some of the men will hang hammocks or occupy floor space while visiting. The remainder of the troops, having relatives or close friends among the inhabitants of this Rhade tribe, will be spending their time visiting, helping in the fields if necessary, and joining in on hunting trips. Challenging each other in the skills of the cross-bow, these people are cautious in using firearms near their village, not wishing to alert any unwanted, unseen guest to the fact that they are armed, well-armed.

Wherever Bigelow goes, he is followed by every child in the village, almost. A few of the younger ones are hanging on to their mothers breastfeeding. Some offering a stomach churning sight, betel nut, being chewed by some of these mothers, is producing purplish saliva that is drooling out the corner of their mouths, running down their chin, down their neck, across and down their breast and nipple, being consumed by the suckling infants.

Commotion due to their arrival has hastened the ending of the work day. Moving from the fields, teenage boys are taking the buffalo into a nearby stream to cool down and for cleaning before returning them to their night enclosures. As more people descend on the village, there is a parade of clasped praying hands, head bows, and a variety of smiles—golden, purple, and white toothed. From some of the older residents, they get a pink-gummed no-tooth grin. Lt. Bigelow is becoming the center of much interest. He finds himself wedged between Ung and Bao, who are explaining the round eye's presence and the importance of keeping his visit a tribal secret.

Bigelow, to some extent, is enjoying this attention. As of late, not being able to partake in the human need to socialize in a mixed grouping of peoples, his inability to communicate with them directly seems to have little or no effect in their enthusiasm when meeting and interacting with him. Bao is pleased with the reception and response they are receiving, knowing that this meeting might not have been this accepting on their part. This tribe of Rhade Montagnards has been driven far from their native mountain villages in Southern Vietnam by the conflict just ending. First by the French, then came the South Vietnamese government prejudices, then the Americans come along with their rounding up villages full of Mountangnards and placing them in what they called resettlement villages for their own protection. The US government, not realizing they were combining rival tribes, people that for centuries have been raiding each other's villages, killing, kidnapping, simply put, not being nice to each other.

Fighting for independence and the freedom to live their nomadic lifestyle, these groups migrating up north placed themselves in the jurisdiction of the Northern Vietnamese, long an adversary and enemy of theirs, making for an isolated, defensive, and untrusting group of people.

Using these mountains as their sanctuary, also the base of operations for their tribal group's militia activities, including ambushes on government targets of opportunity, raiding parties on distant warring rival Montagnard clans and local small security patrols, has not gone unnoticed by the advancement of woodcutters, hunters, and the recent government forays into the high mountains. With the war ending in the South, the North has been able to use more troops in their own backyard. Mountain regions along the borders are being heavily patrolled, indoctrination centers[1] are being built in the higher plains, ever closer, sometimes infringing on what the Montagnards consider to be their personal tribal hunting grounds.

The military, in conjunction with local hunters, have reached high into this tranquil forest searching, tracking, and killing deer, wild pig, and monkey. Sounds of hunting can be heard echoing up the valleys, flooding the ravines with drum rolls of death, which can be heard coming out of the lower jungles and grasslands.

The evening meal consists of deer, monkey, and rice, along with an unrecognizable chicken concoction with fresh vegetables topped with a hot sauce of fermented fish heads called Nuoc Mam. The smell is enough to gag a maggot, but this does not stop these people from pouring it on all they eat. After the meal, Bigelow, framed by Bao and Ung, is escorted to the open pit fire ring and seated on a log of prominence. They spend this night in a whirlwind of greetings and hurried conversations with Lt. Bigelow doing a lot of hand clasping, head bobbing, and bowing. By evening's end, he believes he has met every man, woman, and child, at least twice.

Early morning finds the communal hut full of children, standing, sitting, giggling, sniffling, jockeying for an up close look at the round eye yawn, stretch, and fart his way into a new day. After a morning meal, Bigelow along with Bao, Ung, and a score of young children head out for an extensive tour of the village. Bao, being a little concerned with security, did not like being unchallenged on his approach yesterday, finding only young children on the village outskirts.

In the early morning's light, with the smoke from so many fires fighting its way through the trees, clogging the air with a heavy layer of smoke, they move through the shadows of this place like a ship moving through a fog bank, slowly seeking solitude on a distant shore.

Taking on the role as inspecting general, Bao is fastidious in his approach, being cordial, polite, with a friendly attitude. Finding

---

[1]   Essentially prison camps.

lapses in the care and maintenance of personal weapons, explaining that a dirty rifle, corroded, rusty ammunition will not serve well in battle without being properly maintained, cleaned, and oiled.

This is one of the villages that Bao helps protect, along with two or three others. Periodically, Bao will pay unannounced visits, not only checking equipment and making sure security is adequate, most importantly, that the needs of the group are being met. One of the ways to keep harmony and contentment among the people is to feed them, but you must have a secure environment for this to happen. Bao is more than aware of this, leading him to question why his group was not challenged on their approach to the village. Talking with the two young sentries who manned yesterday's listening post on the uphillside of the village, they explain that they saw the approaching patrol, recognized Bao and his men. They also knew two young boys were in their direct path and would make contact with them. They chose to stay in their concealment, ambush ready on the slight chance that Bao's group was being tracked and followed. With a stern look from his cold dark eyes, a small gradual grin, Bao accepts their explanation.

With their tour completed, the children are now losing interest in the grown-up's business moving off to more interesting adventures playing kid's games, eating and the all-important midday nap. Bao and Lt. Bigelow are sitting on the deck of the communal hut; Bao expresses his point of view on the lack of any formal challenge given his patrol by the two young men yesterday.

"I believe those young men were asleep or otherwise impaired while on guard duty. I would like to think they are diligent in their capabilities and duties. We will see. Bigrow, I have spoken with the three elders of this tribe. Tomorrow evening, they would like to induct you into their tribe with a festive rice wine ceremony, much to eat and drink. We all dress in traditional Montagnard trappings, head and arm bands, loincloths."

Bigelow lashes out. "You want me to wear a dress? Bao, that's not my style. Besides, I don't own one."

Bao, sliding off the deck, beckons the pilot, "My friend, it's off to the dressmakers."

Bigelow gives a startled response. "You're serious!"

This evening is sedate compared to last night's frenzied introductions, with all the confusing and unintelligible but rather delightful conversations. Tonight, these people are engrossed with the cleaning and decoration of the communal hut, the location of tomorrow's celebration. A rainbow of flowers, colors stolen from a painter's palette cover every bamboo post and beam. The drip line of the roof overhang; along with the outside edge of the decking is strung with greenery. The fragrance from this Rose Bowl float can probably be smelled a hundred miles away.

Most of the women and young girls are gathered round the fire pit, working individually or in small groups, readying their tribal adornments, head and arm bands, decorative woven sashes they will wrap around their waists, all being done for the highly anticipated celebration. The night slowly drifts away in communal good spirits and laughter with bedtime stories for the young ones, hunting and war stories for the old, as the fire burns long into the dark still night.

The early morning sun finds the village in a frenzied state of preparation, off to one side of the fire ring; teenage boys along with some of their younger siblings are digging a fire pit, a rather large deep pit. There are young women and girls moving about the compound going to and from vegetable gardens, delivering their baskets full of produce to their mothers and grandmothers, who are chopping and slicing, mixing and cooking the ingredients, making all the preparations for tonight's feast.

Bigelow, trying to focus through the thick fog of flower vapor, rolls up his sleeping mat. Looking for Ung, seeing there is no sign of him or his belongings, he asks, "Bao, my friend Ung seems to be missing this morning."

"Early, Ung stored his equipment under floor, covered with palm fronds. Please you to do same. No need to worry, these people do not know to disturb someone's belongings. For security, it's better for our gear not to be lying around. Ung and some others formed a hunting party. Their objective is to bring back pig, monkey, and hopefully, one live fat tender buffalo for the fire pit.

"You and I will go and retrieve some containers of rice wine from a nearby winemaker. This rice wine has been in the making for quite some time, fermenting and gaining potency inside large ceramic jugs. We will be drinking from five. This is going to be a big celebration."

Finishing the morning's tasks, Bigelow, along with twelve, maybe fifteen men led by Bao, march off in the direction of the winemaker's hut. Moving through the village, the men are singing out, vocalizing in their high-pitched clattering, receiving chuckling laughter from their wives, daughters, in some cases mothers. Nearing the stream, Bigelow can see a number of young men carrying rocks, dragging branches with leaves still attached, into the water. Holding the braces down with the rocks, they are damming this portion of the stream upriver from the buffalos wallow, giving the villagers a clean, cool pool of water to frolic in, being sure to leave shallows for the children.

This expedition is easy and relaxed on marching orders, small talk, short bursts of grab ass and laughing, even smoking, Bao not seeming to care. Reaching a small clearing, they come to the edge of a clump of palm trees. Bao stops the group, signaling for quiet. Dropping to one knee, rifle still slung across his back, hands cupped, pressed to his mouth, he yells something. No reply, no movement except for the sweat running down Bigelow's forehead, over his brow plugging into the right eye, stinging while blurring his vision.

Wiping, dabbing his eye into focus, his recaptured sight has revealed a small little person standing smack dab in the middle of the sun drenched clearing, hands on his hips with a big purple smile, wearing nothing but a loincloth—no decoration, just a plain somewhat dirty loincloth.

Bao approaches, hands raised, babbling in a language Lt. Bigelow is not familiar with. Closing the distance, moving closer to this little man, Bigelow can see he is neither Vietnamese nor Montagnard. He may be small, but he's built like Ung, well-defined and muscled. He has a weathered face and is sporting a long crop of black hair with gray specks sprinkled throughout. Dark beady little slits for eyes with betel nut stained front teeth.

The babbling being spoken by Bao and the little man is not babble at all; it's a Mandarin dialect of the Chinese language. Bao explains that this rice winemaker migrated to the vast reaches of Vietnam's northern high mountains because he was rudely driven from his village in the southern steppes of China, a region known for its production and consumption of a very good but a rather intoxicating mixture of rice wine.

Discovered and admired by the Montagnards, he has been able to make a good living trading and selling his brew, which has become a prized commodity for yearly celebrations. Moving from the clearing into the far tree line, they come across two women tending three-foot tall ceramic wine jugs; there must be twenty or so, some uncovered, others covered with a grass and tree moss stopper, keeping the fermented liquid from overflowing.

These jugs, vases, whatever they're called, have the looks of ancient Roman times. They have that bulbous bottom, round body narrowing into a long slender graceful neck with a smooth flat one inch thick lip. Curled beneath this lip are two, one on either side, large thick round rings, about two inches in diameter.

After spending time in negotiations, a short sampling with the encouragement of the vintner, devilish little man, they prepare for the return trip by cutting and gathering bamboo poles, sliding these six-foot long spears through the ring holes affixed to the jug's neck. Shouldering these poles gives two people the capability to carry these heavy, cumbersome beverage containers back home.

An almost songlike sound is heard filtering through the forest, it's rhythm broken by bouts of laughter and squeals of delight produced by teenagers while playing and swimming in the newly built pond. Crossing the stream, negotiating their way through the congested village, they place the five wine jugs in the communal hut side by side, all in a row. In front of each is placed a small squat little wooden stool. Each jug has a long straw made from a thin small diameter piece of bamboo pushed through the moss stopper, penetrating deep into the depths of this potent mixture.

By early afternoon, most all the children have returned from their water play searching out food. Mothers, grandmothers, and older sisters are chasing them away, most only getting off with a scolding and a cold rice ball, toddlers faring better, clinging to their mothers' breasts.

The children, most enjoying their afternoon nap, what every kid around the world does most every day so they're fully rested and able to pester their parents all evening and into the night.

Now is the time for the adults to play. The pond has been refreshed and replenished by the flowing stream. Its waters are a cool, almost a clear blue jewel of ridiculous childish behavior among a bunch of naked adults, the men more so than the women as both groups are enjoying themselves in a moment of carefree frivolity. Bigelow, most always the recipient of much laughter due to his lily white butt, this time is no exception, far from it. The men think it's funny; for the woman it's a curiosity, one that can't be passed up, one that must be touched in some cases spanked, pinched, and patted like a child's. All this with giggles and a chuckling laugh of silliness. This play is fun, relaxing, and rather revealing. We have people of varying ages, sizes, and shapes, which is not considered a moral issue among these indigenous men and women. It's not an issue for Bigelow, but it is having an effect on him. He stays low in the water trying to remain submerged from the waist down, hiding the fact that he is highly affected. This affectedness problem was somehow perked by the appearance of six eighteen to twenty-year-old beautiful, vivacious right out of *Playboy*, white-toothed, naked native girls. Not knowing what to do, other than stay in this pond until dark, Lt. Bigelow is rescued by Bao. "Bigrow, pay attention to the old women, should help in your situation." He lets out a laugh and a smile of gold. "My friend, your dress awaits. Let us ready for tonight."

Having this old seamstress help the pilot into his loincloth is not the most pleasant of experiences in his condition, but he muddles through and survives another awkward, embarrassing moment along the path of life.

Now dressed in full Montagnard attire, he walks through this village among his newfound friends. Lt. Bigelow has a feeling of pride and profound gratification in his accomplishments. This is the accumulation of almost a year's survival and endurance while living and almost dying in a naturally hostile environment, not to forget having his plane brought down by a missile and living to tell about it. Considering the odds, you've got yourself a happy, content, ready to party Lt. Tom Bigelow US Navy wearing a dress.

Voices raised, shouts coming from the downhill tree line, young boys and girls are running in that direction. Men by the fire pit are stacking logs, readying the fire. Bao and the pilot move to the edge of the clearing, in time to witness Ung, helped by two others bring in a young, very much alive water buffalo. Ropes around his neck and front feet are being used to help guide this snorting, bleating ceremonial sacrifice. They tie his restraints to a thick seven-foot tall pole buried in the ground.

Others from Ung's hunting party are drifting in with their contributions to this night's glorious feast. Lashed by the hocks, swinging to the porter's gait, a huge wild boar with its tongue hanging out the corner of his mouth like an old used dirty sock, eyes wide open in a blank stare covered in a milky white glaze, attesting to its death.

There's another pig being brought in, followed by two young men carrying an untold number of dead monkeys strung along a bamboo poll hanging down with their little hands tied together over their heads, giving them the appearance of a chorus line of head-bobbing leg-jerking macabre dancers.

Preparations are at a frenzied pitch. Things are being done in a military manner, platoons of women converging on the hunter's offerings, stripping hide, intestines and fur, butchering, wrapping the pigs in palm fronds with vegetables, spices, and a generous dollop of Nuoc Mam. Running thin bamboo skewers through the stripped, flipped, and dipped little dancers, ultimately resulting in a tasty monkey kabob.

The packaged pigs are laid on a bed of rock and palm-covered red hot coals, covered in another layer of palm fronds and hot rocks, finally covered with dirt. The deeper bigger pit is being readied for the young buffalo.

People are starting to gather in the vicinity of the restrained wild beast now standing as docile as can be, proud but dumber than a brick. Not moving, just the swishing of its tail warding off flies. A gathering of pink and white globules forming in the corners of its big brown cow eyes, using its tongue to flick flies off its nose.

As Bao and Bigelow approach this throng of jubilant villagers, they are greeted by Ung with traditional Asian respect, head bows and hand clasping, smiling his approval of Bigelow's apparel. Closing in beside Bao, Ung engages him in a lengthy, almost one-sided conversation; once finished, Ung moves toward the staked out buffalo. Bao, holding Bigelow back, stops short of the gathering. "Bigrow, Ung has told me that there are government troops not far from here, not in numbers to be of any consequence at this time. Hopefully, they will just look on from a distance then move off. Until we have evidence of that, please stay within the village proper. No wandering into sunlit clearings. This should not pose too much of an inconvenience. Seeing as most all of today's activities, we'll be within these confines."

Continuing his conversation, Bao goes on, "I should at this time give an explanation as to what will happen today and this evening. Starting with our little tethered friend, after drawing blood the old shaman, you might call him a witch doctor in America. He will say some blessings. I don't understand it all myself. Just smile and bow your head every once and awhile. Once finished, he will drink from the blood cup. You being the honored one will drink next. Smile and pass the cup back to him. Is there any questions?"

Lt. Bigelow observes his surroundings, again feeling the attention he is attracting. "Not so far, stick around though, this party is just getting started. There might be a question or two sooner or later down the line.

"I'm most assured of that, Bigrow. After the blood sharing and the old ones ranting, the animal will be swiftly killed and butchered. This chore will be performed by the men. Women are not allowed to help in the preparation of a sacrificial kill. You, my friend, being the honoree of today's celebration, will do the honors of slitting the buffalo's throat. You grab that big chunk of fleshy hide hanging under the animal's throat. With one quick motion of the knife, cut through hide, windpipe, and jugular vein. One quick motion, knife will be razor sharp. Step back, as there will be an abundance of blood splashing onto the ground."

Taking Bigelow's hand, Bao leads them through the parting crowd, giving head way not only to Bao but for the man to be honored, Lt. Tom Bigelow.

At one time, he was considered their enemy, a purveyor of fire and death. He is a man who can fly—a man who has come to them from above, floating to earth under a cloud of cloth; the same man who has lived their life and understands their ways; a man who needs to become a Montagnard so he may become a true spirit of the mountains.

The buffalo, standing nonchalantly, drinking water from an old US Army steel helmet, hasn't the slightest clue to its fate. Approaching the beast, Lt. Bigelow stands back as Ung aims and fires a short, sharp-pointed arrow into a blood vessel running the length of the animal's neck. Quickly removing this projectile, the old shaman reaches under it's now bleeding throat, filling the cup with its life-giving nectar. Moving to the pilot's side, he starts his rant, waving the cup of blood around like it was the Holy Grail. He starts blessing not only Bigelow but everyone and everything in sight, being most careful in not spilling any of this thick red-anointing fluid. After completing his rantings, the old wizard raises the cup toward the heavens with both hands, yelling some unknown phrase while being egged on by the villagers. Suddenly, he brings the cup down to his lips and drinks in the dark purplish red fluid that is the true nectar of life itself. This done, he turns, with a big purple grin, blood staining the corners of his mouth, beckoning Bigelow to follow after being handed the ceremonial cup. The villagers go quiet. All eyes are on Bigelow, not disappointed they give a shout of joy as he drinks, letting some of the blood run down his chin. Handing the cup back to the shaman, Bigelow rubs the spilled blood from his mouth and chin with the back of his hand and receives more cheers of acceptance.

After this ritual, Ung and Bigelow stand on opposite sides of the bull. Ung gingerly coaxes the animal's head to a raised position, allowing the pilot easy access to the buffalo's vital life-sustaining jugular. Handed a machete, Bigelow grabs the mass of dangling flesh and hide, getting a low bellowing from the now interested wild beast, eyes wide open in a look of questioning alarm, tongue hanging out its mouth, saliva pooling with blood dripping from its bloodletting. Ung pulling on one of its ears, a loud cheer of jubilation rushes over the death scene. The machete, cutting through to the spinal cord with such force, almost severed the head. Stepping back, allowing the dying animal plenty of room to collapse. In a single motion, it crumples to its knees. No death throes. The animal just lies there bleeding to death, dying the way it stood, proud but unquestionably oblivious to its fate. Not all animals will let you take their life so easily.

The moment the great beast's head fell to the ground, it was assaulted by a number of male villagers working like a surgical team in a ground-breaking operation. They proceed in rendering this buffalo fire pit ready in short order. After this blood-gorging, blood-splattering, butcher's fest, most of the adult males head for the stream to wash away the reddish sticky residue from the buffalo's slaughter. They are accompanied by a few of the women. Bigelow has noticed some of his earlier bathing companions, this time wearing loincloths, matching patterned arm bands, gold bracelets, gold anklets, nothing more, beautiful bare-breasted young ladies, promising nothing, wishing for more. On their return to the village, the festive mood has picked up. The fire pit is nothing more than a mound of dirt-leaking smoke. Monkey kabob, along with other assorted animal parts, are being cooked in the open fire ring. All this smoke is filling the air with wondrous smells while bringing out millions of tiny black buzzing flies.

"Bigrow, good job with the buffalo. Now come with me. We have one more task to perform before we can enjoy our meal." As Bao moves in the direction of the highly decorated ceremonial hut, which by now is nearing capacity, the open-sided building is surrounded by villagers. The old wizard or witch doctor, Bigelow doesn't know what to label him, is passively standing next to one of the wine vessels.

Stopping short of their destination, Bao explains, "As before, my friend, the shaman will spout some words, shake some magic dust around, and then he will point to you. At this time, you sit on the stool in front of the first jug of rice wine, the one on the right. He will say something, and I'll tap you on the shoulder. You commence sucking up wine through the straw until the old one yells and claps his hands. You move on to the next jug. I replace you on the first stool. The old man will do his thing again, then we both drink until he yells for us to stop. This is repeated until we have drunk from all five jars. That's it, my friend. But beware, this wine. is intoxicating. Be careful when you get up, or you could end up on the floor for the night, and you would miss, as you Americans say, one hell of a party."

Entering the communal hut, all eyes are on Lt. Bigelow, dressed as one of them, acting as one of them. In a short time, they will know if he is a true man of the mountains or simply, a lost round eye.

The old shaman is standing at the ready with feathers, along with some kind of plant matter in one hand; in the other, he holds a leather bag. Bigelow approaches the line of wine jugs stopping in front of the old man. Quiet whispers cease; the only sound now is the pilot's heartbeat, drumming loudly across his chest. Raising his feathered hand, shaking and screaming, the shaman starts shouting something to Bigelow as he dances around in short hopping steps. Reaching into his leather bag, he starts sprinkling some white powder in Bigelow's direction then suddenly stops, points a boney black-nailed finger at Lt. Bigelow, signaling him to take a seat in front of the first jug of wine. Slowly moving around the jugs as he rants on, the shaman suddenly stops movement and sound. Bao taps Bigelow on the shoulder, indicating that he should start drinking.

Lt. Bigelow has had more than his share of wine. He has had his fill of all types of alcohol. This wine, well, this wine is similar to what paint thinner must taste like, burning all the way down. *Yell and clap, you little bastard*, the pilot's silent thoughts said. As his head starts to spin, sounds are floating back, not yelling or hand clapping, it's the laughing roar of the entire village. Finally, a little bit of yelling and a really loud hand clap, it's done but not over.

After the fifth and final jug has been drunk from, trying to stand, Bigelow is helped to the sidelines by Ung. Seeing the world in a dizzying flurry of faces, all smiling, laughing faces, the pilot sits down to regain some composure and try and get the feeling back in most parts of his body.

Bao, now done, sits on the log next to Lt. Bigelow. Both men need a few minutes to catch their breath. Bigelow is the first to speak. "My god, Bao, how can you drink that crap?"

Bao replies with one of his golden smiles, "My friend, this is not a nice thing to say about our beloved national beverage. Now you understand why we only celebrate once or twice a year." Laughing, Bao goes on, "Bigrow, I have something for you. Normally, after a young man goes through this same rice wine ritual, the family gives him his first gold bracelet, replacing the brass one he has grown up with."

Standing, a little shakily, Bao reaches into a small leather bag and retrieves a beautiful shiny gold bracelet. "This is from my brother, Dinh. He got this from my father after being accepted as a Montagnard. Dinh gave this to me before we left the mountain. He said he knew you were worthy. He said you were a good warrior. I agree."

Sliding the bracelet over his wrist, looking admiringly at his new acquisition not knowing if it's the wine or the feelings he has for Dinh or just the present situation, Bigelow wipes away a small tear, definitely a tear.

Food is the next order of business. There are row after row of woven baskets and palm fronds full of assorted edible delights— fruits and vegetables of all types and colors, shapes, and sizes. There are hard boiled eggs—white, blue, speckled. You have your monkey kabobs, strips of deer jerky, finely cut pieces of raw deer meat. Fish cooked whole, dried fish and just plain raw fish. They're in the process of unearthing the pig, the buffalo staying buried awhile longer.

"Bigrow, enjoy your meal. You may revisit the wine jars at your leisure. Try the mixing of blood with the wine. It really does help with the taste."

Bigelow mingles with the people as he selects his food. Using a small palm leaf as a plate, he gathers what he feels is a good choice for his condition: bananas, a few carrots, some deer jerky, one half monkey kabob, and two hard-boiled eggs. He always liked eggs and had a craving for them the moment he saw them being laid out. Moving to the fire pit, he takes a chunk of pig along with a scoop of rice covered with broth, politely refusing the Nuoc Mam sauce.

This is the pleasant part of each day; the sun lazily drifts over the horizon, letting coolness spread throughout the forest. Birds slowly sing their good-byes to another day and the children, finished with their meal, play out their last vestiges of energy before night envelops them in slumber.

Sitting on a log, surrounded by natives enjoying their meal, Lt. Bigelow decides to start with a boiled egg. His neighbors show interest in his selection as he peels back part of the shell. Smiling to his guests, he bites into his egg. He is instantly repulsed. It seems that Asians like nothing better than cooking their eggs with a little bit of protein. Spitting out his first mouth full of the meal, seeing the severed body of a feathered fetus imbedded in the remainder of his egg almost makes the pilot sick.

Bigelow takes the rest of his meal with dedicated interest, surveying, probing, and poking, making sure there are no further culinary surprises. Finding none, he enjoys the remainder of his meal. Bao approaches Bigelow with a cone-shaped cup made from a small palm leaf and offers him a sip. "Refreshing, is this blood, wine mix?"

Bao smiles, handing Bigelow a folded cup made from a leaf. "Just dip this in the wine jug. The bowl of blood is by the post next to the porch. Help yourself, my friend."

And he does. Bigelow is a little more wine friendly after the addition of this acidic sweetener, somehow neutralizing the burning properties of this paint thinner elixir.

He seems to be the topic of conversation with every one; each person he comes across reaches out to touch him, feel the hair on his arms. Shy young girls cover their mouths and giggle, lowering their eyes, blinking in that all over the world sign of flirtatious embarrassment.

The night wearing on, children, married couples, and older adults are slowly disappearing from the fire ring. Lt. Bigelow, feeling no pain, is sitting next to Bao. Both are surrounded by not-so-shy, bare breasted, non betel nut chewing, rice wine drinking lovely young ladies. Bigelow doesn't think there's a chance in hell that something's not going to happen here, with all the wine, the place, the pulsating blood running through his brain, blurring all reasoning. An arm, a strong wise arm wrapped round his shoulder.

"Bigrow, take one of these young ladies to your sleeping mat. The night will not last forever. Enjoy, be nice, let her guide you to a place of privacy and pleasure. The best of luck and good night, my friend." Getting up, Bao reaches out and takes a young slender hand in his; with shiny gold teeth sparkling bright in the firelight, Bao smiles down at the pilot and then departs with his beautiful young maiden.

Lt. Tom Bigelow, a little more hesitant than his friend, is confronted by the offering of a hand to assist in him standing. A delicate hand attached to a wonderful arm, connected to a most beautiful young, light mahogany brown-skinned Montagnard goddess. She has jet-black sparkling bright eyes and hair, cute delicate nose, soft damp lips staggering into a dream-come-true smile, showing crystal white teeth. His first thought, *There must be a God*. His second thought?

In every man's life, there will be that morning when he reaches almost full consciousness knowing he did something the night before, not quite sure what it was, finding it difficult to open his eyes, leaving him to use his other senses to test the new day. He can feel a sleeping mat under him; it's not on a dirt floor, this surface is cooler, a little more forgiving. There's a slight chill, the air is brisk, and he can feel the radiant heat from another body, a naked body up against his. Somehow, this newfound realization has helped in the opening of his bloodshot blurry eyes.

It's not full daylight. There is a subdued smattering of misted light, shadows not yet reveled, sound none, just the breathing of two people and the incessant buzzing of a tiny black flying insect. The air is fresh, as it should be on a new day.

Slowly rolling over, resting his head on his hand, he gazes upon the sleeping face of a young girl—no girl, this is the woman who trimmed his horns last night, stole his innocence, and tamed the beast within yet so young, so beautiful. He reaches out, stroking her long black silky hair, tracing the outline of her delicate shoulder, down her naked slender back over her firm flawless buttocks.

Awakened, this beauty turns to face Bigelow, covering her breast with her hands, not out of embarrassment, just a young woman's shyness. She smiles at him—no words, just a big bright twinkling within her dark eyes, a comforting glimmer of happiness and delight.

A volley of three shots, spaced out, calculated, deliberate coming from the far wood line down and across from the clearing. Movement all around him, Bigelow dashes for the communal hut, wearing nothing but his sleeping mat. This comedic scene is highlighted by a number of totally naked men and women running out of the bushes all in different directions, headed for hooches, stashed clothing, and equipment.

Reaching the hut, Bigelow dives under its raised floor, searching for his shorts, his Colt .45 and some explanation as to what is happening. At that very moment, sliding under the floor next to him is Bao, hanging onto his partially affixed loincloth. "Good morning, Bigrow. Seems we have been caught with our pants down, my friend."

Sounds of startled children, mothers speaking in a reassuring hushed tone, foot beats of men scampering into positions. Now in his shorts, armed with his AK-47, Bao tells Lt. Bigelow to stay put, don't move until he or Ung comes for him. Message conveyed, Bao is up and headed for the edge of the clearing.

Quiet now, even the small children have stopped their wailing. What seemed like hours, in reality, it's only a few minutes that have passed before Bao comes walking up, kneels down, speaking quietly.

"Bigrow, we have unexpected guests I do not wish to explain your presence to. These are Buddhist monks. They roam the countryside, saying their prayers to the gods, forests, and jungles all over Asia, living hand-to-mouth receiving food and sometimes shelter from villages they come across. We don't mind their visits, their prayers, and chants comfort some of the villagers, mostly the old.

"My main interest in talking with them is strictly directed to the gathering of up-to-date intelligence on the location and numbers of government forces, groups of hunters, and woodcutters they might have come in contact with. They really do help in these matters, so if you could be so kind and remain here, out of sight, I'll send Ung by with some food and water. Thank you, my friend."

Lying under the communal hut somehow reminds Bigelow of his youth back home, playing every child's favorite game, hide-and-seek. Crawling to the far corner support post, covering himself with palm leaves, he now has a good vantage point from which to view the three new arrivals.

What a sight! These people are dressed in long flowing bright orange colored robes and wearing small leather sandals. All three have shaved heads; one is older, the other two look to be in their late teens. Besides each having a cloth carry bag slung over their shoulders, the old one walks with a staff, not a cane, not a walking stick, a six-foot tall hook on the end staff. How religious.

As the villagers start their morning routine, some bring food to the three seated monks. Taking refuge on the front row log, directly across from the smoldering fire ring, they seem content with the attention and service they are getting. Not thirty feet away, comfortable in his relaxed observation position and being tended to by Ung, who has brought a little food and water along with a companion for company, the sweet young lady the pilot spent the night with is now dressed in the typical black pajama pant and shirt work uniform with rolled up cuffs and sleeves. All the young women are now thusly dressed. Most of the men are sporting black pajama bottoms, pant legs rolled to the knee without bothering to put on shirts.

Finished with their meal, the two young disciples start pulling out colored cloth, four or five incense sticks, and a small statue of Buddha from their cloth carry bags. Using a portion of log to fashion a small shrine, lighting their incense, pounding on a small tambourine sized drum, these monks are ready for business. Add in some chanting, hell, you've got yourself a revival. Most of their followers are the very young and the old. The young adults and members of Bao's troops are more or less showing some interest, but from afar with quiet reservation.

The old monk along with elders of the tribe are being led away from the village center by Bao and two of his armed warriors, one being Ung and another man Bigelow has seen but does not know. He must be highly trusted and respected to be part of this security detail. Their direction of walk has temporarily put them out of the pilot's view; he is now limited to the two practicing monks performing their ritualistic duties and his young companion who is content just lying next to her round eye lover.

As the day moves on, the heat starts building under the communal hut, twice the young girl has had to replenish their water supply. The two young monks, after concluding their mass, or whatever they call it, simply string up their hammocks and crawl in for a snooze.

Finally, the elders, Bao, and the old monk return. Not bothering his companions, the old religious man spreads out a colorful sleeping mat and lies down for an afternoon nap as the tribal elders scatter to their individual hooches. Ung and the other guard start roaming through the camp, notifying Bao's troops to prepare for departure.

Bao advances on the communal hut, sliding under, lying next to Bigelow, quietly telling him of their conversation with the old monk. "Bigrow, this old man has given us some very good intelligence on the numbers and direction of movement for the government troops. As we observed earlier, they have been training new recruits in these mountains for deployment down south. Large numbers of men are moving southwest out of our line of march. He knows of three woodcutting camps that are in our path, but they can be maneuvered around. The only real unknown is their hunting parties. They could be almost anywhere, silent and in small groups. We will have to be very careful, diligent, and wise in our traveling. Say good-bye to your little friend. We leave at first light."

How do you say good-bye to someone you cannot converse with? Not in the verbal sense, they say their good-byes in the universal language of lovers. The conversation is long, slow, and meaningful; in their covered little hiding place, they spend the night in total disregard to the world around them.

The morning shines bright and brisk, without monks. They have departed before first light, leaving as they came, quietly. Like three orange ghosts drifting through the confines of their forested home, walking across Mother Earth herself. Voicing aloud, chanting their cries of woe, their cries of faith, testing their karma, hoping for deliverance, trying to glean a pathway to Nirvana. A goal hoped for but apparently not easily attainable. Theirs is not a perfect world.

This morning, Lt. Bigelow awakes somewhat chilled, lying on his sleeping mat partially covered by palm leaves. Funny, it didn't come as a surprise, yet lying here among all these seemingly happy people, these family-oriented people, these people who took him in as one of their own, he feels apart, distant, very much alone.

"Bigrow, it is time to leave. But before we do, there are some changes in our marching schedule. We will not be taking the women with us. We will share in the carrying of equipment and food stuffs. You will walk behind Ung. You may bring your crossbow, but I request you carry an AK along with spare magazines. After the morning meal, get with Ung. He will give you a quick rundown on your weapon. He will also find you a pack for the carrying of your share of equipment and munitions."

Finishing his meager morning meal, after two nights of rice wine, Bigelow finds it difficult to eat; even more difficult is leaving this idyllic hideaway. After his meeting with Ung, getting his equipment and weapon, Bigelow spends time with some of the villagers, their children, and then says thanks to the elders. He looks for his female friend. Not finding her, he asks Bao, "Have you seen my friend from last night?"

"Bigrow, shame on you. You don't know her name, do you?"

Surprised by this, Bigelow goes on, "It was not something that came up during our relationship the last two nights. Maybe I can find out when I say good-bye."

Bao, with a serious look, replies, "My friend, you have said your good-byes. Your companion, Lai'Kim, is now working in the terraced rice fields across from the clearing. You're not venturing out to see her. From the tree line, you may spot her and wave. I'm sure her farewell was said last night with sweet love. It's time to ready yourself for our journey. We leave shortly."

By the time everyone has assembled, said their departing words, smiled, bowed, and hand prayed to everyone, it's late morning, later than Bao anticipated. Now a little agitated, in a rather stern-officiated voice, he barks orders, expecting and getting immediate results.

The point duty is being taken up by Ung's guard partner from the monk conference. He and Ung exchange looks, a few words of caution and encouragement before starting off in an roundabout way, not cutting across the clearing, staying well within the tree line, passing the terraced fields too far to recognize faces. The pilot waves to five black clad figures, none witnessing nor returning his final good-bye.

Spaced intervals, rounds in chambers, safeties off, weapons carried at the ready, not slung, it seems Bigelow is involved in some serious shit. Working their way east, moving higher with each step, the pace a little daunting, spirits still high, sun fading to shadows the deeper they get into the thick underbrush and tall canopied trees. The heat bringing sweat to the brow, this pace and altitude has Lt. Bigelow huffing and puffing as well as his fellow travelers.

They have walked into the late afternoon, stopping only for short water breaks as Bao keeps the procession moving forward. Using quiet persuasion, moving his way up and down the column of men helping to rearrange a load, helping someone through a tight or difficult spot, he is a leader—a leader of men who will follow him into battle, men who will kill and possibly die for him because he leads with his brain, his heart. Most importantly to his men, Bao leads from the front, never asking of his men to do anything that he himself would not do.

Almost last light, just a slight flicker of the sun's rays reach seventeen weary, bone-tired and hungry men. After stopping and resting for a short time, Bao dispenses with sending out night-listening posts and instead, orders everyone to place unneeded equipment in the center of their wagon-wheel defensive position. Each man laid out, face down, legs spread, each man's foot touching the man on either side, every other man on a two-hour rotational guard shift. A cold meal is eaten as the long day crosses over into pitch-black night.

When you're dog tired, your tail won't wag. Sleep is quick and easy. Morning dawns quietly, the air is chilled, movement slow, birds not yet awake and active. No fires, cold rice, dried deer jerky, and fish. Bao, going from man to man, a short chat, pat on the back on to the next, finally reaches Bigelow. "Good morning, my friend. I hope this morning finds you rested, refreshed, and ready for another long day." Looking up from his morning's cold rice ball and dried fish breakfast, Lt. Bigelow's reply sounds sarcastic. "Only if it's all uphill, my friend."

That's how the day starts, an uphill climb, two hours of jarring, leg cramping, straight at the hill assault. The only saving grace is the weather; the sun's still low in the sky with a cool breeze out of the south. Not truly a crest, this jungle-covered forest just petered out; the thinning of trees was as gradual as the incline of the slope. They're now on a high plateau with the surrounding mountains forming a box canyon. There's only two ways off this grassy bald spot: up a cliff-like mountain face or down into a narrow, steep-sided ravine. They plunge into the abyss.

Grabbing whatever they can use as hand holds, they lower themselves into a dank-congested dungeon, smelling like rotten eggs and garbage. It's middle morning; light is a stranger to this hellish pit. They stumble their way in the dark confines of this narrow passage, finding only leech- and mosquito-infested swamps at the bottom. They follow this course, moving through the moss-covered trees, tripping over dead and fallen tree limbs, vines as big as your wrist. Hacking through the thick vegetation with machetes, they continue in a relentless struggle to be free of this deplorable circumstance.

Sweaty, tired, not much stamina left, every step, every minute upright is sucking up their strength like a sponge. Finally, there is sunlight breaking through the trees, lighting their way out of this jungle cavity of rot.

After hours in shadows, short periods of blinding darkness, the sun's splash of brightness is stunning. The vista laid out before the pilot is breathtaking—a panoramic postcard picture of a large, flat, lowland rice bowl, hundreds of individual rice fields separated by narrow raised earthen dikes. The shimmering reflection of sunlight playing off the rice paddy waters is giving it the illusion of being the world's largest checkerboard.

Taking in his surroundings, Bigelow can see they are in a slight depression surrounded on three sides by imposing cliffs. The ravine they just followed out of the mountains was ugly but by far the easiest route.

Not really in the open, this place is tucked behind a small knoll. Trees and palms surround this little grass covered clearing. Bao decides to remain here for the night, stopping their advancement early, ignoring again his habit of posting guards. Bao explains, "With cliffs below, cliffs to our backs, not much point in guards when it's almost impossible to achieve this bivouac without being seen or heard, we will maintain light discipline, small cooking fires only, all fires out before sunset."

As the sun starts to set beyond the distant mountains, the shadows it is casting are slowly marching across the vast expanse of rice fields, bringing total darkness in its wake.

With no fires interfering with a clear midnight black sky, one cannot count all the stars. You lose track of comets and shooting stars; the constellations standing out like rest stops on a road map. Bigelow can think of only one thing missing, blinking strobe lights from planes. Not a one, he's looking at a lot of sky, and there's no commercial or military aircraft. Strange maybe, who knows? He's never been in this part of the world before.

Bao interjects his feelings on this spectacular light show being played out before them. "Breathtaking, my friend. A man could live a long peaceful life under a sky like tonight's. Not often you can see so far into the house of the Lord."

Lying on his back, totally engrossed in the stunning star-studded overhead light show, Bigelow simply did not hear Bao approach. Looking in his direction, he cordially responds with, "Bao, this is the busiest sky I have ever seen, not one blemish to distract from its wonder." He stands with his rolled-up sleeping mat under one arm, holding the leather thong attached to a water jug in the same hand, carrying sack over his left shoulder, his ever-present AK-47 in his left hand. "Mind if I share this little piece of earth with you, Bigrow?"

"Not at all. I welcome the company. Throw your mat out. We can talk."

Once settled in, the cool evening brings but a slight chill to the two weary travelers. Bao lies back to enjoy this spectacle of celestial bodies, playing out across the night sky. "Bao, this question is right off the wall. How did you come to have four gold front teeth? Sorry if this offends you. If I am being rude, you have my apology. My curiosity has gotten the better of me."

"Not at all, my friend. It's a simple story of slow reaction. Many years ago, walking the Ho Chi Minh trail north, minding my own business, walking with maybe twenty, thirty trail watchers, older people left behind to make road improvements and repairs. When out of nowhere, bombs started exploding all around us. Shrapnel, chunks of trees, rocks, and dirt were flying through the air. The jungle was filled with dust and smoke; fire was everywhere. We had been caught in a B-52 airstrike. Confused, dazed, and totally unprepared, many of the workers were killed. I was in shock, could not move, just stood there. I could not believe what was happening around me.

"Long story shorter, a blast of dirt and rock swept over me, taking me to the ground. When I gained consciousness, my face was on fire, not with flame, with unbelievable pain. A rock or dirt clod hit me right in the mouth. There was very little bleeding, but it did knock out three of my teeth, breaking another. My face and lips swelled so much I could not talk for two or three days, couldn't eat either. When I got back up north, the government sent me to Hanoi where I received these shiny gold teeth."

"That hit to your mouth sounds painful. I've seen other Orientals with gold teeth. Are they customary?" Bao let out a little laugh. "Necessity, we just don't have the equipment, material or the expertise to do porcelain work in our dental offices. Gold is plentiful and easy to shape into teeth. They don't corrode, stain, chip, or peal. And they don't conduct heat or cold, damn good teeth."

"Bao, before we left the village, you said that if government troops were headed south, this was a good opportunity for us to move through the lowlands. Why?"

"Well, the main reason is that when they go through a populated area, the population moves out of the way for a few days. The government forces are indigenous, but they treat their own with disdain. Women have been raped, young men forcibly conscripted into the military, their thievery of personal property and the confiscating of large portions of food stuffs makes life hard and miserable for these simple peasants. I'm using this as an opportunity to move through these rice fields and villages with little or no interference."

Standing, Bao beckons Lt. Bigelow, "Come, Bigrow, I will show you what lies before us and why we do not wish to hurry all that much." They walk up to and over the little knoll at the base of their clearing, looking out over this ocean of rice fields that are now reflecting star light off their mirrored waters. Scattered along the paddy dikes are small cooking fires used by the government troops that are now camped below them.

"We stay close enough to gain secure passage through the village but far enough back not to be detected from their vantage point high in the tree line. These villagers can see us passing through. Normally, they don't do anything or even acknowledge our presence. They're just happy to have the government troops passing on." Turning, walking back toward his sleeping mat, Bao continues, "We have never followed this large of a group before. Of the ones we have followed, none have set out flankers or rear guards. For that matter, they don't even send out a point man. They're much too relaxed in their approach to patrolling and their personal security. Look at all those fires, what I wouldn't give to have an 81mm mortar tube with ammunition right now."

Finishing the night's talk, Bao explains to Bigelow what their initial plans are. They should reach a river within two to three days, barring any unforeseen circumstances. After their initial climb onto the flatland rice paddies, their trek should be an easy one, easier than the last two days anyway. Once on the river, they will try borrowing some small two-man-dugout canoes—these little boats are made of indigenous hard wood. They are heavy, sturdy, swift, and paddle-powered. They will journey to Ha Dong, their final destination, about a three-day trip from their debarkation point.

Before sunrise, they watch the Northern troops spread out far below them breaking camp, some stumbling out of native huts, stacking their personal equipment along with looted civilian property on the ground, waiting transport. Coming through the village are flatbed, two-wheeled carts with slated sides pulled by a single water buffalo; men are throwing their military gear and ill-gotten gains aboard as they amble by. This mass of humanity, after more than an hour of trying, manages to resemble a cohesive formation and moves out, being prodded by the loud, echoing commands of their officers.

Already part way down an impressive seventy-five to a hundred-foot cliff face, Lt. Bigelow watches the departing columns, glad for their poor security. Bigelow feels like a real big target, slowly zigzagging his way off this wall of stone.

As promised, once on the floor of this great plain, the going is easier. Skirting the paddies, sticking to the north side tree line, sometimes using the earthen dikes to travel across, they are gaining large pieces of real estate. Passing the villagers and their hooches, Bao's group can see the end result of the government troops' overnight stay: a few of the structures are still smoldering, chicken and pig pens torn apart, vegetable patches dug up and trampled upon. Senseless destruction, no people should suffer these kinds of meaningless acts of hatred. This is what fuels Bao's passionate desire to defend and protect his beloved mountain people.

Another long day has ended. The trip was tiring but a little less grueling. They stop on the side of a small jungle slope. Not more than two hundred yards from a two-lane asphalt-covered road that the NVA troops are strung out along awaiting transportation, they're probably headed back to a base camp.

As the trucks pull up and start loading equipment and men, Bao and three others, taking only their weapons, move among the group collecting hand grenades. Bao stops at Bigelow's position. "Bigrow, I cannot let these people go without a parting gift. Ung will stay here with you and the others. Take his lead. When you hear explosions, move with Ung. He will be headed up into the higher ground supporting my withdrawal. Hopefully, these dumb bastards will not move far off the road. With night fast approaching, we should have the advantage of surprise. Stay down if firing develops. Only fire if you have a good clean target. Good luck, I will see you in a little bit." Bao smiles his golden smile. With his three friends, he heads off in the direction of the asphalt road.

Moving down a jungle incline, not a sound from the four native warriors, Mother Nature being on their side in this matter, all the vegetation is lush green full of water, no crunch, snap, crackle or pops as they creep toward their intended victims.

Gaining over one hundred and seventy-five yards rather quickly, Bao hand signals his men to stop and spread out. He alone will continue the advance.

This portion of highway was possibly the worst place to load trucks. The jungle bordering each side acts as a wall, only the passing of trucks keeps the jungle from reclaiming this patch of roadway. The rain drainage for this road is carved into the natural slope of the hill, no ditch on Bao's side, just a thick covering of congested jungle plants right up to the road's edge. Parked at the very edge of the blacktop are the tires of diesel engine, idling, two-and-a-half ton, canvas-covered troop transports.

Moving swiftly, with little or no concern for noise discipline, there are truck motors, laughing and talking soldiers drowning out any sounds being made by the slow slithering creature bringing death to their parade. Picking the last truck in the convoy, Bao can see under the truck as the troops marching feet pass by. They board their assigned vehicles. Shouts from their officers bringing a quick smile to Bao, they are telling the troops to unload weapons and to use caution in the handling of their munitions.

Finding the right spot, Bao takes one hand grenade, pulls the pin, and wedges the device under the back side of the front tire, spoon handle up against the tire treads. Pulling his hand carefully back into the foliage, Bao moves over to the rear axle repeating this same procedure with the back tires. When the truck moves forward, the grenade's spoons will release, lighting the fuse. Within three seconds, a charge igniting packed powder encased in a little metal pineapple will explode, sending out hundreds of jagged, sharpened metal shards of shrapnel, searching out things to destroy, victims to maim and kill.

Sound from the first truck's revving engines, gears grinding, sudden whooshing of air being released from parking brakes, chatter, clatter, and joyous song from weary troops on their way home. Bao silently, and as fast as possible, vacates the surrounding vicinity. Bao scampers up the embankment, rejoining his three companions in time to witness a huge lighting flash and loud explosion, then another followed by a few single rifle rounds cooking off due to the blast and ensuing fire.

These hand grenade detonations cause the truck to be lifted two feet into the air, coming down hard, rupturing the fuel tank, spurting out gas, igniting spreading flame into the troop area resulting in panicked, screaming, stampeding, flame-engulfed soldiers trying to escape a hideous and horrible fiery death.

Quickly moving up the incline they are on, Ung has the remaining troops, along with Lt. Bigelow, head for the high ground and a rendezvous with their four excited and much-winded comrades.

The commotion from down the hill is chaotic: trucks coming to hurried stops, officers yelling, men running, shots being fired in desperation, tracer rounds going high over the trees. All sounds of a confused and disoriented people trying to make sense of a devastating and tragic occurrence resulting in mayhem, destruction, and death.

With no signs of a pursuing enemy, Bao takes command once more. His first order is to abandon their defensive positions and form up in a marching column, flankers out, point man Ung leading the way. Although dark, Bao wishes to distance himself from their ambush site. Their trek through the darkened jungle is a steady, slow, and treacherous uphill advance.

The echoing sound of small explosions and frantic shouting is withering in the night, diminishing the farther they continue in this southeasterly direction. Once cresting this challenging little hill, they find themselves in a flat open area next to an old stack of tree stumps. Old because of all the vine growth moving over and through the remains of these once massive hard woods, they have come across an abandoned logging camp.

Not wishing to push his luck, Bao sends out three listing posts, limits the use of fires, revoking smoking privileges for the remainder of the night. With a slightly angered enemy within striking distance, there will be no slack in security. Voices at a whisper, their night goes well. Morning finds a clear sky; the air is cool, not crisp. Leading one to believe this day too will be hot and humid.

The next day, night and following day are typical tropical adventures featuring forested jungles with native fruits and nuts, wild game animals, monkeys and lizards; all this under clear, hot, and sticky humid skies. They are accompanied by an almost constant chorus of calls from the birds, warning the other animals in the jungle of this group's unwanted presence.

That second night is spent in the wood line, separated by a field of planted vegetables across from a small village sitting on the banks of the Song Hong, known throughout North Vietnam as the Red River.

This impressive waterway gets its start in Southern China. Known as the Yuan Chiang, it cuts through deep narrow gorges while flowing southeast, gathering large quantities of silt rich in iron oxide, giving the river its rust red color, eventually spilling its clouded red waters into a great delta before entering the Gulf of Tonkin.

It's from this village that Bao will try and secure river-worthy craft for their journey down river to Ha Dong, their intended destination. Procuring eight boats is by all reasoning an impossibility; a village this size could ill afford that many dugouts. Bao must beg, borrow, or steal the transportation he needs, all the while hoping for a non-confrontational solution to his dilemma. The village they are near is small; family farming and fishing support their needs. Any outside materials needed for sustaining life is traded or purchased down river in the biggest town this far north on the upper Red River, Sa Pa.

He knows that he must, at some point, divide his force before reaching Ha Dong. One cannot go walking into a North Vietnamese town with seventeen armed Montagnard tribal warriors. That would be fun but something Bao can only dream about in private thought.

Apparently coming to a decision, Bao spends a good part of the evening talking to his men. The conversation seems at times heated. Bao, always the tactician, calms his dissenters, bringing smiles and head nods. Working his way to the pilot's sleeping area, Bao talks to Bigelow about their future plans. "Bigrow, I was going to wait until Sa Pa, a town farther down river before sending most of my people home by a land route. I missed that mark by a few miles, ended up here. Now we must part company. They have a longer walk. We have a longer more difficult task ahead also."

Both men lie under another beautiful star-lit night. Bigelow not responding with his eyes wide open to the spectacle above, Bao continues, "We will take only three men, besides ourselves. You, so sorry, must spend most of your time undercover during daylight hours. This river is heavy with boat traffic and NVA check points. The check points are arranged along the shore line most times. They just have the boats move close to shore so they can see your cargo. It is easy to divert their attention with a small bribe or some evasive action, such as a diversion while other boats pass."

CHAPTER 5

I N THE MORNING, among the small group of men, three stand apart from the rest. They are saying their good-byes, all the happy backslapping, head bowing, hand clasping taking place with subdued enthusiasm, not wishing to expose themselves to the awaking villagers.

Starting out, this departing group displays their learned trait. They move off in perfect military manner, silent, flankers and point men out, spaced intervals, weapons at the ready. In no time, the jungle has swallowed them whole, vanished, simply no more. The ever-present birds call out a parting early morning serenade.

In this early morning light, five men, one slightly more nervous than the others, are scanning the village for any sign of human life. Pigs, chickens, and ducks have been awake for some time now; the dogs have not yet picked up the five's scent, sound, or movement. That will all change when the first man steps into the clearing. Bao grabs Ung by the shoulder, saying something very quickly. Bao turns to Lt. Bigelow. "Go with Ung and the others. Stay in the dark wood line and move down river, maybe one hundred one hundred twenty yards, and wait in silence near the riverbank."

Turning in the other direction, carrying only his weapon, Bao hurries off, staying in the dark shadows, using natural cover when he can. He is scurrying through this early morning quiet, trying to outsmart and outdistance the dog's keen senses. Nearing the river's edge, Bao can see four or five craft tied to a bamboo-covered dock, only twenty feet from a small hooch built on five-foot tall stilts. That's not Bao's real problem. It's the mangy, little rat-looking dog lying next to the entrance.

Not finding any natural projectiles, rocks, or good-sized sticks, Bao reaches into his pocket and retrieves two 7.62mm rifle rounds. Holding one between thumb and forefinger, he flicks it overhand, sending it buzzing fifteen feet over the dog's head into some bushes. Alerted to the sound on landing, the dog lazily stands, sniffing the air, looking in the direction of the bushes, lets out with a low pathetic, half-assed bark but does not leave his position next to the hooch.

With sunlight fast approaching, Bao wings another cartridge into the same bushes. This more than intrigues the mutt, wagging it's almost hairless curly tail, ears perked to the sound. Getting up with no haste or hurry, he ambles over to investigate.

In a flash, with stealth, Bao glides into the cold morning waters next to the dock. Ducking down, submerged to his chest, wading his way across the muddy river bottom, he maneuvers his way between two dugouts. Placing his weapon in one of the boats, he unties the ropes. Placing himself between the two vessels with a hand holding onto each boat's gunnel, he starts walking the dugouts to deeper swifter waters. Hanging on for his life, Bao uses a kicking motion in trying to steer his little armada to a safe shore. Struggling in his efforts, gulping dark drown, brackish water, suddenly, with startling clarity, he hears a splash, a big splash. Coming for Bao is Lt. Bigelow, a strong confident swimmer. Reaching the dugouts, he grabs one of the loose lines and starts a labored stroke for the riverbank.

Almost reaching the river's edge, Ung wades out to the pilot. Bigelow tosses the lanyard to him, returning to the river and pursuit of Bao and his runaway craft. Bigelow, using a strong freestyle swim stroke, reaches his friend. Grabbing the stern of the little vessel, the pilot, kicking with all his might, steers the log craft and his clinging friend safely to the far bank. Nudging the boat into shore, Bigelow moves to aid Bao, who is struggling to keep his head above water. Bao is gasping for air, flapping his arms like a drowning rat, and with the lieutenant's help, they both reach overhanging vines and hang on.

Bao and Lt. Bigelow, wet and miserable, suck in much-needed air. Bao, looking like an unhappy wet hamster, starts spitting out bits of greenery along with a mouthful of brown water. "Thank you, my friend. That was more water than I could handle. Thank you."

Not trying to be a smart ass nor rude, Bigelow asks, "You can't swim, can you?"

His answer is logical, senseless yet logical. "No, I thought I could just float these dugouts a short ways down river with no problem. I must have been wrong."

Lt. Bigelow's reply was surly. "You little bastard, you could have drowned! Where in the hell would that have left me? Out here in the middle of nowhere. Damn it, Bao!"

Bao, dropping his head, not making contact with Bigelow's eyes, delivers an apology. "Bigrow, you right. I must promise to think more clearly next time. Thank you again for the rescue."

They turn their attention back to the river; their three companions are on the other side, nowhere in sight. With the turbulent sound of rushing waters, yelling and shouting are not suitable communicators. A rifle shot seems as smart as Bao's jump into the water. They're still too close to the village. Suddenly, a dugout moving down the swift waters carrying Ung and his two buddies, no paddles, all three are hunched over, stroking the water frantically, using their arms and hands. Able to maneuver their craft close to the shore, they stay on the water, holding onto the overhanging tree branches, hand over hand pulling themselves to Bigelow and Bao's location.

With light slowly spreading across the treetops throwing early shadows across the jungle floor and playing games with the river's sparkling waters, five exhausted men try gaining their composure. A sudden rush of adrenalin caused by the excitement of a death-defying adventure can bring the toughest of men to their knees.

With everyone's help, they manage to drag the two heavy, solid hardwood dugouts from the water and hide them among the low, overhanging tree branches and jungle vines dangling out over the water, spending precious energy and time concealing their position. All they are able to do is sit in the mornings quiet, only the rushing water and their own labored breathing can be heard. Once they have their breath, they smile; with some trepidation, they stifle their nervous laughter, one way of releasing frustration in their present situation. Barely off the water, they are cold and wet; unfortunately, building a fire is not possible in these circumstances, with them being so close to a major waterway. The villagers will soon be out looking for their castaway boats; this is not shaping up to be an all-star day for this little group.

Traffic on this part of the Red River is starting to appear: one man homemade wood dugouts, long boats full of cargo being paddled by two people, small and large motor boats now moving past their little island of safety. Tucked under a big tree, its branches covered with rows of small, fine lacy leaves giving good concealment but allowing easy observation of passing vessels. Their most unpleasant adversary at the moment, annelids—elongated, segmented invertebrates, leeches. With no immediate way to safely remove these little bastards, the five shiver with cold and the pain of these finger-length blood-sucking creatures from this dark lagoon.

The only good to be said of their location is that they are on the outer bank of a wide turn in the river. With the water's swiftness and the jungle's tangled interference along the shoreline, boats of different shapes and sizes, cargo and passenger keep their keels in midchannel, staying well clear of the hidden party of five.

These craft are varied, some are most colorful. There must be hundreds of single and two-man dugouts, also two people, beautiful bamboo-woven canoe type boats. You have sixteen-foot Chinese wooden flat bottom, stand up stern tiller, two oar sampans. But the biggest and fastest of them all is the Vietnamese built Ghe Nang, a three massed sail-powered boat consisting of a bamboo-woven hull with a wooden top deck attached. It's from this platform that long handled oars are at times used for propulsion and steering; sails are multicolored sometimes with designs and lettering.

Deciding no action is better than foolish action, Bao decides to spend their first day on the Red River camped on an uncomfortably water-logged, leech, and mosquito-infested patch of rotten decaying compost.

From their hidden lair, comfort at a premium, Bigelow wriggles his way to the nearest boat, the one Ung and his two friends arrived in. Throwing a leg over the gunnel, pulling the rest of his body up and over, coming to rest on top of his and the other's equipment, including his crossbow. Somewhat of a surprise are the two nicely carved wooden oars. Motioning Bao over, Lt. Bigelow asks why Ung did not use the paddles in their river crossing.

Bao squirms over to Ung; the two engage in a whispered conversation. After some length, Bao returns to Bigelow, with a whimsical grin and his golden teeth sparkling in the midmorning sun. "Ung says when he took boat from you, you dove back into the turbulent water and disappeared. They could see me hanging onto the fast moving boat headed down river. Well, he said they didn't think or wish to waste time. After quickly throwing all the equipment into the craft, the three just jumped in and went for a ride. It seems in their haste, they were kneeling on top of all the gear that was covering the paddles. They were no smarter than me, but you could not ask for a more loyal bunch. Yes, Bigrow, we were lucky on this one. That's why I chose to wait out the day here. We have food in our bags. We have our weapons. We shall think of better and more cautious ways to proceed. Sorry for the delay, let us study the river's flow, gain knowledge of its pattern and deadly tricks."

This day spent watching and studying this section of the Red River has been interesting and informative, leaving them to believe that they can strike out in the wee dawn of tomorrow's morning and not duplicate this day's near tragic mistakes.

Just before dark, with the upcoming sun's setting, Ung and his friend Dit Hum leave their tiny circle, searching out banana leaves that can be used to abate the upcoming cold and miserable night. Bao, Lt. Bigelow, and the remaining man, Y-Cie, use a cigarette cupped in their hands, so as not to expose themselves, taking turns burning leeches off each other. They will do the same for the two others upon their return. With a darkened and cold sky covering their damp little camp, three indigenous use the one boat covered in large broad leaves as their night shelter. Bao and Bigelow take over the remaining craft, covering themselves with nature's excuse for a blanket, banana leaves and palm fronds. They are tightly packed in a cramped, narrow little space, smelling of damp wood, and rotting foliage. Everything in this place either smells, is damp or uncomfortable—most of the time, all three.

Butt-to-butt, back-to-back, faces just inches from the wooden gunnel, eyes focused on little bugs, brown with a touch of orange striping that are scurrying over and through the cracks. Bigelow quietly breaks the silence. "This, for the most part, was an all-out exciting day, my friend." Bigelow can feel the laugh building in Bao, yet only a little giggle is emitted. This warrior is not willing to give up his night location for a laugh.

"After some needed rest, we should be ready for some water travel. Our new crew member will be Y-Cie. I have known him for many years. He comes from the same village as my father. His parents were close friends of my parents. When I went off to the university, Y-Cie joined with my brother, Dinh, training as a sapper. They had many missions together, good man. The other one is like Ung's brother. I can never separate them. If I tell one to do something, they must discuss it, determine the best way of gaining success in whatever the task. They are exceptionally good troops on their own, but together, they're deadly, always. His name is Dit Hum. In the war down south. he worked with the American Special Forces as a member of an elite all Montagnard strike force. At times, I think he is a better tracker than Ung, but only some times. US Special Forces liked and preferred working with Montagnards because of their desired keen senses and natural skills in the jungle. Most of all, they respected and admired their dedication and loyalty. They were fearless and most deadly and had an ingrained hatred for the Vietnamese. The hardest thing for the Americans was keeping them and their weapons pointed north."

With the captured warmth of their little sauna keeping them toasty, the mosquitoes have fled for the time being. Lt. Bigelow ponders their upcoming adventure, with little aspirations of ever reaching Ha Dong, he hopes for the best; if not, all he can ask for is a quick and painless death.

Waking with cramping pains, the five discard their night covers. Keeping a few broad leaves for the pilot's camouflaged hiding place, he will lie at the bottom of this moldy old log with three weapons, one on each side wedged between his leg and the side of the boat. The third AK-47 is on his lap, his head and back resting on the men's carrying bags. Bao is kneeling directly to his front. Bigelow can poke his head up through his cover and catch a quick peek at his surroundings, ducking back down for quick concealment when necessary.

Observing the river craft yesterday has enlightened them in the maneuvering of their little dugouts. The water running past this bend flows swiftest in the middle, careening off the upper side of its bank in a fast but smooth current. When the river straightens, it runs wide and calm.

Pushing off before full daylight gives them free access to their watery highway; their progress is steady. The front man uses his paddle to row, switching off sides every two or three strokes. The man in the stern does some paddling; he also uses his paddle as a rudder and for balance, trying to keep their little craft under control.

Bao is keeping to the northern shoreline; he feels that any checkpoints will be on the south side since most of the villages are on that side with connecting roads and trails, giving soldiers an easy route to their checkpoint locations.

Looking for any small village on this eastern bank so he might enhance his men's wardrobe, besides Lt. Bigelow and himself being in shorts, the other three are still in loincloths, no shirts or head gear. Bao is looking for someone's laundry.

Early morning sun making its daily climb high overhead, cool on the water with bow spray and a breeze coming off the river acting as a personal air conditioner, this seems so easy, peaceful, and so out of place. As they progress, the landscape is slowly running out of mountains and hills; forested jungles are slowly turning into banana groves along the river's edge bordered by a vigorous growth of wild berries. The farther they go, the more open the terrain becomes with a grassy fertile plain slowly drifting off to the north. To the south, rice fields as far as one can see.

At one point, along this deserted stretch of shore, they pull their boats to the riverbank. Lt. Bigelow and Bao remain as their fellow travelers go ashore to cut themselves three bunches of bananas. This not only gives them the appearance of having a legitimate cargo, it helps conceal Bigelow, and they also have a supply of readily available food.

By late morning, they're joined by a myriad of boat adventurists: farmers and merchants headed to markets selling their goods and produce, families venturing out to visit family and friends in neighboring villages, people going to market for their daily needs, children and teens on their way to school, maybe some journeying all the way to the South China Sea. It's a great day for a cruise.

For the past two days, the only craft moving against the current on the Red River has been small one or two manned dugouts and bamboo-woven canoes. They are mostly local travelers. Normally, these little craft stay close to the southern shore. With the river flowing against them, they must paddle like hell to make headway, but they slowly gain the distance they need to complete their voyage.

Bao is surprised when from down river, he can see a rather large motor boat approaching at a fairly good rate of speed, not varying his course, forcing boats to move out of its way. Using caution over ego, Bao steers for the shore. The two craft they are in, being the only ones on a northern track, seems to evoke interest from the NVN[1] patrol boat. Bao softly and calmly tells Lt. Bigelow to have his and the other AKs locked and loaded, ready for action. Turning to the trailing boat, he can see Ung readying his weapons. Glancing up, he sees the patrol boat turn off its course midchannel, headed straight for their little flotilla of boats.

Bracing for an all-out confrontation, Bao holds his oar in a steady turn to port toward the thick foliage along the near shore. Their adversary is coming fast and true with no sign of them changing direction. Bao is within seconds of reaching for his AK when the patrol boat's bow jerks to its port side, missing the two little craft by just a few feet, swamping the dugouts with its wake and spraying dirty brown prop wash water over both boats, passing so close they can hear the sailors laughing over the rush of water and roar of the engine. Luckily for the five, they were just being assholes and not diligent troops trying to stop contraband or simple banana toting Montagnards smuggling an American flyer.

After bailing water from their boats, they continue on. Bigelow is concentrating his efforts on the drying of three AK-47s and himself. His little hiding place is now damp, smelly, and most unpleasant after having churned up brownish green and rust red-colored water splashed in on him.

Past midday, Bao thinks he has discovered a target upriver from a good-sized village. On the south bank, Bao spots a small inlet not more than twenty yards wide. There's a cleared shore next to a little village. This must be the launching place for their small fishing fleet, no dock, just a flat beach area ideal for the

---

[1]   North Vietnamese Navy

beaching of their low draft boats. About twenty feet past this cleared spot, just to the right of the first hooch, there are six women doing their weekly laundry. With a grin and a heart full of hope, Bao heads across the wide girth of the Red River, making for the southern shore.

Turning their boats starboard, plowing their way through river traffic and strong currents, they reach the south shore, about two hundred yards up river from the inlet. Coasting into the overhanging bramble, there is no beach or landfall at this point on the river. Swinging their craft about, tying the bow ropes off, anchoring themselves to secure limbs, they waste no time plucking wild tasty berries, a wonderfully welcomed addition to their dried deer jerky, cooked monkey meat, and bananas. The five enjoy a late afternoon meal.

Waiting for full darkness, they allow the village fishermen to return from their day's work, beach their boats, and haul their catch into the village. They are now relaxing and having their dinner prepared. Bao, using this nightly ritual as cover for his laundry raid, hopes the village dogs are not far from their source of nourishment, the village cooking fires begging or sneaking a bite to eat, fighting over discarded gristle and bones.

Untying their little craft, they move to the mouth of the inlet where they reanchor. Removing his loincloth, Y-Cie goes over the side, slicing his way into the cold dark unknown waters with nary a ripple. Staying submerged for long stretches of time and distance, Y-Cie makes quick work of his one-hundred-and-fifty-yard swim for the hanging freshly washed laundry that's not going to be there in the morning. The four shipboard travelers can see the unfolding clothing raid in unobscured clarity. The only thing visible from their vantage point so far is the swimmer's head as he breaks the surface, taking in air.

Once Y-Cie is ashore, he slithers like a snake, making his way to the bushes where the laundry has been hung out to dry. So far, so good. Clambering for cover under these small clumps of green brush, he is now out of his friends' sight. The only thing they can now see are black garments disappearing magically as if being sucked in by a silent vacuum, one after the other. Black splotches are being removed from the shrubs outstretched green branches.

His task completed, Y-Cie comes out from undercover, pushing a ball of cloth blackness in front of him as he makes a hasty withdrawal toward the water. Upon reaching this goal, Y-Cie stops, frozen by an unheard unseen motive, his four boat bound comrades not sure of his reasoning in halting. They watch in disbelief as their friend leaves his ball of clothing, slowly turns, going to a crouch heading back into the bushes he has just exited. Moving quickly with unknown purpose, he disappears.

Just the normal humming and clattering evening village sounds, floating across the water, dogs barking, and growling at each other, but no real sound of alarm. The man's naked; he's going to stand out to any who sees him, a sudden low scampering dash from bush to fishing boat. They can only glimpse little bursts of movement broken by flashes of shadows being sprayed across the beach by the light of cooking fires peeking through the undergrowth.

Y-Cie's next appearance comes by way of a short dash from where the boats are, back down the beach to the water's edge where his black ball of clothing awaits. He is at least a foot taller. Y-Cie has liberated five straw conical hats. Looking like a beehive pushing a large black turtle across the inlet, Y-Cie's progress is slow yet steady. Lt. Bigelow is ready to enter the cold waters if the swimmer needs help. Bao holds him back, not wanting two unarmed men in the water unable to defend themselves.

Reaching the boat, Y-Cie removes his stack of hats, handing them to Bigelow. Maneuvering to the other side of the boat, he pulls a piece of clothing from his bundle before tossing the rest into the dugout. Taking a huge breath, he ducks back down into the black cold depths. Sloshing and wriggling in the dark cold expanse of water, he emerges wearing a big purple-toothed grin and a pair of black pajama bottoms.

Leaving their anchorage, they float past the inlet continuing down river three or four miles, pulling under overhanging tree branches for the remainder of the night.

Predawn, sitting in their concealed dockage, the five watch as the NVN patrol boat from yesterday, search light fanning the banks, storms south midchannel. Again, not giving way to other craft, fortunately, there is little traffic this early in the day on the Red River.

By the end of the day, they should reach the docks of Sa Pa. There they will tie to a massive flotilla of boats of all sizes: large, small, and in-between, Some are used for the storage of goods. Some are used as restaurants, schools, stores, places of ill-repute and playground to the children of boat families. There are hundreds of people who never leave the polluted rust red waters of the infamous Red River. This day's journey proves uneventful. Wearing their new clothing and the addition of conical hats eases their fear of not fitting in among their fellow travelers. Blending with his surroundings is one of Bao's main goals in getting the round-eyed pilot through this throng of Asians.

The banks of this mighty river are slowly being tamed as they near their destination. From its beginning in southern China, the Red River has been paralleled by not only a two-lane highway but also following its course is a rail line, continuing through Sa Pa, moving south, eventually ending its run in the coastal ports of the Tonkin Gulf.

Passing the main bulk of the floating city, Bao makes his way between two old rusting barges tying off on their anchor chains; this will be their night's berth, hopefully avoiding detection with the possibility of getting some needed rest before their push to Ha Dong. Sa Pa is a small mountain town with many French style villas nestled among the green-covered hills. Most commerce is conducted via rail or road. Although local marketing of produce and manageable livestock, pigs, ducks, geese, and chickens are transported to and from villages and towns by waterway. This mode of transportation is the easiest and cheapest means of travel for peasants and small independent farmers along the Red River Valley.

Protected by these two rusting hulks, their night passed peacefully. They finally gain some much-needed rest. In the early morning, Bao transfers to Ung's boat, leaving Y-Cie and Bigelow tied to the barge anchor chain. The other three work their way to a gaggle of boats anchored and tied side by side. Coming alongside this floating market, Bao exchanges a small amount of piasters[2] for some fresh vegetables, some freshly cooked rice balls, along with some cooked meat, thanking the merchant. Once this transaction is completed, they return to their waiting friends.

Bao tells them that their next port of call will be Ha Dong, an easy two-day voyage, barring any unforeseen troubles or unnecessary diversions. Separating from the barges, they start their final run down the big Red. Joining other travelers on a misted muggy morning, they jockey for position near midchannel along with numerous other small craft braking off from the floating city continuing down river on their way south, possibly all the way to the sea.

Their first real full day on the Red River is remarkably quiet and calm with the waters ebb and flow carrying them along. The day's end finds them maneuvering their little craft toward the northern shore again, making for the comfort and safety of overhanging trees fully covered by prickly bramble vines that are full of little berries so tart they cannot be eaten. Most of the other small craft stopping for the night tie off together along the south shore. Tying off to a large tree or by sharing a drag anchor cast ashore by one of the larger vessels, some of the boats' crew gather on a small beach using a communal fire for their cooking and warmth. Most will sleep on shore tonight.

Just before full sunrise, light from the moon rendering the boats across the river in gray flickering shadows cast across the black waters, their night's fire has burned down to embers that is

---

2   Currency of Vietnam

sending spirals of grayish white smoke drifting through the trees. Suddenly, coming up from the southern reaches of this mighty river, the powerful roar of a boat's engine and search light from a government patrol boat is casting bolts of jagged light across the waters, sending flashes of light climbing through the trees along the shore. Coming in fast, rocking the boats with its wake, they pull alongside this rabble of market-bound, produce- and rice-laden craft, shining bright search lights about. Rousting the sleeping crews, the NVN start a thorough search of men and boats.

Huddled in their dugouts, the five seafarers again prepare themselves for combat, as before, hoping not to be found and searched. If they are approached and harassed this time, Bao has decided to defend their honor. Each AK-47 has a thirty-round magazine. They could produce a one-hundred-and-fifty round, unbelievably quick and deadly surprise for the six unsuspecting NVN sailors. He hopes not to be disturbed at his mooring.

The morning light is slow to materialize, not giving them a real good view of the proceedings taking place across the river. The patrol boat is between them and the shore. The NVN's search lights can be seen bouncing swirls of light through the trees, shadows thrown at an angle. Splayed across the boat hulls are the silhouetted figures of bewildered crew members. All they can do is watch as their boats and personal belongings are gone through and searched, desired foods and goods confiscated. The NVN continue their reign of stupid, senseless harassment, amounting simply to nothing less than government sanctioned terrorism.

Finished with their south shore duties, the patrol boat idles its way to midchannel, comes to starboard and powers its way up river, all the while reaching out with its tentacle like beam of light, feeling for more victims, more unsuspecting, innocent, defenseless people to harass and scare. The NVN crew just misses the heavily armed men hidden among the thick brambles. The patrol boats departure gives Bao a good reason to weigh anchor and cut across river to join the fleet of boats moving off the south bank continuing their voyage down river. His motive is to try and blend in with a group of boats that have already been searched in hopes of eluding interception and inspection when the NVN patrol boat makes its return trip.

Telling Bigelow to stay quiet and out of sight, Bao brings his craft up to this cluster of boats. They move among the dozen or so small craft, finding a safe spot almost in the middle of the pack. This morning, there is no chatter between boats. Bao sees people with their heads hung low, their spirits broken, their inventories involuntarily depleted. Paying little mind to the new arrivals, they all paddle on.

Villages and decent sized towns are appearing now all along the southern shore. The north bank showing less vegetation at the river's edge, land is open with a gradual sloping right up to the start of the forest covered mountains. Rice paddies dot the flat areas with canals bringing water to them via wooden water wheels made of slatted, seven-foot diameter wheels powered by individuals peddling a sprocket and chain apparatus resembling a bicycle, crude—a lot of work but very effective.

As the day progresses, their little group of merchants is slowly dwindling in size. Boats, in groups of two, three, five at a time, are pulling into small docks arranged along the shore. The approach to each is being watched over by armed government troops, not searching the craft, just observing the comings and goings of the peasants and their families.

Off the northern shore, there is a large confluence of merging waters, a tributary pushing into the Red River, adding greatly to the undulating currents, bringing more waterborne traffic with it. This new northern shore is starting to mimic the south shore, a congestion of small villages and towns; there is a distinctive odor of humans caused by their inevitable smelly waste. The aroma that is drifting out over the waters is coming from open markets with their fly covered produce, fish, and meats that are flooding the air with a foul odor, congesting the lungs and pores of the people as they consume this polluted and poisoned food. They in turn deposit this same smelly ingredient in the privacy of their own homes, public toilets, and other establishments. Only to have this byproduct pass out into the streets, flowing down the gutters in public view, leaving it to travel down an open sewer system, finally reaching the river ending up as fish food, thus completing the recycling of life.

There are other markers of a vast advanced civilization: sounds of congestion, horns, bells, and whistles; the screech of braking cars, cycle and pedicabs, mopeds, trucks, and the ever-present bicycle. These small farming villages grew into thriving little towns that are now being swallowed by honest to goodness big cities. The amount of boats, people, the smells, sounds, and the heat has almost overwhelmed them as they paddle toward the northern shore. Bao will choose one branch of this mighty river, navigating their way in a slightly southeasterly direction looking for the passage to Ha Dong.

Finding his tributary entrance, Bao, turning to port, finds that they must now fight a strong south flowing current, all the while dodging oncoming boat traffic moving out of this confining channel headed for larger ports of call or into the Tonkin Gulf itself, truly, the gateway to the South China Sea. They stay close to the southeast shore, tucking their little craft among others, trying to avoid oncoming boats and the strong currents that are reduced along the shallows. It's not a free ride like when going with the currents; they have to use their paddles a little more aggressively to make progress.

Nightfall finds the two little boats and four crew members ready for some well-deserved rest. Their passenger, Lt. Bigelow, is a little tense and uncomfortable from the weight and smell of ripening bananas, the long journey, and the incessant heat. They are all hungry. Navigating his way through a congestion of small boat docks, floating channel markers, and anchored boats, Bao takes them toward what Bigelow thinks is a fueling dock for larger craft such as freighters and barge pushers that are headed for the big waters of the gulf. There is a strong smell of diesel, oil, and gasoline. The water around this pier has that iridescent blue and purple reflective sheen floating on its surface; there are heavy black oily smelling globs sticking to the dock's pylons. The holding tanks for the fuel are submerged, half-underwater, with their tops coming level with the pier, presumably built this way to discourage air strikes during the US bombing of the North. Large diameter pipes coming out the top of these storage tanks go up ten or twelve feet above the pier planking before hooking over, coming back down another three feet with an air filter attached to its opening. These are the tanks air vents supplying all the diesel and gasoline smells. Attached to another pipe is a long length of flexible hose for the final coupling and filling of the vessels fuel tanks.

With daylight fading, running lights of boats, docking lights along the piers their only beacon, Bao cuts through the shadows, zigzagging his way through the pylons, finally reaching the slimy oil-covered shoreline. Tying their craft to a pylon with a ladder extending from water line up to the pier's deck, the five languish for a time, familiarizing themselves with the sights and sounds of their chosen mooring, not wishing to be surprised or disturbed later in the night.

"Bigrow, if it would not be too much to ask, I would like to borrow your Colt .45. Ung and I are going up on the wharf. I'll be going into town to buy food and drink from a local market or a small hole in the wall restaurant, and I would like to have a little protection while in the presence of my enemies."

Lt. Bigelow, looking at the golden smile of their fearless leader, the slight glint in his coal black eyes, there is no refusal. "Choose your target carefully, my friend. You only have six shots."

"I hope not to find a target. I'm just hungry. Ung will stay topside, providing security for you three. Please stay in boat, only half day tomorrow, and then maybe we can leave boats for a safe house."

Bao and Ung ascend the metal ladder. The only visible sign that these two are not local peasants is the folding stock AK-47

Ung has slung over his right shoulder, Bao concealing the pilot's .45 in his shoulder bag. Reaching the top, Ung cautiously lifts the wooden hatch cover. No sounds, no movement. He pops up through the opening, runs for a stack of old oil drums, disappearing in their tangled darkness. Bao comes topside, stands, taking in his surroundings, dusts himself off, just like that heads for a nearby lighted street and the sound of commerce filtering through the night.

Walking through a darkened area of waterside warehouses, he crosses paths with a fat black and tan alley cat, really unusual this close to such a populated area. They're considered a tasty addition to anyone's dinner. Lucky little bastard, Bao's looking for a ready-to-eat meal.

Reaching the end of warehouse row, Bao looks in amazement at all the light, sounds, and smells of this congested cross street. It has been some time since he has walked among his fellow countrymen and not been suspect, not been looked on as a possible enemy. Tonight, in his peasant cloths, mingling with others of the same caste, he feels the spirit of the moment only to realize this festive mood is the end result of the war between the North and South. It's over, done, finis, no more open hostilities, or so they say. This does not unburden Bao as he has a private war with the governing powers. He and his people are not free of their resentment, harassment, and old prejudices. He might not look exactly like a Montagnard, but his thoughts and feelings, his heart and soul are all 110 percent Montagnard.

Yet he cannot shake the giddy feeling he has just walking along this street. Some are dressed in military and school uniforms. Most of the women are dressed in the traditional Ao Dai—a front opening, knee-length, coat-like garment with a stand-up collar, slits from the waist all the way to the hem, one on each side, worn over a Quan—a zippered front long pant, usually made of cotton for summer use, wool in the somewhat colder months and fine silk for special occasions. Some of the civilian men are in khaki pants with light cotton shirts. Farmers, fishermen, laborers, along with the lowly peasant, are all dressed in black pajamas.

The passing traffic is a hodgepodge of wheeled vehicles—engine-powered and people-powered; along with water buffalo pulling wagons piled high with produce, bamboo, fire wood, and other goods. There are entire families—mother, father, and small children hanging onto little moped scooters as they weave in and out of this chaotic jumble of horn blaring, tire-squealing vehicles, cycle cabs (a three-wheeled bicycle), one-man peddle-powered people haulers, old trucks, and cars.

The two and three-story buildings lining both sides of the street are built wall to wall. Street level floor space is dedicated to small open shops, markets, food stalls, others used as clothing stores, natural herb pharmacies, book emporiums, small restaurants, pots and pans, nuts and bolts—every type of establishment needed to support a thriving community.

Bao's first indulgence, a snake cocktail purchased from an old woman street vendor. She has a basket full of live snakes. When a customer makes a request, this lady will grab one of the wrigly little fellows, skin him alive, squeezing the blood into a glass by milking the still warm, moving, pinkish red, naked body of the snake with her fingers just like you would with the teats of a cow. Mixing in an alcohol elixir, you have yourself a very popular Vietnamese health potion.

The second floors of these two-story buildings are the living quarters for shopkeepers, merchants, and their families. This second floor is usually connected by a long, cantilevered overhang-ing walkway, circumventing the entire building running from one end of the block to the other. Standing at the railing, you can look down on an open communal courtyard. The third floor, if any, is used as private family patios, in some cases, used as open rooftop seating for a downstairs restaurant.

Walking along this thriving little street, with its hustle and bustle, evokes a feeling of relief, not true happiness, not a true spirit of social freedoms. A country wide war has just ended.

There is a breath of hesitance in the air, that same dark foreboding feeling that comes over Bao when he is not really trusting of his surroundings. You just can't put your finger on it, but you know there is something that needs poking.

The smell of food and the growling of his stomach have awakened his sense of duty, that of finding adequate food supplies and returning to his waiting men. Not a difficult task, it's just that Bao finds it kind of nice being out among the masses, even if it is for just a short time. Standing on the corner, surrounded by bright lights, confusing sights, and loud sounds, Bao follows his nose and enters a small family-owned and operated open pit grilling establishment—a few small tables on the busy sidewalk, no seating inside. There's a short counter with an ice chest perched on one end. Behind this is an open raised fire ring, covered with a grate. All their selections are cooked over this charcoal fed fire. Besides pig, one could order and receive an assortment of meats, monkey, deer, and buffalo, along with a variety of steamed or grilled vegetables, bamboo shoots, soups, along with rice done many ways. They have one of Bao's favorites, Vermicelli noodles. There is an ice chest with soft drinks, juices, Ba Moui Ba and Biere 33—both of these are a bitter formaldehyde-tasting Vietnamese beer. Ordering some pig ribs, rice balls, and Vermicelli, along with a scoop of assorted steamed vegetables, Bao, not wanting to drink the oil-tainted water they're moored in, reaches into the ice chest, retrieving five bottles of beer. Putting his parcels into his carry bag and pulling out some money, Bao, looking up to pay his due, is met by a gaping mouthed, wide-eyed merchant, speaking ever so slightly in Vietnamese. "Sir, I would be more careful with the opening of your bag. Not to alarm, do not let authorities see what you have. Sir, your bill is three hundred and eighty-five piasters, enjoy."

Paying and thanking the man, Bao walks out a little startled but grateful, upset with himself for being lax in his own security, exposing his weapon so easily, grateful that this stranger did not panic or cry out, effectively eliminating himself as a potential target.

Not taking a direct route back to his men, Bao goes to the corner, then moves off in the opposite direction, traveling through an apartment district. There are less people out and about, less traffic in the streets. Passing French-styled walled compounds with guard dogs barking, children's shouts as they play on this warm peaceful evening. He turns toward the river, stopping, looking back down the road he has just traveled. No sign of followers. Turning back, he heads for the warehouse district. Moving through the old buildings, keeping to the shadows, he walks by the stack of oil drums. Not making eye-to-eye contact with Ung and using a steady low-pitched undertone, Bao speaks to the night in his native tongue. "Stay where you are, cover me, come in when you're sure no one has followed." Moving onto the dock, he stops, kneels at the hatch cover, listening for that reassuring sound of silence.

Finishing their meal, the five down their beer, holding the empties under the oil-coated waters so they fill with water and sink, best not to have five empties floating around drawing attention to themselves, Bao informs Lt. Bigelow and his men that they will be departing before daybreak.

They move past the row of warehouses beaching next to a small untended overgrown palm grove Bao spotted the night before. His motive is to throw out the rotting bananas and replenish the pilot's camouflage with fresh vegetation. Taking only minutes, they are soon back on the water, staying close to the shore, avoiding as much of the current as they can by staying in the shallows.

Coming close to their destination, there is more congestion on the waterway; the land itself is disappearing, being devoured by humanity, structures of all kinds. By the stench alone, you could find this place blindfolded. The magnitude of sound near deafening, Bao and his crew mates are a little apprehensive and nervous, Bigelow is intrigued.

They're passing homes that are built on the edge of the land, jutting out over the water on pylons. Family transportation in the form of boats are docked beneath their homes. There are rows of banana trees breaking the landscape into parcels, providing some semblance of privacy for the individual families. Just past these little plots, the riverbank is dominated by a long pier adjacent to rows of warehouses. They dock at this mooring of assorted craft. Tied together are farmers, butchers, candlemakers, merchants of all kinds, selling their goods to land dwellers and boat people, farmer or peasant. This is a big open air market with hundreds of vendors, selling their wares. The food stalls are plastering the air with delightful smells. Whatever you need to sustain life, you will find it here.

Traveling this tributary has brought them to a small but heavily trafficked channel, cutting right through commercial and residential neighborhoods with a shoreline that's maybe ten, twelve feet deep. A cement block retaining wall not more than five feet tall at any given point is erected right along the river's edge. Beyond this wall, almost level to its top, there's a narrow walkway where buildings abruptly spring up, towering at times, three to four stories. The taller structures are used as hotels or government office space; there always seems to be a large amount of government paper pushing personnel involved in every communist takeover or in the wining of any war. The two-story structures are being used as family residencies, restaurants, mercantile shops, stores of all kinds, with living quarters upstairs. Every so often, there are short pylon supported piers.

Just past noon, Bao maneuvers through oncoming boat traffic finally bringing his little craft port side, gliding up to one of the short docks. Tying off to one of its supports, they wait. Lt. Bigelow, peeking out through the gaps in his palm leaf cover for a look at his surroundings, is confronted by a bustling, vibrant society of boat people and the unmistakable stench of land dwellers.

There is no breeze. The sun's glare off the river is causing streaks of light to slither lazily across the water, sometimes curling and twisting in a boat's wake, like a slow wriggling snake moving through the grass with the sun reflecting off its scales.

There are people above on the dock, not many, going about their daily lives, none acknowledging their presence. Children are running the length of the pier, at its end diving into the polluted, murky water, swimming to shore, climbing up the slippery side of a pylon, running, repeating their adventure, screeching and shouting as they play.

After an unknown period of time scrutinizing their situation, finding themselves unnoticed, Ung and Dit Hum leave their little craft for dry land without weapons in the enemy's heartland, brave and foolish at the same time, hoping to blend in with all the other the peasants by wearing their black pajamas and straw hats. The next to leave is Y-Cie. Climbing from one boat to the other, speaking with Bao, he is handed some paper currency. Y-Cie unties his craft and paddles off to be absorbed into the moving mass of waterborne traffic.

Breaking the hot and humid silence, Bigelow whispers, "What next, my friend? I don't know if my legs still work. I haven't moved in so long. They're asleep and numb. Standing, even walking, will require retraining."

Bao, not making visual contact with Lt. Bigelow, replies in a returned whisper, "You funny man, Bigrow, not long. I hope for Ung's return soon. He and Dit Hum went to check on two old friends. He will let us know when we can leave these dugouts and walk again on the land. If Y-Cie beats him back, we will eat!"

And that's how it plays out. Y-Cie returns in his little boat with a day's ration of rice balls and those impressive looking, scrumptious barbecued-skewered monkey. Ung's return comes just before dusk; the waters are calm and on fire with the reflection of the dying day's vibrant purplish-red sunset.

The last NVN patrol boat they saw was miles downriver, long before turning up this channel. The only evidence of government security has been two-man patrols armed and in uniform, walking through the open markets and shops lining the streets. They seem to have little contact with the people; thus far, they pose no threat to the five.

Ung and Y-Cie have now left the boat. They're sitting up on the dock, feet dangling out over the water just above Bao and Lt. Bigelow. Boat and barge traffic has slowed down greatly since nightfall. The only illumination cast across the water is coming from quaint little lanterns swinging from poles attached to the bow of small fishing boats bouncing flickers of light across the waters. They are headed for swampy shallows along the overgrown shore-gathering frogs, night lizards, and turtles by shining a bright light into the animals little eyes. Like deer caught in the headlights of a car, they freeze, and the fishermen scoop them up in a net, bringing them aboard alive.

Pulling himself up into a more comfortable position, Bigelow asks, "We seem to have lost one man. When is he coming back?"

"Bigrow, someone will arrive later tonight. They will lead us to a safe house, a place we can stay for a few days while we try and work things out. This priest I'm to meet with was at one time anticommunist, as were my parents when they were all together many years ago. Wars and time have a way of changing one's thinking. Simple survival plays a really big role. One's religious affiliation must coincide with the ruling government's party. His being Catholic carries no power. His prestige as a priest works in his favor. He is allowed to travel in the name of his church, baptize, say mass, and visit with like-minded officials and government dignitaries. My last contact with him was a short one. We did not discuss any personal matters. I don't know if we can trust him with our problem. I cannot hand you over to him and just say good-bye. I could not honestly live with myself. Besides, my brother, Dinh, would kill me. As we speak, Dit Hum is watching this man's residence. He and Ung will be his shadow for the next two or three days. They will discretely follow and see where he goes, who he visits and talks with. They will try and get close enough to gain information from conversations. I must know more about this priest, more than what my family knew so many years ago. I must be certain about his political and ethical beliefs."

Disturbed by the sudden rocking of the boat, not realizing he had fallen asleep, Bigelow struggles to free himself from his restraints, finally breaking free of the aggressive, cunning palm frond that's been trying to hold him to the bottom of the boat. Sitting up, arms flailing about, in the quiet darkness, he glances out over the water, nothing. Swinging around, he sees Y-Cie handing weapons and other equipment up to Ung who's standing on the dock. Reaching out, grabbing both sides of the craft, getting ready to stand, a firm steady hand stops his movement. "Easy, my friend. You were resting. Our guide is here. Get up on the dock, and I'll hand you our things. Careful, don't capsize the boat."

Quickly as possible, they empty the two little craft. Once this is done, Ung shows the pilot how to sling his AK strap over his right shoulder with the folded stock resting against his side cradled under his right arm pit with the right hand holding onto the gun's barrel, to balance and conceal it.

Carrying Bigelow's crossbow is made easier by removing the small dowels from the bows three-foot crosspiece; this detached member is lashed to the main stock of the weapon and placed into the quiver with the arrows. It can now be handily carried over the shoulder or grasped by the hand tie.

With a numbed staggering walk, due to days of inactivity lying on the bottom of a water-logged, slimy little wooden dugout, Lt. Bigelow heads for the dark shadow of a large warehouse. Ung and their guide are a good half city block ahead of them. Nothing's changed in the way Bao conducts this little stroll. Be it jungle or city, his pattern of patrol is the same. Ung is on point, this time with their guide, followed by Bao and Bigelow, twenty yards back. Y-Cie is carrying his AK-47 and the pilot's compact crossbow.

Staying in the shadows of this block long row of warehouses, being as quiet as possible, they finally reach the end of these buildings. Finding the streets almost empty of traffic at this hour, Ung and his companion cross the road, quickly ducking down the dark recess of an adjoining alley.

Bao and Bigelow follow with Y-Cie not far behind, walking down this narrow eight-foot wide cobble-stoned alley with sewage-filled gutters running its length. This combined with the lingering smells of cooking fires leaves an acidic and bitter taste in the humid night air. Covering their mouths and noses with their hands does no good; nothing can filter this muck from penetrating. With each inhale, it's a rancid choking breath tasting of human waste. Both sides of this passageway are lined with small dirty little hovels, workshops, and empty market stalls inundated with large brown hairless tailed rats, giving this dark dingy alley the sights, smells, and sounds of poverty. Some of the windows are showing the flicker of candlelight, casting an irregular swirling spectrum of colors across the panes of unwashed glass. Crossing two more one-lane black-topped streets, they are now in a more open environment. The cobbled alley has regressed into a travel worn, hard-packed dirt path, family homes not as close together, sitting farther back from this well-traveled trail. Dwellings are now built more like the typical peasant hooch, bamboo with palm frond exterior, no stucco- or terracotta-tiled roofs, no lawns or verandas. These family homes have vegetable gardens and animal enclosures nearby. There is the starting of banana groves trailing off toward the forested hills. No light escaping the hooches of these hard working farmers; they are early to bed and early to rise. The only sounds are the distant yapping of disgruntled dogs. Turning into a grassy field, making their way on a one-man foot path cutting through the night, it's the only clue that they are near civilization, light, sound, and the aroma of man rapidly dwindling the farther they follow this path into the darkened night.

Stopping, going to one knee, Ung turns to his companions and motions them to advance. Moving up the trail, they can all see a faint light coming from a lantern that's tied to a pole outside a very small hooch located just twenty yards off the trail. Not wanting to bunch up, Bao signals for Bigelow and Y-Cie to take

cover and wait his return. He moves to the point position with silent anticipation.

Their little conference finished, Bao and Ung come back to Bigelow's position. "Bigrow, you and I will each carry another weapon. May Ung borrow your .45? He goes back to the city to relieve Dit Hum, would like to do so with a little hidden security."

Reaching into his bag and retrieving the piece, holding it by the barrel, handing it to Ung, looking up at Bao, Bigelow repeats his warning, "Tell him to pick his target carefully. He only has six rounds." Taking the weapon by the hand grip, Ung gives Bigelow a purple-toothed grin and nod of thanks, stuffs the pistol into his carry sack, and heads back down the trail they just came up on.

"You and Y-Cie advance on the hooch after you see the lantern extinguished. That will be my all clear signal." With that said, Bao moves back to their guide's location, slinging one weapon over his left shoulder. Holding the other at the ready, they make the twenty-five-yard advance on the small hooch with the porch light still on.

A figure can be seen in the doorway as Bao moves inside; he lets their guide engage in conversation. Lt. Bigelow can make out hand gestures, but no sounds reach him. The night is still. There's a chill in the air; moonlight is obscured by the occasional cloud. The light has just been snuffed out of the porch lantern.

Their approach is slow and steady. Reaching the darkened doorway, a slight male Vietnamese voice calls out as Y-Cie and Lt. Bigelow enter. The doorway is covered with a blanket or mat of some kind, rendering the little room not only blinding dark but also effectively cutting off any fresh air, making for a humid claustrophobic environment.

Bao's voice, in his native language, is directed toward their evening's guide and Y-Cie. When he is finished, Bao pulls aside the door's covering as they step outside. Once again, a deathlike veil of darkness envelops them. Bao quietly states, "Bigrow, we will now light a lantern, did not want to startle you."

There is sound of a high-pitched solid crisp metallic click, the scratchy scraping of a lighter's flint, followed by the whooshing surge of ignition. A Zippo is used to light the way. Someone is holding its flame to the lantern's wick. Lt. Bigelow can now make out two sets of feet. He's been looking down to avoid the anticipated bright light of flame, causing the immediate loss of his recently acquired night vision. His eyes are slow to adjust, shielding them with his hands until he gains focus.

All are in black pajamas, Bigelow and Bao barefoot, the other man is wearing black high top Converse American-made tennis shoes. This must be the man with the lighter. Looking up, Lt. Bigelow cannot at first make out the man's facial features. His head is still down, shielded by his hat brim. Shifting his gaze to Bao, there it is, that damned know-it-all golden smile, lifting his gaze back to the darkened figure as the man slowly lifts his head reveling himself to Bigelow. "Nhu," is all that comes out of Bigelow's mouth. He clasps his hands to his chest in a prayer attitude and bows to his dear old friend. Receiving the same gestures in exchange, they both step back, reaching out with open arms, surprising Bao, and proceed with a very manly hug.

The three talk through the night, Bigelow telling Nhu about his and Dinh's adventures with a wild and woolly monsoon, how they managed to survive their near fatal encounter with a tiger, all about his rice wine ceremony. Telling Nhu about Bao's attack on the NVA's trucks, Bigelow is excited, not only with the remembrance of the event, but also in the telling of the story itself. Finally, they bring Nhu up-to-date by telling him about their recent experiences on the Red River.

Finished, Bigelow inquires about Nhu's schooling. Not yet fluent in English, with Bao's help in translating, Lt. Bigelow hears a tale not unlike that of others who have been subjected to a new government's rules and regulations. Apparently, passing the entrance exam is not the hardest part of getting into a communist-run school of higher education. They're checking into family backgrounds, investigating wealth, parent's position in society, their ranking among their peers, their loyalties and service during the recent conflict along with the verification of one's nationality. Using his family's name was not an option. He could not use Dinh's family name; he is a wanted man. He is using Bao's mother's maiden name. This has worked for a while, but persistent rumors of his subversive behavior and the undeniable fact that he is of Montagnard ancestry has put Nhu in a rather compromising position.

He admits that he speaks out on government atrocities, the senseless killings, the imprisonment of scholars and anticommunist government officials, those few who spoke out for reforms like giving the people ownership of their land, the land their forefathers fought so hard for generation after generation. It's sacred ground for the peasants and their families; their ancestors are buried in graves dug into its soil. Yet this new ruling class wishes to take over these farms, consuming and joining them into collectives, communal government run cooperatives. Clergy, farmer, peasant, teacher, if you are not in agreement with their ideological ways, you're dead or gone.

Almost daily, there are people from his school or some government official asking questions of him. They are suspicious of his activities and his true identity. Nhu is doing well in his studies, but the curriculum is communistically tainted, stipulating what and how to study. There are other students and friends of his who are thinking about rejecting this indoctrination. They do not openly protest, instead they gather at night in homes, restaurants, darkened dormitories, any place they feel safe to discuss their plight. Security is always a priority. If caught, they know the results and outcome—certain death.

He tells Bao and Lt. Bigelow how he acquired his American-made tennis shoes and cigarette lighter. It all comes from US student aid packages sent by concerned college students from schools like Berkeley, Stanford, UCLA, and others. There are not only clothing and personal use items, there are school books, pencils, pens, and paper. Nhu and his friends cannot understand this blind act of kindness. Why would people of a country that just lost a war, who had over fifty thousand of their soldiers killed, voluntarily send aid in essence to an enemy? Nhu and his friends have no idea of the compassion or type of freedoms people of other countries can enjoy, or how they can exercise their freedoms in any way they deem appropriate.

He and his friends are tired and dismayed at the old guard's attitude. They feel Uncle Ho would be displeased with the actions of this new regime. Not much time has passed, yet the citizens seem not to remember that Uncle Ho placed heavy burdens and unfathomable hardships on his own people during his leadership of the North. His troops tortured and killed their way through the South, committing unspeakable atrocities, terrorizing village peasants by beheading, and the disembowelment of village elders and their families, mass killings of the wealthy and educated members of the ruling upper class. During the Tet Offensive in Hau, thousands of civilians were found with their hands and feet tied, shot in the back of the head execution style, their remains dumped in shallow mass graves.

Nhu is understandably confused, disillusioned, and markedly upset with the circumstance he finds himself in, not only his, but his fellow student's futures as doctors, lawyers, bankers, architects, engineers, business leaders, scholars, and educators. Their hopes for the future are being swept aside for the sake of government and political idealism. He feels this is fundamentally wrong for this new merging nation now unified by the blood of so many, at last one Vietnam.

Bao asks him what he's planning to do. Bigelow blurts out, "Stay in school, I hope. I sure would hate to see all the hard work and time you have spent in your early studies wasted, not put toward some form of productive use. It would be a shame. Nhu, you have the ability to go far in your chosen field."

When Nhu left the mountains for school, Bigelow remembers Nhu's hopes of becoming an engineer. He was set to help rebuild his beloved country, restructuring the many bridges, roads, docks, and ports, mile after mile of destroyed rail line, new tracks to be laid to new frontiers. He was excited to be part of the generation that would not only rebuild but move forward with a vigorous society of free-spirited educated people who would hopefully contribute greatly to the needs of their own country, never again succumbing to another countries meddling in their internal affairs. It seems they will have to weather the storm of communist change, like it or not.

Nhu believes there are only limited options available to him at this time: he can continue, try, and finish his second semester by staying out of sight and minds of school staff and those annoying government fact finders. He can stay here with friends and fight a battle against communist oppression or return to his beloved sanctuary in the jungle-covered mountains of the highlands while biding his time, hoping for a quick end to these tumultuous times. After seeing his old friend again, Nhu wishes to aid in Bigelow's flight to freedom.

The next few days consist of Ung returning every evening, briefing Bao of Father Alexis Agustes's daily routine: where he went, who he saw, talked to, what he ate, where he dined. He and Dit Hum are, if anything, thorough in their duties, explaining that Father Alex leaves his French-style-walled villa each morning after a short breakfast of two locally baked pastries and one rather large cup of a dark brewed tea. This villa and compound are also the home and quarters of three elderly nuns. It is visited each day by a woman who arrives in the early morning, staying most of the day, departing in the late afternoon. This person seems to be the cook, washer woman, and house cleaner. The nuns, teachers at a nearby catholic school for young children, depart the villa in the early morning each day, walking to their destination.

Father Alex's workday varies little. His early morning duties include going to a small church located across the road from his villa. Ung believes he might be saying a mass. Attendance is no more than ten or twelve, mostly older people. When finished, he comes out of this chapel wearing his standard white frock with a wide rope as a belt, more like a sash, sandals, and a very easy-to-follow, wide-brimmed, low-crowned straw hat, a petasus, dating back to the ancient Roman times, sometimes called the winged hat of Hermes.

Over one shoulder is a carry bag made of an unknown woven material brocaded with a decorative gold cross, its only outstanding feature. He also carries a leather briefcase containing a game; our friend likes to play backgammon. The stakes in these games being wine, fine, expensive French wine. The battles waged for this wine are normally fought over in the shade of an old olive tree growing in the courtyard of a local bar restaurant, a pub if you will, that is run by an old French and Japanese woman. She has been here doing business in this same place for the past forty-two years. Her name is Dotti, and she does not play backgammon, but she might possibly have the best French wine cellar in Southeast Asia.

His daily opponents consist of local merchants, small shop owners, and two old weather-worn, sun-baked rice farmers. Arriving precisely at high noon, both are wearing the same thing—black pajamas, straw conical hats with worn thin rubber-soled shower thongs. Not playing alone, the two combine their collective knowledge in opposition to the good father. In the four days of observance, neither they nor any of his other opponents have won a game. Seems he has mercy in his heart though; he shares with them a bottle of Dotti's selected wine.

In the early afternoon, there comes along one player who comes closest to defeating him. This man's roll of the dice out of the cup catapults the little ivory-numbered squares in a frenzied spectacle of spinning cubes, sending them banging into the leather rails of the playing board. They too share a bottle of wine, this one selected by Father Alex and paid for by the loser, a fiftyish slightly built, balding, pasty-skinned, beady-eyed, pencil-mustached military officer with the rank of major. He must be part of the garrison of NVA security forces billeted at an old three-story rundown hotel in the heart of Ha Dong. Its only saving grace is its five-star French-inspired fresh seafood restaurant located on its rooftop open air patio.

As darkness looms, Father Alex returns to the sanctuary of his small chapel. Once done with the evening prayers, he returns to the walled compound of his villa, safe in the night from unwanted visitors or prowling animals. He has had none since Ung and Dit Hum have been on watch.

At no time during their vigil did the two ventures close enough to gain any insight as to the good father's conversations with the major. Their gaming location is too out in the open for them not to be noticed. They can only report that the attitude between the two men seemed congenial and friendly.

On the fifth day, Father Alex does not go to Dotti's wine cellar. After his morning duties, without his leather-bound board game, he walks to the city's dockside business district, visiting the offices of merchants involved in the importing and exporting of household goods, refrigerators, kitchen stoves, small standing, and window air conditioners, gasoline-powered generators, farm implements. Never staying longer than thirty minutes, Ung and Dit Hum have no idea of the reasons nor the intentions of these private meetings.

In the early afternoon of the same day, Father Alex takes a cycle cab across town for lunch at a little darkened café off a side street alley. Dit Hum stays outside with the cycle cab driver. Ung waits for a while before entering. When he does, he finds the father sharing a meal with a fortyish sophisticated-looking gentleman, dressed in a western style light tan suit, white-starched shirt with a green-, yellow-, and red-striped silk tie.

They are seated at one of the four tables in this tiny ill-lit eating establishment. Ung moves to the vacant three-stool counter and orders a small bowl of soup. Consuming this chicken-flavored vegetable broth, he leaves before the father and his friend. While in their company, Ung could not understand a thing they were saying. They spoke English. Once reunited with Dit Hum,

Ung tells him to keep following Father Alex; he will follow the American stranger.

Ung's adventure across some of the most heavily pedestrian-trafficked streets he has ever seen is fraught with the distinct possibility of him being discovered. He's feeling more and more out of place the further he follows his prey. They cross into an office-congested business district. Besides the cycle and peddle cab operators, he is the one starting to look out of place wearing his peasant clothing. Just as he is about to put an end to this foolish behavior, the tan-suited stranger turns off the main street and walks halfway down the block, stops, pays his respects and maybe the time of day to one of the entrance guards stationed at the bottom of a wide staircase. This is the approach to a newer looking government building occupied by the district office of the French and Swedish embassy. Besides these two countries, there are flags of other nations, Great Britain, Australia, China, Korea, Japan, but no American flag adorns this structure. The large red with a giant yellow star flag of Vietnam is the largest one, prominently displayed flying from a twenty-foot pole anchored between the two main entrance doors.

The American's disappearance into the inner sanctum of this white stone building releases Ung of his duties for the time being. Not seeing any handy usable hiding place, there are no sidewalk food stalls or open-fronted shops to duck into nor alleys to duck down. Not knowing when or even if the tan-suited stranger will reappear, Ung abandons his task and begins the long and perilous journey back across town and a rendezvous with Bao.

Bao is given detailed information on Father Alex's exploits, with the inclusion of Ung's dangerous adventure into the heart of enemy territory. This insight to the good father's dealings leads Bao to believe that his family's old friend is playing both sides to the middle. He is either surviving on what he has in material goods or in useful intelligence he has been able to gather, passing this information to both sides. Could be that his survival is mutually provided by what he is owed or paid from each side.

The father's game-playing-friend, the major, must know about his relationship with the tan-suited American. Every Northern government agency in Ha Dong must be watching and following any and all foreign diplomats along with any embassy employees, noting their contacts, establishments they frequent. Secretaries, staff workers, embassy-office cleaning personnel—all will be contributing to this flow of information. In an extreme case, phone conversations are spied upon, letters opened and read. Nothing would go unnoticed. All this intelligence would be shared throughout the governing agencies. Bao dismisses Ung, warning him of the pitfalls he could have brought not only on himself but to the others if he had been followed. His trek into the land of Ha Dong's financial business and government center was a dangerous and risky thing to do. Ung knows he again has done what he was asked to do, gather information regarding Father Alex.

"Bigrow, I have received information about the good father that needs confirming. It is time for a visit. My mentioning of your presence will not be broached until I am most assured of his allegiance and political beliefs. You will remain here with Ung. Again, please follow and react to his instincts. We are not in the best of situations here. Nhu and Y-Cie will travel with me. I wish to have in my possession your .45. Thank you."

With a nod from Bigelow, a few words from Bao, Ung reaches into his bag, retrieves, and relinquishes the pistol.

"When I arrive at my destination, I'll send Dit Hum back here. He needs rest, has been on watch for a long time now. Be careful and alert to his early morning arrival. Good-bye, my friend."

Bao steps out into the darkness, with a glance in their direction and a wave of his hand. Nhu and Y-Cie take up their AKs, slinging them under their arms out of sight. They follow Bao down a dark moonlit path to see a man who talks with God.

In the early morning darkness, there is an eerie hollow silence. No man-made sounds, no sounds from nature, not a dog, lizard, nor cricket, just their faint footsteps on the cold earth, accompanied by the rhythm of their own heartbeat echoing in their heads.

Coming close to Dit Hum's location, Bao and Nhu move across a wagon-worn dirt trail leading through an older varietal Changying Chinese olive grove. These gnarly, squatty trees are old; most of the fruit is used in the making of oil, but the fresh ripe fruit is crisp and can be eaten right off the tree. The first few bites may taste a little bitter, but it turns sweeter the longer one chews. This orchard of trees is within sight of Father Alex's villa, the one he will be leaving in the morning's first light, walking the short distance to his little cathedral across the street for morning prayers. Before heading off for a day of games and the drinking of wine, Father Alex will spend a few moments in the courtyard of his villa discussing matters of ethical, political and religious importance, with an old friend.

Y-Cie is just a few yards from the little church in his hiding place. Dit Hum has left. The sun is starting to bathe the earth in an immersion of undiffused clear light, not yet tainted by the disruptive filth of man. Looking past the villa into the olive grove, Y-Cie cannot see Bao or Nhu. They are veiled by the lingering gray shadows of a rapidly fleeting night.

After the three nuns have departed, the father is being occupied with his church prayers. Nhu moves from the orchard to the back gate of the villa, checking it, making sure it's locked. Finding himself a section of the back wall lavishly decorated with ferns and an assortment of ornamental fruit trees, Nhu settles in as security for the upcoming meeting.

As Father Alex emerges from his chapel, Y-Cie breaks cover to intercept him. Coming to the father's side, he is acknowledged with a "Good day, my son." Y-Cie directs the father's attention to a figure coming into view on the opposite side of the street. With a wave and a golden smile, the three men enter the main gate of the father's villa. Bao tells Y-Cie to return to his hiding spot as the two old friends seat themselves at a courtyard table. When the housemaid arrives, she is told to bring a pitcher of water and two glasses. Father Alex thanks her, telling the women she has the morning off and to please return in the late afternoon to begin preparations for the evening meal.

Placing his leather-bound game case on the tiled patio floor, pouring each a glass of water, Alex greets Bao with an open-mouth grin. "You were here not that long ago, Bao. You returning to Ha Dong so soon puts much importance on this visit. If I can be of assistance, by all means, I'm at your disposal."

Taking a sip of his water, Bao wastes no time in his effort for the simple truth. "I wish not to keep you from your long busy day. I would ask but a few questions I feel need answering." Both men are starting to notice the warming of the upcoming day. Leaning back in his chair, Father Alex removes a white kerchief from his carry bag and wipes the sweat from his brow.

"Bao, you're rather tense this morning. We have known each other for many years, since you were a boy really. Your mother, God rest her soul, was the most beautiful, loving, and intelligent woman I have ever met. She ran not only a school but an orphanage, almost single-handed, and did so in some of the worst of times. Your father, she adored. He was, in my eyes, not just a father, devoted husband, not just a provider, he was a scholar of the earth itself. He was never more at home than when he was in his forested jungles. They were both my mentors. I learned to be open, honest, and straightforward with them, as they were with me. You ask your questions, my friend. I'll be more than happy to answer, if I can.

"I have been here for six days now. Not to be disrespectful, I have had you followed. Your trail crosses many paths. What I need to know is to whom are you allied. I have reports of your drinking, playing games, and conversing with a northern military officer with the rank of major. There are reports of your travels into the heart of the city for a clandestine lunch meeting with a tan-suited American, who's working out of the French or Swiss consulate here in Ha Dong."

The good father's retort is quick. "I also play backgammon with friends who are merchants, local shop owners, and my favorites—two old peasant farmers that your parents knew and I have known for thirty years. They travel many miles, two to three times a month to replenish supplies and enjoy an afternoon at Dotti's wine bar and café. We all enjoy a good game of backgammon to keep the mind sharp. We enjoy good conversation to gain insight on the everyday gossip that flows through a town's veins. We all enjoy a good bottle of wine. You have good intelligence, my friend. Use it wisely. What one looks at is not at times what it seems. There are obstructions to the truth in any matter."

Slowing down, trying to be calm and steady, Bao continues, "How do I ask without offending? My purposes in today's dialogue was to establish your loyalties and alliances. At one time I and my family knew you as an anticommunist, a defender of the people's rights. You seem now to be dividing your loyalties. My question is, how deep a divide and why? I have information regarding a missing American pilot. There is no way I will release this information without being positive of your feelings, in this a most delicate matter."

This bit of information has perked a noticeable reaction from Father Alex, using his kerchief once again to wipe sweat from his face and neck, dabbing at the glistening moisture on his upper lip.

"Bao, my loyalties lie in my devotion to the Heavenly Father, a lifelong devotion to my faith. Any government affiliations I have are survival-oriented. You of all people should know that one must first know his enemy before doing battle. My battle is my little parish and the sister's school. I do what is needed to get us through these hard and difficult times. I do not play one side to the other. I use my collective information and knowledge to gain favor with no one. I just wish to get by with as little trouble and interruption to our daily lives as possible. I do, at times, work my friendship with the two sides of this issue, using my status to mediate, sometimes broker deals, nothing overwhelmingly important but just starting a dialogue is just that, a start. The North Vietnamese government has not yet come down off their euphoric high of winning their country's independence. This struggle has been going on for over forty years and cost them well over a million people. They are a resilient and a patent people. They will survive this transitional phase of their current history. I am sure they will move forward in their relations with the West.

"For the time being, I use my neutrality in the best ways I know how. The major feeds me details of downed aircraft. He informs me of artifacts and possessions found by farmers, hunters, and woodcutters who stumble across wreckage and remains of US pilots. I in turn pass this information on to my American friend, Perry, the tan-suited man you had followed to the French embassy. The Americans are most interested in the recovery of lost pilots and their remains. They pay generously for this information. Especially lucrative is the return of dog tags, personal weapons, and pieces of uniforms. I stay out of the money matters. To me, there is no price one can be paid to let a mother, wife, or child know that their loved one's remains have been found. The two parties donate to my church and our little school, which is my just reward in all of this."

Father Alex excuses himself, leaves the patio, and enters his white stucco villa. Bao, uncomfortable not receiving a definitive answer to his question, ponders his next possible move. He cannot approach this American, Perry, on his own. It's out of the question. He knows he will need the help and assistance of his family's old friend, Father Alexis Agustes.

On his return, the good father has with him a flowered motif, hand-decorated ceramic dish with a small pile of sliced yellow cheese, round wafer crackers, and a small assortment of fresh fruit with a short, thin-bladed, pearl-handled paring knife resting on the edge of the plate.

Neither man breaks the silence in the ever-growing hot afternoon. Father Alex reaches over, picking up the pearl-handled knife, selects a small pinkish red with blush red stripes, sweet and juicy apple. Not bothering with skinning the fruit, he simply quarters the sphere then slices a piece of cheese. Placing both on a cracker, he shoves the entire thing into his mouth. Cracker crumbs, apple bits, and small amounts of juice is forced from his mouth as he chews, dribbling down his chin to be wiped away with his now sweat-soaked handkerchief.

Before drinking his water, Alex asks, "Bao, I know your loyalties, your devotion to your Montangnards. They are your flock. This information of yours could have been delivered to a number people in a number of places in a number of ways. Why me and why here? The remains must be skeletal by now. Do you have an identity on this pilot? My only interest would be to notify the American representative of this man's discovery, nothing more. If you wish, I will say nothing of this to Major Trong, my North Vietnamese friend. My guess, there is something more to all this. You personally are risking a lot just being this far north in your travels. Your last visit was very brief. You did not divulge nor request anything from me. It was more of an 'I was passing through, thought I'd stop by and say hello' visit. Bao, if there is something specific, if you think I can help, do not hesitate. Tell me what you desire of me. We are friends, that much you and I both know!"

Bao realizes that Father Alex is right. They have known each other many years. The good father has always been upfront and honest in all their previous encounters dealing in personal and other matters. Bao's parents held this man in high regard. Bao remembers nothing but praising stories regarding the man, at the time, believing their relationship and alliance was based on truth and faith. Bao knows this is the time to stop his doubting, put his cards on the table. Reaching into his bag, Bao retrieves the leather tag off Lt. Bigelow's flight suit. Now dried and cracked but still readable with the black lettering spelling out US Navy, below this, LT JG T. Bigelow. Rubbing this leather tag between his thumb and forefinger, while thinking of his friend's desire to return home, reluctantly, he hands the tag to Father Alex Agustes.

Taking the identity tag from an American navel flight suit in his stubby-fingered hands, Father Alex closely examines this little square of discolored curled edged piece of leather with profound interest. After a few moments of silence, looking up, Father Alex asks Bao just one question. "Is this all you have?"

"We have more in regards to personal and military equipment. We have his web belt with holster and Colt .45 stored in a safe place down in the southern highlands. There are other items. It would have been difficult to bring everything on this trip. We could arrange to have these items brought here, but I think this tag is a good start in the process of notifying your American friend. I would be interested in knowing about this pilot."

"Bao, you and I both know it would take two, almost three weeks round-trip to go back and retrieve the other items. You have come a long way with little to show as evidence to your securing an American pilot's remains. If this is truly all you have brought me, I will be more than happy to deliver this artifact to my American friend. May I keep this?"

"Yes, you may keep the leather tag." Now moving past midday, Bao takes a small bunch of green seedless grapes, popping one in his mouth, enjoying his first bit of nourishment on this hot and humid day.

"Father Alex, I do not wish to stay here in Ha Dong any longer than necessary. How long before you could meet with your American friend?" Finished with his grapes and second glass of water, Bao contemplates, but for reasons not known even to himself, does not divulge the pilot's status or whereabouts.

Clearing his throat, downing another glass of water, Father Alex leans back in his chair, fingering the leather tag in one hand, grabbing up his already damp kerchief, wipes his brow, and dabbles around the corners of his mouth, down and across his chin.

"I shall leave after morning prayers tomorrow. I will travel to the embassy, hoping he has not gone for the day. I was told the phone is not a safe way to convey delicate information. We should try and keep this off the radar as long as we can. This will assure less interference from Major Trong."

With a questioning look on his face, Alex continues, "With regards to Mr. Perry, I don't know what his response will be, if he has one at all. He is a poker-faced man. In all our dealings, I could never tell from his expression what the man was thinking. He gives no indication of fear or apprehension, just a straightforward, all-consuming look."

Standing, slinging his carry bag over his shoulder, Bao delicately fingers a stem of grapes. "May I take these to give a hungry friend?"

Father Alex remains seated. "Take all you need. You do not wish to stay for supper?"

"No, I have been here too long already. I have upset your schedule. Thank you for not only your time but also for the grapes. I will not have you followed tomorrow. In two days' time, I will have someone contact you here at your villa. You can pass him your information or arrange a meeting for you and myself. I do not wish to meet here again. It's nice and all, but it's a hard place to secure with the few men I have, hope you understand."

Pushing out his chair, starting to rise, Alex is gently persuaded to remain seated. Bao places his outstretched hand on the man's shoulder. He looks down on Father Alex with his jet-black eyes. "Father Alex, thank you. I hope your trip tomorrow is not wasted. If you don't mind, I will leave through the back gate. Good day, my friend."

Relieving Nhu of his AK, giving him money and instructions to purchase food and drink, Bao hands the grapes to Y-Chie as they head back to the safety of their secluded little hooch. Their trip is hampered by children, farmers, and women all headed home from schools, markets, and town on this two rut road beside the olive grove. Concealing their weapons and staying to the shadowed tree rows, being as invisible as possible, the two finally reach their destination just as the long shadows of a dying day brings on the quiet of darkness.

Once Nhu has returned, the food devoured, bottles of beer and sodas consumed. Bao explains that they will stay hidden another two or three days. At that time, there will be a meeting of minds,which will ultimately decide a course of action regarding the Bigelow situation.

Lt. Bigelow is nothing more than a bundle of nerves; he's feeling the ill effects of being cooped up in this little hut for so long. Bao decides they should take a short venture into the hills, not only for the exercise, but also to get Ung, Bigelow, and Dit Hum out of their dark little hiding place for a while. They will try some hunting with the pilot's crossbow.

Early on the second morning, short of the sun's rising, Bao and his troops head off in search of game. With strict marching orders, Ung on point, followed by Bao, Lt. Bigelow is followed by Nhu, Dit Hum, and Y-Cie. Flankers out, not as far out as they normally would be, they are concerned about the possibility of coming across locals headed to town and the markets, school children headed to class. This will be a constant struggle considering their closeness to Ha Dong.

It feels good to be out in the fresh air, to have the aroma of the forest filling their nostrils and heightening their senses with its inviting musky fragrance. The decaying and rotted plant matter is giving rise to new growth under their feet. The early morning dew glinting off this virgin grass looks like a bed of diamonds spread across a green emerald sea. It's nice to be out.

Now moving through an old unattended banana grove, large-fanned leaves, which were broken down, bent over, and turned a dark yellowish brown, made limp due to the sun's relentless heat. Clogging the rows between trees are bunches of black-rotted fruit giving off a sweet thick banana smell. It's a short grove ending at a small but rather fast-moving stream. They refresh themselves, each in turn at this little place sheltered by the canopy cast over it by a giant hardwood tree. On the opposite bank, its massive trunk and above-ground root system form a natural bridge for crossing the swift running water as it snakes its way under and around this old wooden obstruction.

Once over the stream and past the tree, the land starts turning upward in its approach to the thickly forested peaks that have stood sentinel over Ha Dong for eons. The climb is gradual in this early morning coolness. They all find this walk rather invigorating, lifting Bigelow's sprits, giving them all the opportunity to stretch long unused muscles. People of the mountains like nothing more than doing just what they are now doing, simply placing their bare feet one in front of the other, moving across the warm earth carpeted in a three-inch layer of decaying leaves.

Early midday, with the terrain starting to raise sharply, the thick jungle forest is starting to block out the sky. They encounter tangle vines, two and three feet high. There is no reason to penetrate this wall of green. They turn east, avoiding four very talkative woodcutters traveling in the opposite direction. Ung warned everyone in plenty of time; he could hear them coming for almost twenty minutes, giving notice to their direction of movement.

This little trip will end without bringing down any game; being so close to this much civilization has left this part of the woods denuded of any of nature's fuzzy little critters. Even those ugly little pigs so plentiful in their own southern highlands are nowhere to be found. Monkeys, deer, even the forest's voice of alarm, the birds, have not been in these trees for so long that large bunches of nuts and a variety of fruit have fallen to the ground from sheer weight. This now easy to reach food is being unceremoniously consumed on the ground by the only rodent able to live among man. Large hairless tailed rats, ugly big bastards that show little or no fear of man. Pugnacious and disease-ridden, only as a last resort will man ever eat one. They spend time diminishing the abundant rat population with Bigelow's crossbow. Bao, Bigelow, and Nhu are a little rusty with their aim, a few close calls but no real cigar winners. Ung fares better than the rest, killing three fat rats with the expenditure of only four arrows. The other two members of this expedition are not participating in this competition. They're providing security just a short distance away.

Awaiting the sun's slide from the sky, able to maneuver through the trees and brush without difficulty, still able to observe the shadows of people passing by on their way home after their days adventures, none making contact with the six elusive strangers in their midst.

On the third morning, Bao and Nhu have a long discussion before participating in the group's breakfast—cold rice balls, dried fish washed down with warm water. Bao beckons Bigelow aside. "Bigrow, I'm sending Nhu back into town, not only to meet with Father Alex, but also to bring back some food and drink. Again, I would like to send along your Colt pistol if I may, thank you. We will stay until his return, eat, then leave. We have been in this location much too long. I'm surprised we have gone undetected this length of time as it is. I ask your indulgence just one more day, my friend."

"I can handle another day, Bao. Are we traveling at night now?"

"We might well be doing just that. It all depends on what time Nhu returns and the information he has for us."

Departing shortly after sunrise, Nhu is dressed in clean black work pajamas, rolled to the elbow shirt sleeves, tennis shoes, carry bag, and straw hat. With his school identification papers, a few books in his bag concealing the Colt hand gun, he looks like any other teen headed to school in the city of Ha Dong.

Traveling this well-used dirt path, Nhu is starting to see more and more people as the morning wears on. There are groups of school children with book bags over their shoulders, skipping along with a morning's exuberance, boys yelling at one another, girls giggling and singing as they go.

There are a few mothers leading the tagalong younger kids. Some woman joining the early morning parade are carrying empty woven baskets they will fill with all sorts of produce and other items from the markets. This is an easy and pleasurable walk for Nhu. Not many of the passersby have paid much attention to him. He is treated like a fellow student headed for a day of learning.

Moving closer to the father's villa on the outskirts of town, Nhu can see a military truck parked by the front gate. There are three military clad young men with AK-47s, at the moment, shouldered. One of the troops is talking to a group of young school girls about his own age; the other two are standing by the driver's door, smoking cigarettes. Not stopping, going the full length of the street, and making a quick left exit into an alley, Nhu hesitates, looks back down the street he has just turned off. The school girls have left the young soldiers and are headed for their intended destination. All three young men are now at the front of the truck, laughing and sending puffs of cigarette smoke swirling into the dusty hot morning air.

At the end of this alley, he crosses a rutted dirt trail. Nhu is once again in the olive grove adjacent to and just behind the father's villa. Stuffing his hat into his carry bag, he swings his bag around so it hangs across his back. He is trying to cut down his visibility by removing items that could easily be detected in this darkened place, things like a white straw hat and cream-colored bag.

Nhu feels comfortable in this task as he disappears deeper into the old grove while silently approaching the back side of the father's villa, which is less than a hundred yards to the southwest of his present location, staying deep in the shadows, moving ever so slowly, not wishing to give himself away. Nhu has no way of knowing that he has been in the crosshairs of a US Marine sniper, spotting scope from the moment he stepped foot onto the rutted road on his way into this grove of olive trees.

Nhu is now working his way to an observation point overseeing the back side of the villa where he can view the gate. There he finds two uniformed guards, very relaxed in their posture like the ones out front. They are not alert to intruders; they seem to be content in keeping the good father confined.

Inside the little walled villa, a conversation is in progress, a very one-sided conversation being carried on by a most annoyed, rude, and upset Major Trong. He is not only the head of Ha Dong's military police force, he is also the military intelligence officer for this northern sector of Vietnam, and he thinks Father Alex is not being forthright with him.

"My dear friend, we have had battles in the past, not only on your game board with the roll of the dice. You and I have had political and religious battles, words, and personal thoughts that we've argued and dealt with as friends. We have broken bread and taken wine together, you with your God almighty and I with the humble hammer and sickle philosophy of our new order. We have often laughed, even snickered at each other's ideals and adversities. This, my friend, is no time for battle or games. The war is over. All the players have left the field, all the players."

For the past hour, Major Trong has been telling Father Alex that four to five months ago, a rumor started circulating in the port district about a high-ranking Montagnard tribal leader asking some of the most unscrupulous individuals and questionable captains of tramp steamers, freighters, and tankers as to the possibilities of taking a round eye out of country, delivering him to a safe port, a free port, without notifying any government authorities. Rumor has it, they all turned him down.

The major has told Father Alex that his intelligence indicates the Montagnard in question is a Captain Bao, an educated French and Montagnard engineer from the Thirty-Second Engineer Battalion, which fought gallantly at Diem Bien Phu. Returning north after the war with the French, he found hardship and despair. When Ho's call to arms came, again he returned to the task at hand, fighting the Americans. After being wounded, Bao's war was over. He arrived back up north only to be disillusioned and displaced by a very vigorous and fast moving populace. He disappeared for a while and then resurfaced as the leader of a marauding band of warriors, protecting the tribal interests of three Montagnard villages in the highlands from intruders, including military personnel and woodcutters. With great abandon and zeal, they go after hunters who enter their ancestral hunting grounds.

"There have been many questions regarding missing American pilots. A few on the list have been eliminated. Their remains have been found, or enough evidence has been gathered to indicate that their status is overwhelmingly in favor of death. Found were dog tags, destroyed and burnt equipment—things like that. Now, just two days ago, a leather tag from a US naval flight suit shows up at the French embassy right here in Ha Dong. Hell Alex, you could have come to me first, damn it! You should have come to me first. I had to hear this news from one of my agents that my good friend Father Alex Agustes is the party that brought in the tag of a Lieutenant Bigelow, US Navy. How about that, Alex? No one, not in my military world, not a one has seen or even heard of this lieutenant.

"When his plane went down, our trackers found his point of entry. The report states that they found shards of a parachute hanging high in the canopy, evidence of broken limbs and branches. Yet on the ground, there was nothing—no tracks, no equipment not even a broken twig. Dogs could not pick up a usable scent. They spent the entire day to no avail.

"I and others thought this rather strange. No US recovery team could have done this. It's too deep in the jungle and way too far north. No, it had to be somebody else, a Montagnard or a group of them could easily sanitize an area in short order and move off, leaving no trace of them ever being there.

"Natives are the only logical answer in all this. I know damned well he didn't just clean up his mess and simply vanish into thin air. He was found and taken by some indigenous peoples. For what purposes? I don't have a clue, but you bringing this pilot's tag to the French embassy has me puzzled. How did it come into your possession?

"I'm thinking you were trying to keep this information out of my hands. Maybe this pilot is alive, and you're trying to help, in your righteous way, get him out of Vietnam. Could this be your reason, Alex?"

Somewhat dazed, not shocked that the major knows so much, Father Alex just didn't think he would gather this information so quickly. When in need, the good father can indeed disregard any bothersome commandments, like the one thou shall not bear false witness. He lies to Major Trong.

"I found it in the collection plate after mass the other night. I do not know if it was left the day before or on the day of the night I found it. We only check the plate every other day or so. There are few who can afford to donate in these harsh times."

Not wishing to go into detail about his visit to the French embassy and his eventual meeting with Perry, Father Alex tells a half lie with a little truth thrown in.

"The reason behind my visit to the French embassy was, on my part, selfish. Our little school needs inoculations against contagious childhood diseases, nutritional foods, and medical supplies. Major, not to cast doubt on your ability to supply these goods, I know damned well the French can.

"I do not know of this pilot's status. I have no intentions of helping any one leave this country. My intent was simply a matter of need. My loyalties are with my people. My parish and I share this country with you, and I would not lose sight of the fact that I owe my existence and the freedom of my religion to you and your government. No, my friend, I would not jeopardize what I have for the risky business of smuggling out undesirables."

With a wicked tight-lipped grin, Major Trong's reply is cutting. "Alex, I have spent many an afternoon trying to play through your cynical little mind. You are distrustful of me and what I represent, and just now, you find it difficult to relate your true motives and contacts at your embassy visit. Don't you know by now that I am privy to all goings on at those embassies?

"You came into the French embassy and asked for Special Agent Perry. You went into an adjoining office, and that is where you gave him the leather tag. The office you used is not wired, and we do not know what was said, but I don't think it was about medicine for kids."

Getting up and moving away from the patio table they have been sitting at, Major Trong stands across from the father.

"Alex, your American friend Perry is working with the CIA. He does not have medical supplies. He only wishes to extricate his fellow American. He might arrange supplies as an exchange, but my guess would be monetary retribution. Then you could purchase your needed supplies from the French. No matter the arrangements you have made with your cohorts, I'm doing my best to find answers. If you are not being honest and straight-forward with me, my friend, if this does not finish well for my side, you and your little congregation will be nothing more than a tragic footnote in the history of North Vietnam."

Walking to the rear gate, Major Trong cups his hands to his mouth, with his head tilted back, barks out orders for the two sentries to move around to the front of the villa and make ready for departure. Turning back to Father Alex, the major makes one parting comment.

"Alex, we are going to get to the bottom of this missing pilot thing. Please stay out of it, Alex, for your sake, for the sake of your parishioners, for our friendship. Today, a convoy of strike force troops begins a trip up into the northwestern highlands in the southern portion of or country. This leader of the Montangnards, Bao, was last seen in the vicinity of a large village by a government hunting party not more than two and a half weeks ago. Our soldiers will know in a few days if he and an American were there for a visit. I have well-trained people in the extraction of information. Good day, my friend. Please don't get up. I can find my way out."

From his dug in hiding spot, the man with the marine-spotting scope takes his attention away from Nhu for the moment, placing the crosshairs on one of the young sentries and follows his movement to the front of the villa. From his position diagonally across from the corner of the villa and about seventy-five yards off in the trees, he can view the back side of the building and a portion of the front including the entrance to the small church across the street.

Major Trong emerges from the villa, receives and returns his troop's salute. Standing for a time, not that the troops are slow to load into the truck, just standing there as if contemplating a return trip to the villa, churning up a little cloud of dust with his quick spinning turn, he climbs onto the trucks running board, hopping into the cab, closing the door as the already idling truck moves off.

The hidden man replaces the crosshairs back on Nhu, focusing on his face. He is confronted by a confused young man, curiously looking in the direction of the father's villa, not moving, not looking around, just staring at the back of the villa. A good hour has gone by, nothing from this young man, he just keeps staring at the villa.

Finally, motion in front of the villa, Father Alex has come out of the compound and is headed for his chapel across the street. Apparently, from his vantage point, the young man can see this movement also. He's starting to rise, bringing his carry bag back to his front, and putting his straw hat back on. Just standing for a time, looking around, he steps out from behind the tree he's been using for concealment. Brushing himself off, he heads for the rutted road; reaching the back side of the father's villa, he tugs on the gate. Finding it locked, he moves to the far corner of the walled compound. Slowly, he scans the street and small shops, looking for any government troops or someone standing apart from the normal village types. Once convinced there are none, he turns the corner and casually strolls across the dusty dirt road. With no hesitation, he enters the dark and clammy little church.

There are only three pews on either side. Capacity? Maybe twenty, twenty-four at the most. There are ten or twelve today. Standing at the small pulpit is Father Alex, one lighted candle precariously balanced next to his open Bible. To the left of this is a screened off divided area where he hears confession. It's lit by a small wall hung oil lamp. There is a crucifix on the end gable wall. On either side of this are small round porthole stained glass windows, these and the doorway letting in the only natural light. Taking a seat next to an old woman with three long curly jet-black hairs springing from a large mole just below the right corner of her mouth, making this more exciting is the lack of teeth when she smiled. Nhu will now wait for the father's sermon to end.

Biding his time, the man hiding in the orchard is now using his spotting scope to scan the street where he has picked out a tall, khaki clad Chinaman wearing a backpack; strapped to his belt is a holster in which is stored a 9mm semiautomatic, Russian made pistol. With no insignias or hat for identification, his only military connection is his short shorn hair and his sidearm.

This man's movement through the village is smooth and deliberate. As he passes a food stall or shop, he looks in with an Asian nod and silent greeting, never really entering the premises, just a look and a nod as he canvasses the area. He is obviously looking for one particular person; someone has brought him to this place. He has that look and feel about him.

Crossing the street, standing next to the little church, listening to Father Alex's sermon, the Chinaman moves to the front of the building. His shadow moving with him travels across the ground bending at a sharp angle, moving partway up the church's front wall as he walks past the doorway. His shadow falls off the wall, sending it running straight up the main aisle, stopping just short of the pulpit. The man in khaki continues his journey, his shadow retreating from the church entry, climbs a small corner of the church's exterior wall before dropping down and being lost to a new angle of the sun.

Turning away from the little church, the Chinaman walks to the front of the villa. Not stopping, he keeps moving down the street and out of the crosshairs. Putting his scope down for the moment, with methodical precision, the man in hiding attaches a silencer/flash suppressor to his AR-15 semiautomatic, a US-made assault rifle, preferred by Special Forces, members of the Navy SEALs and Marine Force Recon teams for its accuracy and size. It's a short, lightweight, jungle-friendly killing machine. He slides a thirty-round magazine into the weapon, chambering a round.

Scanning his front and flanks for any discernible movement or sound, the midmorning sun throwing constantly moving shadows across the orchard and like the birds themselves, these shadows take flight into the trees, sending flashes of alarm to anyone trying to detect a person's movement.

With mass now said, Father Alex has moved to the front entry of his church to greet and bid a good day to each of his parishioners. Nhu, in no hurry, lingers, letting all the others leave the chapel. Luckily on this day, no one, not a soul needs the use of the father's confessional.

Spending but a moment together, Father Alex whispers to Nhu that in thirty minutes, he will unlock his back gate allowing him to enter. Adding that he should be careful, someone could be watching his villa. With this on his mind, Nhu clutches his carry bag a little tighter, paying a little more attention to his surroundings, looking at things and people longer, with a more watchful eye. Looking for that one small thing that sets someone apart from the norm, hoping on the one hand that he can identify his adversary, on the other hoping he does not. He wishes only to find friendly indigenous villagers, a young man's naive and foolish thought.

Making his way home, Father Alex sees nothing out of the ordinary. All seems rather normal, a few shopkeepers' wave and nod to the father on his short journey.

Nhu has reached the edge of a building next to the entrance of a narrow-angled alleyway, ending at the rutted dirt road adjacent to the olive grove. Stopping at the corner rather than turning and darting into the dark little enclave, he walks past continuing down the street. He stops at a fresh produce stand. Nhu pretends to test the ripeness of the fruit, smelling for freshness, but really using the opportunity and time to check on his surroundings, keeping an eye on the dark alley, looking for anyone following him, listening for any warning sounds, someone in a hurry, scuffling of feet, anything to alert his defenses—there is nothing. Buying three six-inch cuttings of sugar cane, placing the newspaper-rolled sticks in his carry bag, Nhu exits the stall. Walking off a little ways, he turns back and drifts off the main street, following this dark wisp of an alley.

Defined, deliberate, quick movement farther down the rutted trail, the man in hiding has a new perspective of the khaki clad individual. Two quick leaps and a bound, that fast, he's in the third row of trees. In a crouch concealed by brush and gnarly old tree trunks, he is silent, not moving, watching the approaches to the alley, paying particular attention to its junction with the beaten down, rutted dirt road.

Cautiously looking for any passersby, Nhu timidly steps out onto the road from the confines of the alley. In doing so, he places himself in the stranger's sights again as he slowly approaches the back gate of the father's villa. This small man in black has the full attention of at least two interested parties: one with a simple and definite desire to end his young life and the other individual wishes to keep this little man alive long enough for a short but meaningful conversation.

Moving on down the road to the back of the father's villa, Nhu finds the day's heat a bit sluggish. High humidity accompanied by rising temperatures, the stifling stench of mankind, chok-ing dust stirred up by the passing of so many people shuffling about with gasoline-powered transportation adding their engine pollutants to the mix.

Reaching his destination, Nhu stops. Turning slowly, with a hunter's trained eye, he searches out movement, shadows out of place. Being this close to total civilization, it's hard, if not impossible, to distinguish smells. In a natural jungle environment, one can pick up on a human's scent. With no evidence that he has been followed, Nhu knocks on the old wooden gate of the villa.

Alex has already unlocked the gate, he almost did not, seeing the man crossing the front of his church looking through the open door during his sermon sent a chill up his spine. He seemed to be a Chinese gentleman, dressed in khaki, tall, short-cropped hair, the type of person his friend, the major, would employ.

Nothing more than thugs, killers, these mercenaries come down from southern China for the quick and easy money in this game of death, deception, and intrigue.

Father Alex almost wishes he didn't have to open the gate, not all that sure of who or what might be waiting on the other side; hopefully, it will be his friend. Crossing the patio, not saying a word, twisting the brass latch, he yanks open the massive old hand-carved gate. Standing there, to his relief, it's his friend Nhu; with a smile and a nod, Alex gestures for him to enter. Just as he does, out of the nearest row of trees comes the khak-clad Chinaman with a gun in his right hand, bounding across the dirt alley, quickly moving on their position. Placing his gun to Nhu's head, with a defeated surprised look on his face, Nhu is shoved into Father Alex. They're both pushed through the open gate.

The first words spoken by the Chinaman are French. "You have made my job rather simple, you two." These were his last words on earth. With just the whistling sound of a small high velocity missile blasting its way through extremely heavy air as a warning, the man's head explodes in a shower of red mist, mixed with small pieces of bone, cartilage, and skull fragments along with the grayish matter that was once his brain, some of this residue splattering on Nhu and Father Alex, the majority striking the front side of the old wooden gate.

They're stunned; this sudden experience has left them para-lyzed and in utter shock. Witness to the most unbridled carnage either man has ever witnessed. Lying before them is the absurd, shattered remains of a human being, a fine example from the neck down. The only recognizable feature left of his face is the lower lip and chin, including a very small part of the lower jaw with three teeth still intact. A hideous scooped-out section of skull with a flap of scalp dangling down, the rest of the man's skull is but a tiny scattering of white flecks, floating in a grayish red slime pool, gathering in the soft dirt under the gate.

Dragging these two out of their trance is the sound of heavy footsteps, accompanied by a low grunting growl being emitted by a fast approaching, camouflage wearing man coming directly at them at a flat out dead run, his weapon held in both hands out in front of his chest at the ready. Nhu and Father Alex, frozen like animals, are caught in the headlights of a car, neither one moves.

At a distance of no more than four feet, the man's weapon is thrust up; and out to his left, his feet leave the ground, his whole body uncoils, stretching out and vaulting down to his left, catching the unsuspecting pair at the knees with a textbook, all American flying cross-body block sending all three sprawling across the tiled patio.

On his feet in a flash, his weapon is in the midsection of Nhu, who for the second time in less than two minutes has had his young life threatened by a stranger holding a gun. Not taking his eyes off Nhu, Perry speaks to Father Alex in French. "Throw some dirt on the gate to mask the blood. When done, close the damned thing! Hurry, Alex. We've got a lot to do, and it must be done quickly. Move." Still not removing his eyes from Nhu, bending down close to the young captive's face, he smiles while greeting him in his own Montagnard dialect. "You move, I kill." In an almost unrecognizable undertone, he blurts out in plain, simple English, "I'm an airborne ranger, you little fuck! If you wish to see the light of another day, do as I say."

Finished rubbing dirt on the gate, Father Alex closes and locks it. Turning to Nhu and his captor in a soulful, downtrodden voice, Alex asks, no, begs for his friend's life. "Perry, this young man knows where your American pilot is located. I do not. Shoot him and we are all out of luck."

Again in French, Perry, still with eye-to-eye contact with Nhu, tells Alex, "Remove this man's bag, very slowly. Do not reach inside. Just remove it and lay it on the ground."

Once this is done, Perry swings his weapon into Father Alex's chest. "My friend, you attract a lot of undesirables. If this little maggot truly knows where Lt. Bigelow is, he lives, but he had better do as he is told, and he had better deliver, or he's a dead man. Explain to him the predicament he's in. Do it now."

Cover photo by author, taken early morning at
entrance of Montagnard village, Loc Ninh area, 1966.
All photos taken with an Olympus Pen-EE

Wine ceremony

Author sipping on
wine at ceremony

Typical riverside villages

River traffic

"Sam," author's
Cambodian-Montagnard
interpreter, 1966

"Ung," author's
counterpart in arms
against Vietcong and
NVA, 1966. Ung fought
against the Japanese in
the 1940s, the French
in the 1950s, and the
VC in the 1960s

Local transportation, ox carts, pedicabs, military
trucks, bicycles, private vehicles. Note garbage on street
above open sewer in pedicab photo at bottom

Typical Vietnamese open-air market

Montagnard's shopping in market in Loc Ninh,
note Khmer Rouge scarf on man at far left
and woven basket on woman at center

US Special Forces Camp Hackley-Alpha-331, Loc
Ninh, Republic of South Vietnam, December 1965

Putting his hands up in a surrendering fashion, Alex speaks in French. "Perry, you can converse with Nhu. He speaks Montagnard and understands French."

Now that they are all on the same page, as far as language is concerned, Perry starts with, "We will, when Alex is certain that all is clear, carry this dead man's body into the orchard and bury him. I have a hole already dug. Alex, you go out front, check for any more of Major Trong's troops. Do something normal. Don't draw attention to yourself. Scrutinize the little trail that runs behind your villa. We need a good three to four minutes to dispose of the remains. We do not want any innocent bystanders complicating this little ceremony. Go, Alex."

Again, he places the silencer-tipped rifle barrel into Nhu's midsection. "Shake your head up and down in a yes posture if you understand my French." Getting a positive response, Perry continues, "I'll be going through your carry bag. You got anything to declare before I do?"

With a sheepish, shy little grin, Nhu's first words to this brazen round eye brings a smile, albeit a brief one, to Perry's dry, chapped lips. "You will find Bigrow's Colt pistol, nothing more of interest to a Neanderthal."

With a quick flick of his wrist, Perry slams his weapon's barrel up and into Nhu's chin, causing pain, anguish, and sending a little blood trickling down the side of his neck. "Get smart with me. I don't give a fuck what you know. I'll blow your funky ass away. Do you understand me now, you little prick?"

Upon his return, Father Alex tells the two that all seemed normal for such a hot and dusty day. No one paid any attention to him as they hurried off to their midday meal and afternoon nap. The streets and shops are all but empty. If there was a time to move and bury a corpse, it is now, before the school children start their homeward journey, before women begin their daily migration returning to the family home laden with baskets of fish, meats, rice, and vegetables they purchased from local shops and open air markets earlier in the day.

Perry and Nhu have come to a temporary truce. Perry is giving direction and orders to the other two. "The boy and I will carry the body. Alex, you open the gate step out and make sure no one is present. We will need a little time. Make your observa-tion diligently." Grabbing the Chinaman's feet, Perry tells Father Alex to unlock and open the gate. Turning in Nhu's direction, Perry orders him to move in and take the man's arms. They lift the corpse off the ground, ready for their mad dash to deposit this heavy lump of useless dead matter into the warm embrace of Mother Earth. Not really useless, small bugs and flies will survive and flourish by scavenging morsels of tissue and blood while leaving their larvae behind, becoming the scourge of all decomposing matter, maggots. these little bastards, along with massive cat-sized rats can and will dissect and devour human remains within days, aided by the high heat and humidity. The only problem will be the smell. In the short time it takes to decompose, the stench will give its location away. Perry has already told Nhu of their intended destination, five rows straight into the olive grove, turning to the left, going down about four more rows of trees. He admits his lack of resolve in not counting the exact number but feels confident that he can find their intended target —Perry's abandoned fox hole hiding spot.

Only once in their struggling journey did Nhu falter; stumbling, he almost drops the headless Chinaman. Nonetheless, they make their mark undetected. Reaching their destination, Perry drops his share of the load, causing the Chinaman's boot clad feet to dig into the dirt, bringing the procession to an abrupt halt. This sudden stop folds the corpse at the waist, flinging his arms up where his shoulder should be. With Nhu's iron-like grip, making damned sure he did not drop his share of the load, this unexpected articulation of the corpses arms sends Nhu in a headlong, half summersault into the Chinaman's chest, his head coming to a rest in the vacated remains of the dead man's skull cavity.

Retrieving the remaining belongings from his two-night, one-and-a-half day hiding spot, Perry stands over a kneeling; sick to his stomach, Nhu, who unceremoniously fouls the Chinaman's khaki shirt by throwing up on it. Putting his backpack down, Perry grabs the corpse by the legs and stuffs it deeper into its resting place. He turns to Nhu. "When you're done, start covering him with dirt and scatter some of this brush around. I'm going down a ways and pick up his backpack." On his return, Perry can see that Nhu has almost finished his task. Moving up to the tree where his equipment is located, he softly tells Nhu, "When you're done and able to, head back to the villa, and we'll discuss a future strategy for our dilemma. I think that's your best choice, but if you would rather run, go for it. But it will not help you or your friends with this Lt. Bigelow problem, now will it? I'm taking this stuff to the villa. You're welcome to join me."

Taking the two backpacks, Perry heads off down the tree line in a military crouch, stopping at each gnarly old tree trunk, silently listening and looking for any intruders, with no inter-ruptions to the muggy afternoon, Perry goes on. At the last row of trees, before crossing the two-wheeled rutted dirt road, Perry, for the first time, looks back to see Nhu making his way toward Father Alex's villa.

Standing at the patio table, Perry dumps out the contents of the dead man's backpack. Tumbling out is an assortment of per-sonal and military items; the most startling is the large roll of bills, paper money. There are hundreds in Vietnamese currency, but most surprising is a single American one-hundred-dollar bill, in this day and age a most unusual site in North Vietnam. On the black market, this one green piece of paper is worth around three to five hundred in the North's money, depending on which black market currency exchanger one deals with. There's a tan leather pouch with five Chinese coins, two of which appear to be gold. There are no military or official type papers. There is no identification at all, nothing telling them the who or the why of this man. Perry reaches in and pulls out a tightly rolled US-made camouflaged poncho liner, seemingly an abundant commodity all over Vietnam. There are two Chinese-made pull ring wooden handle hand grenades plus five magazines for his 9mm Russian-made pistol. One pair of heavy wool boot socks, no explanation for the thick socks, strange when considering the climate. One light loosely woven cotton T-shirt and a little plastic-wrapped package held tightly together with two rubber bands; inside they find a small piece of black tar heroin, two small but rather nice smelling marijuana buds along with a box of wooden matches and a short stemmed smoking pipe.

Rummaging further, Perry comes across two leaf-wrapped bindles of cooked rice balls that have been smashed flat, along with his leather belt and holster, – that's not much equipment. This man was not far from what he called home or some type of base area. He was not going far with what he was carrying. He did have plenty of money to eat and entertain himself. Before the quick burial, Perry patted the Chinaman down and found nothing in his pockets; no external adornments, wrist-watch, rings, or necklace. This man was clean for a reason. His assignment was a simple assassination or kidnap attempt; that's how Perry sees it, sure as hell was not a robbery or a by chance encounter. Was he following Nhu? Was Father Alex his target, or was he doing the same thing his killer was doing, just waiting for a Montagnard to show up at the father's villa? Well no matter, it's all speculation now!

Breaking the awkward silence, Father Alex tells the two about his visit with Major Trong and his revelatory disclosure of him taking a convoy of trucks full of troops into the highlands south of the Red River. Their objective is the Montagnard village where Bao and some of his followers were last seen, the same group that the American pilot is suspected to be traveling with. They intend conducting an investigation and plan on using barbaric techniques while doing so. These methods sometimes result in the death of innocent villagers, a poor yet happy people just trying to eke out an existence.

This information has Nhu on edge. He was not with Bao on that trip, but he does know the village and a number of its inhabitants. Just knowing there are government troops headed in that direction has him most concerned and upset.

Speaking in French, Nhu states his purpose in visiting Father Alex. "I came into this town to see Father Alex and collect facts and guidance with the Bigrow situation, that and to buy food for myself and my companions. Mr. Perry, you have saved Father Alex's and my life, for that I am thankful and profoundly grateful. This information that Father Alex has just divulged is alarming and changes our priority in an unexpected way. I would ask what your suggestion or advice would be. Whatever it is, we must act quickly."

Taking a moment, Perry starts stuffing articles back into the Chinaman's backpack. Unrolling some of the Vietnamese paper money, Perry reaches out, handing the money to Nhu. "Buy food and supplies, bring back ready-to-eat things that are easy to pack and transport. Buy for however many people that will be going, enough to last several days. I will be joining you for the trip south. Go now, keep a low profile, and make sure you're not watched, followed, or otherwise compromised. We don't have any more graves ready. Go now and leave through the back gate."

Perry is rearranging his equipment so he can carry the Colt .45, filling his backpack as full as he can, placing the remaining items into the dead man's pack, leaving room for the bundles of food Nhu will bring back. Looking up suddenly with a perplexed look on his face, Perry blurts out, "Crap, I can't go walking around dressed like this."

Turning to Father Alex, Perry shrugs his shoulders. "Alex, do you have any thing I can wear?"

The good father thinks for a few seconds. "I do have an old black frock coat that I haven't worn in years, could be just the right garment for the occasion. I'll get it for you." Leaving the patio, Alex goes inside to retrieve the coat. Perry, now alone for the first time since the firing of his weapon, allows himself a moment to ponder all that has happened in this short span of time: he has killed a man, buried him, met some young Montagnard punk he knows nothing about, liberated a .45 caliber Colt pistol belonging to a mysterious missing pilot by the name of Bigelow, has volunteered himself for a good three-to-four day long forced march to some yard[3] village he knows not where and might have to do battle with NVA hard line, experienced troops when he gets there, and his friend, Father Alex, is trying to find a frock coat for him to wear. Throwing his hands up, speaking to the heavens, he growls in an almost inaudible voice. "Why do I do this to myself. Why?"

Returning to the patio, Father Alex is carrying the old black coat. "What?"

"Nothing, just talking to myself."

Father Alex holds up the garment for Perry's viewing. "Looks big enough. It is rather large and flowing, should be able to hide your weapon. You can put your backpack under or over it."

Arranging the coat with his weapon hanging upside down over his right shoulder, Perry, in a moment of need, can swing his weapon into action from under its cover. There are no front buttons on this old thing; it buttons down the back. Perry chooses to pull the garment already buttoned over his head, selecting to wear his backpack externally so he has quick access to it. He will put the .45 Colt in a side pocket of his pack. As they wait Nhu's return, Alex and Perry, in a roundabout way, say their good-byes.

"Perry, I'm almost sorry I got you involved in all of this, but I can't think of a better person than yourself for such a task as this. I will miss your competition in Backgammon, but most, I will miss our conversations. You are rather blunt, brash, and to the point, but you are amazingly open and honest. We will not be seeing each other again. May you go with the blessing of the Lord and my personal blessing of peace and safety in your journey. Good-bye, my friend."

Perry, taking his pack and carry bag off, slides his weapon out from under his frock coat and sits down in one of the patio chairs.

---

[3]   US Special Forces slang for Montagnard.

"Alex, I'll be back, maybe not for a few years. This is my home. I was lured here by war. I've stayed because of the people and the beauty of the country itself. The lush green jungle is the pulse my heart beats to. It's like a drug to me Alex. I can't live without it. That's why I stayed after the war's end. If this thing with the pilot had not come along, I would have found some other trail to follow. Our time together has been productive. I have really enjoyed your company. My only worry is the dead Chinaman. He's buried almost in your backyard. when Major Trong returns, play dumb. You had nothing to do with his death. Thank you for your friendship and caring manner. Keep an eye open, Alex. I'll be back. It may be some time, but with your Lord's help, we will meet again."

They embrace. As they separate, there is a faint knock at the back gate. The young Montagnard has returned.

Entering the compound, Nhu smiles in the direction of Perry. "Nice robe, round eye." He sits down the burlap bag of food he has purchased from the market, and as Perry looks on, he starts stuffing the food items he's purchased into the dead man's backpack.

"It's not a robe, you little puke, it's a frock coat, and my name's Perry. Use it."

Once finished, Nhu confronts Father Alex. "I do not know what to say, Father. I think you have helped me with this pilot thing. Should be interesting when this Mr. Perry and Bao meet for the first time." Smiling, Nhe looks at Perry. "I will tell Bao how he saved our lives, which should smooth over the fact that I'm returning with not only food but another round eye. The news of troops moving into the highlands to attack the village is going to set him off. Father, you know Bao. He's going to be pissed and will want to try and intercept them. Mr. Perry, I think that you and I will be in for a fast-paced journey into some of the thickest, heavily tangled, double and triple canopied jungle that this country has to offer, none of it downhill."

Standing, Perry hikes up the front of his frock, slings his weapon upside down over his shoulder. He puts his pack on, replacing his carry bag over his left shoulder, and turns with a devilish smile on his face. "Nhu, I love nothing better than a good walk in the woods." Reaching down, grabbing the dead man's belt with the holstered pistol, he holds it out for Nhu. "Here, put this on under your shirt. Arrange your backpack so you have easy access to your spare magazines, and hurry before I change my mind. Alex, good-bye, my friend. It is getting late. We must go. Thank you again."

CHAPTER 6

SLOWLY OPENING AND looking out the villa gate, all seems clear. With a nod of his head, Perry steps out onto the little rutted road. "Let's go, Nhu. You lead the way. Stay in the shadows off any trails when possible. I'm in no mood for any bullshit,from anyone."

Nhu starts them off in a westerly direction into the old olive grove, keeping five rows of trees between themselves and the rut-ted road. No passersby as yet, the late afternoon sun is starting to cast long shadows across the road. The orchard has already fallen into the late day with the graying of dusk helping greatly in their desire to remain unseen in their journey.

They are now approaching someone's family farm with pigpens and chicken coops, children and vegetable gardens. The adults are going about their end of the day rituals; food preparation, feeding and the managing of livestock. For the young, it's the last run, the last ball thrown, no more hide-and-seek, the last stick fetched by the family's mangy dog. Stopping about a hundred yards from this obstacle, Nhu removes his straw hat, handing it to Perry. "Put this on. It will help cover your face. We will wave if anyone acknowledges our presence, but we will just keep moving."

After twenty-five yards, the first to look in their direction is the father, just a look, no wave or smile. The next to see them is the small boy and the two little girls playing with a dog, which, for some reason, does not pay the two travelers any notice. As the young boy starts in their direction, the father hollers out, stopping the little one's advance. He waves to them, giving up a child's innocent smile. The young boy returns to his play.

Another hundred yards or so, the old olive orchard ends at a well traveled foot path running diagonal to the rutted road. As it turns north following the gnarly old trees in their march to the hills, this new trail is adjacent to an unkempt old banana grove. Turning southwest, Nhu heads for the neglected grove of trees. While crossing the little foot path, he is surprised by three wood-cutters stepping out of the olive grove with their axes and saws slung over their shoulders quietly headed home after a hard day's work. All five are startled, none more than Nhu. Perry just drops his head a little and in a fine North Vietnamese dialect, blesses the three men and wishes them a good day, to which they quickly bow their heads in acknowledgement. Without saying a word, they move off toward home, never looking back.

Again staying among the trees, keeping to the shadows, the two men are seeing more people as they move down the worn path. If they have been seen, chances are they have, no one has made that apparent—no waving of hands, no vocalization. They just seem to stay focused on their personal journeys.

Across from the banana grove, there are plots of cleared jungle. These cleaned areas are being used for crops such as corn, squash, beans, and other food staples. Some of these fields are rich with the aroma of exotic spices. There is another small foot path now separating these productive little patches from the disheveled banana grove. Stopping across from one of the open fields, Nhu goes to one knee. Perry, knowing the laws of the jungle follows, closes the gap between them and waits Nhu's explanation. "There's movement across from us, don't know if they are following or just a coincidence, or even if it's human." Straining to hear or see anything, Perry raises his head just over Nhu's right shoulder, nothing. The late day shadows are now blotting out sections of open terrain, giving anyone or anything good, easy concealment by just being still or lying flat on the ground.

Minutes pass, nothing from the field across from them, Parry and Nhu both know it's too quiet for this time of day. There should be some sounds, birds, small rodents, crickets, other insects that are normally vocal. Now it's just an eerie silence. Without hesitation, Perry reaches into the backpack he has slung over his shoulder and removes the pilot's .45 Colt, flicking off the safety. This notable sound brings Nhu into full alert as to not only the situation they find themselves, but also to the assertiveness of his traveling companion. Minutes pass in deathly silence; it's a huge relief when a family of wild pigs makes their presence known by moving out of the shadows into a sunlit cleared section of field. Their appearance also produces three screaming, yelling, rock and stick throwing black pajama clad teenaged boys leaping from nearby bushes. They pose no harm to the two travelers as they follow the family of pigs, chasing them back into the darkness of the late day jungle, disappearing out of sight in their brassy stampede.

Pausing, making sure there are no other hidden surprises in the darkening recesses of the surrounding jungle, Perry clicks the safety back on while returning the Colt. Still kneeling next to Nhu, Perry tells him he is ready to continue.

Slowly turning in Perry's direction, Nhu looks him straight in the eye, speaking in a low but strong tone. "You see that tree line down the road to our left, just past that bunch of banana trees? There's a small clearing that backs up to the wood line. Up one side is a single foot path, somewhat overgrown, it has not been used that much. Moving past the clearing, you will be able to see a hooch. My friend Bao and your American pilot are in there, waiting my return. I must also tell you that there are three other people providing security. They are heavily armed and they're good. They're all Montangnards, and they will be at listening posts ready to defend that structure. They are not expecting two people to be walking up this foot path. You pull that gun out while moving toward that building, for any reason, you will die."

Smiling, looking up at the terrain ahead, Perry is not taking his eyes off the distant tree line. "Thanks for the warning. I'll be next to you the whole way. They would likely kill the both of us."

With a quick little snort-like laugh, Nhu gives him a sarcastic reply. "They would not hit me. If I were to die, they know I'd be really pissed off in my death. I would return and haunt them to the grave." Again with a low laughing snort, Nhu gets to his feet, lending a hand to the still kneeling Perry. After helping him up, he just turns to his left and heads for the nearby tree line.

Turning up the single-wide foot path, Perry has all his senses working, yet he can't hear or see anything out of the ordinary. He can see small birds scavenging through the little dusty cleared patch, returning to their nests in the trees with their findings. If there truly are listening posts in close proximity to that little hooch, they would have had to be manned hours ago for the birds to disregard their presence.

Narrowing the gap between themselves and the hooch, only a few yards to go, everything around them is now in full shadow with the darkness of the night creeping in on them. Suddenly, on Perry's right, there is sound and movement. Standing up with an AK-47 held at his waist, a rather stocky gentleman is motioning in their direction with his weapon and making a simple proc-lamation. "Tan suit, it's the man in the tan suit." Perry, a little confused and a little startled, smiles in the man's direction while continuing his advance on the building.

The doorway to the hooch is covered by some type of woven screen; there is a faint halo of light leaking out around its edges. Nhu goes no farther, holding his right hand out, motioning for his friend to take it slow and easy. Standing before the doorway, he speaks for the first time. "Bao, I am back. Father Alex has sent along his friend, a Mr. Perry. He is a round eye who speaks our tongue. He says he can help with our pilot problem. We would like to enter, but I must first tell you that he is armed."

Looking in the direction of Ung, still holding them in the sights of his AK, Nhu glances quickly at Perry. "We have already

had a discussion about how foolish it would be and the serious-
ness of brandishing a weapon in your presence."

The barrel of an AK-47 is thrust between the door opening and the cloth shroud, slowly, with trepidation, the curtain is
pushed partway open. Words spoken in Montagnard for them to
enter as the doorway curtain is parted fully. Perry steps forward,
looking into a pair of the darkest, deep piercing black eyes he
has ever seen. A smile and a quick nod are Perry's only greeting. Seeing another individual standing to his left, he turns; and
this time, he is looking into the pale, baby blue eyes of a fellow
American. Without any hesitation at all, Perry extends his right
hand and asks, "Lt. Bigelow, I presume?" He shakes hands with
the pilot. "I've always wanted to use that line."

Perry turns his attention back to Bao. "Excuse me. You must
be the great warrior Bao of the hill tribes. I've heard of you and
your exploits. It is a privilege to meet you. I am a good friend of
Father Alex. He sends his best to you. I am Perry, your humble
servant." With a bow of his head, he turns back to Lt. Bigelow.
Standing before him is a thin shaggy-haired bewildered-look-
ing man, sporting a two- to three-day growth of facial hair. His
attire consists of an ill-fitting rather dirty and work-worn pair of
Vietnam's infamous black pajamas.

As the two new arrivals are removing their backpacks, Ung
sticks his head into the little hooch, informing Bao that this
round eye is the same man he saw Father Alex having lunch with
in Ha Dong, the same tan-suited man who went up the stairs
and disappeared into the big building, the one with all the flags
out front.

After opening some of the wrapped food brought back by
Nhu, Bao rations out food for the night; keeping three portions
in the hooch, he has Nhu distribute the rest of the offering to the
remaining troops. The flame of the lantern is splashing ghostly
shadows across the three men seated cross-legged, almost elbow
to elbow, facing a small bowl of cooked rice. Lying on top of this
pile of rice are three thinly sliced strips of dried meat along with

an eight-inch fish of some kind, also dried. For a garnish, there is a tiny bottle of Nuoc Mam sauce filling the thick musky air of this two-man hooch with a rancid, fermented fish smell.

Picking up a piece of the dried meat, using a rolled leaf, Bao scoops up some of the rice, leans back, ready to enjoy his meal. He hesitates, with a golden smile and a short laugh; speaking in English, Bao gives a lighthearted apology to his two dinner guests. "Must say sorry for the meal that I now eat with you. It's not much, but I eagerly share it. Being in the presence of two distinguished round-eyed Americans, such as yourselves, right here in the middle of North Vietnam and me being a lowly Montagnard, all I can say is, holy shit! One of your American sayings that always seems to sum up all aspects of any given circumstance." All three share a laugh, a smile, and a frightfully small meal, one that must sustain them during a long grueling night march through the thick jungle just past the neglected old banana grove.

During their meal, Perry relates the events leading up to this meeting, from his time observing Father Alex's villa: watching troops and an NVA officer visiting, then spotting an inquisitive Chinaman, later killing him with a single shot to the head, and meeting Nhu, telling how the two disposed of the Chinaman's body. Perry tells them of the father's alarming discovery—Major Trong, with three truckloads of troops, are headed up into the western highlands, home of the Montagnard village that Bao and his troops visited a few weeks earlier, bringing Bigelow with them. Somehow, this news reached Major Trong, triggering his involvement in Lt. Bigelow's search. Bao, taking all this in, is startled and openly angered that news of Lt. Bigelow visiting a mountain village has reached such a far-off place of interest, as quickly as it has.

"Mr. Perry, there are many, many questions I have for you. Now is unfortunately the worst and absolute wrong time. There is only one thing I need from you at this time, do you intend to accompany us in our return to the highlands? If so, you must follow my orders. I plan to outdistance or at the least catch up with this Major Trong. The addition of your fire power would be greatly welcomed. I do not have to tell you of the dangers involved with this kind of operation. I plan on intercepting and engaging with an enemy of unknown strength. Our trek will be long and strenuous, little rest with minimal food. Are you willing to join us on this journey?"

"When do we start?" These are Perry's only words on this occasion, there doesn't seem to be anything else to say. He knows what to expect, and as with any operation involving hostile action, Perry knows what is expected of him.

After the three men have finished with their meal, Bao makes his decision known to the remaining members of his small band of warriors, giving them the choice to follow or go their own way. They all stay onboard for the fight.

No time is wasted. Bao sends Ung out on point, followed, on his own request, by Perry. The main body of this patrol consists of Dit Hum, Y-Cie, Lt. Bigelow, Nhu followed by Bao. There'll be no flank security. They will be moving too fast for flankers to keep up, and it's too dark for them to maintain any type of contact. It's just a risk they will have to take. Being so far up north, Bao feels that ambushes are but a small threat.

Their matter of timing is working to their advantage. It is just now turning absolute dark, covering their movement away from the hooch. While traveling through the banana grove, they can hear the sounds of people closing out their day. The yelling for children to come in for the night, herding farm animals into their pens and corrals, a dog's last bark, the dying of the ever present jungle sounds, except for the echoing, desperate cries of howling tree monkeys.

Traveling through a double and triple-canopied jungle at midday can prove a most daunting task. Not much of the day's light reaches the jungle floor, yet there are shadows to gauge depth and field. There are splashes of light filtering through the mass of limbs and leaves. One can make their way without too much trouble, without too many trips and falls, without getting separated from your companions. It's a dark and gloomy place at times but never like the tormenting hell of walking through this massive growth of tangled vegetation in total pitch-black darkness.

The big bumps in the night are the men of this expedition, running into nature's ever-present obstacles like downed trees, clumps of unseen shrubs, half-buried rocks, and the jungle's most hated obstacle, the "wait-a-minute" vine; a thick, low growing green arm with thorns. Sharp little bastards, ready to hinder or outright stop your progress by stretching across the jungle floor snagging and tripping any unwary passersby. This is their world for the night.

Occasionally, Dit Hum and Y-Cie catch a slight glimpse of the only thing luminous in this dark hell. The dial on Perry's Rolex black-faced wristwatch with glow-in-the-dark, phosphorescence painted numbers along with sweeping hour and minute hands. Ung is determined in his leading the way, their movement slow but steady, their objective is to reach a river crossing northwest of Ha Dong. Once across the Red River, they will set a direct steady pace for the small town of Sa Pa, the town Bao missed on their way north. Sa Pa is the only place with a bridge on this section of the river. Roads coming out of the south connect with the main road into Ha Dong. Their group cannot use this crossing. It has two NVA manned checkpoints, one on each approach. The bridge over the river connects to a road, following its path on the northern bank. This is the route Major Trong will be taking with his three truck convoy. Any vehicle trying to reach the highland logging roads must use Sa Pa as their starting point. This town is a hub, not only for a thriving logging industry, it's also a large distribution point for trucks shipping rice and other goods to towns and villages all along the Red River. Starter roads are being built as fast as the trees can be cut down and the land cleared by fire, later to be bulldozed over, allowing for more development and the migration of an ever-growing populous.

The early morning light is playing games with the upcoming day, throwing glints of light and shadows across the breadth of the jungle. Sounds are slowly returning; their pace along with the new day has picked up. Finally being able to see those tree stumps and downed timbers that were so intimidating in the night, their progress is steady and a little easier. They're now moving at a military route step.

By late afternoon, Ung seems to have found their river crossing. There are two hooches built on the river's edge, occupied by a family operating a pole-and-rope-pulled ferry. It's located down river from the bridge; this little ferryboat has been here for over fifty years, a very busy place before the bridge was built. Even today, it is used to ferry passengers and small buffalo-drawn carts taking people to Sa Pa and other small towns, villages, and markets. It's essential in the morning and early evening hours for the transportation of children coming from and going to schools. This crossing is on a narrow point of land reaching out into the calm waters of this stretch of river. This little peninsula forms a small cove on the southern shore where one end of their pull rope is anchored. Once across, there's a little road leading into the southern part of Sa Pa. There's a ramp connecting the road to the little docking facility where they have the ferry secured. Bao and Ung spotted this ferry and short finger of land while paddling their way to Ha Dong almost two weeks ago. They took note of this place as a readily available means of crossing the mighty Red River.

The column of seven can now afford to break for food. From the start they had been taking water when they could, but not food, now is a good time for eating, along with a short rest. Staying in the concealment of the late afternoon shadows, hidden among the lush fragrant foliage, they wait for darkness to overtake their surroundings before appropriating this small ferryboat.

Darkness once again has beaten back the day. With no clouds in the night sky, there is nothing to blot out the reflective image of a million stars and a huge crescent-shaped moon from bouncing off the ripples in the flowing waters in front of them. Keeping to the cover of the near tree line, Bao and his men ready themselves for a swift dash to the waiting ferry. There is no sound from the two hooches, for unknown reasons, these people have no watch dog. Silently, they approach the craft. Three men board, two pick up poles, and the other one grabs hold of the pulling rope, a rather thick heavy braded hemp, looks and has the feel of being homemade. The four remaining men are making loose the mooring lines and starting to launch this big chunk of wood. Once moving, the four throw their weapons onto the ferry and clamber aboard. Two more are now poling, the remaining three, with their weapons at the ready, scour the west bank for any unwelcome or unwanted guests.

On the west bank, the ferry's pulling rope is anchored to the base of a big tree; next to this tree is a very well-traveled dirt and gravel road leading into town. Directly across from this stately old tree is a rather large building, maybe a small warehouse, no lights but there are dogs. Bao can see two of them standing at the edge of the water, a third one up the road a ways sitting on his butt, scratching vigorously at what must be the world's largest flea infestation. There are other smaller single-family homes dotted up and down the road, some on the road's edge, others set back, more than a few have light showing. People are not all tucked in for the night. Bao starts telling the men using the poles that they should try maneuvering the ferry down river, avoiding the dogs that are starting to pay a little more attention to them. The two by the water start barking. Taking out a machete, Bao grabs for the pulling rope, intending to cut it, sending the craft down river, missing the road and putting them out of sight of the dogs. At that same moment, Perry sits down cross-legged, knees raised, taking his silenced AR-15, flicking the safety off, steadies the weapon with a good tight two-handed grip. Resting his elbows on his knees, Perry fires his first round, with only a small muzzle flash as witness one dog is down. Its companion not uttering a sound, just looks and sniffs at his dead friend, unaware of the projectile headed for him at this very moment, two dogs are down. The third dog, the one with the flea problem, he's just a little smarter than the average dumb flea-ridden, mangy Vietnamese mutt. Seeing his two buddies blown away, this little puppy dog sniffs the night air, renders one long and lowly howl before running off into the nearest tree line, taking his fleas with him.

Staying the course brings the seven to their intended port of call, the west bank of the Red River on the outskirts of Sa Pa. They must now quickly disembark. Bao insists they make sure the ferry is tied off securely so as not to drift downriver, knowing these people will be in need of their transportation come morning. It will be troublesome enough in the early hours of a new day to find their little raft on the other side of the river.

Ung and Y-Cie are the first off. Ung makes for the darkened hooch next to the tree line. Y-Cie goes directly for the two dead dogs. These will be skinned, butchered, and eaten, a welcome addition to a meal. Perry follows Ung into the tree line; these two will lead the way through the woods and into the surrounding jungle. They must stay off the road, making sure not to be seen by any locals, farmers, or woodcutters. This close to civilization is going to make this an all-out effort testing their combined natural and learned jungle skills.

Moving in behind Perry, Dit-Hum takes one of the dead dogs from Y-Cie, ties the critters legs together with a piece of twine stripped from a hanging vine, ties his future dinner to a stick of bamboo. Carrying this over, his shoulder exposes to the world a sad puppy dog face with its tongue hanging out, drooling saliva and blood out the corners of its mouth. Bao is the last to leave the craft, but before doing so, he wedges a folded wad of piasters into a crack between two floor planks, a reimbursement for the owner's inconvenience of having to retrieve his ferryboat and payment for its use.

The early night air is thick and heavy from the day's lingering heat with its accompanying high humidity, with sweat from his labor clouding his vision. Ung trudges on being followed by the others through a less demanding jungle landscape, just past the tree line. They find this section of jungle a little more forgiving, not as much under brush, not as many tangle foot vines. Their progress is vastly improved on this side of the river.

By paralleling this road, they will bypass the main part of Sa Pa. There are numerous trails branching off this well-traveled road: some of them leading out into the vast jungle; others head into farm areas, orchards of fruit, nut, and olive trees; trails leading to rice paddies, small family garden plots. Some of these trails curve through the hills leading to stately old French villas tucked into the mountainsides with commanding views of the Red River Valley and the Red River itself. They have been here for centuries, built by the French colonialists, taken over by rich and influential land owners, high-ranking government officials, along with corrupt civilian leaders and wealthy merchants.

Not quite an hour into their march, Dit Hum requests a short halt so he can butcher and skin the two dogs before the meat goes rancid. One dog has been shot through the right front shoulder taking its leg off, the bullet then traveling into the lower jaw coming out its snout. The other dog was hit in the abdomen, spilling out most of its intestines including the liver and heart, two of the most desired organs of the animal. Wrapping the usable portions in leaves, tying them to bamboo sticks, with these held over their shoulders, they resemble, in darkened silhouette, American hobos walking the rails in the depression era of the twenties and thirties.

They are not alone in their night trek. The main road they are paralleling still has traffic running up and down it, not many motorized vehicles at this time of evening, just normal people returning home from a distant work location, people going to visit friends or into town for some sort of entertainment, to shop at some of the open air markets or perhaps for dinner. Every once in a while, a motor bike will go by with a young couple aboard, just your typical evening on the outskirts of a well-populated city.

Coming upon many small foot trails, they are cautious in their crossing, Ung only stepping out of concealment after making dammed sure there is no chance of them being discovered. While crossing over the little path, they try not to leave foot prints, never leave evidence to the fact that someone has broken from the jungle cover and crossed at this point. This group is well disciplined in patrol etiquette. Never give an enemy or a possible enemy any clues or indication as to your location or direction of your movement. They never waver in this respect.

The main road they have been paralleling has now taken a turn to the north; they do not follow. Continuing their trek southwest hoping to soon cross one of the many logging roads that lead off into the mountains, they will use this as a quick and easy route to the high mountain village. By now, they have come upon and crossed over three logging roads. As they approach each one, Ung has halted their advance, waited a short time, listening, seeking out any movement, staying just off the road itself. Turning in a southerly direction, he follows each one for a short way, always returning, this not being the right one they all cross. Bao, the last man in the patrol, takes his time making sure their footprints have been obliterated by brushing their crossing point with a branch with leaves still attached, always taking this broom a little way into the jungle before disposing of it.

Their advance is not hampered as much as it has been the previous nights, but tonight is the start of an upward climb that will test their stamina and their will to keep going at such a grueling and painful pace.

Signaling for a halt, Ung goes to one knee. They have come across another logging road. Waiting in silent anticipation, there is no sound or movement. The moonlight is giving an eerie glow to the well-traveled road in front of them. The jungle they are in has them in an almost impenetrable darkness. This bald strip of earth radiates like a neon sign, pulling you into a cheap sleazy, waterfront bar.

After feeling certain there are no travelers coming or going in either direction, Ung steps out of the darkness. Once in the light, he can see not only human foot prints, there are buffalo tracks in the crown of the road straddled by wagon wheel ruts testifying to the large amount of lumber being taken out of these mountains. Most alarming are the very fresh, truck tire patterns imprinted into the soil by the recent passage of more than one heavy motor vehicle.

Stepping onto the hard packed dirt road, Ung sees so many footprints going in each direction that he finds it unnecessary to worry about covering theirs. He simply but cautiously steps onto the crowned center of the road. Standing in a ghostly glow surrounded by the yellowish light of the crescent moon, he starts down the road disappearing around a blind curve; within minutes, he returns the way he left, in the open on the dead center of the road, stopping in front of this group of fellow travelers. "This is the road we have been looking for. It will lead us to the high mountain pass we need to reach before turning north toward the village. Seems to me that we could save time and effort if we maneuver down the center portion of the road, staying out of the truck prints, spacing ourselves thirty yards apart. Maintaining a good rate of speed, we could gain some time and distance on Major Trong and his troops. I believe these are the tire prints from his trucks. They're only two, maybe three hours old. They do not have any footprints overlaying them, so they must have come through here late this afternoon or early this evening after the woodcutters and the wagons loaded with timber had passed for the day. We are only this close to them because they have been stopping to eat and rest. They could be doing just that at any point along this road."

Sitting down, Perry removes his boots, tying the laces together flings them over his shoulder. He is the only one in this group wearing boots; he wishes not to leave his bastard boot prints for all the world to see. Smiling, Bao displays the result of having walked down an innocent-looking road years earlier. A road believed safe and out of harm's way only to have his front teeth knocked out. In his desire to reach the aggressive Major Trong, Bao goes against the side of caution, giving instructions for his men to do as Ung suggests. They take to the trail, in this case, a logging road with Ung leading the way. Each man twenty-five to thirty feet apart, silent, except for the slight slapping sound of bare feet hitting the hard packed center of this well used logging road. The seven move out at a military double time. Last to step out of the darkness, waiting a few seconds for his eyes to adjust to the rush of moonlight, Bao looks down the road. Turning, he follows the others. They have been on a gradual incline for the past hour, moving onto the road seems to have increased the angle of climb, their advance is steeper than before. This does not bother Bao; he is amused solely by the fact that during the war and with most all their previous adventures traveling on the surface of a road or trail was strictly forbidden, you never ever leave a trail for your enemy to find and follow. Maybe, just maybe, this time, it will be all right. Most of the night has left the sky. Early sunlight is starting to throw morning shadows at their feet, bolts of light crossing their path at times startling Ung in their sudden appearance, yet he continues in his relentless pursuit of Major Trong and his troops. As more light is cast on their frantic parade, Bao passes the word to bring this foolishness to a halt and for his people to get off the road. Regrouping in the tree line, he intends spending the early morning of this new day in the pursuit of rest and nourishment. They will eat for the first time in almost two days.

Having traveled an amazing distance during the night, all are exhausted. All are hungry and thirsty. Moving deeper into the woods, they find some thick jungle cover. Once secure in their small hide, Y-Cie prepares the smallest of fires to quickly cook some dog meat. Ung and Perry, along with Lt. Bigelow, remove their packs, rummaging through them retrieving additional food items, some precooked rice balls, bits and pieces of tasty greens, along with a small bindle of spices. This along with the cooked dog is welcomed and devoured by the hungry men.

Placing themselves in a wagon wheel formation, legs and equipment to the center, feet of each man touching his neighbors, facing outward, their weapons at the ready, every other man awake, they will trade off this way for most of the early morning, trying to get some rest before their afternoon push up the mountain.

Sleep is at a premium, sore muscles, overwhelming exhaustion, and now the additional annoyance from the sounds of woodcutters and their carts moving up the logging road will not let these men gain the full rest they need and deserve.

Midday, the sun, if they could see it, is high in the sky directly overhead. The canopy of trees keeps the jungle floor dark, hot, and humid. Their trek again hampered by thick tangled vegetation, old rotted fallen trees, snagging vines that will take a man off his feet if he's not careful. In addition to all this, the steepness of their climb has increased making for a rather grueling, unpleasant, and physically challenging cross-country trip.

Not following the logging road anymore, it has turned north, they maintain a straight approach to the Montagnard village. It's not a matter of finding the easiest passage but whether or not they will reach the village in time to help in its defense. With that thought in mind, they trudge on giving their all, never wavering in their goal, stumbling every once in a while but not stopping. There is no quitting in these dedicated, professional warriors.

In the early afternoon, they can hear the sounds of logging, the roar of chainsaws, the metal ringing of axes. Sounds of big trees going down, bringing smaller trees and neighboring tree limbs with them, cracking and snapping, followed by that final loud thud as it hits the ground. This sound is reverberating throughout the forest and surrounding jungle, letting them know they are not alone.

By late afternoon, the seven have dropped down into a wide ravine, not much light, just damp dankness with a rotting aroma accompanied by large swarms of mosquitoes. The men batting and swatting at these little bastards like they were on fire, smacking and rubbing their arms, their faces in frantic defense of themselves. Any uncovered flesh is fair game for these little black, dive-bombing purveyors of sickness and death.

Climbing out of this deep cavity, they find themselves on top of a bald little hill, leading down to a small flat plain. From their vantage point, they can see what looks like a moonscape. There are a large number of craters running from the small hill they are on right through the flat, deforested plain spread out below them. This trail of craters disappears into the accompanying forest of jungle and trees. Viewing this scene, the stunned silence is briefly broken by Lt. Bigelow's solemn remark. "B-52, Arc light strike."[1] No other sound is heard or uttered as they move toward this field of destruction.

Standing on the edge of this man-made clearing, Bao directs Lt. Bigelow to skirt the open field and proceed along the tree line. Ung, leading on point, only goes about one hundred twenty yards before halting. Not going to a knee, he just stops, now standing in jaw-dropping amazement and astonishment at the appearance of bunkers, lots of bunkers. Some obviously for the storing of ammunition, others are troop and machine gun emplacements. These are arranged facing out, away from the cleared section of field. Some of the munitions bunkers have evidence of being blown up from the inside out. Their main structure, sides and roofs, opened and laid out like they were once volcanoes, with debris formed up around a huge hole in the ground. The extreme heat from 500- and 1000-pound bombs has ignited the stored munitions, causing large underground explosions throwing dirt, massive logs, shrapnel, and splinters of ammunition crates high into the air as the surviving trees bear witness with their broken and burnt limbs.

Slowly surveying the scene, they can now make out what looks like the partially twisted barrel of a .51 caliber antiaircraft gun pinned under the base of a massive uprooted tree. Cautiously moving through the rows of bunkers, they come across an old truck or gun mount trailer wheel, blackened by fire with part of the rubber

---

[1]   Code name given to B-52 bombing missions. Massive retaliation strikes on SAM missile launch sites.

tire melted to the rim. All through this area, there is evidence of shrapnel. There are trees with large portions of bark and limbs missing, deep gouges dug into the soil, big chunks of jagged and twisted sharp pointed shards of metal lying about. This must have been a very unpleasant situation when the bombs were falling.

Just past the string of bunkers, they come across what are the remains of a large missile launcher. Steel pipes, tubing, angle iron, and wiring with metal bracing all burnt and fused together now in the shape of a massive pretzel. They have stumbled upon an old SAM (surface-to-air missile) site, the very same destructive device that brought down Lt. Bigelow's plane, starting this whole chain of events in the first place.

Once past the SAM site, evidence of man's ability of destroying his own environment is everywhere: massive craters, uprooted trees, still standing trees showing injuries in the form of broken, shredded, and blackened trunks with burnt upper limbs. All lower foliage is just simply missing, ground cover, and tangled vines, all gone. Any vegetation once growing at ground level has been burnt completely or scorched black leaving the ground covered in a charred charcoal gray, white and black tinted ash. They are leaving ghostlike footprints as they pass through.

Mother Nature has been busy reclaiming her forest and sur-rounding jungle. This destruction seems to be at least one and a half, maybe two years old. The burnt field has a scattering of young grass shoots. Some of the larger charred tree branches have the beginnings of new leaves. Tree trunks are oozing out large quantities of sap as they try to heal. The ever present clinging crawling vines have started an aggressive attack on the destroyed missile launcher. The open bunkers and all the bomb craters are filled with water, enough to provide an ecosystem for tiny green, black, and yellow spotted frogs, along with their ever present life sustaining meal—those nasty blood-sucking mosquitos.

As they are climbing the ridge of this mountain, it provides them with a commanding view of the land in front of them. To the north, they can see a portion of the main logging road as it pokes out of the far tree line, coming out into the open going around a large outcropping of granite, then going up the side of a small hill before diverting back into the trees. Not many of the older mountain roads in the north are out in the open. Their only defense from air strikes during the war was to hide them among the trees. To the west, directly to their front, is a succession of ridgelines leading into the high mountains to the south. A chain of hills and the remnants of a cascading ridgeline coming off the mountain are leading down to the fertile plains and lowland rice paddies.

Resting a short time on this ridge, they muster enough strength to take the plunge into another ravine. Only two more ridgelines to conquer and they should be able to see the small terraced rice fields and row crops belonging to the Montagnard village nestled among the trees on the mountainside.

Sounds of the wood cutting have diminished; only a few distant chainsaw rattlings can be heard echoing across the far northern region of forest as they start their late afternoon assault on the two remaining ridges. Before they can climb out of the second ravine, night has fallen. They are covered in a black veil of nothingness. It was not a slow takeover of the day. Once they moved off that first ridgeline, the earth doing nothing more than her daily routine, took that last little role in her rotation that finally blocks out the sun's light to this part of the world. Shadows no longer exist; sounds change tone. Down in this ravine, there is no right, left, forward, or back. One is seemingly in a quicksand whirlpool of black despair.

Finally cresting the ridge, reaching their goal, tired, hungry, and a bit anxious, they see before them a tranquil night scene. To their direct front, some three hundred yards, lay the terraced rice fields reflecting what moonlight there is. To their right is a dusting of individual little cooking fires illuminating small shadows of villagers as they move through their tree-shrouded encampment.

Rather than risk a firefight with friendly troops, Bao decides to spend the night on the leeward side of the ridge. They will make their final move on the village after the morning's first light. On the ridge, there is but a light breeze. They find some comfort among the grasses and low ground cover under a lightly clouded sky being filtered by the canopy of trees high above them. Not in their normal wagon wheel sleeping formation, Bao has them laid out side-by-side: every other man facing in the opposite direction, about three feet apart. No farther than an arm's reach, two men awake at all times, one man facing each way so as to cover their front and rear. They are twelve feet off the ridge's crest, mak-ing it easy and quick to rise over the top for a peek in case of any alarming noise from that direction.

Once settled in, they go through their rucksacks, sharing what remaining precooked food they have. No one is left out; they all enjoy a little bit of evening meal. Perry has also taken his small but powerful spotting scope out of his pack, not a night vision scope by any means, but a good device for bringing objects that are far away up close. Even in the dark, things that move can be seen.

Early morning, just a few hours before dawn, a light wispy fog like mist coming off the cool waters of the nearby river and ter-raced rice paddies, Ung is close to the end of his watch. The area below them has been quiet for the most part, except for the occasional animal sounds, like the howling of night prowling monkeys off in the distance, loud chirping of tree lizards, the rustling noise made by small rodents moving through the dried leaves on the forest floor. Now there is a sound not of nature, the slight pronounced crunching thumping of human feet stirring up and smashing through dried vegetation. A distinct clattering of man's inability in his task of maneuvering through the brush in the still blackness of night.

Waking the man next to him, Ung whispers to Bao that they have hostile movement below them, not in their direction. The sound is moving across their front, concentrated in the area below the little cleared field just to the eastern edge of the lowest rice paddy. He has yet to see any suspects. Now Bao can hear the unmistakable blundering, stumbling commotion going on two hundred yards downwind of their hillside perch. All seven men are now fully awake. Y-Cie has crawled to the ridge top, listening for any sound or hint of movement behind them—none is detected or heard. Perry, using his spotting scope, starts scanning the lower edges of the first paddy, moving ever so slowly, trying hard to spot anything out of place, any movement to put a face to the sound. Hard to do in the dark, twice as hard with this low lying fog bank.

Perry asks Bao where the night listening post is located. He is told there is an outpost just above and to the right of the highest paddy just past the dike and dirt trail about ten yards into the tree line. He focuses the crosshairs of his scope in that general direction, no friendlies, but he has spotted something not right, someone out of place. This someone is dressed in an NVA uniform, carrying an AK-47 assault rifle, crawling over the paddy dike. He's headed down a little trail toward the lower section of newly planted row crops. He is in no hurry, taking his time so that his movements are not detected by any early rising villagers.

Trailing back to the lower paddy with his scope, Perry finds two more NVA now daring to poke their heads up and out of the ground-hugging fog. Once they fix their positions, they pull their heads back down. This veil of pale gray fog covers the lower portion of rice paddies and row crops extending right to the base of the ridge that Bao and his men occupy. These people are not at all concerned about what's behind them; their focus and sole concern is the south facing slope of the mountain that the village is built on.

As the man crawling down the little pathway reaches the fog bank, he too disappears back into its cold clouded embrace. Farther south along the bottom edge of the row crop field, there is a flurry of activity. Emerging out of the fog bank are two men with their personal weapons shouldered. They're carrying the round metal base plate for a mortar. They scurry up the hill, heading for the wide flat portion of ground, separating the rice paddies from the lower row crops. This the intended spot from which to launch their mortar attack. It is out of range of accurate rifle fire from the village with good concealment thanks to the three foot high rice paddy dike, along with an easy clear field of fire into the little hillside encampment. With such a clear and open view, they can adjust their own fire pattern. Just a minute or two after the base plate is positioned, four more men break cover: one carrying the bipod bracing for the tube, two of the four men are helping with the support apparatus. They also have the heavy 81mm mortar tube balanced precariously on their shoulders. Each man has a canvas bag with three mortar rounds slung over his other shoulder. The fourth man has two canvas bags of mortar rounds hanging off his right shoulder, one AK-47 slung over his left shoulder, plus he is carrying one AK-47 in each hand. This is a well functioning, well trained mortar crew. As two of the men set up the mortar, the other four become security by taking positions along the rice paddy dike.

The day's sun is still beyond the horizon, not yet lighting up the treetops, no sign of light at all. Tree monkeys have not challenged the nesting, still sleeping song birds; it appears that everything in this world is just waiting the bright warm rays of the sun. Bao is convinced that the mortar crew down the hill directly in front of them is doing just that, waiting for the first wink of sunlight to start their shelling of the Montagnard village.

Bao gathers his people with a hushed calm voice. His words spoken with authority and from experience, he lays out a plan of action. "This mortar crew is not alone. There were three truck loads of soldiers that departed Ha Dong, no more than twelve men per truck. We have six men below us. I'm going to speculate that the three truck drivers along with at least two or three others are guarding their vehicles. That gives us, in roundabout numbers, twenty to twenty-four troops hiding along the tree lines to the west of the rice paddies, with the bulk of their troops probably to the north, among the trees above the village. Nhu, Y-Cie, you two work your way along this ridgeline as far as you can. If they have any troops on this side of the village, either alert us or the villagers. By what means is up to you. We will engage the mortar crew. Go now and be careful."

Grabbing their weapons, stuffing extra magazines into their carry bags, turning to the others with a nod from Nhu, a big purple-toothed departing smile from Y-Cie, they are gone on their silent, deadly trek. In an instant, they are swallowed by the darkened jungle.

The others ready their equipment. Bao continues his planning. "Ung and I will gain the bottom of the hill, move through the fog bank to the edge of its existence. Mr. Perry, you move down as far as you need for a good clear shot at the two men manning the mortar. When you are ready, wait till the first hint of light or if you see them starting to fire the mortar. Bigrow, Dit Hum, you two go with Perry. While he gets set in his location, you two move north along the bottom of this ridge, staying in the tree line until you're within easy range of taking out or at the least keeping the four men on the dike engaged and busy for a few minutes while Ung and I take over the mortar. My intention is to raise the tube's trajectory and fire rounds over the village onto Major Trong's troops. Once the village rallies to the firing, watch yourselves. They don't know we are out here. Identify yourself if need be. We must go now. The sun will not wait for us. It is coming out of its nightly slumber and will be rising soon. Ung, let's go. You three, good luck and good hunting."

With that and a slight golden glint from a quick smile, Ung and Bao take their silent deadly selves down the side of the ridge, making their way to the bottom to start their crawl out into the fog. Perry, Lt. Bigelow, and Dit Hum start their short trip off the ridge, down into the tree line, bordering the cleared field next to the rice paddy dikes. All is silent with their movement. It has to be. Their lives depend on it.

Perry has found his spot, a sixty to seventy-yard clear field of fire into the mortar's position. To the right and an additional thirty yards, he has a good line of fire into the men spaced out along the paddy dike; with his silenced weapon, he is hoping to bring down both men manning the mortar and possibly one or two of the men on the dike before any of the others know what's going on. He is also looking for some added fire power being delivered by Lt. Bigelow and Dit Hum once the Northern troops realize he has opened fire. He is sure Bao and Ung will be firing into the mortar and dike positions as they advance on their goal.

The sun is slowly sneaking up behind the mountains, sending out a dusty orange glow that's spreading over the morning sky. It is time; there is anticipated movement from the mortar crew. Perry takes aim, but before he can get his shot off, a mortar round is dropped down the tube. All in the immediate area recognize the hollow ka-thump, followed quickly by a metallic ring and the whooshing of a mortar round leaving its tube. Perry pulls the trigger. One man is down. His buddy, not hearing the shot, is stunned as his companion crumples to the ground with a gaping hole in his chest spewing out blood, lungs, and chunks of intestines. He was hit in the back just under his lower right rib, blowing assorted needed internal parts and his lung out the exit wound in his front. You could say he is a bloody mess. Before he can lose that funny, startled surprised look on his face, the second mortar crew member is face down in the dirt next to his friend. Perry now adjusts his fire to the men along the dike. From his left, he can see and hear Bao and Ung moving on the mortar position. At the paddy dike, two of the sentries are down. The other two have jumped up and flung themselves over the dike only to be caught in the withering automatic rifle fire laid down by Lt. Bigelow and Dit Hum. This end of the battlefield has been secured.

If anyone is still asleep on this hillside, they must be deaf. After the loud and quick burst of automatic rifle fire, the explosion of the mortar round going off in a tree on the eastern edge of their encampment, no one is left in slumber. Never hitting the ground, the mortar round hit a big ole tree limb about twenty feet off the ground. Known as a tree burst, it has severed a sixteen-inch diameter, eight-foot long piece of limb, sending it crashing through the thatched roof of one of the hooches, crushing a sleeping mother and her young child, killing them instantly. Hot jagged metal shards of shrapnel raining down have penetrated the palm covered walls and thatched roofs of other homes, resulting in more wounds but no fatal injuries. The village is now fully awake and under attack. On the upper end of the ridge-line, Y-Cie and Nhu are staying among the trees. They do not wish to be fired on by the villagers and do not want to be seen by the Northern troops massed in the jungle surrounding the upper portion of the village. They have yet to spot any evidence of enemy troops, but the day is young.

At the mortar, Bao is cranking up the elevation of the tube, moving the whole thing a little to the left. Finished with his adjustments, he slides a round down the tube. Ka-thump, the first round is in the air. Before it arches out of the sky, Bao fires another round, it too is on its way. Small arms fire has now erupted from the northwest corner of the tree line above the rice paddies; the fire is directed at the mortar position. Perry, Bigelow, and Dit Hum are now returning fire from across the open space between themselves and the tree line. Bao and Ung are finding little cover at the mortar position. If the firing from the tree line is not suppressed, they will have to pull back and find cover soon. Dirt and debris are being kicked up all around them as Bao waits for his two rounds to impact so he can adjust his firing.

The sound of an explosion is heard far down into the canyon behind the hill the village occupies; the second round landing is now heard coming from the same location. Bao reaches up to adjust the mortar's angle as puffs of dirt are being thrown up all around him. Finished with his calculations, Ung drops a round down the tube, ka-thump, followed quickly by another. Both men drop down into the dirt, unleashing their own barrage of automatic fire into the near tree line. Perry has moved to the edge of his cover. Some of the firing from across the rice paddies has adjusted from the mortar crew to the area occupied by Lt.

Bigelow and Dit Hum; they are twenty yards east of Perry's location and uphill about fifty feet. The people across the way have not yet spotted the silenced weapon tearing into their position with amazing accuracy.

The two mortar rounds come out of the sky with a piercing high pitched shrill; they slam into the trees forty yards past the last line of hooches. Bao has found the mark and hit his target with only two adjustments to the mortar; now he and Ung are dropping rounds down the tube as fast as they can. The suppress-ing fire being laid down by the three men to their south is working. The enemy fire from the northwest tree line has slackened considerably. With daylight comes a little more understanding from the villagers. They can see the mortar being manned by two individuals dressed in black pajamas, and there is automatic rifle fire coming across the open area in front of the rice paddies. This too is being provided by people wearing black clothing, their heads covered by straw hats. They are all too far away to recognize faces, but they do know something sinister and deadly is taking place.

Members of the village militia are now rallying to the cause, moving out of the trees making their way toward the rice fields intending to engage the rifle fire from the northwest section of trees just above the paddies. The last of the mortar rounds have been fired. Ung and Bao are now fully engaged in a small arms firefight along with their three companions—Perry, Dit Hum, and Lt. Bigelow. Enemy fire has dwindled to the point that Ung, Bao, and the others have advanced their positions. All five are now using the paddy dikes as cover. Villagers advancing in their direction can now make out who has been working the mortar; recognizing their three fellow Montangnards and Lt. Bigelow, they are a little confused by the appearance of another round eye. Two in one month, this is North Vietnam. They are wondering just where in the hell these people are coming from?

The small party of villagers that has ventured out into the grassy open have also been firing into the northwest tree line.

Two or three fire full automatic at the same time while the others reload. This is done without halting their advance. In Perry's eyes, these people are not only brave, good, and well-trained, they are heavily armed. Once in range, they toss hand grenades in the general direction of their foe. The rifle fire is by far more effective and devastating. Once they link up, Bao checks for any wounds or ammunition issues. He then tells his group of fighters they are to spread out along the paddy dike; he intends to move into the northwest tree line. Once established among the trees, they will turn east and move toward the enemy troops scattered in groups on the outskirts of the village.

The booming sound of mortar explosions are but faded echoes through the tranquil valleys surrounding the nearby mountains. Major Trong's troops caught in the mortar barrage are moving in different directions: those on the northeast side of the village are being joined by forces driven from the tree line above the rice paddies, now retreating into their own lines. They are being driven back by a ferocious out pouring of automatic fire, a virtual wall of steel being laid down by Bao and his small group of men. Some of the remaining troops that were hiding among the trees right above the village are headed down the southeast side of the mountain onto the ridge Nhu and Y-cie have been occupying. A portion of Trong's troops had started their advance toward the village, as they too were driven off the mountain crest by the incoming mortar fire, but their advance is being stopped by an overwhelming volume of AK-47 firecoming up at them from the villagers. Bao once said, "No one knows how well armed these Montagnards really are." They do now.

Some of Major Trong's troops are moving through the trees in front of the ridgeline Nhu and Y-Cie are on, starting their push into the village. They too are receiving a massive volume of AK fire directed at them. Nhu and Y-Cie are staying low, not moving, using trees and brush for concealment. The automatic fire coming from within the village is cracking through the air just above their heads showering them with broken bits of limbs and a steady sprinkle of leaves being pruned from the foliage by wayward bullets.

Their advance all but halted, Major Trong's troops are not simply regrouping for a second attack; they're getting together to leave en masse. Their departing route will be up the ridgeline to their rear, the southeastern ridge Nhu and Y-Cie are on. The two start a slow low crawl in a westerly direction, hoping not to be seen by the retreating troops. Their hopes are dashed when one of the Northern troops almost trips over Nhu as he is desperately trying to get out of rifle range of the villagers. The young man's surprise at tripping over a black pajama wearing individual has left him practically paralyzed with fear. Y-Cie, just a few feet behind Nhu, rolls to his left, bringing his AK up in a quick and ready position, and fires one round into the man's midsection. As the enemy soldier staggers to the ground, Nhu and Y-Cie jump up. Bent at the waist trying to give themselves a low profile, shift gears, going into a crouched rundown the ridgeline headed for the trees bordering the open grassy slope just west of the village. They cannot accomplish this without being seen. Alerted to their presence by the close in gunfire and the sound of underbrush being trampled through, some of the Northern troops open fire on the two fleeing men. Because they are moving in the direction of the village the troops firing at them prudently decide not to follow.

With a large amount of rounds passing through the air, Nhu and Y-Cie are forced to take cover, this time dodging both friendly and hostile forces. They are seemingly caught in a deadly cross fire. With no clear targets, they do not return fire. They just hunker down, staying in close among the trees.

Letting out a short shrieking cry, Y-Cie rolls to the ground, grabbing for his left thigh. Bark, splintered parts off trees, leaves, and dirt are being thrown about. Fragmented bits of bullets shower the two men who have to shield their faces for fear of being struck. The volume of fire is overwhelming. Major Trong's people have been outgunned in this firefight, and they know it. The leader of the Northern troops gives the order to his bugler. Over the steady sound of gunfire, there is a high-pitched blaring of a bugle resonating through the forest, trumpeting an echoing retreat.

Now there is only random firing from the fleeing troops, just shots to keep the pursuing tribesmen's heads down. The Northern troops on the northwest side of the village hear and respond to the bugler's call. They too are fleeing the battlefield, headed for a rendezvous on the other side of the mountain. Once there, they will link up with the remaining troops from the southeast side. When they join forces, Major Trong realizes and accepts his losses, directs his men to strike out for the trucks. They will regroup, rearm, and return. He will not let this be the end of their engagement.

The return fire from the villagers has subsided. They do not pursue the retreating troops, but they are concerned about the two black clothed men on the southeast ridge. There have been no sounds or sightings since the bugler's call for retreat. A few brave men from the village venture out into the open area and cautiously approach the tree line at the base of the ridge. Not moving, staying quiet, Nhu, in the absence of gunfire, lifts his head. He can see some of the villagers headed in their direction. Not wishing to be shot, he hollers out a big Montagnard hello and a louder cry for help.

In the village, people are bringing the dead and wounded to the communal hut. The dead wrapped in burial cloth are placed at one end; there is mournful crying coming from relatives and loved ones. The death toll, so far, is eight adults and three children. There is the possibility of more dead resulting from severe wounds suffered by two other village members. Y-Cie is among the twenty wounded laying in the communal hut; he is being looked after by Nhu and Lt. Bigelow, the only two from Bao's group with any medical experience.

There is a lot of commotion throughout the village. Bao has taken control of securing the southern end of the encampment, stationing men on the ridgelines surrounding the northeast and northwest approaches to the village, including the area down by the rice paddies. The number of Northern troops killed is not fully known. They have taken the weapons, ammunition, and any other usable equipment they could from the dead. The bodies of the enemy have been brought down and stacked in the open area between the rice paddies and row crops. They will be covered with dried foliage and set ablaze.

Bao and some of the villagers are investigating why the village night guards did not give an alarm to the approaching forces; they move to the night listening post located among the trees above the rice paddies. They discover a disturbing sight; both sentries have had their throats cut ear to ear. They seem to have been caught napping, a very dangerous and stupid practice when one is on guard duty.

Members of the village militia have posted sentries across the surrounding northern ridges. While moving through the trees, gaining on the village, they are coming across a number of enemy dead. Their equipment is taken. They have their feet tied and wrapped with rope made from vines, two bodies lashed and strung together with a long strand trailing so they can easily be pulled to the funeral fire. They transport six Northern troops this way. Wounded none, knowing if there had been a survivor, he would have been shot and dragged down the hill with the others. As they approach the uphill side night listing post, they are faced with the discovery of two young men in a similar circumstance as their colleagues a ways down the hill next to the rice paddies. There are two more young men dead from knife wounds, all of their rich red blood flowing from their wounds pooling on the ground mixing with the dirt staining the earth a rusty brown color. The same two young men that let Bao pass this very position unchallenged not so long ago, the same two he told to be more diligent in their task. Apparently, they did not heed his warning.

Those who are not tending the wounded or mourning the dead are hurriedly packing their meager belongings. Food from the communal storage huts and underground bunkers is being distributed to families. The remaining bulk of the foodstuffs that is not given out will be placed in burlap bags and lashed to the backs of water buffalo. This village will have no living inhabitants come nightfall. The elders of this and other Montagnard villages always have an alternate village site picked out. They have been doing this for centuries. They always need a place to go when the game runs out, fields quit producing, rivers and streams run dry. The occasional lighting struck fire and being contacted or interfered with by Vietnamese civilians, woodcutters, hunters, or government troops. They will take with them the ashes of their dead to cast into the winds of the high mountain forest so their souls and spirits will always be with them in their eternal search for harmony and peace in this world.

Finished with their task of securing the village, Bao, along with Perry, gather with some of the elders and militia members in a small clearing next to an open fire pit. The elders of the tribe are not real pleased with the tragic results of the day's hostilities. They are displeased that the reason for the government's attack was due to one simple fact: Lt. Bigelow was brought into their village by Bao. In doing so, Major Trong was somehow informed and became involved, eventually bringing death and destruction to these well-armed but peaceful people. They also know that had it not been for Bao's people, this day could have had a total catastrophic end for this village and all its inhabitants. All said, nothing can ease the agony and pain of losing family and friends. Leaving this place behind was always envisioned; this is just an earlier departure date than expected.

Ung and Dit Hum are checking on their friend's condition, finding Y-Cie in good spirits with a nonlife-threatening but rather nasty open leg wound. He was very lucky the bullet tore through the upper thigh, taking out bits of muscle and fatty tissue, leaving him with a rather large gaping wound just above the knee on the inside of his thigh. This is accompanied by a large ugly dark purplish, black and blue bruise covering the entire area circumventing the upper thigh running from his crotch to below the knee. Fortunately, it did not hit bone or severe any major arteries or blood vessels. The bleeding has been subsiding with the use of a tourniquet that was applied and is being tended to by Lt. Bigelow. All the wounded are to be moved shortly to another location for assistance in getting ready for their upcoming trip. The communal hut is being readied for the deceased villagers' funeral fire. Dried foliage, along with as many flowers as they can find, are to be carefully placed on the covered mound of bodies before ignition. Later, the ashes will be gathered and stored in a large, centuries old, hand-chiseled and delicately carved jade urn for their final journey into the high mountains.

The smell of smoke hangs heavy in the air. Besides the funeral fires, there are flames licking the treetops throughout the village. Once the family's home has been emptied of its contents, it is torched. There will be no usable structures when Major Trong returns with his reinforcements. There will be no village to attack, no people to harass, no crops or food stuffs left behind, just a burnt out section of forest and jungle where a proud and thriving village once stood.

Groups of people, families, and friends along with all their belongings are gathered in the tree line north of the open field. Elders are saying their good-byes and blessing members who are not going on the trek to the new village. Some have chosen another route: one group plans to visit a Montagnard village in the southern part of the highland mountains; another group is planning to take three water buffalo laden with supplies and cross over the northwest mountain range, ending their adventure in the southern mountains of Cambodia. That is the site of the oldest Montagnard village in the highlands. With members of this clan moving out in different directions, without a clue which to follow, Major Trong will not have an easy decision.

Even in their haste, these people will not move without proper precautions. All parties will have point and flankers; they will have people dropping back to clover leaf over their back trail looking for any signs of someone following or tracking the main body. Members traveling to the new village will leave back four men with five days rations of food and an ample supply of ammunition to wait the arrival of the Northern troops. Once they are spotted, these men will carry out one of the best means of protecting a back trail there is, sniping. A good sniper can halt the advance of a vastly larger force for an extended period of time by changing location after each shot. The North Vietnamese and Vet Cong used this tactic on the Americans throughout the Vietnam war, very successfully.

As all these preparations are being made, Bao and Perry have migrated away from the group of villagers, walking along the north tree line they are engrossed in an animated discussion. Somewhat frustrated, Bao tells Perry, "You come out of nowhere, align yourself with forces you do not know. Is it your desire to somehow liberate your fellow American? This has been my challenge for this past year. What to do with Bigrow? I'm sure he wishes to return to his home, as he should. It has been a harder task then I ever envisioned."

Perry stops, bends down to retrieve an empty AK-47 shell casing, holding it to his lips, blowing into the open end, forcing it to emit a high-pitched whistle. Moving on, Perry risks it all in his blatant, up front reasoning for his appearance into Bao's life. "Bao, I came to you with one purpose in mind, my desire to relieve you of the burden in finding a way to export Lt. Bigelow. Let me explain myself. Over eight months ago, someone came into Ha Dong, a high-ranking Montagnard tribesman. He was asking ships, captains about the possibility of deporting a round eye downed pilot to a neutral, free port. It did not take long for this lucrative information to reach the office of Major Trong. There is a high price for information of this magnitude. After his office gained this choice bit of information, it spread throughout the embassies open in Ha Dong. The Americans do not have a working office in North Vietnam, so when word reached us, I was assigned to the French embassy. Our investigation led me to Father Alex, a known advocate of the Montangnards. After making his acquaintance and gaining his trust, he confided in me that indeed there was someone trying to find transportation for an American out of the north.

"At one point in our negotiations, Father Alex produced the leather tag off a US Navy flight suit to confirm that he knew the disposition and location of the downed pilot, Lt. Bigelow. He exchanged this information with me for twelve boxes of vaccine and other medical supplies destined for use among his church-run schools and an orphanage. We brokered this deal in what was supposed to be a safe room at the French embassy. Obviously, this was not to be. Within hours, word of the name tag was all over embassy row. I immediately grabbed my hunting gear and headed to the old olive grove behind Father Alex's compound, dug myself a little hole, camouflaged my hide, and waited. A day and a half later, who comes along? None other than Major Trong and some of his troops. After quite some time, he leaves, none too happy, I might add. Following his departure, Nhu shows up, not at first approaching the villa, he moves through part of the town even entering Alex's little chapel. That's when I spotted the Chinaman, very much out of place. He was looking for someone, and it didn't take long to find out who he was looking for. Nhu has told you what transpired at the villa. Less than an hour later, you and I met."

"Bao, you could not know the ramifications of asking favors of old friends and cohorts. You were not aware of the political changes people go through when a war has ended and a new regime has taken control. Old allegiances are severed, usually for money, always at the cost of others. This is what led to your village being attacked. It's the sign of the times. It's hard to understand one's loyalties and motives these days.

"Thinking back on all this, your first choice should have been to head southwest into Thailand. There are still American advisers working with Thai ground and air forces throughout that country. My idea of a planned escape route would be over this northern mountain range into Laos, overland to the Mekong River, then by water head south along the borders of Laos and Vietnam on to Thailand, where I would aim for the little town of Nakon Phanom, home of a Royal Thai Air Base, also a staging area for US Special Forces patrols running operations in Vietnam, Cambodia, and Laos. It's the same base I used for our intelligence forays into these same countries during the war. I know if we can get Bigelow to that location, he will be safe. I say we. There's a good chance that if you accompanied us, with your caring and thoughtful rescue of one of our pilots, I believe we could work out some sort of reward, not only monetarily, but also equipment to rearm and resupply your troops. You could reap benefits from intelligence reports, aerial reconnaissance photos, and the latest government reports on any area of interest you might have. I do know that first you must talk with your friends before making any decision. Y-Cie is immobile. We will have to carry him to his next destination. This and other considerations must be looked at and talked over."

Not saying a thing, Bao smiles, nods his head, then walks off in the direction of his remaining followers now gathered around the injured Y-Cie laying on a bamboo and broad leafed makeshift stretcher. "Gentlemen, how you are, Y-Cie? Ready for some travel? Men, there are some things we must discuss and go over before departing."

Sitting with his friends, he tells them of Perry's idea and asks for their opinions. The reactions are varied. Each man has his own agenda: Y-Cie and Dit Hum wish to go with the majority of villagers to the new site. They have relatives among this group and would like to help them build a new home for their families and for themselves. They have a desire to settle and stop their wandering. Nhu has said he will help get Y-Cie to the new village site. After that, he will continue on to where he thinks Dinh has relocated. Turning to Ung, Bao with a smile, almost without questioning knows his answer to all this, Ung will go with Bao as he has for the past five or six years. Bigelow is simply intrigued.

The two groups, not going with the main body of villagers, have left, departing in staggered small groups, moving off in different directions, rendezvousing farther along their route in one or two days. They will follow this procedure until they reach their intended destination; they know this practice will confuse and discourage any one trying to track their chaotic trail.

Lt. Bigelow has been carefully observing and watching the villagers leave. He is trying to locate his friend and companion from his last visit, Lai-Kim. Not recognizing or spotting her in either of the two groups now departing has given him hope that he might reconnect with her on this cross country journey. He's been told the trip should last no longer than seven days. That is without any delays for weather, terrain, or human interference.

Bao's group has been assigned a guide, someone from the village who knows the way to the new location, a young man no more than sixteen years old, a wispy little guy already sporting purple teeth. One of the elders told Bao this kid knows his way through the forest and jungles of this northern mountain region. His name is Sam, no explanation given as to how he got this non-Montagnard name.

The six remaining members of Bao's patrol, excluding the young boy, will carry Y-Cie in rotation. This group is just one of six. There are a total of over fifty villagers going on this arduous journey: men, women, and children. There are also squealing pigs slung upside down under bamboo poles, cackling, clucking chickens with their feet tied together in pairs of two and three lashed to bamboo poles balanced over one's shoulder. Women, children, and the old all help in this task. Buffalo, one in each of the first three groups, are being pulled along laden with fifty pound rice bags and farming implements. These large beasts are controlled by the use of a persuasive piece of bamboo and a brass ring the lead rope is attached to, the big brass nose ring piercing the fleshy covered gristle separating the nostrils of the bull's nose. The youngsters and wounded are going to make progress agonizingly slow and difficult considering the terrain they will encounter.

Bao's group will be fourth in the walking sequence. The three groups in front of theirs consist of the village elders, old men and women along with the children and all the livestock. The two following groups are comprised of the village militia members and some of the young would-be warriors. They are all armed and will provide security during the trek.

After starting off in a single long procession, they go straight through the open field into the north tree line coming out above the recently drained rice paddies. Once they reach the stream, running north to south, they break off into their designated groups. Some moving downstream, some up, they will exit the water as far away from their entry point as possible. Not all groups will exit at the same location; again, this is done to throw off anyone trying to follow. Once they are across the stream, they will spend two days traveling on their own; rendezvousing on the third, they will do this all the way to the new village site. As the villagers move out of sight, the four men staying back to harass Major Trong's troops have set the open field on fire; the village itself has been burning all afternoon. This is to not only destroy any usable structures and land belonging to the village, the large grayish black thundering plumes of smoke rising above the tree cover also notifies anyone in the vicinity that this once happy, productive, little village no longer exists.

Early evening of the second day, they are told by Sam that their rendezvous site is still a half day's march. All these men are accustomed to long walks in difficult terrain, but with a stretcher, it's almost impossible to make any headway. They seem to be going five steps forward, two sideways, and one halting backward stumble. Yet they carry on. The farther they go, the heavier their burden, but carry on they must. The rotation is working well; nobody is getting overly exhausted. The only casualties thus far are Perry's tender feet. He removed his boots before coming out of the stream; his intent was not to leave a big alluring trail to follow. With all the barefoot tracks and just one set of waffled soled boot prints, making it an easy choice as to which trail you're going to follow if you're Major Trong.

If they miss the overnight rendezvous point, they were told by the elders that someone would wait there for them if only to check on their condition and make sure they know the whereabouts of the next scheduled stop. As Sam and Bao approach the designated location, they are challenged by a listening post sentry. Once they have established contact, they all gather in a small clearing once used by village tribesman during long range overnight hunting trips. Mashed down tangled grass and two or three small burnt down fire rings with warm ash are the only evidence that a large group of Montangnards spent the evening cooking, eating, and sleeping the night here. This group has arrived in the early morning of the third day, thus far, they have been without sleep or rest and the only food consumed has been dried fish and some precooked rice along with short slurps of water while on the move.

By early afternoon, they all have rested and eaten a warm meal. Y-Cie has had his wound cleaned treated and redressed in strips of cloth torn from an old but clean shirt. He seems to be in fairly good spirits for someone with the size wound he received. He should be all right if they keep the wound and the area around it clean. In this environment, cleanliness is the most important aspect in the fight to stave off an infection. Later at the new village, they will apply maggots to the wound. Maggots eat away the dead and injured flesh resulting in a nice puffy clean surface covering the open sore. Within months, scar tissue will cover the wound, leaving an indentation and the skin will turn an ugly dark purplish color, but the wound will be healed. Y-Cie's mode of transportation has been changed from the stretcher-type carrier to a single bamboo pole with a vine woven sling for the patient to lie in; the original stretcher device was thought up by the two round eyes. It did not work well in the terrain they were dealing with. Y-Cie constantly had to rearrange himself to stay in the dammed thing. The two men holding the handles were working against each other; it had shortfalls. This new one is more familiar to the Montangnards. In the forested jungle, they move most everything this way. Only their politeness and patience kept them from refusing the round eyes' suggestion and help in the first place, but after two days of struggle, Ung simply went out and cut an eight foot section of three-and-a-half-inch diameter green bamboo. With Nhu's help, they had the thing ready in fifteen minutes.

Their desire now is to try and make up some time and distance. The group of village militia that departed after Bao's group is due in camp by tonight or early tomorrow morning. Sam has informed Bao that if they leave now, picking up their pace a little, they could reach the crest of the mountain looming in front of them by midday. Once on the ridge, it would be a short downhill trek on an old hunting trail leading to a high plain that will take them on an easy northwest plunge into a small gently sloped canyon that drops down to a river they will follow until it turns south, leaving them with a one day hike to the second rendezvous. With food and rest, they start the afternoon off with an invigorated burst of energy as they assault this hill with all they have and then some. By the end of the day, Sam and Bao step out of the forested jungle, gaining the crest of one more mountain. As the others come out into the twilight, they hear the first echoing sounds of faraway gunfire, two spaced reports, combat, or warning signal? Only time will tell. No answering shots, no automatic return fire, just one more mystery from the deep, dark secretive recesses of this vast jungle.

Spending the night on the ridgeline next to the old hunting trail has been rewarding. Rewarding in that they are witness to the most beautiful night long celestial display one sees only once in a lifetime. A meteor shower so vividly bright and bedazzling it has kept monkeys, birds, and other creatures from their night's sleep. Keeping the weary travelers awake most of the night with a constant serenade of screeching howler monkeys along with the cries and moans from hundreds of unseen creatures. With a constant chaotic chattering sound resonating from thousands of song birds.

Eager to start, they break camp at first light with an assured easy day's trip. Sam has told them, "No problem. Tonight we eat and sleep long time."

Perry just rolls his eyes at Bao and falls in behind Sam in the patrol order. He is followed by Nhu with Dit Hum and Ung carrying Y-Cie followed up by Lt. Bigelow and Bao providing rear guard duty. It's one of those warm sunny mornings in Southeast Asia that you know is going to turn into a scorching, 105-degree, a hundred percent humidity ball buster. Drenched in your own sweat most of the day, chafing where you don't want chafing, and you'd rather not scratch there days. But the thought of a good hot meal and some well-deserved rest outweighs the hardships.

Moving out of the tree line parting the waist high grass, they blaze a trail northwest through this green breeze blown sea. The winds send the grass tops swirling and swaying like white caps dancing across the waters of an ocean. Verbal soundings from birds and the ever-present monkeys has been slow to materialize this morning; they all seem to be sleeping in after last night's spectacular light display. No matter, the eight travelers start their march across this open field. Most are glad to be making such easy and good progress, yet all are cautious, even in the relative safety of the high mountains. They don't like hanging it out like this, and they all know you become a target of opportunity being exposed this way.

It is a gently sloping field with mountains starting to rise on the south and northern flanks, at its widest this plain must be three quarters to a mile wide and a good two miles long before the mountains converge leaving a gap, a small pass that advances a little before dropping into a canyon bordered by mountains on both sides. This downgrade is more of a challenge, steeper, shorter grass but thicker. There are small stones scattered about making their walk a little more challenging.

Almost to the bottom of this canyon, the sound of water can be heard, giving these hot sweaty men an incentive to pick up the pace. As they near their goal, the sound of voices can be detected. Sam and Perry go to the ground. Once they have been spotted by the others, they all follow, gently putting Y-Cie down. Ung quickly moves to the front, joining the two men already in position, all three ready their weapons for action. Listening carefully, they suddenly realize that the sound to their front is chatter and laughter of children. One of the earlier groups from the village has been following the river ever since reaching it from a southwest mountain pass they came out of earlier in the day.

With the sun still high in the midday sky, the eight men lying in the grass must try and make contact with the group of villagers without causing any one to be startled. They don't want to unduly alarm their guards. No one wishes to put children and women at risk by engaging in a friendly firefight. Nhu has seemingly come up with the perfect solution; it is brilliant in its simplicity. He slowly, and in a soft voice, starts singing a Montagnard children's nursery rhyme. After the second verse, Ung joins in. The two gain the interest and attention of not only the children but their parents along with their armed guardians. Once in contact, they all gather at the river's edge where the two groups take a short break for a refreshing dip in the cool waters. It's what they needed before their final push to the night's rendezvous.

By the end of the day, this little overnight site will be full of people. There must be thirty, thirty-five villagers: men, women, and children, along with their livestock. The second group arriving has with them a body; one of the wounded has died. A few of the elders, along with two or three young warriors as guards, will stay back in the morning to cremate the deceased, recovering his ashes so they too can be spread in the winds of the high mountains along with the other remains from the old village.

As the camp is being set up, some of the younger tribesmen, crossbows in hand, head out on a late afternoon hunting excursion. Sam has gotten permission to reassemble Bigelow's bow, the one Y-Cie has been carrying. He'll try his hand at procuring the night's meal. This virgin forest is ripe for a hunt.

After the best meal they have had in a long time, Lt. Bigelow and Perry excuse themselves, take a walk into the surrounding woods out of ear shot from the others. The two have not had any free time to sit and talk; they are both needing answers to many unasked questions. Lt. Bigelow starts the conversation off with a question Perry gets asked a lot. "Who are you, and how the hell did you get involved in all this?"

"Let me start from the beginning. Years ago—"

Lt. Bigelow interrupts, "Please spare me the whole story. Give me the short version, basics like who are you and who do you work for? I know you're with the CIA, but what the hell are you doing in the north running around the jungle shooting up people. Is this sanctioned by our government, or do you just do this to get your kicks?"

"Lieutenant, I do get my jollies doing this. I run operations for Clowns In Action, commonly referred to as the CIA. I'm a member of the United States Army Special Forces. No, our government does not know that I'm running around the jungle shooting up people. Now is that enough information for you? Has the short story brought you up-to-date? Anything else?"

"You must excuse my impatience. I have been here for quite some time. It's not been easy, but I have survived. I have managed to walk all over hell and gone. I've been from the mountains to the sea, and now I'm almost back where I started, so long ago."

Perry goes on, "I'll accept that as an apology and try not to bore you with too many details. About six months ago, I was working on a government project with some colleagues of mine. We were running a training operation in Okinawa. Through our intelligence network, the government received information coming out of a French embassy in North Vietnam that a Montagnard chieftain or warlord was trying to make arrangements to smuggle a downed American pilot out of the country. This, of course, piqued every one's interest. I, being the lucky one, close to Vietnam, experienced in jungle warfare and the winning factor, I speak Yard. After a short briefing on the possible identity of the MIA, I was given a list of downed pilots spanning the last seven years. Your name was among them, and that's all the information I had.

"Within two days, I had in my possession a French passport and embassy credentials allowing me to enter North Vietnam as a French government employee. Through my investigating, I found a friend of the Montagnard in Father Alex. Long story short, here I am."

"We all appreciate your help with this village incident. You definitely put your life on the line for these people and myself for that matter. I guess my question to you was the same one I had for Bao when I first made his acquaintance. Where do we go from here?"

With a smile and a satisfied gleam in his eye, Perry says just one word, "Thailand."

Lt. Bigelow is told that Thailand is their best bet in getting, not only himself out of Southeast Asia, it's also Perry's best hope of getting back to normalcy. He explains that Bao made a mistake trying to gain Bigelow's freedom through a Northern port. The people he was forced to deal with are unscrupulous opportunists, untrusting in the state of political and financial unrest they find themselves in. Once word spread that a live round eye was trying to be smuggled out of country! "Shit fire and save the matches, Bigelow. Once this information hit the proverbial fan, everyone, and I do mean everyone, has been trying to get a handle on it."

Perry gives Lt. Bigelow a somewhat lacking in detail, run down on a tentative plan of action—stay with the villagers for a short time, making themselves useful in the construction of the new village, possibly of going with Nhu in his search for Dinh's new location, if it is in the direction they need to take in achieving their own goal. Perry wishes to stay, as much as they can, among the high mountains and jungles moving eventually across the border into Laos, following the mountains until they come to the infamous Plain of Jars. Once through this undulating, high altitude grass plain dotted with hundreds of man-made stone jars, they will then drop down off the high ridges following the ravines to the largest continually flowing body of water in this part of Asia, the Mekong River, then simply float their way down to Nakhon Phanom, Thailand, the home to a Royal Thailand airbase and headquarters for Air America, a venture solely owned and operated by the CIA during the Vietnam conflict. The base is still being used by Special Forces and other government agencies. It has become the starting point for many covert operations into Cambodia as well as extended operations throughout Vietnam. Perry knows that if they can reach this location, they will be able to contact friendly forces.

With just a one day trip ahead of them, most of the village members are in a festive mood, a lot of talking and laughter with a little bit of music thrown in. The children not so much. They are all tired of the trek; even the prospect of just one more day does not register with these little bone weary creatures. Most are in a deep sleep, infants still cling to their mothers breasts in a slow, suckling dreamlike state.

Bigelow has been walking through the groups of people in hopes of finding Lai-Kim, the young lady he kept company with during his last and only visit among these tribesmen. Just smiles, head bows and hand clasping, no Lai-Kim. Finding Bao, Bigelow is informed that the young lady he is searching for is a member of the large group of villagers making the journey into the southern mountains of Cambodia; chances of them seeing each other again are slim to none.

As the light of another day starts its methodical dance through the trees, rendering the foliage in brilliantly hued colors, reaching the forest floor kissing the earth with its life-giving warmth, the adult villagers are organizing for their last push into the high mountains. The children almost unresponsive in the fresh early morning light, they will respond better with the introduction of food, a little prodding and the hurried actions of people packing and readying their belongings all around them.

They will not spend the day in their normal group order, instead they will travel in one, single file column. Leading this procession will be point guards and scouts, followed by handlers with their rice laden water buffalo. A safe distance behind will be the women and children intermingled among the walking wounded. At a much slower pace are the three wounded who are being carried, followed by the remainder of the men and young teenaged warriors in training, all armed with AK-47 assault rifles. They're expecting to hear from some of their fellow militia group members any time during this last leg of their journey. Any contact will be established at the rear of this long, constantly moving column.

With a clear wide trail being blazed before them, the job of carrying Y-Cie has become simpler. Water buffalo and the passing of so many people has cleared out most obstructions. The people in front of the column have been moving aside small downed trees, clearing limbs, along with large stones from the path. They've been chopping and hacking away at the snagging tangle vines. Their progress unimpeded by nature's obstacles has made things much easier much less tiring for Bao and his men.

Midday brings the sound of distant gunshots, again, two quick shots in rapid concision with maybe a three-count interval then two more shots. A moment of silence, one of the rear guards raising his rifle to the sky, fires one single, solitary round. Apparently, a challenge or signal has been answered. There is no stopping the column, no discussion or action other than the single shot being fired, everyone simply keeps moving.

Coming off a gradually sloping incline, turning to the north, moving through moderately congested jungle with a forest of twenty to thirty-foot tall trees covering them in a green canopy. Not much sunlight is reaching ground level. The filtered light is casting irregular-shaped elongated shadows across everything. In the treetops, the sun's rays are being defused by the twisted, shivering leaves, rending it into bright blinding bursts of short-lived light, like the blinking of night stars seen through the flowing motion of the trees foliage. The light appears here, there, and everywhere, gone, back again moving, dancing, throwing you off and fooling your mind. Confusing your perspective of how things should look and be.

As they reach the edge of the tree line, they're facing a short plateau with three to four foot tall grass covering the entire thing. It's not that wide, but it's open to the sun's light, it's a warm and refreshing change from the dark and damp confines of the forested jungle. Within minutes, they are facing a steep climb onto another mountain. Some of the children and walking wounded have fallen back, their pace slowed by the sharp incline challenging their abilities. The two Americans start helping with the wounded, while Bao, Nhu, and Sam are doing what they can for the struggling children helping them through this last uphill surge.

Cresting this last pinnacle finds them looking out over a high mountain plain. Slowly drifting down into a shallow little valley, they have reached their new home. On the opposite side of this valley, hidden among the trees, is a deep natural cave. Water from hundreds of years' worth of monsoon rain has tumbled down this little valley carving out a cave of massive proportions. The opening is at least twelve feet tall, twenty feet wide running about forty feet in depth with the end wall tapering into a small but very deep pool of clean fresh water. It's also an ideal dry place to store ammunition, weapons, and their food supplies. Until their homes are built, this cave will be lodging for most of the women, children along with the elders and the wounded. All others will sleep, eat, and carry on with their daily lives in the relatively open space of the valley floor.

To the west of this valley, a ridgeline forms one side of this open space. There is a fairly large stream that will eventually be partially siphoned into the valley floor for the flooding of rice paddies. Small irrigation canals will be dug and used to water row crops after the fields are made ready. With plenty of bamboo down by the water, homes will be built on the south slope of the valley. They'll have plenty of space for their animals. They have virgin forests to hunt with an abundance of land for farming. The people of this village have chosen an ideal place to relocate.

Over the past three days, militia members have been trickling into camp. The first returnees have told a story of how they repelled Major Trong's troops with sniper fire and ambushes. Losing two of their own, they calculate approximately nine to ten of Trong's people lost their lives in the ill-fated attempt to follow this group of people to their new village site. The dead have been taken to the last rendezvous and are to be cremated; their ashes will be brought to the new village and scattered along with the others once the communal hut is finished.

The paddies and dikes are moving along rather quickly, with the use of buffalo attached to crudely built wooden plows and earth scrapers they have been able to gouge out three terraced paddies along with a dike network connecting them all together. They have also been working on a berm that is being constructed in front of the cave entrance to keep the monsoon rainwater out and provide a bulwark against an enemy attack. The elders, women, and children are working, building the communal hut. Some of these women sit for hours, weaving sleeping mats and other handy useful items out of thick-bladed grass and strips of bark taken from nearby trees. Other groups, including teenagers and adult males, are in the tree line, erecting family dwellings. These people share in all the work. Within two weeks, they have settled into a very functional and highly efficient village life.

At no time has the security of this place been overlooked or jeopardized. They have outposts surrounding the entire area including the highest point overlooking the village along with all its approaches. This is a rotating shift kind of thing, twenty four hours a day, seven days a week. The elders, Bao, and the top echelon from the village militia picked out the locations and set the scheduling of the man power to run the operation smoothly and efficiently. Their goal is to provide the best security network possible.

Daily hunting parties are sent out to scour the hills and valleys for edible game. They are richly rewarded in these high mountains; it seems no one has hunted here for some time. Every animal needed to sustain life is at their beck and call. Hunting with crossbow is helping in the maintaining of noise discipline. They return from their hunts with monkey, deer, succulent wild pig, along with large turkey-like fowl, including some rather nasty-looking tree lizards, not the best too look at but with that taste like chicken flavor.

The care the wounded are receiving is comforting but rather crude. Lacking in medicine, yet it seems to be working. One man is lingering with a painful lower abdominal wound that is resisting all efforts to fight the infection that has set in. The use of maggots has cleaned the outer portion of dead and rotten flesh, but they cannot help in the battle going on deep inside the man's damaged internal organs.

As bad as Y-Cie's wound was, his progress is just short of miraculous. Most of the infection has been stymied, and the wound has closed itself over with a dark reddish purple, somewhat lumpy scab, in places oozing a yellowish blood mixed pus. With the help of the others, he is able to stand and take short hikes, venturing out among the dikes, overlooking the paddies and the land to the west being cleared and readied for the planting of row crops. He can accomplish these walks with the added help of a bamboo crutch made for him by Lt. Bigelow.

It's been four and a half weeks since they first arrived at this new location; most of the family homes have been completed and are being lived in by their new occupants. Cooking ovens have been built. The cave is providing ample cool storage space for their rice and fresh food. It's also a good dry place for the abundance of meat jerky to be stored alongside their accumulated ammunition stash.

On a cool sunny afternoon, family members, neighbors, and friends have gathered on the west slope of the northwest ridge-line overlooking the river. This is the spot of a short but rather emotional ceremony, honoring their dead. With a slight breeze blowing out of the south, they cast into the wind the ashes of their loved ones.

That same evening, Bao, Nhu, along with Ung and the two Americans, are gathered on the porch of the newly finished communal hut. Not pulled together for any particular reason, they have just finished with the evening meal and are quietly sitting, maybe contemplating the ceremony they witnessed earlier in the day. Some are possibly thinking of what is next for this group of wanderers. Bao brings to their collective attention the fact that the rainy session is fast approaching. It's time for the monsoon clouds to assemble over the waters of the South China Sea, soaking up the waters they will deposit across the forests and jungles of Vietnam, supplying the life-giving force that is this place. "Gentlemen, in no time, the skies will open, bringing heavy rain turning the earth into its yearly muddy mess, making traveling difficult and hazardous. We must decide in which direction to go."

First to answer is Nhu. "I have said before that I will travel west northwest and try and find Dinh's new campsite along the high mountain ridges. I'm sure of its location and will be able to find it in three to four days travel from here. Any or all of you are welcome to follow along, but that is my goal."

Perry is the next to weigh in on the subject. "I intend traveling in the same direction as Nhu, west northwest until I cross the border into Laos. Once there, I'll stay on a northwest track, cutting across the Plain of Jars, dropping down off the high mountains onto the Mekong River. Grab me a boat and head for Thailand, hopefully bringing Lt. Bigelow with me. We could join Nhu for the time it takes to find his friend's camp."

Standing, moving his way to the top step of the communal hut, Bao surveys his surroundings. These are the people he loves. His mother and father said that his family would always be with the Montangnards and their way of life. Even after his schooling and the experience of living in a world of congested city life with the noise, smells, and the elbow to elbow existence, his mind has always been rooted in the far reaching lands of his people with their freedoms and easy-spirited lifestyle. Their total ignorance is truly blissful. Bao turns to the others. "I will have a talk with the elders of this village tonight, explaining that it is time for some of us to be moving on. I, for one, intend to return some day. These are my people. I will continue to help them in any way I can. Mr. Perry has been so kind as to offer me assistance in the procuring of arms and ammunition for our use in the defense and protection of this and other camps. I will talk to Ung, explain his options. I'm hoping he is welcome to join in this endeavor. Gentlemen, I will meet you right here in the morning. I do know that Y-Cie and Dit Hum will not be on this trip. They wish is to stay and live among their family and friends. Gentlemen, good night." Turning, walking back down the steps, Bao silently moves through the village in the stillness of another dying day.

"If I go with you, what's my incentive?" Bigelow is speaking to no one in particular. His vision has captured the images of the twilight colors being splashed across the sky. "This looks to be a rather long and arduous journey. If we do decide to go, should we wait for the monsoons to pass? The Mekong will be the recipient of large amounts of runoff water, which could jeopardize your boat trip."

Standing and stretching, working the kinks out of his sore neck and shoulder, Perry answers the pilot's questions. "Now is the time to move. We have about two to three weeks before the heaviest of the rains reach this far into the northern mountain territory. You are correct in the assumption that the mighty Mekong will be a full to overflowing river during and just after the rainy session. That's why we must leave in a day or two or risk being stuck here for the next month or possibly longer depending on its severity. Incentive, Lt. Bigelow, it's on the way home. It's your passport out of Southeast Asia, my good man, and it's a chance once again to see and thank the man that saved your scrawny little ass, Nhu's brother-in-law, Dinh."

The morning dawns bright with just a whiff of a breeze. The villagers are up, some readying their water buffalo for the day's work, others out in the tree line gathering firewood and edible tuberous roots, mushrooms, wild grains, and grasses. The younger children along with some of the elders are trekking over the western ridgeline on their way to a morning of play in the cool waters of a nearby stream. The remaining villagers are busy with food preparations, village maintenance, or finishing up on the hooch construction. They are teenaged boys and some of the adult males; those who are not out hunting are getting ready to relieve those on night guard duty. The day in this part of the world has started.

Gathering his group of men, Bao informs them of his and the elders' collective thoughts on the possibility of them leaving the village for an extended trek, one that will take them all the way to Thailand. None from this village has ever traveled that far south. They have no maps to judge distance, but they have been told by monks and other travelers that it is a good two-to three-week trip, plagued with hardships and despair. Staying out of Cambodia is a must. The communist leader Pol Pot and his Khmer Rouge troops are insanely dangerous. They are starting to evacuate villages and towns, forcing the inhabitants into rudimentary detention camps carved out of the jungle. Many of these people are dying of starvation and the barbarically inhumane, cruel, and harsh treatment dealt to them by their captors.

"Ung and I will travel along with Nhu and the two round eyes. The elders have said we may fill our rucksacks with jerky and other foods. Their only request is that we allow this young man, Sam, to accompany us. He wishes to be a better tracker and hunter. They feel that if he is a member of this expedition, he will gain valuable knowledge that can be taught and handed down to other young men and boys in the village. Long distance trekking is not one of their strong points. Sam's coming along will not only be beneficial to him and his entire village. It will benefit our group in that they we'll have an extra man to share in, not only the hunting if necessary, but also in the job of security while traveling. If there are any objections, speak up now!"

Looking at each man for any sign of rejection, when none is forthcoming, Bao continues, "The first part of this trip will be led by Nhu. He knows Dinh's new location. After an appropriate time of visiting, we will leave. The rest of us will then follow Mr. Perry all the way to his projected destination someplace in Thailand. If we are all in compliance, we will leave on your orders, Nhu."

Nhu has never been honored or shown this much respect before. Bao giving him the leading role in the search for Dinh's new camp has heightened the admiration and respect he has for the man.

Nhu gives his first order of the day. "Men, this should be no more than a five-day trip, at the most. Supply yourselves for at least six days so we will not have to hunt for food while on the move, unless some tempting meal comes across our path. If we do hunt, I request we do so using crossbows. There is no reason to let others know of our whereabouts. You can carry the amount of ammunition you feel comfortable with. We will defend ourselves if necessary as we've always done. Let us meet at the communal hut at midday. Any questions?" No one responding, Nhu finishes with, "Fine, thank you. That's all I have for now."

CHAPTER 7

A s the sun's arc in the sky nears the midday point, Perry, sitting on the communal hut steps, is a little surprised when his fellow travelers show up, wearing native Montagnard loincloths, intricately woven arm and headbands. Even Bigelow has rolled gold tribal adornments. Perry, it seems, is the only nonnative in this group; he is dressed in the national Vietnamese every day work uniform—black pajamas.

All six of the group are armed with automatic weapons. Sam, Ung, and Lt. Bigelow also carry a native weapon, the crossbow. All have rucksacks full of food and ammunition slung on their backs. They are as ready as they ever will be. Bao has thanked the tribal leaders for their extended hospitality. They all have said their good-byes and hopes of good luck to Y-Cie and Dit Hum. It is time. Nhu gives the order of march. He and Bao will be at the front of the patrol with Nhu leading the way followed by the two Americans, Sam, then Ung. Once they have reached the first mountain range, Nhu will set a rotating schedule for the last man in line, referred to as the slack position. He is to drop off every now and then to clover leaf over their back trail looking for any unsuspecting followers. The rest of the patrol will continue for a measured distance and wait for his return. Once joined back up with the others, he moves up in the walking order. After a given distance, this process is repeated until they are sure no one has detected them and they are not being followed.

Even with the Vietnam War over, there are still plenty of communist guerrilla–type units and regular government troops all over Southeast Asia, constantly roaming the countryside, looking for runaway officials and solders affiliated with the old Southern government along with their families and die-hard followers. This is why Nhu chose to dress in his native garb. If spotted by guerilla or government troops, they might be mistaken for a Montagnard hunting party and be left alone. This far up in the high mountains, running into anybody would be unusual. There are no logging roads or man-made trials. In this pristine virgin forested jungle, you would hear or smell an adversary long before you saw him.

Perry has been going shoeless from the start. He did not wish to leave his prints in and around the new village. Now with the fading of light and the distance they have traveled, he feels it is safe to put his boots back on. His feet are not as tough as his fellow travelers. He thinks it would be rather funny if someone came along and all of a sudden, apparently appearing out of the clear blue sky they encountered American made waffle boot prints crossing their path.

After two days of taking the time and effort of doubling back over their own back trail, never hearing or seeing anything suggesting that they are being followed or that any other humans are even in these high mountains, Nhu stops this back trail checking practice. It has insured their safety but has drastically slowed them down. Picking up the pace, they will still observe and maintain noise discipline, no talking, careful in the placement of their feet and absolutely no smoking allowed. Smell and sound are your worst enemies in this environment; they both travel farther and faster than you can.

They are so far into the high mountain country that visitors are the least of their worries. Danger now lies in the terrain itself—steep climbs, almost sheer drops into dark swampy ravines. The days are sweltering hot, humid and long. Moving through the forest, this high up in the mountains is actually easier than in the lower forested areas. Up here the trees are taller and their canopy cover is almost solid, stopping any light from reaching the forest floor, thus preventing the growth of vines and other man slowing vegetation. Their progress is improving. Nhu has been sure and steady in his direction never wavering in his pursuit of Dinh's new campsite.

During a midday break on the fifth day, Perry takes the opportunity to remove his boots. He does not want to leave waffle prints leading into Dinh's new location. If someone were to come across and follow his trail, it will end here, as much of a mystery as to how the prints started in the first place. Hopefully leaving whoever comes across this trail confused and bewildered.

Late that same afternoon, Nhu stops in a sudden drop to one knee. The others follow, all dropping to a knee, not moving, weapons at the ready. Scanning the trees to his front, listening intently for any sound, turning to the others, signaling for them to stay down and not to follow, Nhu slowly regains his feet and continues up the hill, cautiously ducking behind one tree after the other. Slowly and as quietly as possible, he advances. Suddenly and without warning, leaping from behind a clump of brush not more than ten feet to his front, while letting out a loud nerve-rattling roar, a huge tiger bolts from cover. To the relief of all, it heads off in a westerly downhill direction away from the patrol's intended path. After a few moments of realizing what could or might have happened, no harm, no foul. Nhu, a little shaken, continues his uphill climb with the others following.

Early the next morning, as the group prepares for their sixth day of the trek, the early dawn stillness is shattered by the loud screeching of panicked monkeys coming from the tree canopy high above them. Something or someone has disturbed their morning. Within two to three minutes, the loud sounding has stopped. Things are slowly returning to normal with the sound of birds again filling the air with their incessant clatter. Done with packing and the eating of a light meal, the men are once again on their way.

Midmorning perched on a knife edged ridgeline, spending the early morning hours climbing to this thin row of rocks. Looking out in all directions, not seeing any sign of intruders, Dinh is sure of one thing, someone is on his mountain. Yesterday, the crying roar of a distraught tiger could be heard in the late afternoon echoing up from the hills below his camp; then at first light this morning, monkeys were sounding the alarm of impending danger from a predator, possibly the arrival of trespassers. Looking out from his vantage point, there are no indicators of any pending troubles; yet he knows, with the amount of years he has spent living in these mountains, he knows something's out there. More than likely someone.

In the late afternoon, birds once sitting in the trees surrounding Dinh's camp are now fluttering about in nervous anticipation. One minute, they are quiet and calm, the next taking flight, circling in a noisy clattering above the treetops. Whatever is out there is getting closer. Dinh gathers his arrows and crossbow and heads for the tree line just below the ridge he was on earlier in the day. He stays within the sight of the encampment keeping silent, and out of sight. He will make his stand here, if necessary.

Just as the sun starts its nightly crawl into darkness, all sounds cease. Birds have stopped flying, and there is no more constant clattering. Whatever's out there is very close now. The forested jungle is so still; there's not even a nightly breeze to rustle the leaves. This place is erie when it's this quiet. With the sun so low in the sky, shadows disappear, being replaced by shimmering smudges of gray gloom.

It's loud, it's close, and it's intentional, a single gunshot sending the birds and monkeys into a collaborated cacophony of cries, screeches and shouts. Once they have quieted down and relative calm has been restored, Dinh smiles to himself when he hears his name being called out. It's the voice of his good friend and brother-in-law, Nhu.

Standing in a small grass-covered clearing, the six weary and worn travelers watch as the lone, small, dark-silhoutted man emerges through the gray twilight. Walking out of the northern tree line with his crossbow over his shoulder, as he gets closer, they can see that he is shirtless, barefoot, and wearing black shorts. His easy gliding stride brings him to the edge of the little clearing. It is Dinh; nothing has changed for this native of the hills. The first to be recognized by Dinh is Bao, with the sun slowly dying at his back, the last vestige of its light is being reflected off his front gold teeth making them look like little Fourth of July sparklers. He approaches the clearing with his hands clasped to his chest and starts bowing to each man, pausing in a few moments of recognition in front of each. When he gets to Perry, his welcoming smile turns to utter surprise, confusion, and disbelief. He turns to Bao. "I send you off with one round eye, you return with two. This American, did he fall from the sky also?"

With a smile and a glint in his eye, Perry replies in fluent Montagnard. "Not from the sky. I have walked all this way to thank the man who saved one of our pilots. My country is in your debt."

Dinh returns Perry's smart little grin then escorts his visitors up a small rise not that far into the tree line to where his hooch is located. He tells Nhu that they can build a small fire for cooking and to gather around later in the evening. He and his friend Bao move on up into the trees away from the others. Dinh wishes to know why Nhu is not in school, why his friend Bigelow is still in this country, and the reasons behind the strange and sudden appearance of Perry and the young tribal member Sam.

Bringing Dinh up-to-date on all that he asks takes some time. He is slow to realize how fast and how much has changed since the wars end. In some ways, he understood the problems Nhu would be going through. He faced these same prejudices in the dealing with Nhu's sister, his wife, when she was having trouble with her pregnancy and was refused service in a Vietnamese hospital because she was Montagnard. He did not know of the pressure and strain the communist party and school cadre members would be imposing on minority students. Of course, he had no way of knowing that Bao stopped at a Montagnard village on his way to Ha Dong with Lt. Bigelow in tow. This, he thought was a wrong decision on Bao's part. Knowing full well there is nothing now that can be done, yet he is grateful and thankful for the quick and professional help displayed by Mr. Perry and the rest of Bao's men.

Once this information has been digested, Bao tells Dinh of their future plans to follow Perry into Laos. Crossing and descending the high mountains onto the Plain of Jars, continuing to the banks of the Mekong River. After finding boats, they will then travel south until reaching their final destination in northeastern Thailand, a small town with a Royal Thai Air Base, Nakon Phonom. He includes the details of Perry possibly helping with training, along with needed equipment that he can return with, helping in his fight against the oppression of his Montagnard brethren.

Finished with their discussion, the two head out of the trees in the direction of a small flickering fire surrounded by five men. There are no listening posts or sentries out tonight. They are all much too tired to stay awake in this cool, quiet and real dark environment. Sitting down among these men, Dinh thanks them all in their heroic fight at the Montagnard village, especially thanking Perry for volunteering his knowledge, time, and experience to a group of people he did not know.

In the early morning, all the indigenous head out for a day of hunting. With their crossbows in hand, their quivers full of arrows, they try, not only to bring down game for their consumption while visiting Dinh, there is also a need to replenish supplies for the group headed into Laos. With these men gone from the camp, Perry and Bigelow are left to their own devices. This is the first time since meeting that they have had any time alone. The two have never been together without an outside influence until now. As with most American GIs on their first encounter with another soldier, they seem to always start with the logical, typical, and probably the most asked of questions. Perry begins with the simplest. "Where you from?"

Sitting on an old log covered with tufts of rust-colored moss with his back firmly planted against a big shade tree, Lt. Bigelow takes just a flicker of a second before giving his response. "Midwest, small town in Kansas. Bison, Kansas, population less than a hundred."

Perry answers with, "Southern California, San Diego. I'm a true native son of the golden west. You married?"

Smiling at this question, taking a deep breath, Bigelow answers in all honesty. "To my high school sweetheart, but our life has been a bumpy road from the start. Married too young, neither one of us ever dated anyone else. Staying in Bison after school, we both worked for the county until the day my draft notice arrived. The very next day, we drove to the nearest large town stopping at a Navy recruiter's office. I signed up for a four year hitch until they told me with another four year burst[1] I could go through flight school becoming a pilot. Well ! It sounded good at the time. Now I was looking at eight long years of service to Uncle Sam. All this put a huge strain on our marriage and did nothing good for our personal relationship. To make a long story short, we had no kids. We were not living together all that much, so we decided to use my time overseas as a trial separation. It seems to be working. We're both finally happy just being apart. Who would of thought?"

The two men fall silent as the morning sounds taper off. After a few minutes, the ever present combination of monkey cries and bird calls start reverberating through the trees, letting all con-cerned know that whatever danger was lurking in their midst has gone. It's now safe to continue with one's daily routine.

Picking up where he left off, Bigelow getting to his feet, asks, "You married?"

---

[1] A four year reenlistment or a four year hitch added to an enlistment to receive specialized training, such as flight school.

Perry's response is quick, spoken with exuberance. "Married, hell yes, to the service. After high school, I joined the Marines, came out of MCRD² the toughest, most bad ass Marine the world has ever seen. Shipped out to Okinawa with a recon unit in sixty-two, by sixty-four, we were in the highlands of South Vietnam running patrols. I thrived on it. I just loved being out in this jungle hunting those who were hunting me, mano a mano. In sixty-six, while in Saigon, I ran into some Special Forces personnel. They gained my respect right from the get-go. Four months later, I was out of the Marines and into the Army. They shipped me back to the States for jump school, then onto Special Forces training at Fort Bragg, North Carolina. After graduation and upon receiving my green beret, it was back to the Nam, spent time at an Alpha-site running search and destroy missions along with ambush patrols. I found this rather exciting. After two tours in country, I started working with SOG,³ kind of an extension of Special Forces at the time but a lot more clandestine in nature. They basically ran and conducted unconventional warfare operations all over Vietnam, Cambodia, and Laos, as well as in Thailand. I really liked this shit. We did things no one thought possible in a war. While in Thailand, working for SOG, I tagged along with an Air America crew flying support operations out of a Royal Thai Air Base in Nakon Phonom. Through this encounter, I became involved with some CIA⁴ operatives. Now this bunch is absolutely out of their minds. I mean, they do some of the damnedest things and get away with most of it. Well, that's all I needed. I've been working indirectly with the CIA three-and-a-half years, and how crazy is this shit? I'm in the high lands of North Vietnam shooting the breeze with a downed Navy pilot after the war is over. Neither one of us knows if we will ever get the hell out of here. Ain't this some fun shit?"

---

2   Marine Corps recruit depot, San Diego California.
3   Studies and Observation Group.
4   Central Intelligence Agency.

The rest of their day is spent in quiet conversation with the telling of old war stories, even the lurid memories of bars and the women of Saigon's red-light district. Bigelow tells Perry of the horrific missile strike on his plane, of the time spent with Dinh. He speaks of traveling through the mountains with Bao, his initiation into a Montagnard clan, of going down the Red River lying in the bottom of a leaky old dugout canoe. Not leaving out their adventures in Ha Dong leading up to their introduction, seemingly so long ago, in reality not so.

Perry is actually relaxed enough to slip into a short nap. He is a little agitated with himself upon awakening for succumbing to this simple tempting pleasure. They both spend time cleaning and servicing their weapons. Perry returns Lt. Bigelow's .45, the one he got from Nhu back in Ha Dong. In the late afternoon, a sudden change in animal sounds alerts them to possible dangers. As the last of the these sounds is dying out, the two Americans take up defensive positions and wait for whatever is out there to show itself. Gradually, coming out of the tree line, there appears a lone, loinclothed native, built like a fireplug, not very tall just the same width from his shoulders to hips. Ung steps into the sunlit clearing with a small Vietnamese deer draped around his neck, its limp little legs dangling down the front of his chest. The mighty hunters have returned.

The next few days are sunny and hot, but the nights are starting to cool. Dinh and Nhu are staying in camp building an earthen oven into a small hillside as they have done in the past, making their own clay bricks and flue pipe. It is located down by a stream bed a short distance south of the encampment. Bao, Ung, and the young man, Sam, are leaving each morning to go hunting. They're returning with deer and monkey. The first day, they all went out. They brought down a good-sized pig, which has been the staple of their diet for the past week. What meat they are not cooking and eating has been cut into strips to be hung out and dried, becoming jerky for their trip.

Rice has been the only problematic supply up here in the mountains. Three times since he has been here, Dinh has gone down and raided lowland farmers supply storage huts, carting off twenty-five pound sacks of rice each time. Never returning to the same farmer twice, hopefully they will chalk the loss up to poor math.

Waking early on the coldest morning in recent memory, Lt. Bigelow struggles to his feet, trying not to wake the others. Failing in this endeavor, he bids Bao a good morning with a smile and a wave. One by one, the others achieve the state of full consciousness, rubbing, scratching, stretching themselves awake. They all can feel the brisk morning chill. Collectively, they know it's time to leave.

By midday, they've packed and have said their farewells to Dinh and Nhu, thanking the old one for his hospitalities this past week. He in turn, showing his appreciation, gives the departing group a small but nice container of fermented fish heads and entrails, Southeast Asia's favorite food sauce, Nuoc Mam. Bigelow does not withhold the fact that he is saddened having to leave his two longtime friends, telling them if they're ever in his neighborhood feel free to stop by, his door will always be open to them. Nhu gets the meaning of this statement, telling Bigelow he will explain to Dinh its funny connotation at a later date. Before leaving, Nhu gives Bao the 9mm Russian made pistol he was given back in Ha Dong; Dinh does not wish to have firearms in his camp, never has.

The rest of the day is nothing but a steady climb through thick forest. Someday there will be the sounds of woodcutters with their axes singing out with a staccato echoing throughout these hills, accompanied by the clangorous roar of chainsaws. For now, the singing sounds are provided by the birds on high, accompanied by the clattering screeches of tree dwelling monkeys. There will always be some sort of sound coming from these mountains. Which kinds depend on man.

After a four-and-a half days' arduous, high altitude, oxygen depriving journey in sweltering heat, with its energy sucking humidity followed by clammy cold nights, they can finally see off in the distance a vast undulating grass-covered broad high mountain plain. The infamous Plain of Jars, a most mysterious and forbidding place named for the hundreds of stone carved jars, some weighing tons, scattered all over its length and breadth. No one really knows their origins. They are estimated to be over two thousand years old. All are empty, and that is where the mystery lies. What was their intent? Were they for human burial, food, and water storage, maybe for the fermentation of wine? No one is sure. There is no mention in any accounts or records from man's past history, giving a clue as to their original use.

Perry believes that from this vantage point, they still have at least another two-day trek to reach this large expanse of grassy fields. They are calm in their hesitance, staying here where they can study the task before them as they prepare for another cold night without a fire. Any light on the side of this mountain would be easy to spot from down below; this little luxury is forbidden. Their whereabouts remain elusive to any foe. They are all now wearing black pajamas to stave off the effects of the night's chill. Perry gives his fellow travelers all the information he has regarding the place they are about to encounter. "From up here, you can make out some of the stone jars, but what is most prevalent and impressive is the amount of bomb craters and shrapnel pockmarks scattered all over these plains. It was alleged that the US Air Force, along with the CIA, carried out a clandestine war against the Pathet Lao and North Vietnamese troops that were attacking military installations all over Laos and Thailand. This area was under heavy saturation bombing. Every inch of it was targeted because large numbers of enemy troops were staging out of this place, running raids into the country side, attacking compounds, airfields, military establishments, and the vast network of storage facilities. The United States wanted to stop this practice. Look closely. You can see only single, one-man foot paths running through the place. This is because there are so many unexploded pieces of ordinance lying about. It is unsafe to venture off these little trails in the fear of stumbling into an UXO.[5] There are bombs and what we call bomblets still down there. These bomb-like canister devices were jettisoned from an aircraft. While descending from the sky, they would open at low altitude, releasing and scattering hundreds of small antipersonnel devices or bomblets about the size of a hand grenade in a large cover pattern for maximum killing and damage. Lots of these little killers did not detonate on impact. They wait hidden in and among the grasses, armed, ready to explode if disturbed by any-one or anything. It's usually an innocent child or an unknowing adult resulting in disfigurement, the loss of a limb, or the ultimate injury, the one leading to death."

Taking this all in, they ready for another night. Dinner is dried deer, monkey meat, and some fruit they came across earlier in the day. To help with the night cold, they each build them-selves a leaf bed, covering themselves with large fronds layered with more dried leaves, adequate for maintaining a somewhat comfortable and warm night's sleep. First light brings with it an ominous warning of what's to come, clouds—light gray clouds for now turning darker and darker as the day wears on. Within a day or two, it will be raining, heavy drenching monsoon rains. They know they must be off the Mekong River before the annual flooding begins.

After gaining the ridgeline of the mountain, they find them-selves climbing down to a soft green-grass covered saddle or dam connecting one mountain to the other, bridging the steep ravine on the south side and holding water back on the northern uphill side. A good amount of water, this little lake is being retained on the northern end by bumping into the crotch where the two mountains merge. This earthen dam has, in all respects, the look

---

[5]   Unexploded ordnance.

and feel of being man-made. They halt their advance. When something just doesn't look right, it's time to analyze your situation. Just blundering along is not an option. Bao knows when you're feeling comfortable and safe things can change quickly and being stupid out here, well, they all know stupid can get you killed.

Perry and Bao are in agreement that they should run a little recon on this site. The two start slowly moving down the south side, looking and listening for any sign of man. Bao leads off with Perry twenty to thirty yards behind, both staying in the provided concealment consisting of scrub brush, clumps of tangle vines and elephant grass. This grass is good cover because of its height, its only fault being in its razor sharp edges that shred clothing and cut into flesh. Moving close to the base of this thing, they find that it was constructed using large boulders stacked one overlapping the other angling toward the top. Water seeping under and around these rocks help keep the lower portion covered in vines; the upper slope has a large amount of earth and small stones covering the boulders. All this has a dense growth of brush and grass, covering its entire surface, indicating this structure was built many years ago.

Bao starts slowly climbing the wall of grass headed for the top. Reaching his goal, he carefully parts the grass in front of him with no startling revelations, just a large pond of brackish, murky green water with seven black ducks swimming near shore. They scurry across the water gaining speed, aiding in their taking to flight after being startled by man's intrusion. Bao, slithering to the water's edge, waits for the jungle sounds to return after being interrupted by the noisy ducks taking off, silencing the tree dwelling birds chaotic chorus of songs. Once the sounds are back to normal, Bao starts to recon the shoreline. He finds a small building or possibly a boat storage shed with an eight-foot long dock connected to it. Both look abandoned and are in a state of disrepair. The little dock has rotted beams at water level, and the hooch roof has caved in. Vines cover the walls and are now starting to grow over and through the collapsed roof. Snaking their way down to the dock, they find no boats, without any signs of humans at all. Bao signals for Perry to join him. Once united, with weapons at the ready, they advance on the hooch. Their suspicions are confirmed; no one has been here in some time. The small building and surrounding area are void of man's presence; whoever was here did not abandon this place in a hurry. It seems they packed up everything and moved out in an orderly fashion.

Perry moves to the top of the rise, signaling the others to join them down by the water's edge. Once they are all together, each man has his own idea as to the use of this place they have just stumbled upon. Only Sam has the definitive answer to this puzzling dilemma. He and some of his fellow villagers, while out hunting, have come upon this type of structure before up in the highlands of North Vietnam. The NVA, with the help of forced Montagnard labor, built dams of this same type for the use as a ready supply of food for their troops. These high mountain ponds were fish farms. This one most likely supplied some of the nourishment for the troops gathered down below staging from the Plain of Jars, feeding them while waiting to strike out on their assigned objective along with their needed supply of dried fish while on the move. Convenient and practical, it's not known how many of these were built or how long they took to construct. They had the time and plenty of manual laborer to do the job. If there were roads used for the conveyance of building material for these dams, either leading into or from these sites, they were covered over and replanted so surveillance aircraft could not detect a possible target. From the air, these sites looked like small natural lakes not deserving of an air strike.

Due to the easy crossing between the two mountains, not having to maneuver down into a ravine and face a hard climb back out, they find themselves by midmorning standing on the last ridgeline before dropping onto the Plain of Jars. The sun is high, along with the obsessive heat and muggy humidity. They are staying in the shadows of the trees on their downhill trek, about halfway down Perry calls for a halt. Being this close to their objective, he would like to take some time studying the network of little trails running across the undulating grass-covered plains down below. They are paying particular attention to the footpaths running north, northwest the direction in which they are headed. Area farmers, hunters, woodcutters, Pathet Lao, along with NVA troops, during and after the war, forged these trails, leaving a safe lane for others to follow, helping them stay clear of the dangers of UXOs. The trick is not to venture off your chosen path.

The setting sun is splashing the sky with a reddish purple glow. A light wind has picked up; this will be a night of a full moon lighting their way across this deadly field. Perry out front, Bao last man in the line, each man is paying judicious attention to the steps the man in front of him is taking. This night will be a most strenuous and exhausting trip. They don't really enjoy traveling at night, and they detest being out in the open like this. The jars that this place is named for will be their only cover if needed. Their advance is progressing methodically and slow, but steady.

This journey cuts through the heart of the so-called Golden Triangle, an area known for its drug and precious stone smuggling. Some refer to this place as Bokeo, the land of sapphires. For centuries, this is the home to some of the most unsavory characters in all Southeast Asia. They must all be diligent in keeping their senses sharp and in tuned to the night sounds around them. Instead of silence, one will hear the trumpeting of alarm when the presence of a large predator or man is detected at night. Cutting through this open plain may not be the safest route, but it is the quickest way to reach the other side of these mountains, which will bring them closer to the border of Laos and Thailand, so they can start their journey down the river on the mighty Mekong.

First light is peeking over the mountain tops, not yet reaching the men moving down below. As the light creeps its way over the earth, its brilliant crisp rays overcome the sluggish haze that once covered these fields in a low fog-like mist. The sun's morning brightness is spraying a golden hue across the grassy fields. With the introduction of light, they can now recognize that what they thought to be tree stumps or small jars in the mist shrouded moonlight are in reality, 500 pound unexploded bombs buried nose down in the earth. They are the deadly sentinels of this place. Almost out of this field and its dangers, they will soon be in the forested jungle. They must be cautious when traveling through these hills as they are also dotted with hundreds, if not thousands, of UXOs. These dangerous obstacles will not abate until they are much closer to the Thailand border.

They see the flash first, feeling the shock wave and hearing the blast milliseconds later. They are all flat on the ground trying to figure out what just happened. Making sure they stay on the little dirt path they have been following, just the one explosion then a second or two of deathly silence. Now in a rush, the birds and their tree-dwelling friends, the monkeys, begin sounding, filling the morning air with a roaring crescendo the likes of which they have never heard before. Coming out of the southwest tree line, scampering in all directions, is an extended family of seven squealing little piglets along with three adults. One of their group must have accidently triggered the explosion by stepping on or running into a UXO. Staying down until they are sure that the pigs were the cause of all the morning's excitement, they gradually gain their feet, brush themselves off, and continue with their task, keeping a wary eye on the wayward family of pigs.

Stepping out of the bright light of day, crossing over into the shadows of the near tree line, there's an unmistakable feeling of accomplishment and relief as they continue following the little path they've been on most of the night. At trail junctions during the crossing, they changed paths five times, always switching to trails pointing in their direction. The panicked little herd of pigs has disappeared into the grass, hopefully, following one of the many paths to safety. The men take their first break since the start of this adventure, eating a quick meal and drinking some of their water. Many don't realize that parts of Asia's forest and jungles are arid and parched toward the end of the dry season, after enduring many long months without rain, this being that time of year necessitates the rationing of their water supply until they come across a tributary leading to or the Mekong River itself.

This day is spent climbing a thickly covered mountainside. Approaching late afternoon, they come across a bald knife-edged ridgeline. Not wishing to silhouette themselves against the skyline, they hug the shadowed tree line, skirting the open rock-covered crest with its desolate little knob sticking out of a green expanse of trees. They have had enough of being exposed to the world for a while. Dropping into another dark mosquito-infested ravine, Perry suddenly finds himself face-to-face with a very surprised and agitated wild boar. This happened so fast none of the men can get a shot off as the pig runs through their column, disappearing into the underbrush beneath the trees. Startled and stunned, they fill the air with a short blast of relieving laughter. The rest of the climb out of the ravine is uneventful. Reaching this new crest, they hear the unmistakable sounds of rushing water, not yet visible. They know now they're not far from the Mekong.

The source of the Mekong has been debated for centuries. Most believe its true starting point is the Jifu Mountain glacier in Eastern Tibet. Traveling through China known as the Lancang Jiang, changing its name to the Mekong as it flows into the territories of other foreign countries. This being said, let us end this debate by saying that the head waters of the Lancang Jiang[6] is in Zayaqu, originating in the Guosongmucha mountains. If one were to send a post card, it would be addressed, Zayaqu, Zaping County, Yushu Tibetan Autonomous Prefecture, Qinghai Province, Tibet. Thousands of miles long, this river runs from Tibet through China, establishing the border of Laos and Burma, cutting southeast into the interior of Laos before turning due south headed for Vientiane. The Mekong again defines

---

[6]   Mekong River.

a border, this time between Laos and Thailand, passing through Cambodia, eventually dispersing into and creeping its way across the Vietnamese Delta, exiting the country by dumping its brown silt laden waters into the South China Sea.

Their first glimpse of the Mekong is from high above on a narrow ridge. The river is fast in its descent, crashing around into and over huge boulders. The murky brown waters erupt into a white mist of foam that from their vantage point looks like a slow moving fog bank. The sun's rays are being turned into a colorful, gorgeous rainbow as it is reflected off the crystal droplets of water being thrown high into the air by the violent collision of water and rock, sending a deafening roar echoing through the mountainside. From its origin the Mekong thus far has been unnavigable, its twists and turns, rapids and waterfalls, has kept boats off the river. Perry knows the town of Loung Prabang is the location of the first safe place from which to launch a boat if you are traveling south. This north central Laotian city sits on the confluence of the Nam Kan River and the Mekong.

Nearing this populated area, they hear their first sounds of civilization—the high pitch, rattling growl of woodcutter's chainsaws, cutting their way through the jungle forest. Some of these centuries-old trees will go to primitive sawmills to be turned into dimensional lumber for building permanent structures along with the making of larger timbers used in the construction of bridges and train track ties. The remaining chunks of limbs, branches, and split trunks are slowly kiln-dried into charcoal for the use in individual households for the purpose of cooking and keeping their homes warm during the cold chilly nights of their winter. Small twigs and little branch stems are gathered for kindling, with some going into compost piles. Once decayed, it will be tilled into the soil of vegetable gardens to aid in nourishment and to simply help hold in moisture.

Staying well into the covering tree line, the column of men are following the river southwest. Once the river reaches Thailand, it turns due south just a few miles above Vientiane—the capital city of Laos since 1563 when the Lao government thought they would be invaded by the Burmese. Like most large cities or large areas of population in Southeast Asia, they have gone through centuries of turmoil and armed aggression. The French, with their colonialism, guaranteed this city's status as a capital in the late nineteenth and early twentieth century. It was much later used by the CIA as an Air America base during the Vietnam war and finally taken over by the communist Pathet Lao. They had fought a lingering battle for Laos throughout the fifties and sixties. This group pushed through Laos with the support of the Chinese, Russians, and the North Vietnamese. Finally winning their goal after the withdrawal of American troops from Asia and the end of its financial support of the Royal Laotian Army.

The Pathet Lao were on their way to gaining control of Laos as early as 1953. With support of the North Vietnamese leader Ho Chi Minh, the communist Pathet Lao were in control of the northern countryside. With France's defeat at Dien Bien Phu sealing that country's fate regarding Vietnam, it also changed the political structure of Laos. With the rest of the world's help, the 1954–1955 Geneva International Conference demanded that the Southeast Asian countries affected by this agreement of peace should hold free and open elections. This upset all the parties concerned, resulting in violence among the anticommunist and communist supporters over once French-held territory. When the communist rebels started their insurrection in 1955, the US-established a military mission in Vientiane, disguised as a People's Program Evaluation Office. It was nothing more than a front for providing equipment and training of the Royal Laotian army and the indigenous anticommunist Hmong tribesmen who would carry out more than their fair share of the fighting during this war for Laotian freedom. With the communist countries supporting the Pathet Lao, this was shaping up to be one hell of a bloody fight.

While all this in fighting was going on in Laos, the North Vietnamese were quietly establishing safe havens for training troops. Along with building vast storage depots, some in caves, others in underground bunker and tunnel systems filled with ammunition, food stuffs, and medical supplies. Connecting all these sites was a transportation network running the length of Laos, Thailand, and Cambodia's mountain covered borders with many small roads and hidden trail junctions funneling supplies and combat troops to the war in South Vietnam. This network of trails and roads was later known as the Ho Chi Minh trail, becoming one of the war's most bombed targets.

The years 1964–1968 saw most all of Laos as a battleground between the American-backed Laotian government forces and the North Vietnamese supported Pathet Lao. By the end of 1968, the government structure of Laos itself ceased to exist, with the direct help from North Vietnamese forces. The Pathet Lao communists overwhelmed the Royal Lao army and found themselves in control of the entire country. While the Pathet Lao secured the countryside, the North Vietnamese concentrated their efforts in overthrowing the South Vietnamese regime in their war for unification and independence. The Americans spent large amounts of money, time, and wasted political rankling, along with the senseless loss of so many young lives, all to no avail.

The infighting among the anticommunist and the communists came to an end as the Americans disengaged from the conflict in Indochina. The Pathet Lao, following other government take overs by the communist party, stopped holding free government elections, shut down all political freedoms, purged the Laotian army and police forces, rounding up civil servants, business people, and educators, throwing them all into "reeducation" camps scattered throughout remote parts of the countryside. Many were outright killed, with thousands dying of hunger and disease due to the inhuman treatment and the deplorable conditions they were kept in. This is the one thing this group must be aware of while traveling through Laos, Pathet Lao troops. Once you've been spotted, they will try to either apprehend or detain you, maybe just flat-out kill you.

Staying on the Laotian side of the river has presented the group with an easier trek—the terrain not as steep, a few less trees, yet there is adequate cover in the way of low to medium-sized brush and shrubs along with scattered ferns nestled in among clusters of rock formations. Also available for one's protection, if needed in a hurry, are four to six-foot tall, somewhere between three and five feet in diameter termite mounds made of a dried clay mud. These tiny critters create these by applying layer after layer of mud. The construction is so densely packed that they will stop a bullet or two although many a combatant who has used these handy mounds as a shield eventually discovered that a constant concentration of automatic rifle fire will shred one of these things into a pile of dirt clods and dust.

Looking down toward the south from their mountainside vantage point during the day, they can see the columns of smoke lofting in the distance, indicating the encroachment of civilization. In the night, it's the lingering orange glow from the fires of slash and burn agriculturalists, dirt poor farmers who have clear cut the timber on their land and are now burning off any evidence of life ever existing on that patch of earth. Once the fires are out, a team of buffalo will be brought in to plow level and furrow for the eventual planting of crops. The smaller flickering dots of light scattered throughout the hills below them are cooking fires of those involved in cutting down the trees.

Getting ready to move off the ridgeline where they spent the previous night, Ung is the first to sense danger jacks a round into the chamber of his AK. The others, startled by this loud metallic disturbance to the quiet morning, turn their attention in Ung's direction. Seeing him frantically signaling and pointing to a small clearing not more than fifty yards east of their position, they are all straining to find the cause of Ung's excited behavior. From their cover, they watch in silence as two elderly women emerge from a stand of trees. Both are dressed in black pajama bottoms with filthy dirt-stained white cotton shirts. They're wearing woven baskets with arm straps, a ridged open-topped backpack.

They are picking up little sticks, twigs, while breaking branches into small pieces before stuffing them into their basket/packs. These old women are kindling gatherers—elders and children of a village are delegated the task of collecting kindling needed to help start coal fed fires. There must be a village close by or a woodcutter's camp. The stand of trees they came out of surrounds this pie-shaped clearing covered with brown waist-high grass. The women have stepped out of the morning shadows into this sunlit clearing, just standing and talking while taking in the warming morning rays of heated sunlight, gaining a little comfort after a chilly night. They are joined by the cackling, high-pitched sound of three snotty nosed kids rambunctiously scrambling out of the tree line into the clearing, their tiny black haired heads barely showing above the grass. If this bunch of people continues through the clearing and move into the woods at the base of the hill in front of them, the women and children will be on a collision course for trouble. Bao grabs his crossbow, getting ready for a silent kill. Ung works quickly, attaching the cross arm to the bow he has been carrying. Lt. Bigelow, not sure what is expected of him, readies his crossbow for action. Almost automatically, the five men form into a small L-shaped ambush position just inside the shadows of the tree line. The three men with crossbows make up the long side of the *L* while Sam and Perry, with his silenced weapon, anchors the short leg. They're all hoping things will turn out for the good of all those concerned.

Coming within a few feet of Ung's position, one of the old ladies stops, reaches down, and picks a small handful of mushrooms. Turning to her companion, smiling only to have her friend frantically wave off her intentions, telling her in their native tongue, a Laotian northern mountain dialect, that the mushrooms she has gathered are not a good variety, they're death caps, deadly poisonous if eaten. The old woman drops the mushrooms, almost in Ung's face. Rejoining her friend and the young children, they retrace their steps back through the clearing, never looking back as they disappear into the shadows of the trees from whence they came.

As the normal sounds return to the morning, Perry stays in his concealed position, keeping guard for any more visitors as the rest of the group starts stowing away their gear. Perry finally joins Bao and the others to finish his packing and start helping in the sterilization of their overnight site. They never let it be known, if possible, as to being where they should not be, a practice Bao and Perry swear by. When done, they head off through the woods, a little more alert to sounds and movement than they have been the past few days. They have decided to head directly for the river, with all the woodcutters and their support people the group's chances of running into civilian or possibly Pathet Lao troops is mounting.

With the colder nights and overcast days, the monsoon rains are barking at their heels. They must make a concerted effort to get on the Mekong and head south.

Keeping a steady, sometimes grueling, pace through the forested jungle, they are coming across more and more evidence of civilization. Areas that are clear cut, no pattern in their destructive behavior, an area of two-foot tall, three to four-foot diameter stumps, maybe a dozen to eighteen in each spot. Could be a certain kind or type of tree cut down for its color or hardness. Who knows? Just a quarter acre bald spot in the middle of the forest with wagon trails lead into and out of the clearings, covered with plenty of buffalo tracks and dung littering the ground, attesting to the fact that these people are well organized and quick in their work. No campsite or evidence of a cooking fire anywhere, they came in, did their wood cutting, loaded the logs, and departed. By midday, they have come across three such locations, each time they stay in the cover of the jungle, not wishing to be discovered. They are still on track, headed for the river but dodging these little clusters of woodcutters is taking time and expending their energy, continually pushing them off course.

They are close to the river now, so close they can hear, smell, and almost feel the water. The sounds of the river's ever churning, fast moving water is now starting to echo through the trees. The smell of dank, soggy, water logged grasses, and clammy plant matter is wafting through the cool shadowed darkness of the forest. The river's constant rambling flow is generating a cool lofty mist of dampness, splashing water into the humid hot air pushed into the forest as a low rising mist. All day they have heard muffled, reverberating rifle shots coming out of the higher mountains. These are suspected to be the reports from hunters, no automatic bursts, just single-spaced shots chasing down any available target worthy of a meal. There must be quite a few hunters out with all these people in need of feeding come the end of a long day's work. Up until now, they have been rather fortunate, staying out of every one's way. They know this cannot last. At some point, they undoubtedly will stumble across and startle some unsuspecting woodcutter or other innocent civilian. Hopefully, it will not be a group of Pathet Lao.

Now situated in the cover of a rather large, overgrown bramble of berry bushes full of big nasty thorns and bunches of inedible fruit. The men are draped between two large trees that have an enormous root system that seems to be clinging to a rock-faced ledge about eight feet high with its life supporting roots, reaching out, coiling around, and burying themselves deep into the rocks cracks and crevasses. Some of these fingerlike appendages are as big around as a man's arm. Covered in a spongy moss unlike the hard, rough, woody bark covering of normal tree roots whose outer layer is dry to the touch. It's from this prickly perch that they get their first real close-up view of the Mekong River. This could possibly be their watery road to safety. It's late afternoon; the hillside they are on is approximately one hundred yards from the river's edge. There is no easy or clear approach to the riverbank. They can only watch as the water ends its run through rock encrusted canyons and steep gorges. The upper section of the river has been a long valley of raging rapids and unnavigable white water, but at this particular location, the waters tumble off the rocks, crashing headlong into a large pool of emerald green cold water before calmly forging its way farther south.

Because of all the detouring they've had to do, trying to avoid woodcutters and hunters, they find themselves farther north than they intended when reaching the river. The steep banks are covered in a tangle of jungle vines, creeping to the edge and beyond making it impossible to enter the water for miles around. Add in the fact that they don't yet have any transportation suitable for a water voyage. They must travel another one or two days before the terrain begins its metamorphosis from a wild jungle environment into small rolling hills and open grasslands; some of which have been turned into farm plots and rice paddies with clusters of peasant homes nestled among the stands of palms. They will be going from dodging woodcutters and hunters to avoiding farmers and villagers.

Facing their last night in the comfort of the thick jungle that they are familiar with and very much used to, the five weary travelers decide their best bet is to simply rely on plain old fashioned luck while traversing in the open. Wearing black pajama peas-ant clothing along with straw-woven conical hats makes them appear to be just another hunting party or group of men headed for some work in the fields. The only thing out of place with this deception is the height of the two Americans. Bao has suggested they stoop over when being viewed from afar. If anyone's unfortunate enough to encounter them up close, no bending over or stooping is going to help in their disguise. If discovered, they will most likely have to shoot their way out of any close encounters.

With the sunrise comes the realization that they are standing on the fringe of a new frontier. They have run out of forest, jungle vines, and the dark shadows of concealment. They stand looking out over a changing landscape flowing to the far horizon. Mountains that have been broken down by time and weather into rolling hills gradually drop into a flat grassland plain dotted with clumps of Areca palms. Some are surrounded by small swampy marshlands that are producing tall clumps of bulrush swarming with black clouds of buzzing mosquitoes and a steady chorus of croaking frogs. The lay of the land is slipping into the Mekong River. There's a thicket of trees intermingled among a variety of palms. All of which are being overgrown by prickly covered sweetbriar brambles, reaching out forming a canopy that is overhanging the water, making it hard to find where the land ends and the water begins.

The trek is much easier on this flat open terrain. Their progress has improved, even though they are keeping close to the tree line that's following the riverbank. There is a well-traveled dirt road just to their north. It's a humid, muggy day, leaving a sticky coating of stinking sweat clinging to their bodies. The sun is out, but the clouds obscure its full brightness. They are not in darkness, but they feel comfortable in the dim, shadowy haze provided by the overcast, a true sign that the rains will soon be on them.

Ung, out front on point, signals for all to get undercover. They do, staying low among the trees. They watch as five buffalo-pulled wagons head northeast up the dirt road. There are women and children in the carts along with woodcutting equipment. The male members of the group are walking beside their carts, leading the animals with a rope, running through a ring in the buffalo's nose, giving the animal a little added encouragement from a bamboo switch he carries. No weapons are seen; they make no sound other than the creaky clanking clatter of wooden carts and the heavy clomping and slow steady plodding of water buffalo hooves in a rhythmic beat that reverberates with an echoing across the grass-covered hills. Once past, the silence envelops them for the remainder of the night.

The early morning light is at play. Mother Nature is hurling bolts of bright iridescent sunlight, surging through the forest of trees, flickering in a brilliant and dazzling display only lasting for a short time before clouds blot out the sun's light. Shadows are now enveloping the world around them. Bao, last man on guard and the only one of the five awake, is shockingly startled and surprised by a loud, shrill, desperate cry closely followed by another. This time, it's a high pitched shrill, gobbling, followed by a resounding blast, not a ringing whoosh like that of a rifle shot, a booming blast from a shotgun accompanied by more squawking and the unmistakable sound of gobbling. Someone real close is hunting Laotian turkeys. From all the commotion and clatter, it sounds like whoever is doing the hunting has scared up a whole rafter of birds.

The four men who were asleep are now in a confused state of alertness, not yet fully awake.

Just the one shot, but they hear two, maybe three people talking and not in the lowest of tones. One individual seems to be shouting at the others to pursue the now frantically fleeing birds that are scattering across the grass-covered hills. Bao can now clearly see the hunters as they chase after birds they've just flushed out of hiding. All are dressed in the universal black pajamas, straw hats, wearing sandals. Only one has a weapon, a breech loading, single round, long-barreled shotgun. They are about twenty to twenty-five yards northeast of Bao's position. He can see that two of the men are trying to outflank the runaway birds. They're in their late teens or early twenties. The third one is an old man, skinny as a rail sporting a Ho Chi Minh mustache and a long and scraggly goatee. He just stands there, looking out over the river in the direction of the group's overnight bivouac site as if he knows something's not right. Breaking open the old shotgun, he removes the spent shell casing, dropping it into his carry bag, reloads the weapon, snapping the breech closed with a distinctive clicking sound. Walking over and picking up his kill, the old man starts after his two companions, stops, and turns back, looking in Bao's direction one more time. Just standing there, knowing something or somebody is watching him. Some people just have that sixth sense.

On his trip across the short open field, the old man once again stops, looking in the direction of the tree line in which five men are hidden, no sound, no movement. Could have been the sun's glittering display of light or the wobble of a shadow emulating an animal's movement? When the old hunter reaches the crest of the hill, his companions have disappeared over the rise. He again stops, looking back toward the river, not sure what it is but his instincts have him concerned. As he slowly disappears over the grass-covered knoll, Bao turns back to his fellow travelers.

"Gentlemen, we have been compromised. That old man has heard, seen, or smelled something that is not to his liking. Let's get the hell out of here." Bao didn't think he was spotted, but he's always trusted his instincts. This is not the time or place to question them. Moving south through the trees as fast and as quietly as possible, Bao knows the old hunter is more than just a little interested in their overnight site. He would like to put some distance between themselves and that location without making any stupid or wrong moves. Being stupid in these circumstances could get one killed real quick; they must be diligent in their actions. As the morning slowly evolves, some of the dark clouds are pushed to the north by an onshore breeze, leaving them with a bright sunny afternoon. They can see more and more foot traffic on the little dirt road about fifty to sixty yards to their north just above them. Peasant field workers, mostly older men and teenaged boys, a few women, not many, animal owners herding their water buffalo. They're taking them to their daily assignment of plowing through the muddy and wet rice paddies. There are no children to be seen, very unusual in this part of the world. Children will normally follow a parent or sibling into the fields. If not old enough to do any work, they will play nearby. The village these people live in must have a school. Most of the river traffic they have observed up until now has been single and two-man paddle-powered dugouts loaded to the gunwale with rice, fruits, and vegetables headed for some down river market. Not many boats are challenging the currents by going north on these waters.

They have made good progress up until now. It's midday, and they are facing their first big challenge. They've come upon a small village built along the water's edge, with boat access to the river. There is a small inlet with a tiny beach off to one side. There are two wooden docks, each reaching about twelve to fourteen feet out into the water. One pier has two single man dugouts tied to it; the other is unoccupied. There are several women on the shore doing laundry with some young children playing along the river's bank. Bao knows they might have to stay hidden until the darkness of night.

Not long after arriving, they hear the sound of truck engines, followed shortly by three military trucks coming up from the south. They are full of armed troops. From their hiding spot, they count twenty-five to thirty people, some wearing black pajamas; about a dozen have on full military fatigues, no insignias, wearing boots. All are armed with AK-47s. They have two crew served weapons, medium-light machine guns. Four of the uniformed men, probably members of the gun crew, have bandoleers of cartridges draped over their shoulders and across their chest. Not the smartest thing to do in a potential battle situation, if one takes a round to the chest or any other area that has live rounds exposed, that person will go up in a ball of exploding flame and shrapnel like a Roman candle spewing fragments of metal causing mayhem, injury, and possible death to any one close to him. Not all the men get off the trucks. Those that do walk the short distance to the dock area where they seem to be taking a break. Some sitting by themselves, others in groups, most are smoking cigarettes. Civilians and a group of peasants are gathering at the first truck. Bao is not surprised to see the old skinny turkey hunter leading this group. Voices are heard, but conversation at this distance is unintelligible. The surprises don't stop. Stepping out of the passenger side of one of the vehicles, dressed in his full North Vietnamese military uniform, is Major Trong. Bao grabs Perry by the arm, pulling him in close so he can whisper into his ear. "That officer is our old friend Major Trong from Ha Dong, the one we drove off back at the Montagnard village."

Perry takes his spotting scope out of his backpack, handing it to Bao, adjusting its focus, pointing it at the two men of the most interest—Major Trong and the old hunter. The old man is animated in his conversation, frantically pointing up river in the direction of his turkey hunt and the area of the group's overnight bivouac. Perry whispers to Bao, "This isn't a social gathering. Trong being here makes me believe we are the target of a coordinated, multi-country hunt. The major would not be here if he didn't think we were in the neighborhood. Bao, we've got to get across the river and back into the jungle. We will be sitting ducks when they start their search. They will pick up our trail and follow it right back here. It shouldn't take them any more than one and a half to two hours. That gives us very little time. They'll be back here before nightfall."

Up from the south, adding to their dilemma, is the arrival of motorized flat bottom watercraft capable of discharging troops to a shore via a large drop down ramp. These boats are not US Navy surplus. They're left over from the French Colonial Navy. These diesel-powered vessels are from the 1940s. As they tie up to the two little docks, troops are formed into columns and board the landing craft, eight men per boat. All these men are uniformed, most likely, Major Trong's NVA regulars. The remaining troops, believed to be Pathet Lao, are loaded onto the first truck. As they ready for departure, the old turkey hunter, along with ten or twelve of his friends, not all carrying firearms, some bringing along wooden clubs and long-handled grub hoes (big wide-bladed tools for fieldwork), are climbing aboard the second truck. Little bastards are looking for a fight. The predicament in which they find themselves keeps Bao's group from obliging this gang of peasants. The five find they are outnumbered, outgunned with their backs to the river. All they can do is wait in hiding for an opportunity to flee or fight.

Major Trong jumps into the lead truck, signaling the start of their adventure. As the two trucks move north up the dirt road, the two-boat attack force unties and shoves off, heading up river. After their departure, the remaining villagers go about their daily routine. The remaining truck sits parked off to one side of the road with two remaining troops, both armed with AKs. They're starting to make themselves comfortable by sitting on the ground with their backs to the truck tires while leaning their weapons against the truck frame. Both light cigarettes and start a conversation. These are not disciplined Northern troops; they are Pathet Lao rebels, lacking in security.

Speaking in a hushed whisper, Perry tells his companions, "They must have known the only place we could find refuge would be the closest location to an American outpost in Southeast Asia, that being Nakon Phonom in northeastern Thailand. But how in the hell did they get this close to us this soon? That skinny little turkey shooter didn't go over the hill and get on a pay phone and ask Trong to meet him at this village. No, Trong had to have been in the area already. With those two boats showing up right after the three trucks full of troops, now that's a well-planned and well-coordinated piece of military planning. Fuck, we had a good two to three days start on them, and he still caught up to us. I still think our best bet is fording the river, eluding our pursuers in the jungles of Thailand. Don't matter if it's another country, Trong won't stop at a border. Hell, he's traveled across Laos wearing his North Vietnamese uniform, traveling with his own armed troops and is working with Pathet Lao rebels. The little shit has no shame."

As Bao translates a shortened version of this message to Ung and Sam, Bigelow moves over close to Perry. "I haven't interfered with any of the decisions you people have made, but this one is wrong. Have you seen these people swim?" He sweeps his arm in the direction of the three men in hushed conversation. "I have. Bao swims like a frog with a big rock tied to his ass. This section of the river is at least 175 yards wide. The water's cold, deep, and swift, and we're carrying a lot of weight. I don't think stripped naked, we could all make the crossing. The current will bring us floating into the open in front of the village and those two Pathet Lao. We have the same problem if we tried to reach one of the dugouts tied to the dock. It's all in the open. We will have to expose ourselves for quite a distance. Once spotted, we would have to shoot this place to pieces. Now I'm just a jet jockey, but my thoughts run along the lines of a truck ride. If we're going to be reckless, somewhat stupid and brave, why not do it in style? Take out those two guards, grab the truck, turn it around, and get the hell out of Dodge, heading south till we find something better or a narrower place to cross. I'd rather take my chances on the road over jumping into the water here."

Perry is a little surprised by this idea; it never occurred to him. This is definitely a small jolt to his ego. The pilot has voiced a fascinating and practical idea. "Very good, Lieutenant. Your idea just might work. Let me run it by Bao." Interrupting their discussion, speaking in yard, Perry quizzes his three indigenous companions about Bigelow's proposal of commandeering the truck. When he's finished, there's a noticeable look of relief and joy on their faces. It seems they would rather fight than swim the river.

Quick plans are made. Bao and Ung will travel north back up the tree line and find a spot where they cannot be seen from the village, then move up to the dirt road turning south headed back into the village. Perry, Lt. Bigelow, and Sam will remain hidden. All the weapons and equipment are with these three. Bao and Ung are carrying only crossbows, bow strings stretched tight, arrows in place, ready for the kill. Perry is positioning himself for a silenced shot. Just as Bao and Ung reach the truck's tailgate, Perry plans to take out the young man, leaning against the front tire, aiming for his chest, not the head. He could mess and puncture the tire, or the round could go through the skull and do the same thing. To prevent this from happening, he'll go for the chest, which is almost dead center on the truck's steel rim. Once that shot is made, Bao and Ung will bring their bows off their shoulders and dispatch the other guard sitting up against the rear wheel. This man is partially obscured by underbrush, hidden from Perry's sight. They will have one chance to make this all happen. The element of surprise is on their side. The women and children on the little beach will be no problem. Once they break cover, headed for the truck, they will have to keep their eye on the five or six men gathered at the dock. Up until now, the two Pathet Lao are the only ones with exposed weapons; hopefully, there'll be no others introduced once the action starts. They truly don't want this developing into an all-out, full-fledged firefight. Seeing two men dressed in peasant clothing, carrying cross-bows over their shoulders, is a common sight for the two young men stationed at the truck. As Bao and Ung reach the rear tail-gate of the truck, the Pathet Lao, sitting with is back to the front tire, is lifted straight up off the ground. He is still in the seated position, his arms jerking up in spastic contortions, his legs locked rigidly at the knees, staying stretched straight out in front of him. The only sound he makes is a low muttered intake of air, nothing more. His chest is now a red soaked mass of blood and lung with little bubbles of whitish red material gushing into his lap and covering his thighs. He is dead before his ass comes back down, slapping the earth with a hollow squashing sound, like that of a juicy ripe melon that has been dropped on the ground. The other Pathet Lao, for just a brief moment of time, gawks in disbelief at the prompt and sudden death of his friend. No mat-ter, without any reaction, he is choked out of life with an arrow through the neck, one in the left quadrant of his upper chest near the heart, and a third under his right arm pit just below the fourth rib. He too dies, moments after being knocked into the dirt by the impacting force of the arrow's velocity. Before the dust has settled, Bao and Ung have grabbed the two weapons leaned against the truck frame and are in the process of climbing over the tailgate as Sam joins them, slinging equipment, weap-ons and himself into the back of the truck. Perry and Bigelow have reached the running board on the driver's side of the vehicle. Perry moves across the seat into the passenger's position, while Bigelow moves into the driver's seat behind the steering wheel. He is now looking for the power on switch and start button to get this thing moving. There are no keys or a place to insert one, just some buttons and a few switches. Finding a switch labeled *démarreur* ,[7] flicking the pointer in that direction, looking farther on the dash, he finds a button with a label that reads *début* ,[8] pushing on this starts the grumbled whining of the diesel engine. As it begins to come to life, the women and children, who were at the little beach, are all in a quiet state of shock at the activity they have just witnessed. The six men gathered at the docks fled in many directions as soon as they saw Bao and Ung taking shots with their crossbows, killing the Pathet Lao. They never noticed as the first man's chest erupted in a shower of lung fragments and fleshy tissue; they only noticed him after he was lying on his side in a pool of blood soaked dirt. Lt. Bigelow guns the engine, puts the vehicle in first gear, and heads for a wide space in which to turn the truck around. Reaching a spot large enough for this maneuver, he throws the gear shift into reverse. With the grinding and groaning of misaligned cogs, finally with some effort, it clunks into gear. He backs up to one of the hooches. With smoke bellowing from the exhaust, he slams the transmission into first gear, spinning the steering wheel in a herculean effort, turns the truck in a southerly direction. Mashing the gas pedal to the floor, with a huge puff of grayish black smoke pouring out the exhaust, they head away from the village on a very rough, unpaved road south.

Not a road in the true sense, it's basically a single cart and pedestrian trail that is uneven, rutted, and narrow. They must stay below twelve miles per hour just to stay seated. Any faster and they risk the chance of being thrown from the vehicle or simply losing control and crashing. Managing only three to four miles before forcing their first cart off the trail, they anger the old farmer walking beside his buffalo-drawn cart filled with bamboo stalks, enraging the old man to the point of him giving a one fingered salute to Lt. Bigelow. One wonders what went through his mind as he saw this crazed round eye drive past, almost upsetting

---

[7] Power
[8] Start

his cart and running down his prized water buffalo. His little one finger salute of frustration has Bigelow and Perry laughing. In the truck bed, the three indigenous are hanging on for their lives, trying to keep themselves and the equipment onboard.

Approaching a group of black clad individuals, Perry can see that more than one has a weapon. As they draw near, now moving at about three to four miles an hour, Perry leans out his window with Bigelow's AK-47. As the men on foot start to move aside for the traffic, weapons still slung over their shoulders, not expecting their ultimate fate, passing within five feet, two of the three soon-to-be dead men have that dumb "caught in the headlight" look as Perry cuts lose on full automatic, expending a twenty-round magazine in a matter of seconds. All three of the men go down; four others on the driver side of the truck hear the eruption of gunfire but do not as yet understand its implications or consequences. Bao and Ung open fire when the truck passes them. Both firing their AKs, they leave seven dead men next to the road. This is going to put the fear of God into their pursuers or put vengeance in their hearts and souls.

Besides the grumbling vibrations being funneled out of the diesel's exhaust pipe, they have now added a crescendo of rifle fire, warning any one ahead that chaos and danger is coming their way. Picking up speed, they barrel through a changing landscape. The cleared land and little plots of row crops have been given back to the forest and jungle. Once again, the riverbank is nonexistent; overgrown vines and scrub brush clogs the water's edge. Driving on, they find the northern flow of carts and pedestrians has subsided. Could this be due to their firing up the trail with automatic fire or in part due to the time of day? It's almost dark. Thick black rain-laden clouds have been advancing on the sun, blocking its light for the better part of the late afternoon. They feel the coolness in the air; they sense the change that will shortly bring the rain. Staying steady and true to their course, Perry, shouting to be heard over the truck's loud roar, tells Lt. Bigelow they must find a place to abandon their ride and evade on foot into the jungle.

Coming over a small rise, they are confronted by two large logging wagons, both being drawn by double teams of water buffalo. These carts are larger than most. They have four wooden spoke wheels instead of two. Each wagon is loaded with cut and split wood, all their logging tools, along with family members, wives, and children. A cow is tied to the back of the first cart with two big domesticated pigs tied behind the other. These are logging camps on the move. Bigelow quickly turns, running the vehicle into an opening between two large trees, stopping short of hitting one head on. With the engine idling, the truck is spewing black bellowing smoke out the back. They have laid down an effective smoke screen. The two wagons pass without any contact; these people must consider this a normal occurrence. Backing onto the trail ready to continue their trip south, Bao leans over the railing, sticking his head into the passenger side window, and yells to Perry. "We need to ditch this truck. It would be best if we could find a spot to run this thing into the river. I would like them not to have any access to it or ever be able to use it again."

Lightning strikes with explosive flashes of dazzling luminosity, thunder louder than their clattering old diesel truck. These flashes and rumbles bring with them rain. Big drops of water are splattering across the dirty, dusty wind shield obscuring their view with streaks of reddish brown mud. Soon the truck is washed clean by the violent torrential rains of the late afternoon monsoon. It's the start of the rainy season.

Rivulets of muddy water are starting to flow off the hillsides, cutting into the trail as it crosses, washing out sections of its surface, causing large ruts to suddenly appear, making travel rather bumpy and dangerous. Their top speed is now less than three miles per hour. They are actively searching a spot to run the truck into the river, and they find such a place just around the next bend. The little road turns sharply to the east through the forest to their left. The brush-covered riverbank has dropped off, leaving a fifteen to twenty-five foot overhang where part of the mountainside has detached, sliding into the river, leaving a vine covered cliff face. Stopping the truck, Perry yells for the three in the back to off load their equipment, as he grabs his and Lt. Bigelow's weapons and gear. Telling Bigelow to be careful, Perry joins the others in the damp darkness of the tree line. The pilot moves the truck into position, backing up against a big tree, putting the truck in first gear, cranking the steering wheel so that the front tires are pointed toward the river; letting the clutch out, he slides off the seat, stepping out onto the running board. Hanging onto the open driver's door, he jumps off as the truck slowly makes its way over the edge, falling down the cliff, plunging into the water. Not disappearing as one might think, as it rolls down the cliff, it entangles itself in the underbrush and vines that are snagging the undercarriage, almost stopping its momentum. The sheer weight of the vehicle drags a large amount of vegetation off the cliff face taking it into the river with it. Once the water reaches the still running hot motor, a massive column of steam envelopes the cab, giving the truck a ghostly appearance as it floats upright into the main channel of the river surrounded by a huge clump of vegetation. It takes a few minutes for it to fully disappear from sight, leaving a swirling tangle of vines in its wake. Lt. Bigelow, covered in mud, makes his way to the tree line, joining his friends. "Well, that was an exciting ride while it lasted. Let's get back into the woods. Is everyone okay with staying here for the night? Let's find a good RON."[9] They form a line of march and head into the dark-forested jungle looking for that perfect night refuge, not only from Major Trong and his men, but also from the ravages of the ever increasing rain. With help from lightning flashes, they find a stand of palms from which they start cutting fronds to be used in the construction of quick waterproof one-man shelters. They finish as the rains increase, turning everything into a muddy and soggy mess.

---

[9] "Remain overnight" a term used by Special Forces and Marin Recon teams to designate overnight sites.

The night is long, cold, muddy, and wet. One cannot distinguish between night and day with dark rain-laden monsoon clouds filling the sky with a swirling mass of energy, throwing out jagged bolts of lightning with the sound of canon fire blasting across the jungle, echoing through the trees.

They look out from under their frond-fringed shelters. With little sleep and not much to eat, they spend the early part of the day just listening to the rhythmic beat of the rain pelting their cover. Much of the day is spent making adjustments and repairs needed to keep the water out of their shelters. Bigelow has dug a shallow trench around his shelter to help drain the water away from the piece of earth he is occupying, a trick he learned long ago at the mountain home he shared with Dinh. The others struggle with muddy waters streaming through their shelters. Eventually, they slip out to quickly trench around theirs, trying to avoid being miserable the rest of the day.

For two days, the rain is relentless. The trees around them have lost a lot of leaves and branches. Termite mounds are being washed away, broken down to lumps of mud, pulverized by the constant bombardment of water, slowly disappearing in a flood of red tinted mud mixing with the tree rubble. It's all running down the hill, cascading over the cliffs into the river. During the third night, the rains subside enough for them to finally get some needed sleep. They're not comfortable with no one awake, but sheer exhaustion overtakes their concern for security and safety. Besides, this rain must have slowed their pursuers. They haven't heard or seen a single soul for the past two days. The road has been made impassable for motor vehicles; even buffalo drawn carts are going to have a hard time managing this muddy washed out trail.

The early morning sounds have stopped; the rain has quit its tattooing of the trees. No birds or monkeys sounding. Crickets and lizards have vanished; there's just an uneasy eerie silence hanging through the mist-covered forest. It's not the end, maybe just a short break in the storm as the sun tries to make a half-assed attempt of appearing in the dark gray sky. As Bigelow and Perry get together with Bao to discuss plans for moving, they hear a sound none have heard in a long time; the air popping, whooshing noise made by the rotor blades of a helicopter. It's coming out of the north, about fifty feet off the treetops scouting the river trail. Its whoop, whoop, whooping sound echoing down the river as it gets closer. They hunker down in their shelters scanning the skies for a quick look. When it reaches their location, they see an all-black HU-1B[10] aircraft with crew-served door guns. On the nose, under the front wind screen, there is a red painted flag with a big gold colored star in the center, the new symbol of the now unified Vietnam. It's another piece of American machinery left over from the war. They realize they are being sought by an extensive array of equipment and manpower from the air, on the land, and in the water. This is getting to be some serous shit; they really want this American pilot and his friends. They would definitely like to stop his fleeing their country and seem to be sparing no expense in their efforts. The chopper moves south, barking out as its rotor blades slice through the still, cold morning air, fading into the distance.

They now have some hard choices to make. With all these resources dedicated to finding them, they must consider a number of different options: do they continue following the river looking for a safe crossing? They could return north, doubling back over territory they have already traveled. Knowing that Major Trong and his people have been there, taking the chance that they have finished their search and moved on. Is it wise to reverse course? They wait until dark then head off in a southeasterly direction, staying well away from the river. The past two days of rain have aided in their escape by washing out any and all traces of wheel tracks or foot prints they might have left on the now muddy and

---

10   Manufactured in the USA by Bell Helicopter Textron, called a Utility Helicopter (HU) nicknamed "Huey" by the military because it was easier to say than HU

impassable river trail. Under the cover of darkness and heavy rain, the five men trudge off looking for a crossing. Walking these forests at night is challenging in this heavy rain; it's a treacherous journey. Soggy, dead foliage entangling each step, ankle deep mud leaves one's legs heavy with pain. They fall and stumble, silently complain and move on. There is no alternative; they must get to the other side of the Mekong to reach Nakon Phonom.

Their trek southeast has landed them in a thick canopy covered jungle, making it almost impossible to be seen from the air. They've moved far enough from the river that their only risk now is land troops. With all the rain, there's not much chance of being followed or tracked. Food and clean palatable water is their immediate problem. They have gone through their supplies; each man has but a small amount of cooked rice, no meat or greens. Late in the morning of the third day, Ung has come across an easy and quick treat, bamboo larva. After starting a small smokeless fire in a shallow pit, the men rummage through a stand of six-inch diameter bamboo. Splitting open damaged stalks, recognized by a whitish tan appearance, along with numerous small holes with white powdery sawdust looking residue extruding through the small openings made by the worm like larva. They gather hands full of these little one to two-and-a-half inch yellowish orange creatures, running thin slivers of bamboo through their wiggling bodies before placing them over the fire. When done, they have a quick and tasty, rich in protein, high energy meal.

Late afternoon under darkening skies, Bao spots movement exposed by a wavering flicker of dying sunlight. The target of opportunity is a twenty-two-inch long blue tree lizard clinging to the trunk of a towering eucalyptus tree. It takes three tries from Bao's crossbow to bring this fat lizard down. Once on the ground, he is quickly dispatched, gutted, tied to a stick, and roasted over a small fire. This, along with their remaining rice, makes for another meal. The returning heavy rains have them again going to ground, they chop down small saplings for the construction of a single lean-to type shelter. Waterproofed by interwoven palm fronds as shingles, it was quick to construct and works well. They now have an opportunity to discuss their future plans. Perry is insistent they cross over into Thailand and try making it to Nakon Phonom where he is sure they will find a small contingency of American intelligence and special operations people at the Royal Thai Air Base. The air base is located just off the main road outside the eastern section of town; it has been active since the early fifties. It was used for all sorts of clandestine operations throughout the Vietnam and the American-backed French war. After the French defeat and surrender, the Americans moved in escalating the scope of the base's operations. During the Vietnam War, Nakon Phonom was attacked by the North Vietnamese more than a half a dozen times. It was a real thorn in their sides with Air America[11] and the US Air Force using the runway for the staging of missions into North Vietnam, Laos, and Cambodia. Each time, they were repelled with a high cost in casualties. On two occasions, US forces pursued their attackers back across the river into Laos, stopping short of entering the village of Thakhek, chasing the northerners into the jungle-covered hills.

Two days of incessant rains, the ground they are on is a soggy quagmire. If this keeps up, they won't have to walk back to the river, they'll slide down to it along with the rest of the forest. Trees, along with huge sections of the hillsides, are being washed away. The flood of mud is so deep in places, trees are not tumbling down the hill; they're sliding down in the upright position, bumping into other trees as they go by. It's a strange sight. They have chosen their spot with care, away from large trees on a small rise covered in a short yellow-tipped green grass. The ground they're on is soggy with water, but the grasses seem to be holding the soil, resisting the temptation to break away and slough off. For now, they just try and weather the storm as best they can. They are looking at another hungry, wet, and miserable day in the exotic Far East.

---

[11] CIA-run air operation for supply and personnel insertions, among other things.

CHAPTER 8

ACROSS THE MEKONG River, in northeast Thailand, there's a small nondescript, unpainted clapboard-sided building with one door and no windows. It's about twelve by fifteen feet with a rusty corrugated tin-covered gable roof, situated on the southwest edge of a Royal Thai Air Base runway located in Nako Phonomm. It looks like some kind of equipment storage shed; that's the intent. There's an old dilapidated black Citroen motor car parked nearby. Inside this claustrophobic box are three men; two dressed in civilian clothing, the other in camouflaged tiger-striped jungle fatigues. They are working with Thai security forces. They're the last vestiges of American forces in Southeast Asia. All are Special Forces members of MAC-SOG.[1] One is a major, the other holds the rank of captain, and the third man is an old hand at this clandestine undercover type operation. He's the one in tiger stripes, Master Sergeant Tony Gratton, a Special Forces detachment leader during the Vietnam War.

He was the team leader of numerous Alpha camps[2] along the Cambodian border that ran from Three Corps down to the Delta. He is now working for SOG, attached to the MAC com-

---

[1] Military Assistance Command–Studies and Observation Group also known as Special Operations Group. Their mission Covert operations throughout Southeast Asia.

[2] A Camps, 12-man Green Beret Special Forces units working with indigenes troops.

pound at Nakon Phonom monitoring activity along the Thai-Laotian border. This operation is a bit different in that they are actively looking for a group of people they think is trying to cross the Mekong somewhere near Nakon Phonom. From intelligence received, this group consists of two Americans along with two or three Montagnards. The US personnel, one a Special Forces operative from the military working with the CIA, the other an alleged downed US pilot. Their companions are said to be tribal leaders wanted by the North Vietnamese for resisting the new government's policies and rules imposed throughout the countryside. They do know the man running the search for the North. He is a ranking Northern security officer, Major Trong. He has been given free reign and full support not only from his government but also apparently that of the Laotian government.

It seems someone shot and killed a Chinese army intelligence officer invited by Major Trong to help work on a case involving the reported escape attempt of a US pilot. It was uncovered that an American agent working in conjunction with the French embassy went missing about the same time as the Chinaman's death. This same man was later seen at a Montangnard village and gave assistance to the villagers in a firefight with Major Trong and his troops. Defeated, Trong withdrew seeking rein-forcements. He has been searching this group ever since.

Looking up from the map laid out on a small wooden folding table, the young captain starts things off. "Major, we don't have a positive fix on these people. We do know they're close to Thakhex because of all the air and boat traffic in that area. Our patrols report escalating military boat traffic on the Laotian side of the river. We think the US personnel across from us are trying to acquire some form of transportation for a run across the river into Thailand. Perry knows we still have people here. I'm positive this is his intended target. Where else can he go?" The two officers concentrate on the map. The only sounds are the hissing of burning fuel being used to keep the lantern lit, static from a radio receiver sitting over in one corner, and the ever-present rattling clatter of the heavy rain pelting the tin roof.

"Sergeant, our patrols report having seen two black painted Huey's in the search area along with a number of patrol boats and two old French landing craft full of North Vietnamese troops. They really want Perry this time. After finding the dead Chinaman in Ha Dong, the games have been on." He turns to the captain. "Frank, you give Tony all the support you can. If we have to bring down those choppers, so be it. Who the hell are they going to bitch to? Those are US aircraft, and we will bring 'um down if they pose a threat."

The radio in the corner comes alive with a voice barely audible over the static and the thumping of rain splattering the roof. "Digger one three, this is Swamp Rat three two, over."

The captain takes the handset. "Go ahead, three two, this is Digger one three." Releasing the handset talk button brings back a rush of static. "Digger, we have an old French landing craft full of NVA troops patrolling the river adjacent to and in front of our AO.[3] We have not seen, I say again, we have not seen but have heard choppers to our north and south. They must have two aircraft aloft. The boats are staying close to the Laotian side of the river. Don't seem that interested in our side of the water for now, over."

"Three two, no change in orders. Keep to our scheduled radio contacts. Alpha four one will be operational shortly. He will contact you when they near your location. He will not cross over into your AO without radio communications. Until your next sitrep,[4] this is Digger one three, out."

Turning to the Master Sargent, the major adds, "Tony, you've got our blessing and support. Find those people and bring 'um in.

---

[3]   Area of operation

[4]   Situation report

That's it, gentlemen. Good hunting, Sergeant." The major leaves the two to finish the briefing.

"Sir, I get air support if needed?" the captain answers. "With two choppers and boat loads of armed troops, affirmative on the air support, but, Tony, we don't want to rekindle a war. You had better be in dire straits if you call us to pull the trigger."

Wiggling into his poncho, Gratton leaves the little building, ignoring the hard pounding rain as he walks through ankle deep mud seventy-five yards into a small stand of palm trees and tall grass. On his approach, three or four poncho-covered heads pop up. These are all handpicked volunteers from the Vietnam War era assault and reactionary group known as Mike Force.[5] Its members include Cambodians, Chinese, and Montagnards recruited from all over Southeast Asia. They were trained and armed by Special Forces to help in the defense and relief of A Camps along the South Vietnamese border that were under attack by overwhelming enemy forces. At the end of the war, many of these troops refused to put down their weapons. They were willing to carry on with their own war. The Cambodians and Montagnards have had years of animosity toward the North Vietnamese people for atrocities inflicted in the South during the war. These same troops now take and follow orders for the sake of the fight. It's in their blood; it's their passion to hunt a cunning and daring foe. One that can hunt them back!

This heavily armed group of twelve, including Gratton, will deploy into the jungle along the Mekong River across from the Laotian town of Thahex in hopes of rendering useful assistance to the group of people trying to flee Laos. Sargent Gratton's unit will be in radio contact with two other teams dedicated to the same purpose. Before striking out, Gratton makes sure his Prick

---

[5]   Special Forces–armed, trained, and lead mobile strike force composed of US and indigenous personnel, used as a reaction and reinforcing unit in support of outlying and isolated Special Forces A camps.

twenty-five[6] radio is fully functional. "Digger one three, this is four one, communications check. How do you read me, over?"

"Five by five[7] four one, this is Digger one three out." The problem this radio had throughout the war was its batteries—not long lasting, with minimal use maybe two, three days. If transmitting and receiving a constant flow of traffic, you could only expect two to three hours. In this hot wet tropical environment, batteries corroded rapidly. You always had to carry replacements.

---

[6]   PRC-25, dubbed the Prick-25 by American GIs, a light infantry field Frequency Modulated radio. PRC means portable radio.

[7]   The best of twenty-five possible subjective responses used to describe the quality of communications.

CHAPTER 9

THE SLACKENED RAIN brings the new day into focus. Along with the early sunlight, there is the thundering, whooshing sound of rotor blades cutting through the thin morning air. They are close, staying undercover. Perry tells the others, "We're in for a long day with this search tightening. Soon they will have ground troops covering these woods. We have two options. We must choose one and stick to it: we can stay here and hope not to be seen. I don't give us much of a chance in doing so. With the road being washed out, foot troops will be in our area by this afternoon. They know we're up in these hills. It's just a matter of time. Or we could start our move to the river, but during daylight, we would be easy to spot from the air. There's a chance we could run into ground forces or simply stumble across a group of woodcutters. I'm sure everyone around here knows we're being hunted. Shit! They probably have a bounty on our heads. My suggestion would be to find a better hiding place for today, possibly farther up in the rocky hills where we can defend ourselves a little easier. If we can remain undetected till nightfall, maybe, just maybe we can work or way down to the water and find some means of crossing."

With much trepidation, they leave their shelter of the past few days and move out, reaching higher into the northern hills as the sound of choppers grows closer. They move quickly but with caution into a rock strewn outcropping leading to a jungle-covered rock ledge about fifty feet high capped with large boulders stuffed with clumps of grasses and shrubs. Not only is this a good place to hide from aircraft observance, ground troops would have to expose themselves to find them. It also provides a good platform from which to scan the meadow they came out of. Plus, it has the added advantage of a commanding view of any and all approaches to their lair. Anyone headed into this area from the north or south would be in their sights. Coming at them from above would be difficult, stupid, and suicidal. They have found an excellent hide.

Early afternoon brings with it their first sighting of an aircraft, an American Huey helicopter with flat nonreflective black paint; a red flag affixed to the nose embossed with a gold star. It comes roaring up out of the lowlands, skimming the tree tops swooping directly over the rock formation they occupy. Not sighted, the chopper circles the rock ledge with a low level fly by. With no signs of intruders, the aircraft returns to the forested jungles along the river. Bao, in a hushed voice, tells Lt. Bigelow and Perry that he really dislikes helicopters. During the Vietnam War, they were death on any enemy ground troops they spotted. Being able to stay on target for long periods of time, it was hard to outmaneuver one that was locked on your position. On top of that, when their ammo ran out, there was always another that showed up to continue the assault. The Americans never seemed to run out of aircraft no matter how many you shot down. If you did bring one down, you knew more would be on the way to rescue, recover, or continue thrashing the surrounding area. It was better not to fire on these people if you could avoid it, as the payback was overwhelming.

During the late afternoon rains, Pathet-Lao troops are seen emerging from the forested tree line. They slowly cover the open ground leading to the rocky hills looking for any signs of the people they are presently searching for. With the weather providing a steady downfall of rain, any tracks would be obliterated within minutes rendering this search fruitless. The dozen troops reach the base of the rocky ledge, trying to distinguish between real life movements or just tricks of the failing day. They stand looking up at the rock formation, scanning the undulating boulders for any signs of man's intrusion. Not finding anything suspicious or out of the ordinary, they back off, moving down into the tree line surrounding the little meadow. Turning back toward the rocky ledge they form a line, and on command fire blindly up into the rocks, each man expends a twenty-round clip. They quickly reload their weapons and wait any retaliation. This is called reconnaissance by fire, used by many forces trying to flush out enemy troops. It only works if they receive returning fire, giving away and fixing an opponent's position. These five stay down; they have all at one time or another seen this tactic used. At the least, a ricochet could wound; at the worst, it will kill. Not returning fire keeps them safe for the time being.

The Pathet-Lao forces move into the tree line out of view of the rock formation. Staying put, the five can see the flicker of three small fires by which they can view the ghostly silhouettes of troops starting to cook a meal as others start setting up a night bivouac site. Perry pulls out his spotting scope. In the dark, with firelight in the background, he can see the outline of a man moving against the pitch blackness of his surroundings. The reflection of the fire giving the man a halo effect the entire length of his body, he's easy to follow as he moves about twenty-five to thirty yards to the southwest of his companions. Putting his backpack and weapon down by a tree, he hunkers down beside his equipment, vanishing into the black void of the night. They now know to give this area a wide berth when they start their push to the river. They wait a little over an hour, giving the Pathet-Lao time to finish their meal and start their night's rest while their fire burns down to just glowing embers. They actually welcome the night rain. These rains will be a big help in their being undetected and unseen by uncomfortable enemy troops trying to stay dry under their ponchos. The five silently move out of the rock formation, heading for the wood line just past the clearing south of the Pathet-Lao camp. The rains are heavy most of the night,

conveniently masking any sounds they are making, besides washing out any tracks they might be leaving. The rains subside by
dawn. With the slightest hint of approaching daylight, Bao leads
them into a bramble thicket close to the water's edge. River traffic and foot troops will normally avoid this prickly mess of tangled, twisted vines. Very painful and uncomfortable to be in or try
to maneuver through, keeping your entrance point camouflaged
and hidden will keep unsuspecting passersby from investigating.
Assuring in some degree, guarded safety.

A graying overcast brings with it a long drizzly and soggy day
filled with lengthy periods of boredom, punctuated with anxious
moments when both boat and foot traffic comes close to their hide.
They are always in anticipation of being seen and having to fight their
way out of this difficult position. These interruptions have deprived
them of needed rest as they must be on full alert in their present
location, not far from a well-traveled path. Food has been supplied
by the very bushes and vines they have taken refuge in. Berries are
abundant and plentiful, but they must control their intake of fruit
or risk losing control at the other end, not the most pleasant of
experiences given their present position and circumstance. Finding
potable drinking water is of no concern; it's everywhere.

Perry, the only one with a timepiece, is trying to keep track
of any schedule the river patrols are keeping. At dawn, the two
helicopters come up the river out of the south in a low and slow
fly by. Door gunners leaning out, looking for any movement to
fire on. About an hour later, a single chopper came, screaming
back from the north disappearing downriver. The first of three
patrol boats appear, cruising the shoreline out of the south. Each
boat contains four armed troops along with one boat operator
and a commanding officer. The little craft is powered by an outboard motor that the helmsman is using to maneuver their way
up north. The water level is high as is the current of water flowing south; this upriver journey slows them down and puts a lot of
strain on the motors. The men have their weapons at the ready as
they actively search the shoreline intently. Not only are the boats

being watched from the northeast shore by the little group hiding in the brambles, they are being simultaneously watched by an American-lead patrol on the Thailand side of the Mekong with the call sign, Swamp Rat three two. No action is taken by either party as the three craft disappear up river.

During the daylight hours at least, one boat would pass their location every hour and twenty to thirty minutes. The chopper from the north came through about noon, if he has been in the air all morning; Perry thinks he's headed for lunch and refueling. An hour after the chopper raced by, an old French landing craft moved by their position filled with full uniformed North Vietnamese troops with their heads poking up over the gunwales scanning both shorelines. This larger vessel is armed with twin mounted .30 caliber machine guns and is moving slowly mid-channel as it travels up north. Regular boat traffic, farmers with market-ready produce, small two-man dugouts, merchants transferring goods from one town or village to the next are all absent from the waters. Either from the swollen condition and the rapid flow of the water both due to the torrential rains, or could it be that government troops have a hand in their disappearance? Whatever the cause, the Mekong River is thundering along virtually unmolested by the presence of man.

Midafternoon and the skies are awash with dark gray clouds that keep producing a soaking never-ending drizzle that makes life miserable for those not under cover. The lone black helicopter appears once again, skimming over the river on its return trip up north. The small river patrol boats are holding to their one and a half-hour schedule. As they go by, Bao states that they must leave this place before the light has faded from the day, moving through this tangle of vines in the dark is asking for trouble with the possibility of countless puncture wounds and their accompanying pain. All five are now very uncomfortable and more than ready to leave this prickly thorn and mosquito-infested hiding spot. They make sure foot traffic has stopped along the trail due to the lateness of the day and count on the patrol boats to maintain the schedule they have been keeping all day. Bao leads the way out of this mound of brambles. As they emerge, they're greeted by the sound of automatic machine gunfire and the whooping crack of rotor blades. Coming out of the north the lone chopper is returning south, firing up the riverbanks as it goes by. Bao and his companions have just missed being shot up. Staying down, crouching behind trees, they are spared sudden death with debris, dirt, and ricocheting bullets, flying about as a result of the helicopters random reconnaissance fire.

"Digger one three, this is Swamp Rat three two, over." After a few seconds of light static but no reply, he tries again. "Digger one three, this is Swamp Rat three two, over."

"Roger three two, this is one three. Go ahead, over."

"Digger one three, Black Cloud[1] just came by reconnoitering by fire. We have no, I say again, no WIA.[2] Just before his fly by, we observed movement across the river from our position. We made out three personnel, possibly more. Visibility is down. We're rapidly losing what little daylight we have, but we are certain there are people across the river from us. No contact. We will stay here until morning. I think if they're friendlies, they'll move south during the night, over."

"Roger three two, Digger out."

"Alpha four one, this is Digger one three, over."

"Digger, this is four one, I copy three two's transmission. I'm southwest of his AO, will monitor river south of his location. Visibility's not good, light showers, and it will be dark soon. Will do our best. Black Cloud blew past my position a little while ago, same report as three two. No, I say again, no WIA. I'd sure like to pull the trigger on that little bastard. Four one, out."

"Four one, this is Digger. Stay high and dry. Keep watching for our people they might be headed in your direction. Stay with your scheduled sitreps tonight. This is Digger one three, out."

---

[1] Codename for helicopters patrolling their area of operations.

[2] Wounded In Action

Realizing how lucky they were, Bao and the others set out in a southerly direction to accomplish what they started out to do all along, find a means of getting across the now swollen and fast-moving Mekong River safely. Bao decides to take to the near tree line for cover, still paralleling the little road they have been connecting with for the past three or four days. This night seems especially dark, with the skies full of ominous dark puffy clouds obscuring any light from the moon and stars, building for another day of rain. At present, they're under a light sprinkle, an improvement over the constant heavy drizzle they put up with all day. This close to the swollen river, they have lost some abil-ity to hear the night soundings of the jungle. The noise of the rushing water is echoing through the trees. In less than an hour after starting their night march, Bao halts the column. Going to one knee, the others follow. Moving up to Bao, Lt. Bigelow asks what has captured his attention. With a finger to his lips, he then cups his hand behind his right ear indicating that he hears something while pointing with the other hand in the direction he believes the sound to be coming from. At first, unable to pick out any distinctive unnatural sounds over the rushing waters. Finally, after a few minutes of concerned concentrated effort, Lt. Bigelow picks out the faint constant buzzing, crackle, and hissing of static coming from a radio receiver. Looking to the pilot for a possible answer, Bigelow whispers to Bao, "Static, my friend. Someone out there has a transceiver, two-way FM[3] radio."

In frequency modulation (FM) radios, thermal or white noise is referred to as static; it's caused by interference from radiated electromagnetic noise picked up by a receiver's antenna. When a radio set is on but not transmitting and with the radio's squelch button not set properly, you end up broadcasting a constant ambiguous prattle of static, a dead giveaway in trying to find an enemy force's position.

---

[3]   Frequency Modulation

Ung, carrying just a crossbow, starts threading his way through the darkened night. He is moving from tree to tree, bush to bush, in a crouching bent over posture, keeping his silhouette low, not giving himself up as a target. He drops flat on the ground when the nearby hissing static suddenly stops. Someone has pressed the talk button on the radio's handheld microphone silencing the static, which is replaced by a man's voice speaking Vietnamese giving a call sign. When he starts speaking, he tells whoever he's communicating with that their boat is secure. His four Pathet-Lao troops are set out in a crescent shaped ambush, about sixty feet to his front. They are between the road and river with their backs to the water. He ends the conversation after assuring them his area of responsibility is, at this time, quiet and secure. He must be done transmitting; the static hiss has returned.

In a light sprinkle, almost a frothy wet mist, Ung silently returns to Bao's position, explaining the circumstances as he knows them. There are four armed troops to their northeast; the lone radio operator is separated from the intended ambush site, the road, by sixty feet, which puts him about twenty feet off the river's south bank. He mentioned that the boat was secure, so in all, they must have six men in their party. During their day light vigil in the brambles, they could see six men in each of the small craft. They know what they are up against, and they know or almost know the enemy's location. The challenge will be to get by all these people and abscond with their boat quietly, without turning this into a firefight. At the moment, the odds in man-power are close to being even, but Bao's group has the advantage of surprise. Other considerations include how close and available are their reinforcements. That point is relevant when your opponent has in his possession a radio transceiver; help could be just a call sign away, and they haven't seen the old landing craft yet this evening. It's still upriver to their north. They know it regularly heads south for an unknown port at this time of day, usually following the helicopter's last run south. It's late or it's not coming down river tonight.

Perry tells the others, realistically, that he doesn't think they have a chance of confiscating a boat without some form of resistance. All the people involved in this confrontation are too close to each other. Surprise is important, but this is going to make some noises. Even in the dark, once a trigger is pulled, there is not only a resounding blast, there's the addition of the muzzle flash lighting up the night betraying your position instantly. Even the silenced weapon Perry has will emit a muzzle flash when fired. Crossbows would be almost a better choice in this situation if they had positive targets and could get close enough for them to be effective. That is, close enough to kill.

With the rain starting to intensify and the impending daylight not far off, they must move quickly. The pattering rattle of rain falling through the trees has drowned out the sound of hissing static. They decide on a plan of action: Bao will go after the lone radio operator; Sam and Ung will take on the boat, they will try for silent kills on their two objectives; Perry and Bigelow will move between factions covering Bao's assault, opening fire on any enemy troops trying to intervene. They have decided to wait out the night, striking out at dawn. There are many reasons for this decision: they can't see anything in this black void; those out on the ambush site spent an endless night being rained on and will be extremely tired, miserably cold, and wet even if they had ponchos with them. Assuredly, their only thoughts at first light will be food, warmth, and returning to the river for an easy, relaxed boat ride.

There is not a true dawn this morning; the only sign that the sun has approached the skies in this part of the hemisphere is the lighter shade of gray mixed in with the dark clouds bringing the rains. It's light enough now to see just a few shadowy feet around one's self. This is going to be a difficult hunt. They can't see nor hear their prey. They have lost the hissing static sound due to the rain's return. Bao strikes out in the direction of the last known enemy location, the area from which the radio noises came from. Ung and Sam move to the river's edge heading south hoping to come across the boat and its lone sentinel. Lieutenant Bigelow and Perry creep and crawl their way through brush and shrubs, around trees, slithering across muddy grasses, paralleling the river about thirty yards north of its bank, hoping to stay between the radio operator and the four Pathet-Lao. They all wish it were a little brighter; it's going to be hard picking out a man's silhouette with no contrasting light. Unnatural shapes don't stand out against a background of total darkness.

This is not the best of circumstances or condition to be in; the weather is uncooperative, with dark low clouds bringing a steady cold rain. They have done something every soldier is trained not to do; they have divided their forces and are completely out of contact with one another. If a firefight does erupt, they all must be in complete control of their actions, common sense, and reflexes to prevent any friendly fire incidents. There really is no such thing as a friendly fire death. It's simply and officially called killed in action. Friendly or not, you're still dead. Splitting their force is the only way they could deal with this situation; hitting one objective within close proximity of the others would be impossible. In this instance, they will go with the one objective,the boat. They will respond according to the reactions of the enemy troops. They are desperate men in a desperate situation; their actions now will either save the day for this group or bring this long agonizing and treacherous journey to an abrupt end. Just a river's width away from relative safety.

Sam and Ung are the first to reach their target. The sound of the rain has given them this find. The rain hitting tree leaves makes a light slapping sound as the drops land, bending the leaf rolling off hitting another, then another, on its way to the ground, ending its brief existence in a muddy pool. What they are hearing is a repetitive slapping, rain drops falling on a solid surface, making a drumming slap as the droplets splatter and bounce off this drawn tight, plastic covering like it was a snare drum producing a muffled high-pitched rattling thump. Moving closer, they can now see the faint outline of a small boat with its motor exposed reflecting what light there is off its shiny black paint. They quietly approach the covered craft, convinced the guard will be under-cover, protected from the elements trying to stay dry and warm.

Ung moves to the far side of the boat, inching up to the gun-wale, listening for any signs of life. He is rewarded by a low grunt-ing like snore, this man's asleep on duty. His punishment will be death, a fast, maybe not a painless end to his young life. Ung, reaching into the craft, grabbing the man's hair twisting his head around and slitting his throat from ear to ear with his machete, exerts such force the man is almost decapitated. With the blood flowing freely from his gaping wound, Ung pulls his lifeless body up and over the boat's railing, unceremoniously dumping him into the thick brown mud with a definitive thudding plop.

Ung starts to untie the boat's plastic covering as Sam climbs over the boat's edge to reposition the outboard motor. Sam is suddenly and violently knocked down by a bullet, ripping through his left upper arm, tearing out a chunk of muscle and splintering the long upper arm bone. There are four rapidly spaced shots. Ung lies motionless in the bottom of the boat; the only sound now is the persistent rain and an agonizing moan coming from Sam. The shots were fired from a blackened clump to Bao's right, the blackened clump being the poncho-covered radio operator who is now frantically yelling to someone over the radio that his position has been attacked. His conversation is cut short when Bao lets loose with a burst of automatic fire, eliminating both operator and radio. Ending another life and finely silencing the radio static. Bao has eliminated his target and is now on a dead run for the boat. Perry and Bigelow are surprised when one of the Pathet-Lao troops suddenly jumps up and fires a burst of automatic fire in the direction of Bao's last known position. This lone exposed Pathet-Lao soldier is way too slow on the trigger; his shots are wild and too high to do any good except pinpoint his own location, in this case a testament to his demise. First, Perry must try and locate the other members of this ambush; they know there were a total of four Pathet-Lao set out to watch the trail that runs north to south. One has shown himself, the others should be responding soon. Lt. Bigelow and Perry stay down, quiet and ready for action. Two more Pathet-Lao come out of hiding; both are on Bigelow's left flank, no more than twenty to twenty-five feet from where he and Perry are hunkered down in the mud, using scrub brush and the thick short grasses as cover. They're going to have to act soon or risk the chance of being spotted by the Pathet-Lao as they advance toward the boat. They really can't wait any longer for the fourth man to show himself; the others are getting too close, heading in their direction.

Without a word, Perry signals Lt. Bigelow to take the two men on his left, and that he will eliminate the one to their right front. After firing, they plan to stay low, concentrating on the area to their right, searching out that elusive fourth man. As they ready their surprise attack, the three exposed Pathet-Lao troops open fire in the direction of the boat. Without any warning, Perry opens up on his target; a startled and surprised Lt. Bigelow opens fire on the two remaining men. Back down in the mud, the two strain to hear or see evidence of the fourth man. Nothing to see, no movement from their right or left. They can't hear a thing; their hearing has not recovered from the loud noise produced by the rounds just fired. Gunfire is now coming from the direction of the boat directed to the right of their position. Bao has spotted the fourth man; he seems none too interested in the situation he finds himself. Crashing through the brush, scampering up a muddy incline, he's running as fast as his legs will carry him down the same little road he spent all night guarding. The aggressors have taken their objectives and captured themselves a boat.

Picking up weapons and ammunition from the dead, Perry can't help but notice how young and innocent-looking these Pathet-Lao troops are. They appear to be maybe sixteen to eighteen years old, ill-trained and ill-lead, tough luck in this deadly game. They booby trap and leave the bodies. Booby trapping a body is an easy task; one simply pulls the pin on a hand grenade and slides it under the corpses. When his friends come along to bury him, they too become victims. Moving the body will release the grenade's spoon handle, igniting the device, sending out a deadly spray of shrapnel. Now you have two dead enemies. The battlefield spoils from this encounter are ammunition and three AK-47s. Reaching the radio operator's location, they find a fully uniformed North Vietnamese junior grade officer armed with an AK, along with a 9mm Soviet-made sidearm. Close to the body is a shot up Chinese-made and supplied FM radio transceiver. Nothing can be salvaged from this site. Bao's twenty rounds at such close range has destroyed or damaged beyond repair any and all potential usable items. Bigelow and Perry head for the boat.

"Digger one three, this is four one Alpha, over."

"Fourone, this is Digger. Go ahead, over."

"Digger, this is four one. We have had some sort of disturbance across the river, and to our north, small arms fire, short burst followed by rapid automatic fire. Quiet at this time. We are moving north, will be crossing into three two's AO shortly, four one out."

"Digger one three, this is Rat three two, acknowledge four one's transmission. We also confirm hearing automatic fire south of us on the other side of the river. Understand four one moving into my AO's southern sector, over."

"Roger three two. We are moving south for linkup, over."

"This is Digger one three. Understand three two and four one will try linkup in three two's AO southern sector. Keep me informed. One three out."

The third team on the Thailand side of the river, Red Fish, has been making its regular scheduled situation reports. They have kept silent over the radio network simply because up until now, they have had nothing of interest to report. This patrol is way north of Swamp Rat three two's AO. They too heard the echoing rumble of gunfire coming up the river from the south. They finally have something of interest to report. "Digger one three, this is Red Fish two five, over."

"Two five, this is Digger. Go ahead, over."

"Digger, this is two five. Be advised, we have a French landing craft coming out of a tributary or inlet just to my north. Moved across my front and is at this time powering up for a run south. Will be in three two's AO in about thirty minutes. I say again, craft in three two's location, ETA[4] three zero minutes. It's loaded with troops. There are two personnel manning a deck mounted twin .30-caliber machine gun, over."

"Two five, this is Digger one three. Roger your transmission. Move south, looks like that's where all the action is taking place. Radio your location when you reach three two's AO. Give them a heads up. One three out."

"Three two, four one alpha, this is Digger. You will have visitors shortly, an old landing craft full of Pathet-Lao troops. It is armed and manned with deck mounted twin thirties. ETA your location thirty minutes, I say again, your location three zero minutes. It's time for our intervention. Try and stop landing craft from reaching shore at sight of firefight. Suspect our people are involved with this morning's disturbance. Keep me informed. One three out."

Joining the others at the boat, Lt. Bigelow leans over the railing, placing the confiscated weapons in the bottom of the craft, hesitating doing so because of all the blood splashed across the floorboards. There's the dark purplish red thick blood from the man killed by Ung, mixing with the fresh foamy crimson red blood flowing from Sam's shattered arm. Bao is in the boat tying a strip of cloth around Sam's upper arm, using it as a tourniquet, slipping a stick through the knotted end, and twisting it tight to constrict the flow of blood. Ung is at the far starboard side of the boat ready to shove the craft off the beach, hoping to launch it for a quick trip across river. If it could only be that easy. As Perry throws his extra weapons over the port side railing, he suddenly stops. They all stop what they're doing. The faint sound of multiple rotor blades can be heard coming out of the southern skies down river. Helicopters

---

[4]   Estimated Time of Arrival

are not yet seen, but their presence will soon be felt. Perry yells for Ung and Lt. Bigelow to assist him in recovering the boat in its plastic tarp, leaving Bao and Sam where they are.

"Digger one three, this is Alpha four one. We have the sound of choppers coming out of the south. The Black Cloud flight is on its way back. Would like to request a SPAD,[5] over."

"Four one, this is Digger. I have Sandy seven on deck. Will be airborne in zero five. Go to reserve frequency and give him your coordinates. Over." Gratton dials in the aircraft's frequency. Depressing the talk button on his handset, he begins his short conversation with the A-1 pilot. "Sandy seven, this is four one Alpha. Do you copy? Over."

"Four one, this is Sandy seven. Request coordinates your location. Over."

"Sandy, four one roger. Coordinates as follows, one seven degrees twenty-three minutes zero two seconds north and one hundred four degrees seventy-eight minutes zero three seconds east. Do you copy? Over."

"This is Sandy. Copy, one seven, two three, zero two north, one zero four, seven eight, zero three east. You are north of my present position. ETA your location twenty-five minutes, I say again, your location two five minutes. Sandy seven out."

With the dwindling rain and the appearance of sunlight breaking through the gray overcast skies, Perry, Bigelow, and Ung hastily cover the Pathet-Lao bodies with readily available brush, making detection from the air close to impossible. Finished, Perry has Lt. Bigelow and Ung move into the tree line north of the boat's position. They hide among the brush and trees, concealing themselves from the choppers but keeping in view the little trail in case Pathet-Lao troops try using it to out flank their position. Perry moves into the near tree line south of Bao's location close to the river's edge, keeping an eye on the beached boat along with being able to deal with any hostile traffic coming up

---

[5]   Single Place Attack Douglas A-1 sky raider

river. This part of the deadly game they are playing is the hardest, the waiting—waiting for the inevitable. When they opened fire on these six people, they knew they were inviting trouble. With helicopters looming in the distance and the possibility of boatloads of armed troops approaching, their position is dreadful. They are isolated in this small area with no plan for escape. Their situation is desperate; they have themselves outmanned and outgunned with their backs to the proverbial wall. In this case, the mighty Mekong River.

With the distant sound of rotor blades still echoing upriver, another man made mechanical sound attracts Perry's attention, the clattering muffled rumble of an outboard motor under full throttle. One of the six man patrol boats is straining against the river's strong southerly flow, trying desperately to reach the shoreline where Bao and Sam are beached. With anticipation high, the five armed troops in the boat have their weapons at the ready, expecting some sort of resistance when they reach the shore. As the craft throttles down, the helmsman brings the boat out of midchannel, turns starboard and heads for the clearing along the bank.

When they pass within range of Perry's position, he opens up on full automatic. His silenced weapon belching out twenty rounds of high-powered, full metal jacketed ammunition. Hitting the front three men kneeling in the boat's bow sends them jerking and twisting in utter agony and pain as their bodies absorb the impact of bullets, all the while showering their comrades with blood, bone fragments along with particles of flesh and intestines. The helmsman cranks on the power, steering the craft away from shore into midchannel on his port side. He's headed for the far west side of the river, trying to get out of rifle range from the eastern shore, just south of the beached boat.

Sergeant Gratton, in moving north into Swamp Rat three two's AO, has also maneuvered his way through the tree line east bordering the river's edge, putting him in a perfect position to witness the action unfolding on the river not far from his location. Not wasting a moment, Gratton sends two men into positions on the river's bank. With the rest of his people behind them scattered throughout the tree line giving covering fire, the two men kneeling at the water's edge extend their launcher tubes and each fire a LAW's[6] rocket. These high explosive warheads tear into the unsuspecting boat and its crew with two devastating explosions, tearing apart the boat and killing the helmsman throwing the remaining two crew members, wounded, into the river. The troops giving cover protection stand up and riddle the two Pathet-Lao still alive, plus the bodies floating near the wreckage making doubly sure none of the enemy troops survive. Across the river, Perry is shocked by the explosions followed by the massive volume of automatic fire directed at the patrol boat. He has no idea who his savior is, and at this moment in time, he doesn't care. He's just thankful they showed up when they did.

Perry can't make out any real distinct shapes from the other side of the river; he's right at the edge of the water about one hundred and thirty yards from the Thailand side. All he saw were explosions and muzzle flashes; he never saw who fired them. Thinking that he should try and get a better perspective of what's going on across the river from him, Perry makes a quick run for the covered boat to retrieve his spotting scope. When reaching the boat and pulling back the plastic tarp, he finds himself looking down the barrel of an AK-47 held by a very confused and frightened Bao. "Damn it! Perry, you should know better. Knock next time. What the hell is going on?"

Taking a few seconds to catch his breath after having his life flash before his eyes, Perry jumps into the boat. "I don't know what's happening, Bao. Someone on the other side of the river just blew the crap out of one of them patrol boats. I opened up when they got close to our location, taking out a couple of the little bastards when they headed across river to get out of my range. They ended up in a whole bunch of deep shit. Bao, they got hit

---

[6]   M-72 Light Anti-tank Weapon, a one shot 66mm unguided rocket packed in a telescoping fiberglass tube.

by rockets and a big load of automatic fire. I didn't see anybody doing the shooting, but they've got to be friendlies. I came back here to get my spotting scope. Maybe I can pick someone out." Rummaging through his pack finding what he was after, Perry asks, "How's the kid?"

Bao answers honestly, "He needs to get out of here. We all do. He'll be okay. He's young and tough. Aren't you, Sam?"

Sam, lying in the blood congealing on the bottom of the boat, among backpacks and weapons, manages a curt, feeble smile as Perry heads back to the near tree line.

"Digger one three, this is Alpha four one, over."

"Four one, this is Digger. Go ahead, over."

"Digger, this is four one. We have had contact with hostile forces. A boatload of armed Pathet-Lao. They were forced to our side of the river by unknown forces across from us. Whoever did the shooting was using a silenced automatic weapon. No sound, but we could see muzzle flashes and personnel in the boat reacting to being struck by rounds fired from the tree line. We have no casualties. All the troops in the hostile patrol boat are KIA.[7] Four one, over."

"Four one, roger your contact. Keep me informed as to your link up with three two and any further sightings or contacts. One three, out."

"Four one, this is three two. Roger your last transmission. From the sound of you firing, you're still a few hundred yards south of my position. I will move to you, over."

"Three two, this is four one. Roger your last. Will sit tight until we have visual on you. Four one out."

After action silence in a jungle environment is eerie at best. It's an echoing silence peeling back the many layers of sounds as the surrounding jungles dank dark recesses absorb the last stagnate, vibrating waves of battle. With his ears still ringing from explosions caused by the piercing crescendo of gunfire, straining,

---

[7]   Killed in action.

Perry hears the far off whooshing, whooping crack of chopper blades. Only to be confronted by another, closer disturbance to this silence, the chugging, coughing, stammering sputter of an old diesel engine that's powering the French landing craft coming down from the north. Perry only hopes his unknown friends from across the river are as accommodating with their support when this boatload of people arrives. He's also concerned about the two North Vietnamese helicopters fluttering about. Are they waiting to support their ground troops when they come ashore, or will they come down and fight on their own? Perry's vast past experience with Vietnamese chopper pilots was that they were not easily persuaded to participate in a close-in ground action. You could always identify and find the Vietnamese choppers; they were the tiny little black dots high in the sky, staying out of range, like circling vultures, loitering, hovering out of harm's way, waiting for others to make the kill before coming down to earth, indulging in the pillage and plunder of war.

Lt. Bigelow and Ung, covering the northernmost flank on the edge of the road, can hear the approaching enemy long before they are able to see them. Two coming up out of the south, smack dab in the middle of the little mud clogged road. Two men on either side of the road breaking brush, about twenty to thirty feet inside the tree line using the underbrush for concealment, not much finesse or stealth among these young, ill trained Pathet-Lao troops. Most were conscripted or driven into military endeavors because of the extended war in Southeast Asia that was causing many hardships for all its inhabitants. The young men fled their family farms and rice fields for a steady source of food and meager monthly pay from the many communist revolutionary guerilla groups, backed by the Chinese and Russian governments who were supplying plenty of arms and ammunition for their border wars.

The two young men coming down the road must have drawn the short straws, they are nothing more than cannon fodder, a target purposely sacrificed to draw an opponent's fire so their comrades can find and fix their position. Once this is known, they will return fire. From his present location, Perry cannot see the road, but he can hear movement through the brush to his north among the trees bordering the road. Now, just now, he senses and then hears movement behind him. First, a crinkling and scraping, followed by quick footsteps through mud, the kind that sends out a mushy splattering sound when the foot goes down and a slurping, sucking pop when retracted. Turning, Perry catches a slight glimpse of Bao disappearing into the tree line just north of his position between the river and road. Ung also detects noises behind his position. Realizing it must be one of their own, with the river to their backs, no one could maneuver onto the exposed beach without being at least spotted or shot. He tells Lt. Bigelow to be careful with his field of fire, they have friendlies to the south and behind their position.

"Alpha four one, this is Rat three two. Be advised I'm moving people down to the river's edge. They will try and intercept boat traffic from the north as it comes down river, just a heads up if you spot movement, over."

"Three two, this is four one. Roger your last. Standing by, out." Sending four of his eleven troops down a small embankment armed with three LAW's rockets and one M79 grenade launcher,[8] along with their personal light weapons, they will be initiating this engagement with a barrage of rockets and high explosive grenades. This action does not go unnoticed by Perry. He has been scanning the far riverbank with his spotting scope and picked out a darkened figure moving off a small rise, maneuvering down to the water's edge, but lost sight of him in the thick underbrush.

The chugging diesel sound is getting closer; the Pathet-Lao troops moving down the little road seem to be pacing themselves

---

[8]   Single-shot reloadable break-action grenade launcher, firing an array of 40mm rounds, sometimes referred to as the blooper by US soldiers for the sound it makes when fired.

to coincide with the landing craft's arrival. They're not moving at this time, no sound from their direction. Only two of the troops, those on the road, have been spotted. Bao, knowing that shortly they will have visitors moving in behind them from the river, decides to act by moving forward through the trees, his advance much quieter than his opponents.

The four men from the Swamp Rat three two patrol are in place. Everyone on this section of the river can hear the French landing craft coming out of the north headed down river making its way to the narrow strip of land that their patrol boat is beached on. Radio communications were lost during its last transmission; automatic rifle fire and explosions followed the severed conversation with the patrol boat's leader. One of their other patrol boats was sunk with all aboard killed attempting to reach the same shore. A ground patrol was launched; the last report from their position is that all is quiet with no sighting of the enemy at this time. They have not moved on the open beach yet. Their last radio message is, "Waiting cover fire and landing of troops before advancing."

They don't have long to wait; the old landing craft is now within sight of the shore they need to reach. The soldier manning the twin .30-caliber machine guns prepares to open fire, but before he can grab and press the trigger on this World War 2 era instrument of death, the starboard side of the boat is hit by a 66mm LAW rocket that literally bounces off the old thick metal plated outer armor bulkhead. Another ricocheting off the starboard plated stern, a third leaves a trail of flaming smoke across the fantail gun position, missing the boat entirely.

The boat gunner turns his attention to the Thailand side of the river and opens up with his .30-caliber guns, sending out a hellish display of destruction. trees are having their leaves and limbs sheared off. the air is filled with debris, but no one is hit. Not one thing less than six feet tall got touched by all the lead flying through the air. The fixed gun emplacement on the boat can be traversed right, left, and up, but it cannot be depressed or aimed low enough to hit anything or anyone of importance. Once this has been noticed, the man on shore with the M79 grenade launcher gets to his knees and starts his own deadly bombardment, putting two rounds of high explosive warheads into the troop area of the open landing craft, causing death and destruction among the Pathet-Lao troops. Quickly, the helmsman steers the craft toward the north shore on the Laotian side of the river, bringing his guns into a lower trajectory. The gunner is now tearing up the south bank with his own deadly and accurate fire. Three of the four men near the river's edge are hit, two fatally, the third slightly less serious, he might live.

With the gunner's attention directed toward the far shore, Perry starts taking shots in his direction, most of his rounds ricocheting off the metal bulkhead surrounding the lower half of the fantail gun emplacement. After repeated rounds bouncing off and making deafening ringing sounds, the gunner swings his weapons to the north bank and starts firing into the trees close to Perry's position. The personnel manning the twin thirties have the same problem on this side as they had on the other. They're too close to shore to be affective; all their firing is too high to hit anything except trees. The soldiers in the landing craft are now throwing what looks like blooded body parts and still smoldering equipment over the side rails. The troops coming up from the south on the little road take the wild firing from the river craft as if the Marines had landed. They foolishly charge the beach, running head long into a facade of automatic gunfire being laid down by three highly trained, motivated, and experienced adversaries. Of the six man patrol, five die in their tracks. The sixth? In a hail of bullets, he throws his weapon down, turning abruptly heads back down the mud-choked road, slip sliding his way to safety.

"Four one Alpha, three two Swamp Rat, this is Sandy seven on downward leg of my run in on your coordinates. ETA zero two, seven out."

As the landing craft turns for shore, heads are poking over the port side staring in disbelief as a prop-driven plane not more than thirty feet off the water barreling down on them with four, 20mm cannons firing hundreds of rounds per minute. The old French landing craft was not built for this kind of punishment, even with the addition of reinforced metal side plates and bulk-heads. The boat starts to disintegrate just off shore. Troops are now clambering over the starboard side only to be caught in a horrendous onslaught of bullets being fired from shore. As the Sky Raider passes over head, it leaves in its wake a sinking boat and a river full of dead and dying Pathet-Lao troops.

"Sandy seven, this is four one. Job well done. You have a confirmed kill on one old battleship gray, French landing craft. Over."

"Four one, this is Sandy. Roger. Have you seen anything of Black Cloud this morning? Over."

"Seven, four one. Negative sighting but did hear rotor blades earlier to my north. Over."

"Sandy seven, this is Digger one three. Do not, I say again, do not go into Laos after those choppers. Only engage if fired on or they pose a threat to our ground forces, including those friendlies across river. We're not here to restart the mess we just got out of. One three out."

"One three, this is Sandy. Roger your last, understood. Four one, I'll be standing by. Let me know if Black Cloud shows himself. Sandy seven out."

The quiet is slowly returning to the surrounding forest; the only remaining reminder of battle is the lingering smell of gunpowder wafting through the damp air. Ung and Bigelow, along with Bao, have returned to the beached boat. They find it virtually unscathed but covered in tree debris caused by the erratic wild machine gunfire from the French craft. Pulling back the plastic cover, they find themselves looking down the barrel of an AK-47. Sam is very much alive.

Perry has yet to return. He is concentrating on identifying the people across from them. Even with the sinking of the landing craft and the slaughter of its passengers, no one has openly exposed themselves. He has only seen muzzle flashes. Who are they? How did they show up just at the right time, and where in the hell did the SPAD come from? Maybe some answers will be forthcoming when they reach the far shore.

The midmorning drizzle is keeping the air chilly and damp, the sun desperately trying to break through the thick northern clouds. Bao, Lt. Bigelow, and Ung have placed their equipment and weapons in the boat. Bao has checked Sam's tourniquet and dressings, making sure the flow of blood has stopped. They have pulled back the plastic boat covering; all three are now engaged in launching the craft, pushing it back into the river. Perry, upon hearing the commotion, heads toward the little beach when he hears the not-so-distant rattling rumble of a helicopter coming out of the north at treetop level. When a pilot is flying 90–110 miles per hour at treetop altitude, it's hard, from the ground, to pinpoint his direction or location unless he's right on top of you. The chaotic whooping sound made by the blades cutting into the air rushes through the thick treetop canopy before being dispersed through the lower leaf covered branches and limbs, then amplified throughout the forested jungle in a resonating, confusing clatter of disorientated sound.

From across the river, Sargent Gratton, team leader of patrol Alpha four one can hear and see the advancement of the Northern force's helicopters converging on the beached boat that three men are desperately trying to drag and push back into the water. He can't see the chopper flying through the treetops, but he has spotted another craft northwest at about fourteen hundred feet. This is the high man in the high-low formation. The craft flying treetop level is trying to locate and fix the target. The "high" flight, the command and control ship, will only drop altitude if his fellow aircraft is fired upon. He is the support factor in this deadly equation.

"Sandy seven, this is four one. I have visual on one Black Cloud north, northwest across the river from my location at approximately fourteen hundred feet. I can hear another craft, but he's too low for a sighting at this time. He's flying the treetops from the sound. I'm sure he's close to the beached boat across from me. There are people trying to launch that boat as we speak. Request your return and support at my last designated coordinates, over."

"Four one, this is Sandy. I'll be coming out of your south, southwest, on target in zero five. Sandy seven out."

Perry reaches the boat just as its bow enters the water. "We've got choppers in the air. Every one grab a weapon this could get real nasty." As the boat planes out in the swift moving water, they all clamber aboard. Bao is pulling the starter rope on the out-board motor with no results; the little engine sputters and spurts but does not start. Again he tries; the motor gives a sputtering cough but still refuses to start. Bigelow tries helping with the motor by fooling with the choke lever on the carburetor, pulling the rope again, the engine belches to life for one brief moment, then conks out. Bao continues pulling the starter rope to no avail. With years of fishing experience from a small outboard motor boat, Perry reaches for a small red gas can, the boat's fuel supply; running his hand along the gas line feeding the outboard motor, he locates the fuel supply pet-cock valve and opens the flow of fuel to the little engine. One more pull of the starter rope and the motor roars to a loud smoky life. With tiller in hand, Bao runs the boat upriver, against the current so he can maneu-ver away from shore. His intended target is the bramble clogged bank on the far side of the river directly across from their present position.

Dropping off the treetops like a giant prehistoric wasp, roll-ing out of the mist with a swirling veil of water being whipped up and thrashed about by the rotor blades, the helicopter is just a few feet off the water, four hundred yards down river from the boat's starboard side catching the craft mid-river, slugging its way to the southwest shore. The crossing is not an easy one with the boat struggling as it fights the strong current; their progress is marginal at best. Seeing the aircraft coming at them just a few feet above the swift moving water, Bao starts a zigzag pattern in an attempt to present a more difficult target. They feel hopeless and forlorn as the chopper drops its nose, turns slightly to his port side aligning his door gunner with the little boat, their one and only target.

"Sandy seven, this is four one. I have visual on one Black Cloud southeast of my location just off the water getting ready for a gun run on a boat load of friendlies directly east of me. Four one out."

The four one Alpha patrol is on line and strung out along the river's edge hidden among the brambles and brush over grow-ing the bank. They're anxious, ready, and more than willing to open fire the instant the aircraft is in range. Eleven men with automatic weapons can and do put out an unbelievable amount of sustained continuous fire, more than enough to bring down a Huey. The North Vietnamese managed to shoot down hundreds of very well armed and piloted US helicopters over the past ten years, doing this very same thing.

Flying in a crab like posture, moving sideways at a steady seventy miles per hour, the door gunner is lining up with his target, his M60 machine gun dancing from the bungee cord holding it to the aircraft. Belted ammunition glinting in the defused sunlight. The young North Vietnamese door gunner smiles in giddy anticipation as his target grows bigger in his sites the faster they approach. Suddenly, from the Thailand side of the river, an almost solid wall of deadly steel, rounds are hitting the chopper like moths flying into a car's headlights on a warm summer Nebraska night. The loud dinging on his helicopter takes the NVA pilot by surprise, totally terrifies him as he flies through this hail of bullets.

Working his controls in panic speed, the chopper pilot brings the nose of his craft up while turning hard to port, overflying his intended target. Taking fire, not only from the shoreline, he's now being fired on by three men in the boat who have a choice target, the underbelly of the helicopter as it sails just a few feet directly over their heads. The door gunners can't get any meaningful shots off due to the erratic maneuvers of their craft as it flies almost backward over the zigzagging boat beneath them. The helicop-ter levels out after gaining some altitude. The experienced pilot hovering slowly drops back down to just twenty, twenty-five feet off the water preparing for another run on the boat and adjacent shoreline where the heavy ground fire came from. The NVA pilot once again drops the nose of his craft, this time turning his starboard side to the target, going light on the skids, picking up horsepower by gaining maximum allowable RPM. This maneuver is used to transition from hover into forward flight; he starts his second run on the boat load of people trying to reach the northern shore of Thailand. As he heads south, patrol Swamp Rat three two follows the example of four one Alpha; they open fire with all they have, again surprising the south bound aircraft forcing it once more to change course and head for the Laotian side of the river, out of rifle range but staying within effective killing range of his M60 machine guns.

"Four one Alpha, this is Sandy seven. Inbound your location in zero three, give me status on Black Cloud, over."

"Seven, this is four one. I have one aircraft across river from my location in attack mode. He will be to your northeast just off the water on the river's edge. I have lost visual on the high bird. He dropped altitude while heading northwest from his last known position. Over."

"Four one, roger your last. I'll be coming out of the south tree-top level. Sandy seven out."

With his nerves settled, the chopper pilot gets ready for another try at blasting the boat load of people out of the water. Swinging his craft to starboard while still hovering he drops altitude to just a few feet off the river's turbulent current. Gaining RPMs, tilting the nose of his aircraft in a downward attitude, the two side door gunners start a wild assault on the far shore line from which all the previous ground fire came from. Slowly edging south, trying to get parallel to the boat across from him while dropping even lower over the water. So close that his rotor blades are churning up a spray of frothy mist. The starboard side door gunner brings his M60 machine gun in alignment with the boat and starts firing. A jagged line of water spouts can be seen dancing their way directly toward the target. Just as the pilot starts his run in on the little craft he is suddenly, momentarily blinded by two bright fast-moving red balls of fire passing just inches in front of his windshield. These twenty millimeter tracer rounds,[9] about the size of baseballs, are being fired by Sandy seven as he comes roaring up out of the south. Working his controls in desperation, trying to avoid a sure and sudden death, the copter pilot aborts his advance on the boat, radically and rapidly changing his altitude and attitude. Bringing his nose up sharply, jerking the craft hard to port and putting the aircraft on its tail, he heads for the Laotian jungle. Both door gunners start firing retaliatory bursts from their M60s, but their efforts fall short. The next burst of twenty millimeter rounds fired from the SPAD crash into the chopper's engine cowling just below the housing that holds the transmission to the rotor mast, resulting in a catastrophic explosion, spewing out burning pieces of engine and fuselage. Smoke engulfs the craft. Red hot metal fragments and chunks of debris are thrown throughout the cabin killing the two door gunners: one blown out of the chopper, the other dying instantly at his gun position. The carnage engulfs the forward compartment, wounding both pilots and sending the helicopter into a spiraling backward dive into the jungle on the river's edge. Its rotor blades splintering as they dig into the trees, the tail boom breaking off from the main section of the aircraft with the remaining front portion exploding into a ball of mangled, tangled, twisted flaming wreckage. Sandy seven pulls up sharply, missing the treetops by a matter of inches as he heads for the west side of the river.

"Sandy seven, this is Red Fish two five. I'm three miles north of three two's AO in dense cover two hundred yards off the river. I have visual on your lone Black Cloud aircraft. He's moving slowly in your direction just off the south bank under heavy tree

---

9   Phosphorus-coated rounds that ignite and glow red when fired allowing the shooter to see where his rounds are going.

canopy that he's using as cover. I don't have a shot at him. Out of range. Just relaying his present location, over."

"Red Fish, roger your transmission. Sandy seven out."

The burning wreck is casting eerie shadows through the trees and jungle. A wavering line of orange flame is lapping at the river's edge, its reflection jutting out over the turbulent waters dancing across the white caped waves. There's a popping sound as ammunition starts heating up and cooking off, spitting out trails of smoke into the gray midmorning sky. Water spouts can be seen as spent bullets splash down in the river. Fighting the current of the flooded river, Bao gives his motor full throttle as he heads into a huge overhang of brambles and tree branches. Ung, kneeling in the bow of the boat, starts grabbing anything he can to secure their landing.

"Sandy seven, this is Digger one three, over."

"One three, this is seven. Go ahead, over."

"Seven, this is Digger. Break all contact and head for the barn. Naked Fanny[10] has two, I say again, two fast movers[11] on radar headed in your direction coming out of the north, northeast. That lone chopper is more than likely waiting for their support. He is too low to pick up on radar. We have the fast movers zero two zero ETA your location. Over."

"Roger, one three, Sandy seven out."

"Alpha four one, this is Digger one three, over."

"One three, this is Alpha. Copy your last transmission. We have two fast movers inbound my location, over."

"Four one, roger that. Get those people out of the water and move to the high ground and cover. You don't have a lot of time. Over."

"One three, this is four one. Roger out."

Struggling to keep their little craft at the shoreline is made difficult by the rushing waters trying to pull them back into the

---

[10] Call sign for Royal Thai air base at Nakon Phonom, Thailand.

[11] Jet aircraft.

main channel. Perry is now helping Ung secure their craft. With much effort, the two manage to stop their forward momentum and bring their boat close to land. The boat is not yet up against the bank. Perry and Ung jump overboard, finding themselves in chest deep water. As they try to pull the boat closer into to shore, they hear a voice call out in English. "Perry, get your ass out of the water! We have enemy aircraft headed our way. I'm sending people out to help you."

Bigelow, while helping Sam, is the first to see them—camouflage-dressed indigenous troops carrying CAR-15 and M16s, US-made weapons used by Army Rangers and Special Forces personnel, not your typical Southeast Asian AK-47 like most everyone carries. These are the friendlies that have been supporting them all morning; finally someone to thank. Moving as quickly as possible with the help of their benefactors, the five weary travelers, for the first time, step foot on neutral, safe soil. Not wasting any time, they start to scramble up the river's bank, moving through thick underbrush. They reach the bottom of a slight incline covered with trees and jungle vines. Standing head and shoulders above his men, Sergeant Gratton smiles as he greets his old friend. "Perry, who the hell did you piss off this time?"

Seeing his long time special ops partner invokes a moment of gratitude from Perry. "Gratton, you son of a bitch! I didn't expect a welcoming committee, but I'm not unhappy to see your funky ass."

"Perry, we don't have time for compliments and small talk. We've got fast movers vectoring this location in zero one five. We also have a chopper sitting just north of us waiting for support. Grab your shit. We're heading for the high ground and cover."

Scrambling of the water's edge, Perry tells Gratton, "We have one walking wounded that we need help with."

Sergeant Gratton has two of his men help with transportation of Sam as they move up the embankment into the trees.

As they gain the tree line and start their search for cover, they hear the faint barking of rotor blades coming down out of the north. The helicopter pilot is hoping to mark a target for the two aircraft coming in to support and destroy his findings. He does so using a tried and true method, reconnaissance by fire, simply flying down the river firing up the bank, hoping for return fire to locate their enemy. Two quick passes result in no returning fire. Without positive sightings of enemy troops, evoking no response from the hidden enemy sends the frustrated chopper pilot and his crew into an angry, malicious assault on the tree line, flinging red hot metal fragments buzzing through the trees like a swarm of bees defending their hive. Debris torn from the vegetation masks the air in a cloud of leaves. Pieces of bark and splinters off impacted trees are scattered over the hidden troops raining down like darts. Muted cries of pain and gasps of surprise can be heard as some of the men are wounded by metal shards and wooden missiles. Fortunately, none of the troops sustain life-threatening injuries. There's a lingering smell of cordite[12] hanging heavy over the water. One of the door gunners tosses out a yellow smoke marking grenade as the chopper heads for the far side of the river, giving the two-jet aircraft a marked target to concentrate on and plenty of room for their own safety during the jets' bombing run.

As the chopper hovers on the far side of the river, two shiny Russian-made MiG-23s come screaming out of the northern sky, dropping low over the river right past the yellow smoke drifting along the river where the troops are undercover. "Digger one three, this is four one Alpha, over."

"Four one, this is Digger. Go ahead, over."

"This is four one. We've just had two, I say again, two fast movers of Chinese origin with big red stars under their wings fly over my position. They crossed over the border and are out of sight at this time. Over."

"This is one three. Roger. Two MiGs crossed over your location and violated neutral air space by crossing border. We have an

---

[12] A smokeless powder used as a military propellant replacing gun powder.

RTAF[13] flight of four interceptors on the way to your location eta zero two zero. Over."

"Roger. Good guy's zero two zero. Four one out."

The two Chinese piloted MiGs are coming back, this time out of the southwest about two hundred feet above the treetops headed directly for the yellow smoke that's marking their target. The weather and the river's current has pushed the smoke to the south and partially out over the water, away from the tree line hidden ground troops. The first aircraft lets loose a silver eight-foot long canister of napalm, an incendiary device that spins somewhat erratically when it's released, tumbling wildly in its descent, exploding into a huge fiery ball of flame that sticks to and ignites anything and everything it comes into contact with, sending huge plumes of black oily smelling smoke high into the sky. The riverbank in front of them is engulfed in a roaring ball of flame. There's even fire crawling out over the water, the tops of the trees have caught fire, oxygen is literally sucked from the air leaving some of the ground troops grasping for breath. The second plane, flying even lower than the first, fires up the area that has been napalmed with rapid 20mm cannon fire. Both planes roll out and head north over Laos on their way home to Southern China. The lone helicopter picks up RPMs, gains altitude while dropping his nose climbing up and out over the trees in a northeasterly direction. They have abandoned the field of battle.

A few minutes after the Chinese aircraft's departure, a flight of four older US-made McDonnell Douglas F-4 phantom jets stream out of the southwest sky. Flown by Taiwanese pilots, they pass over the tree line and napalmed shoreline as they fly into Laos. A short time later, they are seen coming back just south of four one Alpha's position. "Digger one three, this is four one. Looks like all the bad guys have headed home. Over."

---

[13]   Royal Taiwanese Air Force.

"Roger four one, the RTAF flight has been recalled. They will not pursue enemy aircraft over the border. All patrols return to Digger one three's location. Is any help needed? Over."

"This is Swamp Rat three two. I have two KIA. We are also carrying three WIA, would like transportation once I reach black top road located northwest sector of my AO. My eta, zero four five minutes. Over."

Major Tanner helps direct an orderly withdrawal. "Rat three two, this is one three. Roger your last. Trucks on the way. Four one, do you roger?"

"This is four one, roger. I also have WIAs. Out one three. Break, break. Three two, this is four one. I'll be in your southern AO shortly. Keep an eye out, do you roger? Over."

"Four one, this is three two, roger. You will be in my southern AO, out." As the fires burn down, the black oily smear of smoke lingers in the higher reaches of the trees. Gratton signals his people to move out heading north from their present location for a rendezvous with the Swamp Rat patrol at the edge of the black topped road.

Nothing is said as they clamber through the trees and head across a small fingerlike ridge that drops into a jungle-covered valley. The trip is made easy by taking a high speed trail[14] that was used during the Vietnam conflict for the purpose of getting troops across the border for clandestine special operation patrols. It is now serving as a refreshing change of pace for Bao's group; they have tried to avoid any trails they came across during their long trek through North Vietnam and Laos. An uneventful forty-minute trip brings them to a ten-foot wide asphalt-covered road. The Swamp Rat three-two patrol is there to greet them. Two poncho-covered bodies lay on one side of the road way; wounded are on the other side being looked after by two US-trained Cambodian medics. Bao helps Sam to this makeshift

---

[14] A trail cut through jungle, three to four feet wide for the quick movement of troops.

medical site. Troops not caring for the wounded are sent out as security, as no one knows what their cross-border enemy might do in retaliation for getting their butts kicked and not stopping Bao's people from reaching safety in Thailand. The sound of trucks is heard coming down the road. The first vehicle to appear is an old US-made WWII Willies jeep driven by Major Tanner, commanding officer of SOG operations in this part of the world. He is followed by three deuce and a half trucks.[15] Two stop at this location, the other continues down the road to pick up the men from the northern most patrol, Redfish two-five. As the dead and wounded are loaded into the vehicles, Major Tanner calls out for Gratton, Perry and Bigelow to join him for a quick jeep ride to Nakon Phonom air base. At Perry's request, Bao joins them.

Major Thaddeus "Red" Tanner, six feet six inches tall, weighing in at 275 pounds, red-haired, all-American linebacker in college. Drafted during the Korean War. At its conclusion, he came away with a Silver Star and two Bronze Stars for bravery in combat, along with a Purple Heart for a leg wound. After his recovery, he was allowed to attend West Point by an appointment from his commanding officer. Upon graduating from the Point, Red requested and was granted an assignment with the Army's newest command unit, Special Forces. After jump school, he was sent to Fort Bragg, North Carolina, where he completed the very difficult and stringent Special Forces training course. Upon graduation, he was awarded his green beret. When the Vietnam War came along, Red was assigned as commanding officer to a border surveillance outpost. One of many Special Forces Alpha camps stung out along the South Vietnam border with Cambodia and Laos. Their objective was to stem the flow of North Vietnamese troops infiltrating into the South via the Ho Chi Minh trail. After two yearlong tours of duty, he was asked and accepted an

---

[15] U.S Army two and a-half ton truck.

assignment with MACV-SOG, a clandestine group sometimes associated with the CIA.

They ran special operations all over North and South Vietnam, including forays across the borders into Laos and Cambodia. When the war ended, he received a voluntary assignment as commanding officer in Thailand, overseeing operations run by a small group of Americans still carrying out cross border patrols into Laos, Cambodia, and Vietnam for intelligence purposes. Gratton and Perry served under Red when he was their Alpha team leader in South Vietnam. They both transferred into SOG at Red's invitation, and the three have been working together for over seven years.

Pulling off the paved road leading to the town of Sakon Nakon, they are now moving west on a frequently used dirt road passing two well-armed checkpoints before reaching the edge of a concrete runway. They're at the Royal Thai Air Base located at Nakon Phonom, Thailand. Red pulls to the side of the road, letting the two deuce and a half full of troops move onto the main base road. When these trucks arrive at the indigenous compound, they will unload the troops, deposit the wounded and dead at the medical facility where relatives can claim the bodies and ready them for funerals. This ceremony is a very elaborate, religious ordeal immersed in age-old tradition and ritual meanings important to the Montagnard people, assuring a prominent place in the afterlife for their loved ones. Ung will stay at the indigenous hospital with Sam, giving him as much comfort and aid as he can. There are no full time round the clock nurses at these facilities, family members, loved ones, and friends take on this role in third world Asian hospitals, sometimes sleeping on the floor next to their charge. This base is first class; Ung gets to spread his sleeping mat out on a bamboo woven cot next to Sam until his recovery.

After the trucks have passed, Red turns in his seat, left arm casually dangling over the steering wheel. "Gentlemen, we need to debrief. There are many questions that need answering, but for now, I would like to take you filthy bastards for a steak, potatoes, and all the beer you can drink dinner. Any objections?" None forthcoming, Red heads off until he comes to a fork in the road, he takes it. Arriving minutes later at an open-sided center post, large military tent with four empty tables covered with clean white linen table cloths, four chairs at each, set with silverware, cloth napkins and clear crystal drinking glasses. This serves as the American officer's mess for the air base. Just a few feet away, on the back edge of the tent is an old, cut in half fifty-five gallon fuel drum on metal legs being used as a charcoal fed barbeque grill. The rest of the cooking area consists of two large buckets of water, a small wooden table, couple of pots and pans, woven baskets full of vegetable greens and herbs, along with a butane refrigerator and freezer. All this is being looked after and used by two elderly women; one Chinese, the other Taiwanese. They do not speak each other's language. They communicate by grumbling at each other, showing no signs of cohesiveness in their work, yet some how, pulling together to prepare some great tasting food, along with supplying a seemingly endless amount of cold beer.

After a real hearty and delicious meal, along with the consumption of untold bottles of beer, Major Tanner tells Sergeant Gratton to meet with the other two patrol leaders carrying out joint operations along the river at the same time as his. The three will write up a detailed after action report describing as accurately as possible the events encountered during their contact with the enemy, including a list of wounded and those killed, signed by all three and submitted within two days' time to the major's office for final approval, before being discreetly tucked away in a secret file where few will ever see or read it. Any useful intelligence gathered will be passed on to the appropriate agencies.

With Bao, Bigelow, and Perry in tow, Red drives to a secure safe house on base. It's an enclosed eight foot tall chain link fenced compound with coiled concertina barbed wire strung along its top. One guarded entrance gate with armed sentries walking the perimeter. This area and building is used by teams preparing for cross border operations. On their return, they gather here for debriefing. The three men whom Red has brought here will be in isolation from three to five days for debriefing, with a little R and R[16] thrown in. "Gentlemen, I will be back in the morning. After some breakfast, we will start our debriefing process. There are towels and toiletries in the latrine along with plenty of hot water. One last thing, the young gentleman standing by the door is Lieutenant Clover, give him your uniform size, and he will get you some new fatigues along with boots, if we have them. If there is anything reasonable that we can supply you, just ask. I can't guarantee you'll get it, but feel free to ask. Good job, men, and good night."

Four days of intensive talks conducted almost like a criminal investigation. Hours going over topographical maps, detailing locations and routes used during their trek from northern Vietnam to Thailand, Major Tanner wants to know as much as possible about the civilian's mindset following the war, how they are dealing with the restrictions and land reforms imposed by the communists. He is interested to know if they can add to the file they are building regarding the North's capabilities and the scope of their operations. They know now that the Northern forces are using captured US helicopters that were left to the ARVN[17] troops when the United States pulled out of Southeast Asia after signing the withdrawal treaty with the North Vietnamese. The North easily achieved victory in the land war, taking the South in weeks, confiscating tons of military equipment along the way; they also know the North has the full support of China, evident by the appearance of the two MiGs that napalmed the riverbank.

These people are the last known American-friendly troops to infiltrate the defenses of a Northern city. Ha Dong is a major center of commerce. It has a large population and is a busy shipping port. The city has a substantial military garrison with gov-

---

[16] Rest and Relaxation, sometimes referred to as Rest and Recuperation.

[17] Army of the Republic of Vietnam, the Southern government troops the US was supporting.

ernment troops patrolling the streets, guarding the entrances to all important buildings with sentries posted on all the docks and at all the warehouses. They're keeping a watchful eye on who and what is going on around them. Perry, even in his hasty and unauthorized departure from the French embassy, was able to move undetected through this maze of security. This is of great interest to Red, as this information, along with other bits of intelligence could be useful if his unit decides to send operatives back into that area at some future date.

On the morning of the fifth day, a jeep arrives, delivering Sam and Ung to the compound. They are greeted warmly by Bao and their round eye friends, Lt. Bigelow and Perry. Sam's arm is covered in a plaster cast, resting in a sling. He has had a small titanium rod inserted, holding his broken arm bone in place. Bandages cover a sutured five-inch long incision. Other than the discomfort of this situation, he is doing fine. Ung was more than ready to leave the confines of the base hospital and the bothersome staff that was helpful in their professional medical duties where Sam was concerned but annoying and troublesome in their curiosity with the two Montagnard tribesmen. They both add small points of interest to the information already gleaned from their fellow travelers. Later that day, Red tells the group of the plans he has in store for them. "Perry, for the time being, you will be assigned to Sargent Gratton's unit. He is working on the orders reinserting your indigenous friends back into the northern highlands. I would like your input and knowledge of the area and situation along with your recommendation for an LZ[18] site. Bao, Sam, and Ung will be going over to the training center to gain knowledge and instruction on the use of equipment we are sending back with them. Lieutenant Bigelow, you will remain in this compound for future briefings. This time, by a member of your own service. We have a senior naval officer from Guam on his way to conduct this interview. As for the Army, SOG, and myself,

---

[18] Landing zone.

I would like to thank you for your cooperative participation and patience these last few days. From what has been said about your actions throughout this ordeal, I would like to say, without any hesitation, that I would be honored and proud to have you on one of our teams. Thank you again, Lieutenant. If there is anything I can possibly do for you, please don't hesitate to ask."

As the men gather for their ride to the mess tent, Red takes Perry aside. "Thought you should know what happened in Ha Dong after your departure. First, the Chinese man you killed was sent to Ha Dong on Major Trong's request. His sole purpose was to help in the capture and detention of an American pilot that was trying to flee from North Vietnam. I'm suspecting he got close to the pilot before he was killed. When Trong returned to Ha Dong for reinforcements, after his embarrassing defeat at a Montagnard village, someone, by then, had found the Chinaman's remains. Trong had your friend, Father Alex, detained. He has not been heard from or seen since. The entire embassy staff at the French consulate was expelled from the country and its doors locked. They have reopened, but the new ambassador is concerned that the entire building has been bugged. Recently, the Vatican has gotten involved because one of their priests has turned up missing. I know you did what you had to do. Perry, this is a prime example of every action has an anticipated and adverse reaction. With all things considered, you did another fine job. Thank you."

Lieutenant Bigelow spends the next few days relaxing, drinking cold beer, making good use of the officer's mess. But they are keeping him on a short leash. He cannot travel on his own; he is escorted everywhere he goes. Things are looking up though; today he meets with a Naval commander by the name of Harley Franklin Wight, an old school Navy man, true salt of the sea who's been in for most of his life. He is not bringing nor delivering the news Lt. Bigelow was hoping for. After some fact finding disclosures about his being shot down and eventual escape from the north, Commander Wight gets down to the Navy's conclusion regarding Bigelow's MIA and assignment status.

"Lieutenant, you've been missing for quite some time. Your records show that you were married with no children. Mother and father both deceased. One sibling, an older sister. Lieutenant, as of five months ago, your wife asked the Department of Navy to declare you dead, taking you off the MIA list and adding your name to the roll of KIA. Apparently, she wishes to move on with her life. She wrote in her letter that the two of you were using your overseas duty as a trial separation, and that your marriage, for the lack of a better term, was on the rocks. She also stated that she was planning to remarry soon. This, in a way, makes our position a little less harsh for the time being. Lieutenant, we really need to keep your escape under wraps for a while. Unfortunately, we can't just send you home, turning you loose back in the States. You must try and understand our position and your predicament. With well over a hundred men missing in action still on the books, news of your recovery would trigger countless inquiries regarding their status. Family, loved ones, and friends would be asking about other missing pilots, wanting to know if ground troops are still out there, running around Vietnam, trying to get home. We both know the answer to that. There aren't any. You were one in a million, a fluke, Bigelow. Your experience in escaping North Vietnam probably cannot and more than likely will not be duplicated.

"You will be sent to Guam where you will be assigned to a flight squadron, standby status. You will not fly for the time being. Your assignment will be in the administrative office attached to the base flight command and control. You will be monitored twenty-four hours a day. Sorry for any inconvenience, but please understand our concern as the Navy would like to keep your profile low and off the radar. We need time to work up a plan for your reintegration into a social environment. We've never covered this ground before. It's new to all of us. We are thinking maybe eighteen months. I'm assuming you still know the standards and protocol of being a naval officer, Mr. Bigelow? On your arrival to Navy Headquarters Guam, you will be promoted from lieutenant junior grade to full lieutenant. Congratulations, Lieutenant. That should do it for now. I know you're not overly thrilled with what's been said, but I would be more than interested in any views you have on the subject."

Stunned silence, the pilot is blindsided by this revelation. He understands the Navy's reluctance to just send him back to the States, letting him tell the public his story of survival and in doing so putting pressure on the government and its dealing with the ongoing sensitive and delicate MIA situation. At this early juncture of their peace treaty, the United States has no bargaining chips or leverage in their dealings regarding this subject with the new Vietnamese regime. They have just recently opened meaningful negotiations dealing with the returning of known POWs.

Being isolated and monitored in a corner of some island, doing busy work does not sound all that appealing to Bigelow, especially after the adventurous challenge he has gone through over the past year. Lt. Bigelow knows he must find a way out of this horrible assignment he has been handed. "Commander, that's what you have to offer, really doesn't sound all that inviting, sir."

"Lieutenant, it's the best we can do for now. This is all new territory. We have few options with little recourse right now. This mess has just ended, and we need time to establish a mutually acceptable dialog between our two governments. Sorry, young man, this is going to be tough on you and the Navy."

After a few moments of unquestionably tense apprehension, Bigelow thinks fast on his feet. "Commander, my only request would be seeing my Montagnard friends before they return to their homeland. I've become somewhat attached to them this past year. We've been through a lot together."

"Certainly, Lieutenant, I fully understand your attachments and feelings for those you've been in combat with. Very commendable. I'll speak with Major Tanner. His people will convey to you the decision we reach regarding your request. If there is nothing further, thank you for your time and good day, Lieutenant."

Early the next day, Bigelow is visited by some old friends: Major Red Tanner, Perry, and Sergeant Tony Gratton. They come into Lt. Bigelow's compound dressed in Army issue olive-drab green fatigues with unit designation and rank sewn on the sleeves, over the left breast pocket are sewn CIB[19] and Jump Wings[20] cloth insignias above a US Army stenciled logo. All three wear green berets. Over the right breast pocket of each man's shirt are stenciled name tags, Tanner, Gratton, and Scopes. Bigelow is a little confused. "Scopes, your last name is Scopes. You're a Periscope?"

"No, Lieutenant, it's Scopes, Perry Scopes."

Persisting, Bigelow adds, "All this time, I thought Perry was your last name. Even the major calls you Perry."

With a whimsical smile on his face, Red interjects, "I call him Perry because Scopes always sounded like I was addressing a piece of military equipment."

Speaking up, Perry adds, "When I use my full name, the reaction is usually the same. Some asshole will inevitably joke about me being part of a submarine. Would you like to say something stupid or just let it go, Lieutenant?"

Not wishing to get on this man's bad side, Bigelow lets it go, simply finishes the subject with as few words as possible. "Perry, we've had a good relationship so far, hell let's keep it that way."

"Thank you, Lieutenant, and congratulations on your promotion." Major Tanner breaks in, "The two sergeants and I thought we would celebrate your promotion by going into town and toasting a few. You in, Lieutenant?"

Lt. Bigelow asks, "You've talked to the Commander." The Majors replies. "That I have, we'll talk tomorrow. You ready?"

It was a night to remember. Bigelow had heard many stories about the bar girls of Thailand, told to him by fellow pilots who were either stationed in country or visited there on R and R dur-

---

[19] Combat Infantry Badge signifying the wearer has been in combat.
[20] Signifying the wearer is jump qualified.

ing their tour of duty in Southeast Asia. After a scrumptious lobster dinner, the four start a bar tour of Nakon Phonom, eventually ending up at the Morning Star Bar, the only American owned and operated establishment in this corner of the world. They serve real, honest to goodness black label Jack Daniels Tennessee straight bourbon whiskey. This is where Bigelow learned an important lifelong lesson—never, under any circumstance, try to out drink a Special Forces trained, combat veteran, master sergeant, airborne ranger, *never*. His head reeling, his motion and sight impaired, newly promoted Navy Lieutenant Tom Bigelow paved the road back to base with a lobster and whiskey infused chunky pinkish white and dark tan-colored vomit. The last they saw of Lt. Bigelow that night was the top of his head while bending over the porch railing of his barracks, puking into a flower bed.

Major Red Tanner pays Lt. Bigelow a visit the following afternoon. He has met and talked with Commander Harley Wight before he flew back to Guam early that morning. Red knows of the Navy's plans to keep Bigelow under a bubble refusing to return him to the States. He personally disagrees with their decision, but he understands their predicament. He is rather uncertain what he would do in their place.

"How you doing, Lieutenant? Did you get your head screwed back on?"

"I think so sir."

"Good we need to talk. There is nothing I can do about your orders from the Navy. I'm to keep you here until the indigenous return from their training, maybe another three or four days. At which time, you will be allowed to see your friends before they leave. We are to return you to those two Navy shore patrolmen hanging out by the front gate. They will escort you all the way to Guam. We did a little bribing last night, didn't have to take them with us."

"Sir, with all due respect, the Navy's orders are bullshit. I'd rather go back to the highlands with Bao than face being penned up like some animal on an island. Yes, sir, I would!"

With a surprised look on his face, the major asks a profound question. "Lieutenant, if you, I'm just saying, if you had the chance, would you go back up north with Bao?"

" Major, if I did, the Navy would have your ass in a sling, and they would probably shoot me."

"Lieutenant, my ass is always covered. I'm not worried about your Navy pukes. What are they going to do, report you AWOL?[21] You're already on the MIA list. Bigelow, I could use a man in the northern highlands. We have been putting operatives in Vietnam since the war's end but never this far north. We are sending weapons, ammo, and medical supplies in with Bao. We would love to have one of our own personal go in with his group to insure accurate and reliable information to base future operations on. If you did go, and that's a big *if,* you would definitely be in harm's way. There will be no back up support and very little chance of resupply. The mission command orders call for three helicopters: two slicks;[22] one with troops, the other loaded with equipment; the third craft is a gun ship just in case the flight runs across any bad guys. The selected landing zone is only big enough for one aircraft at a time. The first one in will be personnel. They will secure the LZ. The second craft will bring in the supplies. Most of this equipment will have to be stashed until Bao is able to bring troops back to uncover and distribute the arms and medical supplies to his people. If you were to go with them, you'd be looking at five to six months in the jungle. If, for some reason, you were in need of an early extraction, well, that would be a problem. It could take two maybe three days to get into your location. Lieutenant, you will be the one with his ass in a sling if the situation gets nasty

---

[21] Absent without leave..
[22] Unarmed helicopter.

and out of control. There are many things to think about. I'm going to send Perry over to talk with you after the evening meal. Think on what we've talked about, Bigelow. Just for the record, I don't know nothing, didn't see a thing. Thank you, Lieutenant. Have a good afternoon."

With hope of an alternative to his dire situation, Lt. Bigelow ponders the possibility of returning to the challenging, inhospitable jungle. With long hours of walking over difficult and treacherous terrain, exposed to extremely harsh unpredictable conditions. With all the bad and worst figured in this is looking like a plausible alternative to eighteen months of confinement on the island of Guam. The risks are greater, both to his life and his overall health but his freedom and the exuberance of the whole experience. Being out in the wild untamed forested jungle is somehow naturalistic to him. He really thrived on its simplistic ambivalence toward man and his quest for an idealistic life. For some unknown reason, he liked the serenity and understood the unbridled vastness of it all.

Leaving the mess tent after dinner, Perry and Bigelow, joined by two rather large, sweaty naval shore patrolmen, walk back to the pilot's compound on a breezeless hot and humid night with clear skies full of stars and one bright, really big full moon. The shore patrolmen stay at the gate entrance as Bigelow and Perry ascend the stairs of the billets, moving into the cool breeze of a ceiling fan in the entrance way. After opening two cold beers, Perry starts the conversation with a question. "Lieutenant, are you out of your fucking mind?"

There's a heavy silence as Bigelow sips his beer. Again, Perry questions his sanity. "You just got back from that hellhole. Do you truly believe you can go out and do this all over again? Bigelow, think about it, you know or should know this is no game we play out here. If Major Trong thought for a minute that you had returned to the Highlands. He would stop at nothing in his search for you. He will use every resource available to him, and he has many. If he finds you, my friend, he will take you all out. You,

Bao, the whole damned lot of you. This man's upset. Not only did he lose a considerable number of men in his encounter with us at the Montagnard village, he had one of his helicopters shot down, one of his trucks stolen and destroyed, not to mention what happened to his Navy. He has lost tons of credibility with his government and his Chinese counterparts for letting an American pilot escape his grasp while fleeing the country. Not to mention the pressure he must be under regarding Father Alex's disappearance. You can bet your sweet ass this is one pissed off major."

Finishing his beer, Bigelow breaks his thoughtful silence. "You know, for the longest time, I thought I was just getting accustomed to my new environment. Then I realized that I was enjoying the adventure. I was working hard to stay alive, not only for the sake of my survival but also for the love of the place and the people I was with. My desire to return has nothing to do with Trong. I'm sure he would like another crack at me. The trick will be for him to find me. No, my desire is the anticipation of the unknown held by the forested jungles of the northern highlands. It's Dinh, Nhu, and the bond I have with Bao and Ung. These people not only saved my life, they showed great care and deep compassion in dealing with my desires to flee North Vietnam and return to my homeland. Along the way, patiently teaching me the skills needed for jungle survival, all the while treating me as one of their own, when in fact I was the root of a lot of their problems. Were it not for me, their village would not have been attacked leading to the deaths of family members and friends, ultimately resulting in the abandonment of their village. Yet these people kept their loyalties too me. I, in turn, have a strong sense of admiration and respect for them and would like nothing more than to return with Bao and the others. It is not all fun and games. There's always a new energetic and stimulating experience at every turn. Maybe I just like the excitement of the unknown in the highlands. With its massive stands of trees and its thick jungle environment, every step is an unknown. The air is filed with the smells, sights, and sounds of unknown and unseen creatures. Even the colors are more vivid. Your senses are alert to all of this. It simply flows through your veins. It's sucked up through your pores and pumped throughout your body, making you tingle with anticipated exuberance. Perry, I liked it! I really liked the experience, every minute of it! I'm not willing to endure the crap the Navy has planned for me, no thank you. I would rather face the unknown and take my chances with these people. I truly became one of them. I was even ceremoniously welcomed into the Montagnard society. I became a brother of these people, and I'm damned proud of that fact. Could be I'm just lost to the jungle's mysterious dark beauty."

Perry knows these feelings and thoughts; he could never explain nor understand the physical and psychological hold a jungle environment has over man. Is it the exotic lure of the unknown or the excitement in its mysterious dark dangers that seemingly lurks behind every bush, tree, or clump of bamboo, whatever or how is never clear? He just knows that after nine years in Southeast Asia, the addiction is strong. This place gets under your skin, pulsating through your entire body making one dizzy for more.

"Lieutenant, the purpose of this visit was to determine if you were blowing smoke up our ass, or were you dead serious about returning to the Highlands. Now that I have a definitive answer, let me explain how you might achieve this goal."

Perry tells Bigelow that in an anticipated four days' time, three Montagnard tribesmen will be repatriated into the northern highlands of Vietnam to gather intelligence on North Vietnam troop activity and movements in general, specifically any and all actions pertaining to or regarding the highland Montagnard tribes still in the area. The US forces in Thailand would like to help these people in their quest for some sort of peace, either in their own country or by an emigration process to another country. They were loyal to the American forces during the war, leading patrols through hostile territory, participating in numerous firefights. Many times, saving the lives of their American counterparts, sometimes sacrificing their own lives so their round eye friends could make it home. At wars' end, the US Government pulled her troops out but did nothing for the people who for many years fought alongside Special Forces and Special Operation solders with profound loyalty and respect. These same people have been harassed and persecuted by the North Vietnamese ever since. Killing and relocation into repatriation camps has been the Vietnamese solution to the Montagnard problem, very much unacceptable to Bao and his fellow tribesmen. They would rather fight on, defending their historic way of life, regardless how persistent and powerful their enemy is. With the advice and help of the Americans, they might someday find that elusive freedom and way of life they lost so long ago. If Bigelow were to return with these people, he would become the liaison between the Montagnards and Americans—the only source of reliable information between the two peoples. Perry asks Lt. Bigelow if he knows or has he ever used Morse code. His answer is affirmative, once in a while in the Boy Scouts, long enough to receive a merit badge and a brief mention of the process during a course in communications while at school during Navy flight training. Most all communications involving a pilot is voice.

Lt. Bigelow is told that if he were to return with Bao that an AN/ GRC-109[23] crystal modulated frequency radio set with a hand cranked generator would be sent in with them. Communicating with short, cryptic encoded text messages in a blind broadcasting[24] situation. This small light weight radio was used by Special Forces and CIA operatives during their time in the jungles of South Vietnam. They referred to it as the little black box. It has a built in sending key for Morse code. There are no voice capabilities with this radio. Bigelow is told to spend time going over the

---

[23] Army/Navy ground radio transceiver.

[24] Sending information out over the airwaves on a designated frequency, at a certain time and date, expecting no response or direct contact with the station receiving the message.

dits and dahs representing the Morse code alphabet, along with the operating instructions in the 109's radio manual.

As for Lt. Bigelow's escape from the compound, Perry tells him that the night of departure, he will be taken to the mess tent for dinner, where he will be outfitted with his equipment, given weapons, and taken secretly to the helicopter pad, joining Bao and the others for their flight into the Highlands.

Naturally, Bigelow asks, "What will be my military status upon returning from this mission, Sergeant?"

"I was told that you would no longer be a member of the United Sates Navy. Through his connections with the Pentagon, Red will have you transferred into the Army, assigned to his SOG unit headquartered here in Nakon Phonom, Thailand. Lieutenant, you would be a captain with the pay grade of zero three. To counter your MIA listing, you would be given special operations status. As far as the military is concerned, you have been on secret long range, long term mission patrols in the north working with indigenous Montagnard troops loyal to the Americans. That's two promotions in a year, Lieutenant, not bad."

With a tight thin-lipped grin on his face, Bigelow ends their meeting. "Not bad, if I live to collect my pay."

The next four days are busy for Lt. Bigelow who is studying the 109's radio operating manual and working with Perry trying to familiarize himself with the Morse code alphabet. It's not coming back so easily to him after all these years. Sending Morse code using a telegraph key is a large part in the coding and encrypting process; the remaining part is in the rhythm and speed in which the message is being sent. Lt. Bigelow has a way to go before he is anywhere close to being efficient at this task. They keep trying.

A few days later, on a balmy late afternoon, Major Thaddeus Tanner pulls his jeep to a dust clouded stop at the gated entrance to the compound. Stepping out of the vehicle, he salutes the two Navy shore patrolmen now standing at attention in front of the sandbagged guard station. Red is escorting three indigenous troops wearing new tiger-striped camouflage uniforms, along with mesh and leather-covered American-made jungle combat boots. He leads them up the stairs, disappearing into the building's entranceway, out of sight from two curious gate guards.

As the sun starts its daily plunge behind the western mountains, a thin smattering of clouds is slowly turning purple, giving the sky a blush of color. A 1942 Dodge G505 half ton military ambulance pulls up to the front gate of the compound. The Taiwanese driver gets out, moving around to the rear, opening the vehicles two back doors while smiling at the two naval guards. He just stands there like a cabbie waiting for his fare.

Shortly after his arrival, Perry comes out of the barracks, approaching the two shore patrolmen. "Gentlemen, today we've had fresh lobster flown in from the coast. The major and his friends are headed for the officer's mess for dinner. If you are so inclined, I'll drive us to the NCO[25] mess tent for a T-bone steak and lobster dinner, including baked potatoes, washed down with good ole American brewed, ice cold Budweiser." Jumping into the driver's seat, he starts the engine. The two men hop aboard. The ambulance, when not fitted for stretchers (two hung from ceiling brackets, the other two litters were hooked into the flooring system), has folding bench seats running the length of its two interior body walls. Major Tanner joins the driver in the cab, while his four troops climb into the back of the vehicle closing the doors as they get in. Two men on each side, all their equipment and personal gear, along with their weapons are stacked on the floor between them. As they drive off, Lt. Bigelow changes from his olive-drab fatigues into a new tiger-striped camouflage uniform while replacing his black, all leather Army boots for a pair of lightweight jungle boots. These people are not going to dinner. They're headed for the helicopter pad.

After sitting down and ordering their meals, Perry tells his companions he needs to check on something with the major and

---

[25]   Noncommissioned officer

excuses himself. Perry is headed for a helicopter, getting ready for a night run up north.

It's dark early, no shadows remain, objects and people are a light shade of gray as Perry pulls up to the helicopter's sand-bagged revetment. Parking the jeep next to the ambulance, getting out, he walks over to the craft being loaded with duffle bag-sized containers. Placing his rucksack and weapon behind the port side crew chiefs seat located next to the cargo bay, he helps finish with the loading.

Once the aircrafts are ready, Major Red Tanner gives Lieutenant Tom Bigelow a pat on the shoulder and thumbs-up to the three indigenous, reassured by their calm, almost shy grin in anticipation of returning to their beloved highlands. He gives Bao a wave of approval, receiving in return a golden smile, golden, even in this almost totally darkened environment.

Stepping back, Red salutes the helicopter pilot, then holds his hand in the air twirling his finger, signaling the choppers to start engines. With a deafening high-pitched whine, the rotor shaft slowly starts to spin as the jet turbine roars to life, whirling faster and faster running up the RPMs for liftoff. Nose down tail rotor angled up like a scorpion ready to strike, they move down the runway, skids just inches off the runway, creeping higher and higher until they are fully airborne.

With the gun ship in the lead, the three aircraft head north along the Mekong River on a clear dark moonless night. Once in the air and out over the river, all the running lights, except for the pilot's instrument panels, are extinguished. They are now three loud fast-moving black shapes zooming through the night at treetop level.

Returning to the officer's mess tent driving his own jeep, the ambulance has already been returned to the Taiwanese motor pool parking lot. Red finally starts eating his lobster and steak dinner when he is interrupted by two confused and very distraught naval shore patrolmen asking if he has seen either Sergeant Perry Scopes or Lieutenant Tom Bigelow. After a short discussion,

Major Tanner informs the two Navy representatives that they will be flown back to Guam the following morning so they can explain to their commander H. F. Wight how they lost track of the man they were guarding. Major Tanner tells the two shore patrolmen that he will take no responsibility for their failure and steadfastly maintains he did not see or hear a thing— end of conversation. As the two men leave, Red asks the old cook woman if she would please reheat his steak.

CHAPTER 10

THE FLIGHT PLAN for this mission calls for three helicopters to depart Nakon Phonom Thailand, fly north-north-east following the Mekong River. At mile two hundred and thirty, no map coordinates are available, just mileage and a written description as to what they should be looking for; a large valley full of rice paddies surrounded on three sides by massive tree covered mountains. Twenty miles deep and three miles wide at its end along the western bank of the river, north of these diked paddies, they will find a flat stretch of cleared land. Nearby is a docking facility for the loading of rice onto barges and boats bound for ports and villages all up and down this watery highway. The flat area is used during the harvest season to dry rice hulls and for bagging the finished product before shipping. It's not being used this time of year and the fact that the main village is located at the headway of the valley backed up against the mountains, makes this an ideal spot to refuel the aircraft. As the helicopters land, they encounter three large dugout canoes, each carrying two fifty-five gallon drums of aviation fuel. These boats are manned by three US-trained indigenous Laotian freedom fighters. Each boat will unload and roll their fuel containers down the dock and up to the helicopters, refueling as fast as they can by using hand operated pumping devices. It will take about twenty minutes per drum, per craft. They should all be refueled and airborne within forty-five minutes if all goes without any equipment problems, mistakes, or unwanted company. This fuel has been stockpiled for months just for such a purpose. Once done, the Laotians will sink the drums in the river and paddle off to a safer shore. On the return trip, the three helicopters will refuel again; they will be doing so farther south.

Fueling completed, Bigelow and his three friends return to their helicopter. They've been about forty yards out on one of the paddy dikes acting as security; they observed no movement or action from the far off village other than a few lanterns seen slowly coming to life, only to be extinguished moments later. Perry and the other crew chiefs have done a quick check on their aircraft for leaks, loose nuts, and bolts or any sign of wear and tear to mechanical components. The pilots ignite their turbines to begin the second leg of their trip.

The final destination is about an hour and forty minutes out on an east by northeast heading. They will be leaving the river taking a more direct route to a mountainside landing zone blasted out of the jungle over two years ago by a B-52 strike. It was used only once as an insertion point for a seven man Marine reconnaissance team; after being on the ground for only four hours, they made a scheduled radio contact before vanishing. Flying over trees tangled in thick vines is making it hard to see anything but varied shades of gray. They have the coordinates for their recommended LZ. If there's a clearing to land in, they will find it.

This new course is more of a challenge; they are now flying over tall mountains and snaking through valleys and deep rock faced canyons. They're doing all this with just the light of a few stars on a moonless night. They fly farther in an easterly direction; the horizon is starting to show that early morning glow. The northern highlands seem to jump up out of a green sea as they rise, dragging with them great stretches of forested jungle along with rocky slopes and jagged cliffs that are being swallowed by a ravenous jungle growth. Their altitude is higher, the air cooler, coming up out of a step wide ravine and cresting the ridgeline they are hit by a blast of startling bright sunlight. Beautiful bright morning sunlight is flooding the mountains in glorious color, golden orange puffs of clouds float across the sky creating shadows of dark purple that hide among the jungle's nooks and crannies. Every color of green is being displayed in its finest hue with the sun bathing each color in the best of the day's light.

"Dragonfly, this is leader one. I have visual on our target. I'm going down to find an opening, over."

"Roger one. I'll be above and to your east, out."

Flying just a few feet above the trees looking for an LZ, the first helicopter, the one carrying the ground troops, finds its intended landing zone. It's not an open field or even a clearing. It's basically a large hole in the canopy big enough for one aircraft at a time to descend into. This is going to take nerve, patience, and plenty of flying skills to get these troops and equipment on the ground and then getting their aircraft out safely. With the fuel situation critical, they can't linger in this area for more than ten or fifteen minutes. Dragonfly one swings his ship around facing the uphill side of the opening. This looks to be his best approach. The trees to his front are taller due to the steep slope of the hill. Dropping the tail while still hovering over the abyss, he cuts power instantly sinking below the treetops. His main rotor missing the trees to his front, but they can feel and hear the sounds of tree limbs being snapped and shredded by the tail rotor as it glides through the over grown branches and vines. The cabin of the helicopter is being showered with leaf foliage and broken stem fragments. The air is clouded with all this debris, making things that much worse for the pilot. Pulling full power, bringing the tail up, leveling out his aircraft, the chopper pilot is regaining command of the beast. Once through the overgrown opening, he finds a fairly good sized landing zone on the forest floor. After getting his aircraft under control, he hovers about two feet off the jungle floor. Bao is the first to put boots on the ground in the highlands of northern Vietnam, the others follow. They all sprint to the wood line looking for concealment while providing security for the LZ. Their transportation starts running up its turbine's RPMs for a quick ascent through the hole in the canopy from which it came. Pulling full power the aircraft reaches for the light above, popping up out of the dark confines of the forested jungle bringing with it a giant spray of green leaves and severed pieces of limbs and vines.

"Dragonfly, this is leader one. Angle your approach from the downhill side, then break power. Once through there's plenty of room. Watch your descent. You've only got thirty to thirty-five feet before bottoming out. Good luck. Leader one out."

The pilot of the second helicopter starts his descent into the black hole cut into this sea of green; his strategy is a little different. He comes in from the downhill side, but instead of dropping the tail of his aircraft into the hole and sliding through at a backward drift before cutting power, he simply hovers over the opening, then puts the brakes on by cutting power and trying to drop straight down. It doesn't work. His craft starts going into an out of control autorotation spin. He slides through the hole facing downhill putting his windshield in direct contact with the trees. His main rotor blades follow, sending out a loud thwacking sound as they start slicing their way into the landing zone flinging debris everywhere. He wrestles with the collective and cyclic control sticks while pumping the tail rotor pedals, trying to bring his helicopter's spinning under control before slamming into the ground. Pulling full power, bringing his airship to a normal attitude, the crew braces for a hard landing. Recognizing that this is not going to be your typical helicopter landing, Perry reacts swiftly by throwing out his rucksack and weapon before grabbing one of the duffel bag containers and heaving it out of the aircraft as it smacks the ground with amazing force. It's a wonder that it didn't explode into a ball of flaming wreckage. Instead, it bounced almost four feet into the air, only damaging the starboard side landing skid. With his hands full, the pilot gains some control as he slams back down. Perry and the other crew member continue throwing out bundles as the helicopter starts to bounce back up. The helicopter pilot pulls full power starting his ascent. At just four feet off the ground, the pilot looks over his left shoulder in time to see the port side crew chief leave the aircraft. Unable to stop his climb, he punches through the small opening, ripping and tearing his way through the trees into bright sunlight. "Leader one, this is Dragonfly. I've lost one crew member, over."

"This is Leader one. You've lost a crew member. Did you receive enemy fire on the LZ? Over."

"This is Dragonfly. Negative, it looks like he jumped out. I was on my ascent and could not abort my liftoff. Should I return for him?"

"Break, break. Dragonfly flight, this is Digger one three. Negative on your return to LZ. Stay with your original scheduled plans. Proceed with your homeward refueling stop. I'll deal with our missing crew member. Digger one three, out."

Putting down the radio handset, Major Tanner tells his second in command, "Put Sergeant Perry Scopes in your mission report as a US member of this North country observation and reconnaissance patrol working with friendly Montagnard units attempting repatriation before submitting it to SOG headquarters, understood?"

The reply is rapid, simple, and to the point in a military manner. "Yes, sir."

Early morning bolts of sunlight dancing across the forested jungle floor, particles of dust, tiny bits of leaf and tree matter swirling in shafts of light defusing its brightness. The echoing roar of helicopter turbines and the whooping sound made by rotor blades cutting through the morning air has faded, leaving them in utter silence. From his vantage point, flat on his back, Perry can see that he is in the midst of a wide circular clearing beneath and surrounded by a tall stand of trees. The glowing aperture of light at the apex of this dome high in the trees gives one the feeling of being in a colossal cathedral. His release from the helicopter was a little higher than he had anticipated, resulting in his having the wind knocked out. Rolling over onto his hands and knees, grasping for air, he scans the tree line looking for any movement, none found. It's common practice for members of a helicopter insertion team to "lay dog," simply staying low, hidden out of sight, quietly for at least thirty to forty minutes after landing. Making sure there are no landing zone watchers, woodcutters, hunting parties, or military personnel in the area that would be attracted by the sight and sound of low flying helicopters. The early morning sunlight brings with it short ever-changing shadows to the forest floor. Birds, lizards, and the sounds of monkeys can be heard in the distance returning to the fold. Perry has always enjoyed this clean, crisp fresh morning jungle aroma with a slight hint of aviation fuel that's drifting through this place, plant matter mixed with the dank musty smell of rotted and decaying vegetation decomposing beneath the trees. This rancid sweet smell gives permanence to this place.

As the morning sun starts climbing across the sky, Perry senses movement to his right front. Lying on his stomach, he reaches down fingering his model 1911 Colt .45 strapped to his right hip. His main weapon, a CAR-15 is somewhere in this open field with his rucksack. Suddenly, the birds have quieted, and the monkeys have fallen unusually silent. Something is afoot. Perry unsnaps the leather flap covering his pistol, running his fingers over the grip. He clicks the safety to the off position. The figure moving out of the tree line is a short stocky man wearing a native loincloth with ceremonial arm and leg bands, barefooted, carrying an AK-47 assault rifle. It's Ung, headed toward one of the duffle bag containers. Another figure is emerging from the shadows. He is wearing tiger-striped combat fatigues and US jungle boots, also armed with an AK-47. It's Bao, making his way to one of the canvas bundles.

As he gets to his knees, the two men in the open make eye-to-eye contact with Perry but say nothing continuing their task in silence. A third figure is moving out of the dark shadows of the tree line, stepping into the sunlight. He walks past the equipment bundles and is headed straight for Perry. Stopping just a few feet in front of him, Lt. Bigelow, in a controlled voice of authority, asks, "Scopes, what the hell are you doing? Please tell me you fell out of that chopper."

Answering with a sheepish grin on his face, Perry replies with his typical bravado. "Lieutenant, I can't lie to you. I jumped sir."

Lt. Bigelow is not really surprised, seems this man definitely marches to his own drummer. "I would like to know the why, Perry. Why in the world did you jump out of that perfectly good aircraft?"

"Sir, I will give you my military answer first. I really do not think you are capable nor qualified to send accurate, precise, and intelligible radio traffic. My personal reason is that I love this shit and this place. Garrison duty sucks. Training exercises are boring and get old fast. I'm all for the real thing, you know the adventure of the hunt, the thrill of the chase. I certainly didn't do this to piss you off, sir. I was hoping to be of some help."

With a disgruntled but accepting look on his face, the lieutenant mutters, "I'm sure you will, Sergeant. I'm sure you will."

Getting to his feet, Perry locates his rucksack and weapon. Ung and Sam are just inside the tree line on the downhill side of a small rock formation using entrenching tools[1] to dig a slit trench in which the equipment and medical bundles will be buried. Lt. Bigelow and Perry each bring one of the duffle bags over to the rock formation. Bao greets Perry with a curious smile. "Welcome, my friend. It is good, and I am glad that you are with us."

Ung looks up from his work, giving Perry an Asian hand clasping nod. Sam smiles quickly as he keeps shoveling dirt filling over the bundle laden trench. Without a word, the others start gathering leaves and small branches, along with other debris to cover and camouflage their hidden stash until they can return with more people and retrieve them for distribution among the villagers.

Midmorning, the heat and humidity are already starting to claim the day. Birds and monkeys are vocalizing again, filling the air with their songs and calls. It's time to move out. Ung, as usual, takes the lead as point man, followed closely by Perry. Third

---

[1]   US military issue, folding shovel.

man in line is Sam with his AK slung over his good shoulder; he must endure his cast for a few more weeks. Behind Sam, Bao, the fourth in line, will take his place as patrol leader. Waiting for Sam to move off, Bao turns to Lieutenant Bigelow, flashing his golden smile. "Bigrow, this good you come back. Much to do. We find village and return for our medical supplies and weapons. Then we look for Dinh and Nhu up in the highlands. Could be long trip. No matter, Bigrow, you maybe last man home." He turns, following the others through the trees, disappearing into the mysterious dark depths of the forested jungle. He leaves Lieutenant Tom Bigelow standing alone in a far-off land with the silliest grin on his face, realizing that he is absolutely and emphatically satisfied with his decision to return with Bao and the others. Having Sergeant Scopes with the group only adds to their credibility as a small but lethal fighting force. Looking around, making sure the area they are leaving has been sterilized, no traces of human intervention. Slinging his AK-47 over his shoulder, Lieutenant Tom Bigelow moves off following his comrades in arms, into the true unknown.

AUTHOR'S NOTE

THIS IS A work of fiction. Names, characters, places, and incidents in this book are the products of the author's imagination; any resemblance to an actual person, living or dead is entirely coincidental. Except for the following names:

- Tom Bigelow   Close family friend.
- Dotti   My dear Mother
- Harley Franklin Wight   My Grandfather, Lieutenant Commander, USN
- Ung   My Cambodian counterpart at Loc Ninh, Republic of South Vietnam. 1965–1966
- Sam   My Cambodian interpreter at Loc Ninh, Republic of South Vietnam. 1965–1966
- Perry Scopes   Character from a 1930's radio show written by my Grandfather, H.F. Wight

         (Sam and Ung were Montagnard tribesmen.)

ABOUT THE AUTHOR

Ex SPECIAL FORCES Sergeant, Vietnam veteran, spent nine months at the Special Forces Alpha camp on the Cambodian border located near the town of Loc Ninh in the Binh Long province, Republic of South Vietnam known as the infamous "Fish Hook."

Born and raised in Southern California, after the military, moved to Northern California working 35 years as a carpenter/contractor building custom homes. Married 32 years, one son, four grandsons and two great granddaughters.

This book being my first and only written work was in its own right my Personal PTSD therapy, my experiences in the jungle runs throughout its pages, the jungle and its mysteries are always with me, the battle scars are healed, but the memories linger.

As with most veterans I am proud of my service and honored to have served my country.

—De Oppresso Liber
Charles David Wilkinson

Made in the USA
Columbia, SC
06 August 2023